Annie Maria Barnes

Matouchon

A Story of Indian Child Life

Annie Maria Barnes

Matouchon
A Story of Indian Child Life

ISBN/EAN: 9783337215576

Printed in Europe, USA, Canada, Australia, Japan

Cover: Foto ©Andreas Hilbeck / pixelio.de

More available books at **www.hansebooks.com**

—*Frontispiece.*

MATOUCHON:

A STORY OF INDIAN CHILD LIFE.

BY

ANNIE MARIA BARNES.

Author of " Children of the Kalahari," " The House of Grass," " How
Achonhoah Found the Light," " Ninito," " Life of David
Livingstone," " Some Lowly Lives," etc., etc.

———

PHILADELPHIA :
THE AMERICAN SUNDAY-SCHOOL UNION,
1122 CHESTNUT STREET.

NEW YORK BRANCH: 111 FIFTH AVENUE.
1895.

TO

MY FRIEND AND BROTHER,

REV. J. J. METHVIN.

PUBLISHER'S NOTE.

The customs, habits, and family life of the native American Indians are fast passing away. They are of great interest and value, not merely to the student of comparative religion, and of ethnology, but to every reader of American history. Aside from its thrilling incidents, this work has a peculiar value, because it gives faithful and graphic delineations of wigwam and tribal life among American Indians, and of customs and habits that will soon cease to exist, and be known only in history.

The engravings are from real life, and have been selected with great care from a wide number of trustworthy sources.

CONTENTS.

MATOUCHON:

A STORY OF INDIAN CHILD LIFE.

CHAPTER I.

UNKAMA.

ONE bright spring morning, in 188-, Dr. George Holley, physician to the Government, was on his way to one of the camps of the Apaches for the purpose of attending an old woman who was ill. The Doctor was a tall young man, with a broad chest and a pair of very strong, long legs that could carry him for many miles over the plains without weariness. He was nearing middle life, but as yet there was very little gray in his dark brown hair; and his eyes were as keen and sparkling as they had been when he was a boy. He was walking very fast, for he was in haste. There were several sick Indians around the Agency, and he felt that he must visit them all that day; the most of them before midday, if possible.

The sun shone with a pure, gold radiance from a deep blue sky. The air was very bracing and the pungent odor of the wild sage, just putting forth its blooms, was very pleasing to the Doctor's keen nostrils. All around him stretched the boundless prairie; not a tree nor a shrub was to be seen, save the waving grass and the bright patches of wild flowers. He was walking directly away from the river, or the line of low-growing cottonwoods and willows marking its flow would have been visible. Some Indian ponies, with their fore legs hobbled, were grazing

(9)

very near his path. He turned a little out of his way to give them a caressing rub across their glossy flanks with the palm of his hand, for the Doctor loved all animals and children.

He had passed a Comanche camp, and was two or three hundred yards beyond it, when his ear became conscious of a faint sound like the feeble wail of a child. He at once looked about him, but could see nothing. The grass was not very tall along this portion of the prairie, so he could see well in every direction. Again he heard the faint sound, and was now quite sure it was an infant's cry. Directly in front of him there was a slight depression in the earth, which was almost bare of verdure. He recognized at once that it was a dry water hole. Very soon when the spring rains would begin to come in earnest, it would fill up and the cattle would gather here to drink. But now it was perfectly dry, and there was a collection of sand at the bottom. A third time the cry was repeated, and the Doctor distinguished plainly now that it proceeded directly from this water hole. He took a few steps forward, descended to the bottom, and then stooped down, listening intently. There was no further noise. The Doctor, thinking he had assuredly been mistaken in the location of the sound, was on the point of rising, when a slight disturbance of the sand to the right of him attracted his attention. He at once made his way to the place, crawling on hands and knees.

"I think I know what it is now!" he said aloud, as he began rapidly but carefully to scoop up the sand with both hands. As he did so the stir beneath became more and more perceptible. In a few seconds, he had removed the sand to the depth of about a foot and a half, and there, in full view, was the tiny body of a baby wrapped in an old piece of blanket. Though it had given utterance to such a distinct wail several moments before, the baby was now very nearly suffocated from the pressure of the sand, and the Doctor had all he could do to revive it.

"This is the work of some Comanche mother," said he, as he sought vigorously to bring life back to the baby. "The

poor woman has given birth to twins, and following the prompt-
ings of her mother-nature she has sought to put one out of the
way in order to save the other."*

In a short while, the Doctor had so restored the baby that
it could feebly open its eyes. Then he unbuttoned his coat,
and, throwing it off, took from beneath his warm flannel vest,
and wrapped the little creature snugly therein. This done, he
replaced his coat, and, sitting down upon the sand, took the
tiny bundle in his arms, and gravely contemplated it.

"Now what is to be done?" he asked himself. "This is a
queer sort of a find for an old bachelor without a chimney
corner of his own, and with little time to stay thereby if he
had one. There is little doubt," he continued, "that this
baby came from the Comanche camp yonder, and it would be
little trouble to locate the mother, though she, poor woman,
would do all the lying she could to get out of it. If I carry
the baby back, I but carry it back to certain death. If the
father hasn't returned yet, the mother will bury it again. If
the father has returned, then out go its brains against the nearest tepee pole! Poor little outcast mite! What am I to do
with you?" His kind eyes filled with moisture, as they were
fixed once more upon the baby's face. "All the white families I know, have as many babies now as they can care for.
Oh, I have it," and in his joy at seeing his way clearly through
the difficulty, he sprang to his feet and began swinging the

---

* Among the Comanches the terrible custom of destroying twins is still
prevalent, for it is thought to be animal-like and unnatural to give birth to
them. If the father is absent and the mother does not herself destroy
them, then the father, on his return, will dash their brains out before her,
or throw them as he would blind puppies into the river, never minding
how piteously the mother may plead. Sometimes, when twins are born
in the absence of the father, the mother will put one of them out of the
way herself in order to save the other. More than one child has thus
been unearthed by a kindly rescuing hand from the pit of sand where the
mother had buried it. There is now among the Apaches, near to the
Agency of Anadarko, a little Comanche girl of thirteen years who was
thus rescued.

baby back and forth in his arms after such a hearty fashion,
that it opened its eyes wider than ever and its mouth too, with
a smile that rippled all over its face.   Truly, it had never been
rocked in such a delightful cradle before.   "I have it," he repeated, "Unkama!"   The very sound of the name seemed
to give him encouragement.   Truly this Unkama, whoever she
was, dwelt on the sunny side of his heart.   "Come *ma-tou-*
chon (little child)," he said, again tenderly regarding the baby.
"Come and let us go and find just the best mother that ever a
baby had, Indian or white."   So saying, he took the muffler
from his throat and fastening it about the vest, the better to
secure its folds, set off at a rapid pace across the prairie, over
very much the same route he had come.

The Government Agency of Anadarko (*An-a-dar'-ko*) Indian Territory, stands very near the center of the beautiful
Wichita (*Wich'-i-tah*) Valley.   To the north of it, flows the
shallow but picturesque Wichita River; on the south, it is
bounded by the low-lying, cup-shaped Keatchei Hills.   Not
more than a dozen white families live at the Agency; all the
rest are Indians.   The Agency is about twenty-five years old,
and is the supply station for nine Indian tribes; principally,
the Kiowas, Comanches, Wichitas and Apaches; between four
and five thousand Indians in all.

To the right of the Agent's house, and only about a fourth
of a mile away, there was a cluster of three or four tepees,
much whiter and nicer looking than the majority of those that
dotted the plains.   Their poles were very tall and straight, the
canvas itself strong and every rent neatly mended, while the
windward flaps were always so arranged that the smoke could
find free outlet without being driven back to fill the eyes of
those within or begriming the sides of the canvas with soot.
Near the center was one tepee, larger and taller than the
others.   It was made of heavy yellow canvas and the top and
base were each encircled by an ornamentation in red paint.

These tepees belonged to a band of Kiowas all of whom
were more or less related.   In the largest tepee, dwelt a

Kiowan chieftain, Tohausin, with Unkama his wife, and three or four squaws who were either his nieces or hers.

They were a very quiet, contented family, intelligent and cleanly, and far more thrifty than the average Indians. The head of the family, Tohausin, had been a great warrior in his day, and his body was covered with the scars of the wounds he had received in battle. In all the tribe of the Kiowas, there had not been a single brave, fiercer, bolder or braver than he. But poor Tohausin could be neither fierce nor bold any more, for he was dying with slow consumption. Yet there was enough of the old fire and spirit left to tell what he had been. He was still as straight as an arrow, despite the disease that had seized him. His eyes were so strong that he could gaze for a second or so at the sun at noon. Tohausin and Unkama were devoted to each other; indeed on her side it was little less than idolatry. He had never had but the one wife, despite the custom of his people, and her he had always treated kindly and with consideration even in the fierce old warrior days. Doubtless, this was one reason she loved him so, and, considering the treatment generally bestowed by the Indians upon their wives, she had cause.

Unkama and Tohausin had no children of their own. Both their little ones had died years before. They loved children dearly, especially Unkama, and thus it was that the two papooses in their tepee had just the nicest time in the world. And so had the dogs; particularly Tinhim, who was Unkama's special pet. Unkama and Tohausin had a nice little ranche of their own on which there were several ponies and two or three nice cows. The ranche was about fifteen miles from the Agency, and Unkama and Tohausin had lived on it until within the last few months. It was on account of Tohausin's failing health that Unkama had moved to the Agency, so that he might have the constant attention of a physician. It was in this capacity, that Dr. Holley had so endeared himself to Unkama, and she would have crawled on

hands and knees to serve him. He was an intelligent and
conscientious young man, well up in his profession, the very
best physician the Agency had ever had. Tohausin's case
had peculiarly touched him, and he had worked so faithfully
and so well over him, that he had patched him up considerably. But the skilled eye of the physician could see that it
was only for a time, and so he had frankly told Unkama.
But she, living only in the present, let her heart go out in
gratitude and devotion for what she fondly believed he would
make a permanent cure.

Dr. Holley, with his strange burden carefully concealed in
his arms, skirted around the Agent's house and made his way
direct to the tepee of Unkama.

An Indian's wigwam has neither bell nor knocker. Literally, he keeps open house and is always prepared to see a
visitor. So, without ceremony, Dr. Holley lifted the canvas
curtain falling over the entrance, and stepped within the
tepee ; only his head went in first and then his feet followed.
"Greetings to you, my friends," he said in Kiowan the moment he was inside.

"The same to you, friend Doctor," a cordial voice replied, and there was Unkama, her broad face beaming with a
smile of welcome and both hands outstretched.

The Doctor had to sit down the moment he had shaken
hands with Unkama, for if he had not done so, the smoke
would have made his eyes smart. You would soon learn this
about an Indian tepee if you didn't know it before. There is
no standing ceremoniously within one. You have to give up
dignity the moment you have entered, and sit down ; that is,
squat almost flat, upon the ground. If you don't, you'll soon
wish you had done so.

The inside of the tepee was neat and clean, and everything
well arranged. In the center, a fire was burning in a small
hole scooped out in the earth. Two upright forks held a
slender rod of iron and a pot of meat hung to boil. Reaching high above this, was another set of forks and a cross-piece,

all of wood; on which strips of beef were hung to dry and
to be seasoned by the constantly ascending smoke.

The beds, which also served as seats, were arranged in
a circle around the fire. They were almost flat on the ground,
there being under them only a frame work of willow poles
bound together with wisps of stout grass. Grass was also
heaped above the pole-work, and on this, the blankets were
spread. Every Indian slept with his feet to the fire except
Tohausin and Unkama. They slept on a kind of raised
couch at one side with their feet pointing toward the entrance
of the tepee. It was on this couch, where Tohausin was now
lying, that Dr. Holly seated himself, and taking the hand of
the chief in his, asked him how he felt. Tohausin replied
that he was not quite so well to-day, that he was afraid he had
taken cold again the day before.

"He would go over the river," said Unkama, at this point,
"and we were late coming back. I told him I was afraid it
would be too chilly."

"Well, he must be careful," said Dr. Holly. Then to
Tohausin, "I can't afford, chief, to have you taking cold.
But I'll give you something directly to make you feel bet-
ter."

At these words both Unkama's and Tohausin's eyes glowed
with gratitude.

"You are so good," Unkama said, looking at him with
lips that quivered.

"Not half so good as I'd like to be," he returned quickly;
"especially, as I have come to ask a favor, a very great favor
indeed, of you."

"You cannot ask anything in my power that I will not do,"
she said as quickly.

As she spoke, she bent her dark, earnest eyes upon him.
Her face was broad, and its features rather heavy; but despite
this, it had a pleasing appearance. You felt instinctively that
she was one you could trust. Her eyes, too, gave you a favor-
able impression. They were bright and strong and could look

at you without wavering, though they often drooped with a fringe of tears upon their lashes, as they were doing now. She was unusally intelligent for one of her race, for Unkama had lived a great deal among the white people. That is, before Tohausin's sickness, she had spent weeks at a time in the white families at the Agency, giving them such assistance as they needed, and in turn, learning their ways. Thus she had picked up many useful things as well as gained a knowledge of the English tongue. She preferred her own musical Kiowan, however, and rarely spoke English when she could make herself otherwise understood.

"I am well aware of your readiness to serve me," Dr. Holley said with deep feeling. "I know your readiness, therefore I hesitate, for the favor I am about to ask is a great one."

"There is no favor you could ask that would be too great for me to grant," and now two diamond drops from the fringe of tears had fallen upon her lap.

It was only too evident to what she alluded, for as she spoke, she reached out and placed her hand upon the thin one of her husband which lay outside the blankets.

"I know that, Unkama. God bless you for it! And now see here."

As he spoke, he opened his coat and there, lying upon his broad chest, snugly wrapped in the folds of his vest and muffler, was the little Indian baby sound asleep.

Unkama threw the palms of her hands together and then outward as an expression of surprise. Then she moved nearer and held out her arms for the baby. The other Indian women, even more overcome with surprise, crowded around, squatting upon the ground at the Doctor's feet, each one gesticulating after her fashion, and murmuring words of astonishment. The noise aroused the baby and it began to cry.

"It is nearly starved," said Unkama to one of the women. "Here, Tagano, take it and let it nurse with your own papoose. But, first, wait! It is not so comfortable in these things as it could be made."

With these words, she stooped over the baby and removed the vest and muffler. Then she took a bright strip of woolen cloth from her basket, about a yard in length and a half yard in width. This she folded together, and, cutting a round hole near the center, drew it over the baby's head. Then she brought it together at the waist—taking care to leave the little one's arms out—and tied it with a string. And so, in three minutes, time the baby had been dressed and snugly too; that is, for an Indian baby!

" We'll put some more on her after a while," Unkama said, as she handed the baby to Tagano.

" And is the favor you wanted about the baby ? " she asked, looking again at Dr. Holley.

" It is."

" Well, Unkama is ready to hear."

" I found the little one only a half hour ago. I was walking across the prairie on my way to Howling Wolf's camp, when I came upon the baby buried in the sand. But for its feeble wail, I should never have known it was there. It was just a few hundred yards beyond the Comanche camp."

" It came into the world so, I suppose ? " said Unkama, holding up her two forefingers together.

" Yes, it was born one of twins, I am satisfied of that, and the mother sought to destroy it."

" Poor thing ! I know it hurt her to do that," and Unkama sighed, " but that was much better than having its brains dashed out before her. And have you brought the baby to me because you did not know what else to do with it ? " Unkama continued.

" Yes, Unkama, that is just it. I am not married, you know. I have no home of my own. It would be impossible for me to care for the child. I would have carried her to one of my white lady friends, but all of them are overburdened with household cares now. Just as I was in the deepest of perplexity, not knowing what to do, I thought of you. I know you love children and I thought you would doubtless take the little

2

one in and care for it until I could decide what to do, only I
do so hate to give you the trouble."

"It will be no trouble. The little one is welcome. Tagano
has a young papoose and can care for this one too. Besides,
I'd do this and much more for your sake," and again her dark
eyes were fixed gratefully upon his face.

"But I do not mean to burden you with the support of the
child, only with the care of it. Whatever is needed, you must
let me know. I'll bring down something for the clothes to-
morrow. And Unkama," he added as he was going out, "call
her Matouchon, for the present; that is the Comanche for
"little one," you know. I judge," he went on, turning around
for a moment to look toward the baby, "that she is only about
three days old, so Tagano must be very careful with her."

By the next day, it was all over the Agency that Dr. Holley
had found a little Indian baby in the sand and that he had
carried it to Unkama to be nursed. More than one mother,
with whom the young physician was a great favorite, reproached
him for not bringing the baby to her; but for all of them he
had the same answer, "I thought you already had care enough.
Unkama has no little ones, and she loves them dearly. Besides, I thought it might be best to have the baby brought up
after the ways of her people."

Truth to tell, he was proud of his baby and his great warm
heart had gone right out to her, from the very moment that he
had scooped her helpless and almost dead from her grave in
the sand. He felt that she was indeed his very own, for had
he not given back life to her? Thus the young physician did
not feel in the least teased nor did he even blush when he was
joked about his baby, but took it all very gravely and quietly.
The only time he did blush was when he went to buy some
cloth to make clothes for the little one, and, being asked the
number of yards he desired in each piece, had not the remot-
est idea. He finally left the store quite abashed, wisely deciding that he would leave it all with Unkama.

He was quite overjoyed to meet Unkama as she was walking

towards the Agent's House. She was very carefully dressed as though for a special visit, and Dr. Holley soon learned that she was on her way to meet an agent of the Smithsonian Institution, who was negotiating with her for the war bonnet and full warrior costume of Tohausin. Unkama's leggings and moccasins were resplendent with beads, but beyond these, her attire was quite civilized, being of bright calico, well made. Over her head she wore a light shawl instead of the typical blanket. She soon arranged to go with the Doctor, and in a little while they had purchased everything necessary for the baby.

In the meantime, the Doctor had been making close enquiries with reference to the child. He had even visited the Comanche camp and gone from tepee to tepee, but if any of the women knew anything with reference to the parentage of the child, they would not disclose it. There were two women each with a baby only a few days old ; but both appeared so wholly innocent and unaffected, that Dr. Holley was finally convinced that their innocence was not feigned.

"An Indian mother has too tender a heart," he said to himself, "to show no emotion over such a deed as this, especially when it has been done through necessity."

So the little Matouchon, the abandoned waif found in the sand, the bud so mercilessly cast from the parent stem and left to perish, grew day by day into a fat, saucy and good-humored baby, winning her way to all hearts, but especially to that of Unkama, her adopted mother.

CHAPTER II.

SEVEN and a half years had gone by, and the Agency had undergone many changes. A "new administration" had taken hold and removed the old Agent with his assistants, but Dr. Holley was still retained. He understood and accomplished his work too well and was too popular with the Indians to be dismissed for mere political reasons. So he remained at the Agency, greatly to the satisfaction of all concerned.

There had also been an addition to the population of the Agency. The Rev. John Melville, missionary to the Indians, his wife, and six children had been at the Agency now about three years, and in that time, had greatly endeared himself to whites and Indians alike. He had been a "frontier" missionary for several years prior to coming to Anadarko, having served in that capacity among both the Creeks and Cherokees. He was still in the prime of life, small in stature but tough and wiry, with every muscle in his body expressive of energy and determination. His face was not handsome but it was kindly and true; while his eyes, as deeply blue as a sky in midsummer, had an expression when he spoke that made one feel the intense earnestness that possessed him. This was especially true when he conversed on missionary topics. Over his breast fell a well-kept auburn beard, while his thick, reddish brown hair stood straight up from his forehead with a precision that had long ago given his children the byword of comparison, "As straight as father's topknot." Mr. Melville, with his stout little pony Blinko, had been half over the Territory. Rain or shine, cold or heat, he obeyed every summons that came to him. No danger was too great to dismay him, no soul too lowly to receive his ministrations. Hunger

(20)

and privation were as naught to him if his Master's work were done. He had been known to go where other white men had not dared to go. He had suffered peril by flood, by fire, and by ambush, escaping each time as though by a miracle. Yet he knew it to be no miracle, but instead the sustaining power of the Guiding Hand that was ever about him.

This then, was the man who had come on his errand of love and peace and good will to the thousands of ignorant, perishing souls, that up to the time of his coming, had not known what it was to have even a few beams of the precious gospel light. But now many of them had come into the full radiance, and the little church at the mission numbered, in addition to the whites, sixty-five members. There were others earnestly groping for the light, and many that felt within themselves the inexpressible longing for something, they knew not what; something a hundred fold better than anything they had yet known. To all, the missionary was a friend, a brother. Even those who were not as yet within his fold, he was ever ready to advise and help. They came to him with reference to their temporal matters as well as spiritual. When they became tangled in their affairs at the Agency, his was the ever-ready pen that untangled them. When they needed a forceful tongue to plead the justice of their cause, his was at their service. It was no wonder that they grew almost to worship him.

On first coming to the Agency, the missionary had suffered many hardships besides those encountered on the plains. For two years he and his brave wife and little ones had lived in a small two-roomed shanty built of the uncertain cotton-wood lumber, with a partition but little better than pasteboard between them and the howling winds of the prairies. But as bad as was the partition, the roof was even worse, for it leaked like a sieve. Again and again, they had to crawl into trunks and boxes to escape a thorough drenching. It is no wonder that some of the family fell sick, first the devoted wife and then three of the children. One of the boys, Glover, had not

yet recovered from his tough struggle with the rheumatism.
He was a pale, delicate little fellow of ten years, and the pain
and stiffness in his leg kept him in the house a great deal.
Thus, he had become the source of much help and comfort to
his mother while the other children were away at school. She
managed to find time to teach him herself. But the Mission
Board represented by the Rev. John Melville had done better
things for him at last, and now he had a snug, neat cottage of
four rooms with a chapel attached. Yet even these four rooms
were insufficient for his fast growing family.

Unkama and Tohausin were still at the Agency. They had
been the first members taken by the Rev. John Melville into
his church. Tohausin's determinate hold upon life had surprised even his faithful physician, Dr. Holley. Truth to tell,
the Doctor had not expected him to live even half so long.
But that he had lived, had filled the good physician's heart
with joy, especially for Unkama's sake.

"It will quite unnerve her when Tohausin does have to go,"
he said to himself again and again. "How I dread to see the
end come!" But, as yet, it had not come, though, during
the last few weeks, Dr. Holley's quick eye had caught many
unmistakable signs that made him feel it could not be very far
away. Still, the frail threads of life might hold together for
some time yet, maybe a year or so. But to have them do so,
a change was necessary. The air at the Agency was too raw
during the winter and the winds too bleak. Further down on
the grass lands at a point the Doctor knew well, where there
were some dry, wooded knolls, Tohausin would fare far better
than here. So, Dr. Holley had advised the change to Unkama, promising to come to see Tohausin at least once a week.
For many reasons, Unkama was loth to go, but if the change
would really benefit Tohausin, then she could not hesitate.
But there was one bitter thing about the parting; she would
have to leave the little Matouchon behind, for Dr. Holley had
said she must stay and go to school.

Matouchon was now seven and a half years old. She was a

bright, sweet-tempered child with gentle, loving ways, and oh, how she had grown into Unkama's heart! Unkama herself did not know just how dear Matouchon was, until the separation confronted her. To Unkama too, Matouchon was fondly attached. She had known no other mother, though, from the moment she could understand, both Dr. Holley and Unkama had thought it best to let her know that Unkama was not really her mother. It would save her much pain in whatever changes the future held for her. Through all the years that he had been a constant visitor at the tepee, Dr. Holley had taken care to notice the child. Indeed, he had grown more and more proud of his baby, and now he was fond of her too. She well deserved his affection, for she was not only bright and sweet-tempered, but truthful as well. He had early sought to instill this principle into her, and Unkama too, was a faithful teacher.

Matouchon was never happier than when seated upon the knee of her adopted father listening to the words he spoke in the English she now loved so well, or to his reading of some entertaining story in the picture books he brought her from time to time. Matouchon herself could read a little in one or two of the books, for the Doctor had taught her. Her heart leaped for joy when she heard him say that she could now go to school. But over the sunlight of her joy came a dark, dark cloud when she learned that she was to be separated from Unkama. As hard as the child took it, Unkama took it even harder. "It is like tearing out a part of my heart," she said to Dr. Holley, with her eyes overflowing; "I have grown to love the little one so! She is like the bright sunlight that comes into the tepee when the curtain is withdrawn. Now that she is going, it will seem like the curtain is down all the time."

"I know it is hard, Unkama," he replied, his own eyes moistening. "This is one part you and I never foresaw, the growing into your heart, and the pain of a separation. But do not take it so hard. It is not final, you know. In a few years she will be through school; then she will be yours again. In the meantime, I'll bring her every now and then to see you."

This promise cleared away much of the shadow in Unkama's heart. "But have you thought of any one who will take her? I believe you said you wanted to keep her right here at the Agency and not send her over the river to the Government School?"

"Yes, she is too small to send there yet. I want her to have the influence of a home for at least three years. No," answering her first question last, "I have not found anyone yet who could take her. You know most of the families here now are new to me."

"Have you tried the missionary's wife?" asked Unkama suddenly.

"Why, no, Unkama, that is the very last place to which I would think of going. They have a house chock full of little ones now."

"But, believe me, it is the very best place to which you could go, and somehow I feel the good woman would take her. Oh, she has such a warm true heart!" and Unkama's voice was tremulous with tenderness as she paid this tribute; for well she remembered the many little kindnesses and attentions shown the sick Tohausin.

"But Unkama, it would be such an imposition. Think of the number of little ones there already!"

"But there is always room for one more. I heard her say it herself. Besides," suggested the practical Unkama, "if you paid something to them to keep her, how could it be a burden?"

This view of the question put an entirely different face upon the matter; so he went at once to see Mrs. Melville. He found her with three or four women seated around her, busily teaching them how to sew. What a time they were having, rejoicing over a brand-new sewing machine which one of the missionary societies at home had sent out to them! Dr. Holley's sympathetic heart was filled with joy just to see their own.

The missionary's wife was a fine-looking woman. In the old days, before she had encountered hardships and deprivations and unceasing toil, she had doubtless been a handsome woman. She was rather plump in form despite the wear and tear of this frontier life, and she carried erect her shoulders on which was set a fine head with smooth bands of dark brown hair well streaked with grey. She had white delicate features and very expressive hazel eyes. She was glad to see Dr. Holley, for he had endeared himself greatly to her during her own sickness and that of the children. So, she gave him a warm hand-clasp ere she motioned him to a chair. "You came just in time, Doctor, to witness our great joy over the new sewing machine. I do not think anything could have been sent out here that would have given me more pleasure, and I bless from the bottom of my heart, the thoughtful women who sent it. Now we can have clothes made without the wear and tear of flesh."

"It must indeed have been slow work by the old finger process," said the Doctor. "I must compliment you Mrs. Melville, and thank you, too," he continued, "for the great improvement that has come to so many of our women. Such as have come under your influence no longer go with their half nude bodies exposed to the public gaze or what is worse still for them, to the chill of the weather. I feel assured that you have averted many cases of pneumonia and bronchitis among the women."

"The poor things need only to be shown the way and to be helped, for they are always ready to follow instruction."

"Yet honor is all the same due to the one, patient and self-sacrificing enough to teach them! But I came to see you about a little matter this afternoon. I suppose you are pretty well packed—in here," glancing about the small room as he spoke and into the still smaller dimensions of the one beyond.

"Yes, but not exactly after the fashion of sardines, one on

top of the other," she replied good-humoredly, and secretly
wondered what could have prompted such a question on the
part of Dr. Holley.

"I suppose you couldn't take in one more?" he enquired
quite anxiously.

"Well, it would all depend upon the size of that one. If
it were a large one now, I am afraid not; if a 'teenchy, tiny'
one, as my little Lillian says, then maybe so."

"Fortunately, in this case it is a 'teenchy, tiny' one, only
a size or so larger than your own little girl."

She looked at him enquiringly.

"You have seen the little Indian girl, Matouchon, who
lives with Unkama and Tohausin at the yellow tepee?"

"Oh yes, many times. Unkama has brought her here and
my children have been there to see and play with her."

"Mrs. Melville," and now in his great earnestness the
Doctor bent nearer her, "I am going to ask a favor of you.
You know how sick Tohausin has been? Well, he is no better. The end cannot be very far away now, but through a
removal to higher and drier ground it may be held back
several months, maybe a year or so longer than it could possibly be here. Knowing his wife's devotion to him and how
she would keep him every day that she can, I have advised
this change right away. Unkama is ready to go at any time.
There is only one thing that detains her now."

"And that?"

"A home for the little Matouchon, where she will be kindly
treated and have the training of a Christian household. You
know the little one's history. Of course, I am deeply interested in all that concerns her. I wish her to remain here and
attend school. I have made all necessary arrangements about
that with Miss Davis. She will take her with the white
children, as none of their parents object. The only thing in
the way now is the securing of a proper home for her, and
that is really the greatest consideration after all."

"And you came this afternoon hoping I would take her?"

The missionary's wife had a way of going straight to the point that was very gratifying to one of the Doctor's own straightforward nature.

"Yes, Mrs. Melville, I did, and I hope it is not asking too much of you. I know how many little ones of your own you have." Then he added as he had done to Unkama, "I do not wish to tax you with the support of her but only the care."

"I would be willing to take her without a provision of this kind," the missionary's wife said generously.

"But I would not consent to that. You must let me provide for her; I insist upon it. I am fully able to do so, you know. Can it be," he concluded joyfully, "that you will really take her?"

"Yes, I will take her. At first, I could not see my way quite clear, for we are so crowded. But now, I have concluded to let her sleep with my own little ones. I know Unkama has taught her to be nice and clean, and I can continue the lesson. One more can squeeze into Emma's small bed. It shall be the little sand waif, Matouchon."

"God bless you for those words," said the Doctor, with deep emotion. "They come from a truly noble and generous heart! How can I ever thank you enough!"

"There is no need for thanks, especially if I let you provide for her as you insist."

"But will not your husband object?" the Doctor asked, as he was going away.

"My husband? No," with an assured smile. "He always leaves such things to me. Besides, I know him so well he'd say, 'Let her come' as readily as I do. Why, he'd give up his own bed if there was need."

"I am sincerely glad it can be arranged without anything like that," the Doctor said, as he bade her good-bye.

Unkama's joy was great when she learned that her beloved Matouchon was to have a home with the good missionary and his wife. It took much of the bitterness out of the parting, though it was still bitter enough for both of them. Over and over again, Unkama instructed the little one as to just how she was to make herself as useful and as helpful as she could.

On the second day after Dr. Holley had arranged with Mrs. Melville, everything was put in readiness for the departure of Unkama and Tohausin. That night, Matouchon slept in the arms of her dear adopted mother, even Tohausin for the time being partially forgotten. Matouchon felt like sobbing out all her grief at the parting on the dear breast that had been her resting place ever since she could remember. But she was a thoughtful, womanly little thing, and with a great effort, she refrained from showing her feelings, fearing that it would not only increase Unkama's grief, but disturb and distress poor Tohausin who was also greatly attached to her. So, she bravely choked back the sobs, though many were the tears that fell in silence.

The sun was well up, ere the start was made. Dr. Holley had advised this, in order to avoid the morning mists. He came in person to direct the departure and also to carry Matouchon to her future home.

"And will Unkama and Tohausin be long on the way," the little one asked him, as she stood holding his hand and gazing wistfully after the spokes of the wagon wheels.

"Ere the sun has said good-night to the hills, my Matouchon," he said in reply to her, "our dear good Unkama and Tohausin will be at their journey's end. It is only twenty-five miles away."

"It is not so far, then, but that we may go many times to see them?" She asked the question wistfully, gazing up into his face, while the tears trembled upon her lashes.

"Ere another big round moon has come up over the plains, Matouchon shall see Unkama; and every time that moon is as round and full and big as my little girl's eyes were when she was a happy, laughing baby, then she shall go over those plains to where the dearest and best arms in all the world await her."

The sunshine of a smile was struggling through her tears now, and as he stooped and kissed her, she put her arms around his neck and said softly: "I will try to be as patient and as obedient as I can, for, oh, you are so good to me?"

As they reached the mission house, they found that the missionary had just returned from one of his long trips over the plains. But he had been at home a sufficient time for his wife to tell him of the addition that was to be made to his family. "And so I am to have another little girl!" he said cheerily, as Matouchon crossed over the room to shake hands with him.

"May I be just like your own little girl?" she questioned anxiously, as she gazed up timidly into his face.

"That you may, my dear," he responded heartily. "And now, if I let you be like my own little girl, I want you to tell me what you'll do for me in turn." This he said a little quizzingly, and it is safe to say, he had no idea of the answer she would give him.

"I will love you and serve you," she said, looking straight up into his face with eyes that spoke eloquently of the love and faith of which the loyal soul could be capable.

"God bless you, my child, God bless you!" he said with emotion, which others shared besides himself.

And all her life long, those two words were truly indicative of the thoroughly sweet and devoted nature that was hers— love and service.

CHAPTER III.

THE MARK OF THE FINGERS.

"O MOTHER," cried Emma Melville, as she came running in one morning about two months after the events related in the preceding chapter, "there is an Indian woman out here, and she is just going on terribly. She said she must see father. I understood that much, but couldn't understand any more, for she acted as if she were crazy. I believe she *is* crazy, for she made such terrible gestures and her eyes just blazed. She has been in a fight too," the little girl continued breathlessly, "for there is blood all over her."

"Emma," said her mother reprovingly, "you are worse than a prairie wind. You are twelve years old, and must try to be less boisterous. Why, from the way in which you ran in, slammed the door, and fell over a chair, I thought something had frightened you out of your senses."

"Well, mother, I was frightened, and I am frightened now. It is just as I told you; the woman is a terrible sight and she is covered with blood. I believe her fingers or her hand or something is cut off. It made me so sick to see her, I couldn't look long enough to tell what it is."

"Well, did you tell her your father is not here?"

"Yes, mother, I did. I told her so twice, but she didn't seem to pay any attention to it. She said she was coming in here if he did not go out there."

"Well, go and tell her to come."

"But, mother, she is an awful sight!"

"That does not matter. We have seen awful sights before. But, first, go and call Matouchon to watch the coffee so I can have time to talk to the woman. And, do you go to Mr. Cleveland's store for Arthur Keotah to come and interpret for me. Not that I am afraid I can't understand her if only she will talk rationally; but if it is as you say, I'll doubtless need his help. Stay a moment, Emma. Is the woman Kiowan, Comanche, or Apache?"

"Comanche, mother."

"Then go as quickly as you can to the Agent's office instead of to the store, and tell him please to let Charlie Ahatone come here for a little while. As you go out of the gate, speak to the woman kindly and tell her to come in."

Emma's steps had not more than reëchoed from the doorway, when Mrs. Melville heard the woman coming in. A moment or two later, she stood in the room.

She was indeed, as Emma had said, a terrible sight. It was all Mrs. Melville could do to repress an exclamation of horror. She had evidently walked a long distance, for her moccasins and leggings were torn and muddied. In more than one place, the naked skin was showing through, and this was scratched and bleeding as though from stones or thorns. About her waist, was tied the remains of an old blanket, tattered and bedraggled. All the covering the upper portion of her body had, was a strip of calico about three yards long, doubled over, with a hole cut at the doubled end big enough to admit the head. It was hastily sewed together at the sides, with stitches that gaped, a place having been left through which to put the arms. As she was rather a large woman, a gusset had been put on each side to enlarge the garment below. But it was not only her clothes that gave her a terrible appearance. She wore nothing on her head, not even the usually indispensable blanket. Her hair was cut short and reached to her shoulders. It was thick, glossy, and of raven blackness without a single gray hair. But here the appearance of youth ceased, for her face was so worn and haggard, so distorted with emotion of some kind that she looked like an old, old woman. Her face was not only haggard and distorted, but it was smeared with blood. Her clothing too was covered with deep red spots. As she advanced nearer, Mrs. Melville noticed with horror that three of

the fingers of her right hand had been cut away. No attempt
had been made to conceal the bleeding stumps, though a strip
of cloth had been bound tightly about the palm to arrest, as
far as possible, the flow of blood. Overcome with pity as well
as horror at the woman's appearance, Mrs. Melville pushed a
chair towards her, motioning her to be seated. But she did not
do it. Her emotions were doubtless too great to allow of her
sitting down quietly.

"What can I do for you!" asked Mrs. Melville kindly. As
most of the Indians around the Agency and in her husband's
church were Kiowas, she knew very little Comanche.

At the question, the woman began gesticulating frantically
with her hands, and hysterically uttering words, among which
Mrs. Melville distinguished that of *cumufpa*, which she knew
meant husband. "I suppose that you want to see my husband?" she said enquiringly. "I am sorry, but he will not
be here before this time to-morrow. Can you not come back?"
But the woman did not understand her, and still kept up her
gesticulations and mutterings.

Mrs. Melville was in despair. How was she ever to make
herself understood? She certainly could not without an interpreter. Would Charlie Ahatone never come? Going to
the window, as though to find an answer to the question, she
felt her heart sink as she saw Emma returning alone. Neither
Charlie nor Arthur were in town. This was the message Emma
brought. Charlie had gone to Fort Sill and Arthur to the
railroad. The woman was still muttering, though her gesticulations had ceased, and she had sunk into the chair, doubtless
overcome at last by exhaustion.

Mrs. Melville thought quickly and her face brightened.
"Run, Emma dear, to the river where John is cutting wood,
and tell him to come just as fast as he can. He has been a
great deal with Willie Conover who understands Comanche
thoroughly, and he can doubtless find out what it is the
woman wants."

In about ten minutes, Emma returned with John. Both,

in obedience to the mother's injunction to hurry, had run until they were nearly out of breath.

John Melville was a bright, manly lad fast nearing his fourteenth year. He had always seemed the oldest boy of the family, as Mabin, who was really the oldest of the children, had been little more than an invalid all his life. John was not only bright and manly, but he was steady and reliable as well, a great help and stay to his parents, who almost idolized him, especially his father.

"John, dear," said his mother as soon as he came into the room, "here is a poor Comanche woman who is in trouble, and who has had her fingers cut off in some way. She wants your father, but I can't make her understand that he is not here and will not be until some time to-morrow. See what you can do with her."

John removed his hat, for every woman was a lady to him, and went and stood close beside the squaw, laying his hand upon her shoulder. As though the touch compelled her, she looked up quickly. Something she saw in the boy's eyes seemed to attract her, for she continued looking up into his face. "Is it my father you want to see?" he asked kindly.

She muttered an assent.

"Then I am sorry, for you will be disappointed. He is not here. He has gone to Tsait-tim-gear's (Stumbling Bear's), to see his sick son, and to preach to the Indians. He will not be back before to-morrow morning. You come at this time to-morrow, and I feel sure he'll be here."

"I *must* see him," she muttered. "I'll do as you say, I'll come to-morrow." With these words she tried to get up from the chair, but fell back again. John placed his hands quickly under her arm and helped her to rise. Once upon her feet, she seemed to grow steadier.

She was just turning to go away when her eyes for the first time fell upon Matouchon. During all this time, the little girl had been standing by the stove quietly stirring the coffee.

3

Though she had been badly frightened when the woman had entered gesticulating so wildly, and the sight of her bloody garments and multilated hand had turned her sick, yet she made no sound of fear.

As the woman's eyes now fell upon Matouchon, she uttered a quick exclamation and stood as though transfixed. Then she said sternly: "Why did you follow me? Go back home! go back, I tell you! go back at once!"

John, who understood the words, said quickly: "You are mistaking her for some one else. That is Matouchon, my father's and mother's own little girl they are keeping. Come out of the corner, Matouchon, where she can see you well."

The child did as she was told, though she was trembling visibly. The woman's manner and words had frightened her greatly; and now there was a look upon her face, which made the little one's heart beat even more rapidly than it had the moment before.

"Now, you can see that you were mistaken," said John again.

But still the woman seemed unconvinced, for she kept looking back at the child until the door was reached and she had passed beyond.

There was not only a look of incredulity upon her face but also a fast gathering one of terror, as both John and his mother could see. But the poor woman's head was doubtless turned by her troubles. Even after she had gone through the gate, she kept turning around to gaze towards the house, muttering to herself and standing still for a moment or so as though she expected some one to follow her.

"And so she took our own little Matouchon for some one she knows," said John, as he went to where the little girl was again standing by the stove and placed his arm affectionately around her shoulders. "Well, I think I soon convinced her of her mistake."

"Is there not something wrong with the poor woman's mind?" asked Matouchon anxiously.

"Yes, I think so, Matouchon. Her troubles have doubt-less turned her head."

"What could her troubles be?" asked Matouchon, more of herself than of John, but John answered her.

"I think she has a cruel husband and that he has treated her this way. You noticed her fingers were cut off?"

"Yes," answered the little girl, trembling again at the re-membrance.

"Well, I feel sure that her husband cut them off, and she came to my father to see if he could have anything done with him."

"Oh how could he have been so cruel as that?"

"Because he is a brute, but he is not the only one," con-tinued John. "Lots of the Indian husbands treat their wives this way. My father knows of several women among the Apaches, who have not only their fingers but their noses cut off."

"Oh, what makes Indian husbands do this way?" she asked with a shudder.

"Because they are savages, Matouchon, and know nothing of the precious religion of Jesus which fills the heart with love and gentleness."

The next day, the woman came back only about a half hour or so after Mr. Melville's return. It was as John had sur-mised; her brutal husband, Tab-i-to'-sa, had kicked her senseless, and then while in this condition, had cut off her fingers. It was long ere Mr. Melville could convince her that he was utterly powerless; that by a law of her savage tribe, no punishment could be inflicted upon her husband.

"Oh, you white people have such different ways!" she cried from the depths of her overcharged heart, and glancing as she spoke upon the sweet, happy face of the missionary's wife who sat with her husband's hand resting affectionately upon her lap.

"Yes, Amado, we do," he said gently.

"Why is it so?" she asked.

He took her hand kindly in his, and pressed it while he answered : " It is the religion of Christ Jesus that makes the difference. I have it in my heart ; Tabitosa has it not, hence he is savage and cruel. But sometimes where men have not this religion," he continued, " they treat their wives kindly. It is what is in the heart, after all. But every heart, whether it is kind or not, is made all the sweeter and better by having this religion in it."

She sighed and shook her head sadly. As yet she could not understand these words. She only knew there was a vast difference between her wretched lot and that of the happy wife before her.

" But, Amado," the missionary said reassuringly, " I will do all I can. You may trust to that. I will go and see Tabitosa and talk to him myself. If I am kind and gentle, perhaps I may finally win him to see just how cruel and wicked he has been. But I feel certain I can do nothing with him if I try to drive him. He has the temper of an unbroken mustang and the hard head of one, besides. Go home and try to bear things as patiently as you can. He surely will let you alone for a while."

This was undoubtedly hard advice to follow, but all Mr. Melville could do under the circumstances was to give it, and promise to talk to Tabitosa. He knew well that he must not meddle in a case of this kind. Each Indian tribe had its own laws and customs. Notwithstanding how harsh and cruel, how utterly barbarous they might be, no outsider dared to interfere. There might be some redress through the Chief, but even the Chief himself was powerless with reference to certain matters, particularly those relating to husband and wife. The husband was the supreme head ; the one autocrat from whose arbitrary rule there was no appeal. His wife was his servant, his slave, his dog. She had no existence of her own; everything in connection with her was absorbed in his. He could kick her, beat her, mutilate her, nay, he could all but murder her, and she would have no redress.

Mr. Melville knew Tabitosa well as one of the neighboring tyrants. He had several wives, and every one of them had been made to feel his heavy hand, though perhaps he had gone further with this one than with any of the others. Mr. Melville felt that he must be careful in talking to Tabitosa, but he determined to talk to him nevertheless.

Just as the woman was going out of the gate, Matouchon, who had been sent to the store on an errand for Mrs. Melville, came up, and stood for a moment waiting for the squaw to pass. Evidently, the child had not forgotten her nor the scene of the morning before. She turned pale and began to tremble as her eyes fell upon the woman. But there was sorrow in her heart as well as fear, and her eyes were very tender and sad as their gaze fell upon the poor mutilated hand. The woman seemed to have been expecting her, and the moment she caught sight of the child, she turned toward her with an exclamation that was part a sob and part a little moan of pain. The child did not draw away from her as had been her first impulse, but stood still, though she could feel herself trembling. The woman raised her hand, the one that was not mutilated, and placing it upon Matouchon's head, began to stroke it softly. " It is so like ! It is so like ! " she said. Then as though she had seen something that had struck terror to her, she turned and walked away.

The next day it snowed enough to cover the ground to the depth of several inches and to bank itself up on door sills and window ledges. That covering the door sills and the steps of the parsonage, was cleared away by John's ready shovel the moment the fall ceased. But not having time then, he left that on the window ledges for the next day. The little room in which the children slept, next to that of Mr. and Mrs. Melville, had windows rather high from the ground.

The night following the snow, Mr. and Mrs. Melville having seen all the little ones safely in bed, were preparing to retire, when they were very much startled to hear a sudden, sharp cry from Matouchon. On hurrying into the room, they found the

child sitting up in bed, evidently greatly frightened; while
her eyes were fixed in a stare upon the window at the foot of
the bed.

"Matouchon, child," said Mrs. Melville anxiously, "what
is it?" But Matouchon was evidently beyond speech for the
moment.

"Have you seen anything to frighten you, my dear?"
asked Mr. Melville gently. As he spoke, he sat down upon
the bed and drew her head against him. The warm touch of
his arm and the loving pressure he gave her seemed to restore
her.

"It was there," pointing to the window, which had the
curtain partly drawn. "It was there! I saw it so plainly, a
terrible face that was looking at me. Oh, how the eyes
shone! It seemed they would go through me!"

"Why, who could it have been?" questioned Mrs. Melville hastily and not a little anxiously. "I didn't know any
one was in the habit of prowling around here; the Indians
are so peaceful."

"Are you sure it was the face of a person that you saw,
Matouchon?" asked Mr. Melville at this point. "Might it
not have been one of the dogs that had climbed upon the
sill and was looking in?"

"No, sir, it was no dog; I am sure of that. Oh, sir, it
was a person! I saw the face quite plainly."

"Then, I must go at once and investigate," said Mr. Melville determinately. "No such person as this one seems to
be, must be allowed to prowl around here."

But though he went at once and was gone several minutes,
and they could hear his boots crunching the snow in every
direction, he had to report a fruitless search. "Whoever the
person was," he said, "he became alarmed and got away before
I could discover him."

"How did the face look, Matouchon?" asked Mrs. Melville again. "Was it a man's face or a woman's?"

"It was a woman's face," said the child faintly. "Oh, I

am almost afraid to tell you for fear I may be wrong, but I am sure it was—it was—it was the face of the woman who was here yesterday."

Mrs. Melville cast a hasty glance in the direction of her husband. "This is the strangest thing," she said. "The first time the woman came, she acted very queerly the moment her eyes caught sight of Matouchon. She seemed to think her some one she had left behind her, and ordered her rather sternly to go back home. Then Matouchon has told me how, when the woman was going away yesterday, she met her at the gate and began stroking her hair while she muttered something the child did not understand. All of a sudden, she turned and walked away as though she had seen something to frighten her."

"She has doubtless lost a child, and imagines that Matouchon looks like her," said Mr. Melville, by way of explaining the problem. "I noticed in my talk with her that her mind was a little unsettled. Sorrow and trouble have doubtless both weighed heavily upon her."

"Perhaps so," assented his wife, but she was not altogether satisfied.

The next morning, an examination revealed distinct tracks beneath the window, made by the moccasins of an Indian woman. There was something else also, a something far more conclusive than even the tracks. Plainly imbedded in the white bank of snow on the window ledge, were the imprints of three stumps of fingers and two perfect ones. As if this were not enough, there were crimson stains where the stumps of fingers had lain. She had evidently placed her hand upon the window, not heeding in her eagerness that it was her crippled one, and thus drawn herself upon tiptoe the better to look within the room. The strain had undoubtedly reopened the healing wounds.

CHAPTER IV.

ACROSS THE PRAIRIE.

ONE morning, some six months after the visit of the Comanche woman to the parsonage, Mr. Melville said :

" Well, John, my boy, since Miss Davis gives such a good account of you at school and you have striven so hard to help the good mother here about the house, I have decided you may have holidays the balance of the week, and go with me and spend three or four days in the camps. We'll start to-morrow."

John's face showed his delight, and he went at once to get his favorite pony, Spot, in readiness for the trip. Besides rubbing Spot up until his already glossy sides shone glossier than ever, there were his saddle and bridle to mend and a thicker saddle blanket to be looked up ; for John was too much of a plains man not to know that everything must be in ship-shape condition before starting, if he wished to avoid annoyances on the journey. By sunrise the next morning, they were off. Each carried his own stake pin, rope, and pair of blankets. Besides these, they had their rubber coats and a substantial lunch stored away in the pockets of their saddles. It was a morning late in May. The air was crisp and cool, just enough suggestion of frost in it to make their blood tingle. They turned their horses' heads and took a southeast course, directly towards Mt. Sheridan and the Wichita Mountains. All about them lay the boundless plains. Though the air was chill, there was little wind stirring, and everything seemed as if asleep. Even the tall grasses were scarcely moving. The wild flowers, too, were motionless as though deep in the enjoyment of their own sweetness. The purple blossoms of the wild sage were gemmed with dewdrops. As the sun rose higher and higher, the whole plain glittered and sparkled as though with a wealth of diamonds. Nearer the ground, there was a deep green plant with leaves shaped like those of the clover, only much larger. As the sun reached it and rewarmed it into life, the tiny veins running along the leaves glowed like threads of fire. It seemed as though they were on fire; and so too the heart of the plant, where a small mass of scarlet blossoms like the pendant bells of the hyacinth, caught and reflected a wealth of glowing flame. The grasses were as beautiful in their way as the flowers. There was a tall variety, shaped like sword tips, from the glittering points of which a thousand gems seemed tossed.

They rode on in this way for five or six miles. By this time the sun was well up, the dewdrops had almost disappeared, but around them the plains were as sweet and fresh as ever. They had now entered a strip upon which cattle were grazing, and John had to get down in order to open the little wire gate. The air was blowing bracingly from over the plains, the sun was shining from the depths of a sky as deeply, darkly blue as a baby's eyes ere many tears have washed them. All the earth was bathed in magical hues. Even the bare patches of ground, showing in a few places here and there, seemed to glow with a beauty that made them almost dazzling.

"O father," said John, "I feel like I can't ride on a morning like this. I must walk or run, use my own legs and not Spot's. How *can* I keep still?"

"Well, I'd advise your not doing so for a while, John," returned Mr. Melville; "at least, until we get through here. Those long-horned fellows out yonder look particularly vicious, and they have been eyeing us a little suspiciously for some time. I imagine your running would be just the very challenge they'd want."

"Oh, I guess so," said John a little nervously, and taking care to mount Spot as quickly as he could; "I hadn't thought of them."

"Well, I see you are thinking of them now," said Mr. Melville with a smile, as he noticed the alacrity with which John sprang into the saddle. "Oh, there is no danger unless you provoke them. Just wait, my boy, until we are out of this feeding ground, and we'll have a race with the ponies that will warm you up, I think, quite as much as one on your legs."

And so they did, and John had to acknowledge that the exercise was amply sufficient; for neither Spot nor Blinko were ladies' ponies, and the rough shaking-up they were capable of giving when put to the top of their speed, was enough to satisfy even John's ardent desire for motion.

About eleven o'clock, they came in sight of a small band of Kiowas, evidently on the move. But they had stopped to build their campfire and were preparing their noonday meal. "John," said Mr. Melville, "let us stop here, stake our ponies for a while, and go and talk to these Indians. They are some I have not seen before, at least to know them. I think they have come from down about Rainy Mountain, and are going up nearer to Anadarko, so as to be in readiness for next Issue Day."

The Indians received them kindly, shaking hands with them and then motioning them to seats around the campfire. As Mr. Melville was on the point of seating himself upon a pile of tepee poles, he was very much surprised by the actions of a squaw who came suddenly up to him with the light of glad recognition on her face. She extended her hand, clasped his, and, as she retained it in a grasp that almost made him wince, broke forth into joyful exclamations.

"You heap good! you heap savey! You heap medicine, good, good, good!"

She then took a seat beside him and continued talking, making animated gestures all the while. As he still did not seem to understand her, she burst out laughing; then arose, and extended him her hand again. "You not knowy me?" she repeated. "Squaw sick. Heap good medicine. White man make well again."

It now dawned upon Mr. Melville that he had seen her before, but when? A few more words on her part fully enlightened him, and he called to mind that one day, when on a round of the camps, he had come upon this woman out on the prairie, some distance from the camp. She had fallen prostrate upon her face, with her children screaming around her. He had revived her, ministered to her needs out of the little medicine case he always carried, conducted her to her camp, and a day or two afterward visited her again for the purpose of taking her more medicine, and also of reading and praying with her.

The squaw's joy was great when she saw that he at last recognized her. She pointed to the breast pocket of his coat and said something about "the book." He understood that she wanted him to read again to her from his little pocket Testament, and he was glad. He had been intending, in a short while to read to all the Indians, but now was as good a time as any. So, he finally made them understand what he wanted to do, and they all gathered around him with the exception of two young bucks who held themselves aloof, declaring contemptuously that they didn't want to have anything to do with a "squaw's book."

In deep, earnest tones, Mr. Melville read a part of Christ's sermon on the mount, explaining it in simple words as he read. The most of his listeners seemed deeply impressed, especially the squaws. As he finished reading, an old man, who had been among his most attentive listeners, said to him:

"What kind of a book is that?"

"It is a book called a Testament."

"What does Testament mean?"

"It means a last message that is given by any one."

"Well, whose message is that?" pointing to the book in Mr. Melville's hand.

"It is the message of one whom we call Jesus Christ, the Saviour of men."

" You astonish me. Does any one propose to be the Saviour of men?"

" One has not only proposed it, but is such; this same Jesus of whom I have told you. He came to earth to die that all men might be saved."

" Why did he do that?"

" Because he loved poor sinful man and wanted to save him from the wrath of a just God."

" Was God angry with man?"

" Yes, very angry."

" Why?"

" Because he had sinned and fallen far short of the glorious purpose for which he had been made. Jesus, God's Son, felt his heart open with pity, and so, he gave himself to die for the sins of men."

" That was a great thing to do," said the old man again, evidently much touched. " And did he come to die for those who lived then or for those who live now?"

" For both," said the missionary earnestly. " He is still the Saviour of men."

" And does that book contain the last messages that this Jesus gave?"

" It does."

" Well, all this is very strange. I never heard of this Jesus, nor the book—the message you say that was given by him. But your words, the words you have read and explained to us, make something stir here," laying his hands upon his breast, " for they are like no other words I have heard before. I shall ponder them, and some time, I hope to have you tell me again the words that this Jesus has said."

" Yes, my friend, I too hope so. Come to the little church at the Agency, and there you will hear me tell again, once every week—sometimes oftener—of this Jesus, the Saviour of men and of his wonderful words."

" But how am I to know when to come?"

" Give me the stick in your hand. Now, see here: I cut

four short notches and then one long one. When each day passes, trim away a notch, and when you have come to the long one, then you will know that the day that is marked by the long notch is the one on which you are to come and hear me tell more of Jesus and of the wonderful words he has sent."

The Indian seemed much impressed and said he would remember. Then with the Indians all around him, Mr. Melville offered up a most fervent prayer that the light might speedily come to these souls that still groped in the darkness. At its close, they pressed him most cordially to stay to dinner with them, and doubtless he would have done so but for the incident that happened just about this time.

The services over, the squaws went at once to attend to a pot that swung from a cross piece set upon stakes. It was now boiling away as though it contained the most savory meal in the world, and doubtless the Indians themselves thought so. Mr. Melville, however, was of an altogether different opinion, as the sequel will show. One of the Indian women caught up a long-handled spoon lying near, and began vigorously to stir the boiling mass. As she did so, and lifted the meat to the top for a better inspection, Mr. Melville was horrified to see that it was dog meat, and not only dog meat but the hair and hide were still on. It was nothing more nor less than a fat four months' old puppy.* Excusing himself kindly but firmly, Mr. Melville had soon shaken hands with all, mounted his pony, and was riding away.

John's face was a study as he followed his father. There was a feeling too about his stomach that was far from giving him a pleasant sensation. "Just to think, father, if you hadn't discovered the shape of the puppy in time, what would have happened! Ugh! it just makes me sick even now to think of it!"

"Well, in this case, at least, the imagination is far prefer-

---

*Among certain bands of the Kiowas and Apaches, dog meat is still eaten with considerable relish. Indeed, no morsel is considered more toothsome than a fat young puppy. They cook it with the hair on.

able to the reality, John; so get over that sick feeling as fast
as ever you can and be thankful it is no worse. Once the
Indians had proffered us the meat, we could not have refused
it without making them downright angry with us, and thus,
much of the good seed which I hope I have sown would undoubtedly have been lost."

At noon they halted, picketed their horses, and crept into
a thick clump of wild mustard, which grew as tall as a man.
This afforded them a shelter from the heat of the sun, and
then they partook heartily of their lunch. They had also to drink
from the leather bottle they had brought along, as there was no
water to be found. In the meantime, the horses were feeding
upon the luscious grasses that grew in abundance everywhere
around them.

"It is too bad they have no water," said Mr. Melville, "but
I hope to procure some for the faithful fellows before we camp
to-night."

"O father, are we going to camp to-night?" asked John
eagerly.

"Yes, John, that is the plan I now have in view, though
some circumstance may alter it."

"Well, I hope not. Oh, it will be just glorious to camp!
especially if we can get a place to suit us."

"I think I know the place," said Mr. Melville confidently,
"and, if I mistake not, we'll soon strike into the trail that will
lead us to it."

Mr. Melville was not mistaken in his calculations, for about
three o'clock in the afternoon, they began to come upon signs
that he recognized as familiar. In less than an hour, the trail
became very perceptible. Just as the sun was sinking, they
rode up to a little belt of timber and there dismounted. Under
one of the trees, they found a woodman's rough shanty, but
no sign of life. The wood camp was for the time deserted.
They took the trappings off of their horses, watered the animals
in a little stream near by, and then staking them out on the
prairie where they could have plenty of the rich grass to feed

upon, entered the hut. It had a ground floor and a very poor apology for a roof which at one side had been left partly open so the smoke could escape. But as the weather was not cold, only chilly, it was very acceptable shelter. Soon they had a cheerful fire kindled, for there were plenty of chips and small bits of wood near at hand. They warmed their lunch, ate heartily of it, read a chapter each in the Bible by the light of the fire, sang, said their prayers, and went to bed. It was not a very inviting bed, for they had only their blankets between them and the ground and their saddles for pillows. But John, at least, enjoyed it, for next morning he declared he had never slept sounder in all his life.

The next day, as they stopped for dinner, Mr. Melville was in a dilemma with reference to driving down the iron stake-pins so that the ponies could be secured while they ate and rested, for there was not a stone or a billet of wood to be found in any direction. Just as he was in the deepest of the perplexity, John suddenly gave a solution to the problem by calling out,

" Father, why do you not use your boot ? "

Sure enough, why hadn't he thought of it? " But it always takes a wideawake boy for an emergency of this kind," he said to himself. Mr. Melville wore very heavy, thick-heeled boots, and such was their weight that he found no trouble in driving the stake-pins down into the soft soil of the prairie.

The ride for most of that morning had been over a rather cheerless portion of the Territory. In winter it must be exceedingly bleak and drear, they thought. It was no wonder that few signs of life were visible. Now and then, they saw a buzzard flying high in the air. Once, they caught sight of a big gray and brown eagle, but he was making his way off so swiftly toward a clump of cotton-woods in the distance, that they had no more than a glimpse of him.

" He'll be a dead bird as soon as the Indian bucks get a sight of him," declared John with conviction. " Father, what do you reckon is the reason the Indians are so fond of eagle feathers? Fully a third of the Indians who come to the church still wear them, though you have tried in such a kind way to get them to stop.   And they set such a high value upon them too.   I tried to get old Tsaitiente to sell me one of his, as I wanted to send it to cousin Reuben over in the States, but the old chief wouldn't part with it for any consideration."

" I think the reason they are so fond of the feathers," said Mr. Melville, " is because they think the wearing of them lends them such dignity ; and I suspect the reason they don't want to part with them, is because they think it will bring them bad luck."

The only other signs of life they saw, with the exception of one or two small Indian camps they passed, were a couple of coyotes that came very near their path.   They were doubtless hungry and in search of food, which accounted for the rather bold way in which they approached and stood eyeing the travellers, for generally the coyote is very cowardly except when in packs.

" If I had my gun," said John, " I'd get those fellows' skins ! Wouldn't they make a nice rug now for the little mother's feet ? "   She was always " the little mother " to him, though she towered a head or more above him.

" Well, I'm glad you haven't the gun, John," his father said earnestly, "since we are bound on a peaceful errand.   It might seem too warlike."

" Father," said John, after a moment's thought, " do you know what the men at the Agency say?   They say that you are running a great risk in traveling thus over the Territory without firearms of any kind.   Some of the Indians are quite lawless, you know ? "

" Yes, John, and more than once, I have had troublous times with them.   But I do not think it best to carry fire-arms.   Sometimes, the display of them does more harm than not having any.   Besides, most of the Indians know me now, and there is really little danger.   Then too, John, my lad," he said reverently, " there is One above who watches over all our ways."

He had hardly spoken the words, when suddenly they descried across the prairie a mile or so in the distance, three Indians, putting spurs to their ponies and coming toward them at a sweeping pace. Soon they were near enough for their wild yells to be heard. To add to the warlike appearance of the picture, they had guns in cases slung to the pommels of their saddles; while, even at that distance, could plainly be seen the gleam of the knives in their belts.

" O father," said John, turning pale, " now I am sure something dreadful is going to happen. Oh, if I had only brought my gun ! "

" Be still, my boy, and don't borrow trouble. Wait till it comes. I think I know these Indians better than you do. See, they have not even unslung their guns."

" But they are yelling like crazy creatures, and brandishing their arms, and just see how they are riding ! Father," added John quickly " let us do some fast riding too, off here to the left ! I am sure Spot and Blinko can outrun those ugly little ponies. Say, father, will you not ? "

" No, my son, that would be the very worst thing we could do. They would think then we were afraid of them. The best way is to keep right on and meet them."

The Indians were now almost upon them and were slackening their pace. They were in full Indian costume, moccasins, leggings, beaded jackets, blankets, and feathers. Their faces were also painted in a horrible manner. As they drew near, Mr. Melville recognized one of them as Dogoba, an Indian he had seen around the Agency several times. He had evidently constituted himself the spokesman of the party, for he rode up at once to Mr. Melville and said, in pretty good English :

" What you doing out here ? "

" I am on my way to visit some of my Indian friends at their camps," said Mr. Melville composedly.

4

"How long has it been since you left home?"

"I left yesterday morning at sunrise."

"How long it be you expect to stay?"

"Four days in all, my friend."

"What may it be that is your business?"

"I go to carry them a message of love and good will from One who cares for them."

"Which may be the camp to which you are first going?"

"To that of Ta-ta-quit-nam'-se, among the Comanches."

"That will do my friend," he now said in Kiowan. "We are satisfied," and with these words he put spurs to his horse and went flying off again across the prairies, the others following.

"Well," said John, throwing his head back to laugh heartily, "if that doesn't beat all! So, it was only curiosity after all, that brought those fellows down upon us in all their warlike array?"

"Yes, my son, and I suspected their design from the first, and that was the reason I advised our doing just as we did. This is not the first experience of the kind I have had with them. The Indian has a great deal of curiosity, especially the men. But that may be," he said after a moment, and smiling, "because they have less hesitation with reference to showing it. Why, I have had them to stop me right in the midst of my sermon to ask me the most foolish questions, with reference to my dress, the way my hair is parted, and other things equally trivial. But this has always happened at the camps. At the church, as you know, they keep very quiet, for they seem to have a reverence for the place."

They passed several small camps of Indians during the afternoon, at each of which Mr. Melville felt a strong inclination to stop. But he knew that if he did so, he would very likely not reach Tataquitnamse's camp that night, and this he felt he must do.

CHAPTER V.

A T about four o'clock in the afternoon, they came in sight of the Wichita Mountains, near the foot of which Mr. Melville expected to find the camp of Tataquitnamse.

All the mountains in this portion of the Territory are but little more than hills, low lying and with but scant verdure upon them. But the Wichitas at this point were somewhat more thickly wooded than usual, having here and there a dense clump of box-elders, hackberries, cotton-woods, and scrub-oaks. The sun was considerably on the slant, and thus much of the mountain chain was in shadow—dark, purple, mysterious shadows, eloquently suggestive of the warlike bands that had so many times lain concealed within the wooded recesses. But where the sun shone full upon the mountains, the foliage was a very beautiful, rich, deep green, with here and there a flame of color, due to a luxuriant tangle of vine, laden with a mass of scarlet bell-shaped blossoms. Further down the slopes, and almost out into the valley, grew thick clusters of the wild flower known as "Snow on the mountains;" but the snow of these beautiful blossoms had a dash of rich cream color near the heart.

They rode on now through a magnificent growth of wild sunflowers, which, unlike the sunflowers known to us, grew in thick bunches or clusters; sometimes as many as twenty-five or thirty flowers hanging from one stalk. In many places, they grew high above the heads of the horsemen, and it was with difficulty they could make their way through them.

"I think these fellows must have decided to hold their summer convention at this spot," said John, "to judge by the thickness with which they are gathered. Why they seem to be here from all over the country!"

"Doubtless they are," returned Mr. Melville. "You know their tendency to spread, especially if the soil is turned in the least. I should judge that at some time one of the Indians, more enterprising than the general run of his fellows, had up-turned the sod here by way of experimenting with his government plow. Then, you know, too, how the birds can spread the seed."

They came now upon stalks which were as thick as a man's arm, around which they made their way with difficulty.

"I do wish," said John, grumbling again, "that they had made up their minds to settle somewhere else."

"I don't think, John, if it were in the fall or winter of the year, and a cold night had caught you out on the plains far away from wood of any kind, as is so often the case, that you would complain of your ill fortune in having encountered the sunflowers."

"Why not, father?"

"Because they would be your only hope for a fire, and a first-rate one too if they grew like this."

"Well, I should think it would be a pretty poor sort of a fire, going out as fast as it was built up."

"There you are mistaken. If dry, the stalk of the sun-flower, especially when as large as these, makes a capital fire which does not have to be replenished nearly so often as you think. The lives of men almost frozen to death, have again and again been saved by just such fires. So you see, that while to the farmer of the Territory the sunflower is a great nuisance, hardly any field of size being exempt from it, it is to the fall and winter traveller on the woodless plains a blessing indeed.

The sun had set and it was almost dark before they reached the camp of Tataquitnamse. When some distance away, they could see the gleam of the white tepees and hear the hum of voices and other noises. It was quite a respectable village, a

"It was quite a respectable village."

P. 56.

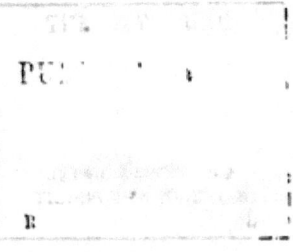

dozen or more tepees, enclosed by a protection of upright poles with flexible strips of willow and oak—the foliage on them—twisted from one to the other.

"Now, John," said his father, "as you haven't had much experience in visiting the camps, I'll give you a hint or two for your future benefit. Always, on coming to an Indian settlement, whether it be large or small, take care to ask for the chief if there is one; if not, ask for the head man. Pay your respects to him immediately, showing him that you recognize and respect his authority, and everything else will be easy. Indeed, you will be treated with great consideration, and the whole village will be placed at your disposal. You can go and come too at your pleasure without having annoying questions asked."

Tataquitnamse did not keep them long waiting. He came in a very few minutes after Mr. Melville asked for him. He was tall, slim and straight, with a fine carriage, and would have been handsome but for the horrid paint daubed on his face. He wore, pushed back from his face, an old cavalry hat that he had obtained from some of the soldiers down about Fort Sill and this was stuck full of eagle feathers. About the upper portion of his body was a kind of short shirt, made of brilliant hued calico, which reached to the waist and was there belted in by a leather girdle resplendent with beads and bits of shining metal. It had also a fringe of buckskin stained with many bright colors in front and at the back. On his feet, were moccasins, which like the girdle were covered with a mass of bead-work, with a fall of fringe over the heel. His leggings of buckskin were adorned with wolves' teeth, beads, and numerous bright brass buttons which were doubtless, like the hat, procured from the soldiers at the fort. Over all was draped a kind of blanket made of red damask, which was also belted in at the waist, and so arranged as to show his brilliant shirt and his beaded leggings; while the long ends, pulled through the belt, hung down before and behind almost touching the ground.

He received the travellers with much ceremony and great kindness, shaking the hand of each warmly and calling one of the squaws to take their ponies. At this point John, much astonished, was on the point of protesting and declaring he could take care of the ponies himself; but a look his father gave him said quite plainly, that he must take things just as they were arranged for him, without refusal or comment. So he had to stand by quietly and see the girths loosened, the saddles taken off, and the ponies carried away to be picketed with the other ponies, where they could get grass and water, and all by a young Indian girl not much older than himself. Though he outwardly gave no sign, knowing it was best to heed his father's warning look, yet inwardly John was raging.

"It is just like these lazy old Indian men to put everything upon the women!" he said to himself. "I should like to let them know that isn't the way we white people do!" and with this, John clinched his hand as though he'd like to give Tataquitnamse a sound shaking with it. But of course he knew this was out of the question. He must now be on his prettiest behavior, especially for his father's sake.

Tataquitnamse conducted them directly to his own tepee, letting them understand that he expected them to spend the night with him. John, and doubtless his father too, would have preferred another camping out, even on the open prairie, to the questionable accommodation at the tepee; for the dogs, women, and children were now crowding about the opening, and they could see that it already had double its share of occupants. But they felt that they must accept everything with good grace, especially as the old chief was treating them with the greatest hospitality. There were five squaws, nine children, and at least a dozen dogs within the tepee; for they had now returned from the outside, and were gathered about the travelers eyeing them curiously.

Mr. Melville spoke kindly to one or two of the women, but soon saw they did not understand him. He knew very little Comanche himself. The conversation with Tataquitnamse had

been carried on partly in English and partly by means of the
sign language.   Mr. Melville expected to preach to the Indians
of this camp through an interpreter who lived only a few miles
away.   He was a young Comanche Indian by the name of
Paul Koto, who had been a student at the Carlisle School in
Pennsylvania.   Paul was expected to arrive every minute, and
until he came, Mr. Melville had to do the best he could in
carrying on a conversation with the women and the two or
three men who had now come in out of curiosity.   Sometimes
the chief helped him out and sometimes John, who really had
quite a fund of Comanche expressions, as has been intimated.
He had picked them up at the Agency and through association
with a lad of about his own age, Willie Conover.   Willie's
mother was a Mexican, who had been captured in infancy by
the Comanches, and who thus spoke the language.   So, when
it came to the every-day phrases of Comanche communication,
John was really an adept.

He soon made himself perfectly at home with the children
and the dogs, though he took occasion to whisper to his
father, with a wry face at the latter, that he was quite sure
they were not going to sleep a wink that night for the fleas.
He already felt them taking full possession of his legs.

While they were in the midst of conversation, they were
suddenly interrupted by the loud beating of a "tom-tom,"
followed almost immediately thereafter by the discordant cry
of, "Hiya! hiya!" and the loud clatter of rattle-gourds.

"My men are going to perform the eagle dance to-night,"
said Tataquitnamse, by way of explanation; "after which
they are to feast upon the bodies of two young calves which I
have had killed for the purpose.   Come, let us go see."

Thus addressed, all rose and left the tepee, with the exception of two squaws who remained for the purpose of cooking the chief's supper and that of the travelers.

On coming outside the tepee, they found about twenty
Indians, principally young men, arranging themselves in a
circle.   They were entirely nude, with the exception of a

waist cloth, which fell about half way to the knees. In the center was the leader with his " tom-tom " and about a half dozen men with rattle-gourds. These rattle-gourds were dressed off with feathers, paint and beads. They were held in the right hand, while in the left hand of each was a wand on which was fastened an eagle's wing. While the men on the outside, or rather those forming the circle, were standing, the men on the inside were squatting down almost motionless. But the moment the leader struck upon his " tom-tom," they jumped up and began swaying their bodies from side to side, rattling their gourds as they did so.

The entire circle now took up the swaying movement of the body. At the same moment, the discordant cry of " Hiya! hiya! hiya!" broke forth again. It grew louder and louder, and more discordant, other guttural words now being added to it and the "Hiya! hiya! hiya!" seeming to serve as a kind of chorus. As the singing grew louder, so also did the beating of the "tom-tom" and the rattle of the gourds. The noise they made became almost deafening, while the bodies of the dancers were swaying back and forth wildly to the music, if music it could be called. But suddenly it dropped to a lower key while the dancing almost ceased. Then the circle divided, a part going to the right and a part to the left and meeting on the opposite side to come down in pairs, exchanging greetings as they did so. In the meantime, the dancers who had been on the inside of the ring had formed a circle around the " Tom-tom " man, and were now marching, with him at the head of the procession of dancers, their wands with the eagle's wings pointed above his head. They marched around three times in this way, and then the circle was formed again and the dancing resumed. Now arms and shoulders and head took up the movement as well as legs, and in a little while, so violent were these contortions, that it was difficult to tell whether these were human beings who were thus engaged, so much like animals did they seem. But now the music ceased as suddenly as before, and also the movement of the dancers, with the exception that those within the circle, now marched back and forth two or three times holding their wands high above their heads and rattling their gourds. Then at a signal, they sprang into the air, uttering two or three times the cry, "Hiya! hiya! hiya!" This done they joined hands with those forming the ring so that the space in the center of the circle was entirely clear. Into this one of the men now stepped and began a speech. It was all about some daring exploit in which he had been chief actor and in which the Great Spirit had favored him with success. As he finished, he flung his arms into the air, which was the signal for another cry of "Hiya! hiya! hiya!" accompanied by a stamping of feet. This finished, another Indian stepped into the ring and began to speak. His speech was also about some mighty deed the Great Spirit had helped him to perform. The beating of the "tom-tom," the rattling of the gourds and the stamping of feet that followed the conclusion of the speeches were all expressive of thanks and praise to the Great Spirit who had thus smiled upon them. The members of the circle broke up to squat around the fire and partake of the feast, and the eagle dance—so called because of the eagle-wings carried upon the wands and the clusters of feathers upon the gourds—had come to an end.

As they were turning to go back to the tepee, John, who was a little in advance of the others, almost ran over a woman who was bringing some wood to replenish the fire. As he drew himself up to avoid the collision, he had a good view of her face. An exclamation escaped him as he saw that it was the Comanche woman with the mutilated fingers who had come to the parsonage.

"Why, how do you do, Amado," he said, extending his hand.

Laden as she was with wood, she could not take it, but showed her pleasure at the recognition by a nod of the head and a smile that broke faintly over her face. She still looked cowed, and so sad, that John's heart was sore for her. How

he wished he could do something for her. He would have
stretched out his arms to take the wood from her and carry it
himself, despite the hint his father had previously given him,
but by this time they had reached the fire and she had thrown
her burden down.

"How are you, Amado?" John said again, determined now
that she should shake hands with him.

"Amado is not well," she said to him in her language.
"This hurts all the time," laying her hand upon her head,
"and oh, it is so sad in here!"

As she said these words, she placed both her hands over her
breast with a gesture, that made John reach up to wipe something very much like moisture from his eyes.

"I am so sorry, Amado. But my father is here. He has
his little medicine chest with him, and I feel sure he can give
you something to help your head. And, Amado?" added
John earnestly as he was going away, "won't you come and
hear him preach to-night?"

Amado shook her head.

"Too much work for Amado. Wood, fire, water, ponies.
No, no, no, Amado cannot come though much she would
like."

"But, Amado, I heard Tataquitnamse tell my father that
he was going to see to it that the squaws came to hear the
preaching as well as the men, even if something was left un-
done."

At these words a pleased look came into Amado's face.
"Where is the preaching to be?" she asked.

"Right in front of the chief's tepee. My father would have
it in the tepee, but he knows it wouldn't hold all those who
want to hear him."

"Well, it may be that Amado will get to listen," she said
hopefully. "Tabitosa not here now. Over about Fort Sill."

"Does he treat you any better, Amado, since my father
talked to him?" asked John earnestly.

A sudden light came into her face and her eyes glowed.

"'Tabitosa is the same wicked, cruel man," she answered. " He is crouching all the time like the panther ready to spring, but I can see that something the good man said to him keeps him back. I know not what it is, but since the good man came here and talked to Tabitosa for nearly an hour, as he did over there in the tepee, Tabitosa has not laid his hand upon Amado, except once, and that was when he took this piece from her ear with the nail of his thumb," showing a small scar as she spoke.

"Oh the mean old thing!" said John indignantly; " he is cruel yet. I do wish he could encounter some man who would treat him the same way. But you must be sure to come to the preaching, Amado," he added, as he was turning off. She nodded her head by way of assent, and then stooped over the fire to replenish it.

As the missionary came out of the tepee and saw the number of Indians that were gathered to hear him preach, his heart filled with gladness, and an earnest prayer went up to the Master whose servant he was that a rich harvest might come of this sowing. There were even many of the eagle-dancers present, their nude forms having now been partly covered by the folds of their blankets. Despite the wild revels in which they had so recently been engaged, they seemed disposed to give the missionary the closest attention, sitting with grave faces and quiet, respectful demeanor.

The chief had been true to his word. He had sent out and commanded that the squaws too should come to the preaching, no matter what they might be doing.

John was rejoiced to see Amado among the others. He wondered if his father also noticed her. But it was likely that he did not, there being so many present and he so engrossed with his sermon. But John was determined that she should be brought to his father's attention when the services had closed. He wanted him not only to give her something for her head, but also to say a few words to her in that sweet, gentle way, which only his father had.

Amado had two children with her, one a boy adout ten years old and the other a little girl of seven or eight. There was something about the latter which impressed John strangely. His eyes kept turning to her every now and then, although he wondered why. She was quite a pretty little creature with large dark eyes and attractive features. Her hair was long and black and glossy, but it was not well kept, so John's quick eye noted. Her clothes too had an untidy appearance, being soiled and ragged and insufficient to cover her body, for the gleaming reddish brown skin was showing in several places. There was a look about the child's face which struck a chill to John, though he had thought her features so pretty a moment before. It was a sullen, cowed look, forbidding at any time and in any face, but doubly so in that of a child. It not only sent a chill to John's heart but a pain also, for he was a gentle, sympathetic lad. He wondered again and again what could have given so young a person such an expression. Then the solution of the matter seemed suddenly to strike him. "Oh, I just know it is all through that horrid, wicked, old Tabitosa!" he said inwardly. "He doubtless beats his children as well as his wives, and don't give them a dog's showing. Poor little creature, no wonder she is cut and cowed! I do wish something could happen to the miserable old wretch," and then John had to pull himself up and give himself a good lashing mentally, for there was his dear, good, gentle father saying at this moment, through his interpreter, "Love your enemies, bless them that curse you, do good to them that hate you, and pray for them which despitefully use you, and persecute you." "My good father little knew he gave me about as hard a rap then as any one in the audience," he said to himself. "Of course I can't say anything more about Tabitosa." And he didn't, though he could keep neither his eyes nor his thoughts away from the little girl. There was surely something familiar about her, but just what it was he could not tell. The more he thought of it the more deeply puzzled he became, till finally he arrived at the conclusion not to bother himself any more about it. Then, boylike, his thoughts went off in an entirely different direction, and the little girl was for the time forgotten.

But John thought of her again, as, the sermon over, he went to bring Amado to his father. Then he learned that the little girl's name was E-chos-chy, which in Comanche meant Red Bird, and that she was Amado's youngest child.

"She is just so many years," said Amado in answer to John's question and his notice of the child, holding up eight fingers as she spoke.

Mr. Melville also noticed the little girl and, like John, he too thought there was something familiar about her. But he did not give it so much thought as John had done, and in a little while, engrossed as he was with other and weightier matters, forgot all about her, though the child never forgot him nor the warm hand-clasp he gave her and the kind words he spoke. Her lips would tremble wistfully many days thereafter whenever she thought of him.

Mr. Melville recognized Amado at once and gave her a cordial greeting. He spoke many sympathetic words to her too, which made her eyes fill with tears. She had followed every word of the sermon closely, literally drinking in parts of it. But oh, there was so much of it she did not understand! How she wished that it could all be made clear to her, as clear as these words the missionary was now saying to her:

"Be of good cheer, Amado. It is hard, I know, but try to bear it patiently. Learn to know God and to serve him. He will make the way plain to you and so much easier to go therein. Come to me whenever it is in my power to help you. And, Amado, there is a promise I want you to make me before we part. It is this: when next you are at Anadarko, I want you to try to stay long enough to come to the church." She did not understand this part at first, and so Paul, who was interpreting for them, had to repeat it. She gave the promise readily. She felt now she would be only too glad to go if she had the chance. There were so many things he had said in

his sermon that were still stirring her heart ! When had she
ever heard the like of them before !

" And now, Amado," Mr. Melville said, stretching out his
hand to take hers, " let me see if I can tell what it is that is
the matter with your head." He felt her pulse, examined her
tongue, and then, deciding it was biliousness, went inside the
tepee to get his little medicine case. He could easily remedy
this physical trouble, but, oh, how powerless he was to alleviate
the other which she had described as pathetically to him as she
had to John, by laying her hands upon her breast ! But he
prayed earnestly that in time, even this " sickness," as deep-
seated as it was, might be healed through the far-reaching,
all-sufficient power of him who has said, " I will have pity
upon thee ; be thou healed."

CHAPTER VI.

THE " BUSK."

TATAQUITNAMSE was very sorry to part with them. He entreated Mr. Melville to stay yet another day and night and preach to the Indians again. Mr. Melville longed to do so, but he felt that he could not, for there were two other camps still to visit. This was Friday morning, and he must be at home by Saturday afternoon.

"And when are your people going to send down here and build a church for my people?" Tataquitnamse asked him at parting.

"I don't know," said Mr. Melville sadly.

"Is it because they can't do it?" asked Tataquitnamse suddenly. "Haven't the people the money to do it?"

Mr. Melville had to confess that he thought they had.

"Well, this is strange," said Tataquitnamse again. "Don't they care for us?"

"Oh yes, my friend, they care for you very much."

"Well, I can't see how this can be. You say they have the money and that they care for us, and yet they do not send or come to build us a church. My people have never heard the gospel preached, only once or twice as you have come to preach it. They have no church. They have no preacher. Now I myself know very little about this religion you preach, but I can see that it is a very good thing. I can tell by the change it has made in those Indians over about the Agency. This makes me want to know more of it, and I want my people to know more of it too. Then I am sure they will quit lying and stealing and beating their wives, as old Tabitosa and others do. Do many of your people know about this religion?" Tataquitnamse concluded suddenly.

"Oh, yes, nearly all of them do," Mr. Melville had to admit.

"And yet they will not help my people to know," the old chief added a little bitterly. "Here are three thousand souls on these plains around here. They go on from day to day not knowing of a single one of the many good things of which you preach. The white people have a God who is indeed a great God, since he can do so much for them. Then why do they not tell the poor Indians about him and let him be their God too?"

"Many of the Indians have been told, Tataquitnamse," Mr. Melville said. "I go whenever I can, and I preach to them every time I have an opportunity. You know my regular work at the Agency takes up the greater part of my time?"

"Yes, my friend, I know, I had no allusion to you. Your hands are full. I can see it. You do even more than your share. You come here, away out here to preach to poor dying Indians. Why does not your church send us a preacher of our own? one that we could have all the time to preach to us?"

"The church, my friend, would gladly do so. It is not the church itself, not the Mission Board, I mean, who is to blame because you have no preacher. They would gladly send one if they could, but the money is lacking. There are other fields you know, where hundreds, yea thousands are crying out pitifully for the light, just as pitifully as you are here. It is impossible to heed all these cries with the amount that is in the treasury and the force that is at hand. Oh, if the people themselves would only awaken to the matter, to the great and crying need! If only one in every ten would but *give* in proportion to his ability."

"Why don't they do it?" asked Tataquitnamse bluntly.

"Because their hearts are not right. Because they need to be born again of the very spirit of missions, to be enkindled through and through with the flame of its earnestness. Because—if I must say it, my friend—they love money better than they do their God. But I suppose," he added after a moment's thought, "all are not so bad. There are some who are only careless. They do not know the crying needs of the work. If only they could come and see for themselves, how quickly their hearts would be touched and their pocket-books opened!"

"Can you not write and tell them just how it is?" asked Tataquitnamse.

"O my friend, how many times I have already done that! And I have not only done that, but I have gone back to the States and plead with them face to face. But keep up a hopeful heart; learn to know God and to trust him. It will doubtless come as you desire in its own good time. The Mission Board is sincerely interested in this work, and is doing all it can."

"Well," said Tataquitnamse, with the air of one who has kept back some very good news to the last, "if only they'll send the preacher, we'll build the church. Some of these Indians are pretty good carpenters. They've learned it by building the white men's houses. They will do the work, I know, for I have talked with them: and Tataquitnamse himself will get most of the lumber. You tell your Board *that.*"

"That I will, Tataquitnamse!" returned the minister quickly, a glad light in his face. "This is indeed glorious news, and shows the interest that has really taken hold of your people. Surely if the Board can ever see its way clear to sending you a preacher, it can see it now. I'll write them the very night I get home."

Mr. Melville was busy with his thoughts as he rode onward. Oh, what a broad field was here and how little it had been occupied! As yet, only about one minister of any church had been sent to from five to six thousand souls. How was it possible for one man, even on fire with the flame of zeal and with a constitution that could stand almost any wear and tear, to break the Bread of Life to so many perishing souls? When would the church, the people at home, arouse themselves to just what it meant to undertake to carry on their Master's work? Never would the thrilling promise of "life

5

eternal" reach unto the uttermost ends of the earth, as he
had commanded it should, so long as millions were spent in
gratification of self and only hundreds for the spread of the
gospel.   Never could the world be won for him who made it,
as long as "dollars for self, and cents for the heathen" was
the spirit that ruled the church.

On leaving Tataquitnamse's camp Mr. Melville and John
turned their ponies' heads in the direction of home; but as
they were going to make a kind of a circuit of the journey,
they passed to the right of the camp instead of toward the
left—the way they had come.

About eleven o'clock they reached the camp of Watch-e-ca'do.
Here they found the men preparing to celebrate the green
corn dance, or "Busk" as it is called.   The Indians engage
in this dance regularly once a year before any corn is eaten.
The dance is under the direction of one who is called the
"band-chief."   Each town has its band-chief.   Watchecado's
camp was considered quite a respectable town, since it had
reached the population of nearly two hundred souls.   Therefore quite extensive preparations were on foot to celebrate the
green corn dance.   Peen-a-bou'-net, the medicine man of the
town, was standing near a huge pot full of herbs and roots
which was boiling as furiously as a big fire could make it.

"Why, it looks like a regular witch's cauldron," said John
eyeing it suspiciously; "I wouldn't be surprised now if the
old fellow had put cats and dogs and owls into it!"

As though he divined something of his thoughts, old
Peenabounet glowered at John as he approached the pot.   Of
course, John resented it.   What boy wouldn't?

"Oh, you needn't be eyeing me that way," said John, half
aloud.   "I don't want anything you have in that mess," and
with a look of disgust he turned away and began watching the
Indians who were preparing for the dance.

Unlike the eagle dance, which had been composed entirely
of men, all the Indians of the town, men, women, and
children were to take part in this.   They were now gathered

in a group near the pot waiting on the medicine man. They were almost nude, having a covering only from the waist down to the knees. In the case of the men, it did not reach to the knees. The men and boys had their hair parted in the middle behind, plaited in two plaits and done up in animal skins or with the tails of animals. At the top of each plait, was a bunch of eagle or buzzard feathers. The hair of most of the women and girls was cut short, merely reaching the shoulders. It was parted in the center across the top of the head, the line being marked by a brilliant streak of red, blue, or green paint. There was also an arch of paint directly above the eyebrows and a line running down the bridge of the nose. The men had their faces horribly smeared all over with rude images of spears, tomahawks, and bows and arrows.

After a while, old Peenabounet seemed to have the contents of the pot to suit him, for he scattered the fire-brands in every direction and then waited for the mess to cool.

This took fully a half hour, during which time the Indians had joined hands in two circles, one within the other, and moved from side to side, gently swaying their bodies to the slow beating of the "tom-tom." Then the band-chief mustered them into line and marched them three times around the town, the "tom-tom" still beating and the rattling of gourds having now been added as an accompaniment. This done, he slowly filed them in the direction of the medicine man, who was now standing over the pot with a huge wooden spoon in his hand.

As each one passed by him, old Peenabounet compelled him to swallow a spoonful of the liquid mess that had been stewed in the pot. That it was not a delightful dose was evidenced by the wry faces of many of the children. Indeed, some of the smaller ones refused to take it at all, at which old Peenabounet gave them a look that frightened them so that they opened their mouths and swallowed down the dirty, bitter liquid before they quite knew what they were doing. They would gladly have spit it out again had that been possible, but he took care to hold their chins up in the air until the medicine had gone down. If they started to cry, he frowned at them again in such a way that they were so frightened they forgot what they had been about to do. When all the Indians had thus been dosed, they formed again into line except those who had been overcome by the sickness the medicine produced. But these were chiefly the women and children, for the men, having a contempt for what they called "squaw weakness," were determined to hold out as long as possible.

The ring being formed again, the dancing was resumed, this time with the violent swaying of the body and all manner of contortions of face and form. All this time the "tom-tom" was beating furiously and the gourds rattling. As an Indian would be overcome with sickness he would fall out. Sometimes, this would be right in the way of the dancers, and, as he fell literally, he was likely to be trampled upon before he could pull himself out of the way. In this manner one or two were badly hurt.

The scenes following the conclusion of the dance were disgusting in the extreme since the medicine was given by the medicine man for the purpose of cleansing them before they began their feast of green corn. It is considered by the Indians a great sacrilege to begin eating the green corn without preparing themselves for it.

Long before the dance came to an end, Mr. Melville and John had mounted their ponies and were riding away over the plains, for the former knew well there would be no preaching to the Indians of that camp that day.

About three o'clock in the afternoon, they came to a small cluster of tepees, and found a band of Apache Indians, who intended to stay only a few days. Mr. Melville was indeed glad to have this opportunity of preaching to them. One of the men he had met before at the Agency. He understood English well enough to interpret plain, simple sentences. Mr. Melville took care to make them as plain and simple as possible. At the conclusion of the services, his heart truly re-

joiced when two of the Indians came up and said to him that
they believed what he had told them; that they felt there was
indeed a God who could do much for them. They wanted to
know more about him and were coming to the church at the
Agency. Mr. Melville knew that it had cost them much to
come to this decision and that they must be sincerely con-
victed, since it takes a considerable amount of moral courage
to enable an Indian to come out from the old ways and attach himself to the white man's church. Ridicule and opposition on the part of his people are the two worst things against
which he has to contend. Only those who have witnessed it
know just how hard it is for an Indian convert to stand firmly
by his convictions. So, Mr. Melville shook hands warmly
with the Indians, told them how glad he was of their decision,
and encouraged them all he could to keep bravely to their decision until he could see them again.

Soon after leaving the Apache town, Mr. Melville and John
passed through quite a strange-looking village, much larger in
dimensions than any they had yet found. There seemed to
be also a multitude of inhabitants, but how queerly they
acted! As soon as the travelers came in sight of the town,
an alarm seemed to have been given. Immediately it was
caught up and sounded in every direction. The inhabitants
were now seen running helter-skelter from every quarter.
Each seemed to be making towards his own domicile. In a
little while every one had disappeared and not a soul could be
seen to give them welcome.

"Well, I must say this is a nice way to treat folks!" declared John. "Now suppose we were depending upon them
for quarters for the night, wouldn't this be a fine beginning?"

"I don't think, if they should turn hospitable and invite us
into their homes, we'd find quite room enough," said Mr.
Melville laughing.

"No, I think not," returned John. "At any rate, I'd not
like to try. But do look at that old fellow back yonder. Now
that he thinks we have passed by, he is sticking his nose out

as much as to say, ' Good riddance to you, and I hope you'll
not disturb me again.' Well old fellow, all I have to say in
return is, that for once you were too quick, for really we didn't
intend to intrude. Do look, father, there they are popping up
in every direction back of us, while in front they still keep themselves securely hidden. Oh, what scary creatures they are!
As if we'd harm a single hair on their precious little bodies!''

"Yes, the prairie-dog is quite a timid animal. He seems
especially suspicious of man and will fly to the cover of his
dwelling the moment he catches the sound of human foot-
steps. But nearer the Agency, I have seen small villages of
them that are not so easily alarmed. Many of them sit near
the opening of their little mound-like houses gazing unconcernedly upon the passer-by. I suppose they have been so
often disturbed that it is no novelty. But I have noticed that
they always take the precaution to place themselves as near to
the entrance of their dwellings as possible. This shows caution as well as instinct.''

The village covered fully a dozen acres, with thousands of
the little mound-like houses showing in every direction. As
they came in sight of a cluster of dwellings the inhabitants
would be seen quickly scurrying to their shelter. As soon as
they passed, the heads would pop up again in every direction.
Thus they passed entirely through the queer village without
making the acquaintance of a single one of its inhabitants.

" Father," said John suddenly, breaking a silence that had
lasted for a mile or more, " did you notice the little girl who
was with Amado at Tataquitnamse's camp?''

" You mean the little girl she was holding by the hand while
I was talking to her after the preaching?'' asked Mr. Melville.

" Yes; that was the one.''

" Yes; I noticed her John, but not very closely. Why?''

" There was something about her that struck me strangely.
I couldn't tell just what it was. It seemed to me that I had
seen her before.''

" I had very much the same impression," said Mr. Melville,

as he now recalled it. "I was very much struck by something familiar in her face, and was just trying to bring to mind what it was when my attention was taken away from her. I had forgotten all about it until your words this moment call it again to remembrance."

"Do you think father, we could have seen her at the Agency?"

"That is very likely. The Indian women and girls are constantly coming into the village you know to get their supplies, and many of them have some errand or grievance that brings them to the parsonage."

"Well, do you think the little girl—her mother told me that her name was Echoschy, and that it meant Red Bird—do you think the little girl would have been likely to come without her mother?"

"No; unless the camp was very near the village. We have doubtless seen her with her mother on one of the Issue Days. You know the women and girls are required to receive and carry away the supply of provisions."

But John was not satisfied. Over and over again in his mind he turned the question as to where he could probably have met Echoschy before seeing her at the camp. He knew that many of the Indian girls looked alike. Indeed, he was acquainted with two or three that he could scarcely tell apart. But he did not think this could be the case with reference to Echoschy. Her face was so different from any of the others. "It would be really pretty," decided John, "if only it didn't have that cowed look about it. And it is an old face too for a child to have, and so sad and despairing. Oh, if I could only just get hold of that old Tabitosa," and in his indignation he clinched his fingers with a force that would have left the print of his nails upon his palm had not the reins of Spot's bridle been in the way. John's face was in a cloud for many moments after that. Then quick as a flash it cleared. Trust a keen-witted boy not to find the solution of a perplexing problem if once he sets his mind to it!

"O father!" cried John, clapping his hands together with all the delight of a child, "I have it! I have it!"

"Well, what have you, John?" asked Mr. Melville much amused. "I hope something that will be of lasting good to all concerned. Maybe now, it is a solution of the Indian problem?" quizzically.

"No; nothing so grave as that father, I have simply found an answer to my own question. I know now why it is I thought I had seen Echoschy before. Well, it was not Echoschy I had seen but some one she looks like. Why, father, don't you know? haven't you seen? Why, it is Matouchon! Yes, Echoschy is just like Matouchon, only," added John loyally, "she isn't nearly so pretty nor so sweet."

"Well, now that you speak of it, I believe that *is* it," assented his father. "It is strange we didn't think of it before. But I didn't have the little one on my mind after that first glimpse of her."

"And, father," went on John, "I have another thought. Don't you remember mother's telling you how strangely Amado acted the first time she saw Matouchon? I was there and witnessed it all. She took Matouchon for some one else and ordered her to go back home. I know now it was Echoschy she was thinking of. The poor woman's head was so turned by her troubles she didn't stop to think of the difference that is really between them when you think of them both together. It is all certainly very strange!"

Mr. Melville too had on his thinking-cap by this time. He knew well every incident in Matouchon's history, for Dr. Holley had long ago told him all there was to tell. The facts were plain now and the story connected. Even John would see it after a while. So he said aloud, "It is not so strange, John, when we sum up the incidents. You know where Matouchon was found? In the sand. You know that she was placed there by her mother. At least, such was Dr. Holley's surmise, and all who know the horrible custom with reference to the birth of twins practised by these Indian fathers and mothers can see that it is correct. Well, Matouchon was found in the sand. She was placed there by her mother, in order to save the life of the other child. The mother was a Comanche woman, and there was a Comanche camp at that time very near the spot where the baby was buried. Now, here comes this woman, she too a Comanche. She has left her child at home and yet she thinks she sees her in another, so close is the resemblance. She goes on so strangely over this other one as to attract attention, as well as to frighten the child. Again the scene is repeated, only the next time it has the element of fear in it. Why? Because the mother, overcome by the remembrance of her deed, is haunted by the feeling that it is the child's spirit. Next comes the attempt to look through the window of the room upon the child. That was the mother heart drawn back towards the object it had wronged! Or, it may be, she wanted to see if the child was well cared for."

"O father!" cried John quickly "you don't mean to say that Amado is Matouchon's *mother ?*"

"It looks very much like it, John. The evidence is certainly strong."

"Oh, I don't want to believe it!" declared John. "I can't! It doesn't seem right. Our dear, sweet, clean little Matouchon the child of *that* woman!"

"But stop a moment, John. Think what Matouchon herself would have been had her lot been the same as that of her mother and sister. She is different; yes, quite different, but what made the difference? The way in which she has been brought up; the influences by which she has been surrounded. I'd want no more eloquent plea, John, of the power of Christian training to make these Indians as thoroughly new creatures, no more eloquent plea, I repeat, than the example of Matouchon, child though she is."

"O father," broke forth John suddenly, "it will nearly kill Matouchon when she finds it out. She is so attached to Unkama, and to Dr. Holley, and to all of us that it will quite break her heart. Yes, I know it will if she has to go and live in the camps with her mother."

" Well, she need not know, John, unless you and I tell her, and I do not see the necessity of that, at least for a while yet."

" But will not her mother find it out and tell her?"

" I think her mother already suspects it, John. At least her actions have said so. I must see her and talk with her about it. But you need have no fears in that direction, John. Her mother would be the very last one to let it be known. She stands too much in fear of her husband."

" O father, you don't think old Tabitosa would do anything real wicked if he found out about Matouchon?"

" I don't know, John. I am afraid so. He is both wicked and cruel. He could do anything he pleased and the Indian law would uphold him. It is from him I wish to shield the little one, at least so long as I can."

" You may depend upon me, father," said John decisively, " to keep silent. There is only one I am going to tell, and that is the little mother."

CHAPTER VII.

THE WORSHIP OF THE MESCAL.

IT was nightfall ere the camp of Psait-chu'-tel, the chief of the Apaches, was reached. Here Mr. Melville had an engagement that was of two weeks standing, hence quite a number of Indians had gathered besides those belonging regularly to the village. Here also his interpreter, Andres Martinez, was to meet him.

Andres had a most interesting history. It read more like fiction than the truth. He was a Mexican, and had been captured when seven years old by the Apache Indians. By them he had been cruelly treated, once or twice almost put to death. On his forehead, was the long scar of a spear thrust which had nearly ended his life. They made a perfect slave of him, trading him from one band to another sometimes for a small amount of intoxicating drink. Such was the life of the poor boy until he was nearly twelve years old. About that time, a band of Kiowas came on a visit for trading purposes to the Apaches who then had Andres. Among them was Tohausin the husband of Unkama. Tohausin was then a great and warlike chief, but even at that time he did not have it in his heart to be cruel to women and children. He saw the little Andres and took quite a fancy to him. He and his friend, Ke-a'-ko, effected a trade for Andres. They gave two mules, two buffalo robes, and three or four blankets. They brought him back to the Kiowan Reservation and made a present of him to Chief Tsait-to'-yo, who had also seen Andres when he had been among the Apaches and taken a fancy to him.

Tsaittoyo declared the boy should no longer be a slave, but should be a son to his daughter, the wife of Yeddle-ke'-ah who was a great Kiowan warrior. Soon after this, in a battle with the Utes, both Tsaittoyo and Yeddlekeah were killed. But the Kiowas proved very kind to Andres. He was quick, intelligent, and industrious, and picked up many things of usefulness to them. When three or four years had passed in this way, the government removed the Kiowas to their present Reservation. Andres was now sixteen years old. He was placed for a time in the Government School and made rapid progress. He soon learned to read and write and became of more service than ever to his Indian friends.

One day, when Andres was about twenty years old, he happened to be in the post-office as the mail arrived from the railroad station. For the first time he saw the mail distributed. The letters and packages handed out to each one aroused a new and strange feeling within him. He had many times thought of his home in all these years since his capture, but though it was always with a heartsick feeling and an intensity of longing, still it was in a vague kind of way, for he could remember nothing distinctly. But now, as he saw the letters given out and made enquiry as to what it meant, new thoughts and hopes and desires sprang up within his heart. This means of communication between widely-separated friends filled him with an intense longing that was soon put into action. Now, that he exercised his mind vigorously, memories that had slumbered for years were suddenly aroused. Names, places, incidents came one by one to him and with a vividness and force that stamped them as real. He recalled now his own family name. He remembered too his brother's Christian name. Then came also the recollection of the name of the place near which had been his home, Las Vegas, New Mexico. He went to Dr. George Holley and told him every circumstance of his history that he could remember. Then he got the Doctor to write to his old home a letter of enquiry. In due time, to Andres' great joy, an answer came back. His mother and brother were both alive, and oh, how they longed to see him! He went to them and stayed four years. At the

end of that time his heart being sick to see his old friends, and his mother having died, he came back to the Reservation and had been here ever since.

On the coming of the missionary, Andres had been one of the first to unite with the church, and had ever since led an upright and consistent life. He was invaluable as an interpreter, for his knowledge of three or four Indian tongues in addition to Spanish and English, put it within his power to hold communication with all people and classes throughout the Reservation.

Andres had arrived at the camp a little before Mr. Melville and John, hence he was among the first to greet them as they came in. They were both exceedingly glad to see him and Andres to see them, for quite an attachment existed among them, especially between John and Andres. Andres was now twenty-eight years old, but his heart was as light and his manner as cheery as though he were still a boy. It was this happy good-tempered way of his that made him such a favorite with all the lads around the Agency. No hunt, or camping trip, or expedition was complete in their opinion without Andres Martinez. And as Andres could be grave and steady as well as boyish and light-hearted, and as he was thoroughly reliable in every way, the parents were always entirely at ease when Andres had accompanied their boys.

Andres was rather small in stature, but he carried himself well. He had light brown hair, a ruddy complexion, and, unlike the typical Mexican, very keen, bright blue eyes.

John swung one arm up around his neck and rubbed his chin across his shoulder which was his way of meeting Andres after some days of separation.

"O Andres, it does one good just to see you! I am so glad you are here and so too is my father, I know. He was wondering, on the way here, how he was possibly going to manage in case that business with the Agent kept you longer than you expected and you did'nt get off."

"Well, it would have done it if I had let it," said Andres.

"I didn't get through, but I told Major Ware I must come. I got Charlie Ahatone to take my place."

"Good Andres!" said John approvingly, and gave him another rub of the chin across the shoulder, to which Andres responded by hugging the lad in genuine fashion.

At this point a messenger came to tell them that Psaitchutel was waiting to receive them. As they started towards the tepee, they were joined again by Mr. Melville, who had stepped aside for a little while to give some medicine to a sick child whose mother had earnestly solicited him.

Psaitchutel gave them a most cordial welcome. He had arranged a seat for them on his own raised couch. Mr. Melville sat in the center, with John on one side and Andres on the other. At the head of the couch was Psaitchutel and sitting on the straw at his feet, his favorite wife. Soon after the three entered the tepee, supper was served. It consisted of pork chopped into small bits and stewed, the rib bones of beef also stewed, bread, and coffee. The meats were served in a tin pan together, Mr. Melville, John and Andres having one pan between them. The chief also had a pan. The rest of the Indians fished up theirs as they wanted it from the pots, laying it upon their bread. The bread which was of two kinds, corn-cakes cooked in the ashes and wheat-cakes baked upon a kind of stone griddle, was placed upon a piece of oil-cloth spread out upon the ground where all could reach it.

As they ate they talked back and forth, Andres interpreting. Psaitchutel had many pleasant things to say to the missionary. Indeed, Mr. Melville felt the impression that he was trying to appease him in some way. He found out what it was, when Psaitchutel, after much urging, finally confessed that he and his camp were going to engage in the "mescal" worship that night as soon as the missionary had finished with his preaching.

Now, this mescal worship was one of the customs of the Apache and Comanche Indians that tried the missionary sorely, for he found it harder to combat than almost any other.

It was like breaking the drunkard of his dram-drinking or the opium-eater of his habit that clung like the arms of an octopus. Indeed, it had all the narcotic influence and the vision-producing effects of the Persian hasheesh.

The mescal bean, Mr. Melville knew was a Mexican importation, and the tribes of Indians celebrating its worship had grown into it through their associations with the Mexicans. It had begun to have so demoralizing an effect upon them of late that the Government Agent had positively forbidden the sale of the bean on the Reservation. Not to be outdone, the traders had now begun to introduce them in the shape of buttons. These buttons had, when chewed and swallowed, all the narcotic influence of the bean itself, for indeed they were nothing else.

It was no wonder, then, that Mr. Melville felt his heart sink when he learned that Psaitchutel and his people were making preparations to engage in the mescal worship. But he was indeed glad of the opportunity the chief had promised him of preaching to the Indians first. He prayed fervently that some influences might result therefrom to counteract the vicious ones of the mescal worship.

Nearly all the Indians came to the preaching, for the chief had so ordered. The most of them were respectful and attentive and two or three of them noticeably so. Mr. Melville hoped much from the earnest way in which they came up after the services and thanked him for what he had told them.

But the chief sat with stolid indifference through the entire sermon. At its close he said to Mr. Melville,

"We will begin directly with our mescal worship, and I want you and your 'talking man,'" nodding his head towards Andres, "to come and see it. I will send for you when we are ready; or, maybe, I will come for you myself," he added with much condescension. "You get your revelation from God through the Book you have just read to us. You can read; we cannot. We eat the mescal, and God talks to us through that and sends visions and dreams that we understand.

Both these ways are good, your way and mine—the way of the white man and of the Indian. We all worship the same God, or, that is, it seems to me that we do from what you tell us of him. But you need not take my word for it. You come and see our worship for yourself. You can stay as long as you please, leave when you get ready, and it will be all right. Then to-morrow morning before we break up, I will come for you again, and you can tell us all that is in your heart to tell us, you can also say what you please with reference to our worship."

Mr. Melville thought this a very fair proposition, so he consented to go.

In about fifteen minutes, the chief himself came for them. He conducted them to a large tepee that stood near the center of the village. Approaching the tepee from the east, he led them once around it before he motioned them to enter. They could hear the "tom-tom" beating within, though in a low, muffled way, while there was also the faint rattling of gourds. There were about twenty-five Indians, all men, within the tepee. They were arranged in two semicircles, one behind the other. In front of them squatted the medicine man. He was perfectly nude with the exception of a cloth tied about the waist and falling in front. The other Indians were either fully or partly dressed.

On entering the tepee, Psaitchutel at once took his place in the center of the first semicircle. On either side of him were arranged the sub-chiefs according to their rank, and at the outer left-hand and right-hand end respectively the "tom-tom" and the "rattle-gourd man." There were also two other "rattle-gourd men," one at each end of the second semi-circle.

Mr. Melville was greatly interested in the "tom-tom" used on this occasion. It consisted of a pot which was filled with tea obtained from the boiling of the mescal buttons. Over the mouth of this pot was stretched a piece of parchment of sufficient tensity to give forth a muffled sound when beaten with the fist.

As soon as Psaitchutel had taken his place he was given a wand dressed off with eagle feathers and a rattle-gourd, one of which he held in each hand. When the "tom-tom" was beaten he would shake the gourd and wave the wand, the others with the rattle-gourd, joining in, while all gave utterance to a harsh, grunting sound.

In the center of the tepee was a fireplace made in the shape of a horseshoe with the opening towards the east. Just at the mouth of this opening was a vessel of water and a tin cup. Next to that, and further within the horseshoe furnace was a pot of boiled corn. On the other side of the vessel of water was a large dish of stewed apples and in front of all a larger dish containing beef.

Mr. Melville afterwards learned that this crescent-shaped furnace was to represent their worship of the moon, and the food grouped about it the good things with which the earth had blessed them, for all the Indians are *object* worshipers, more or less, worshiping the thing created instead of the Creator. On the western edge of the furnace was lying one large mescal button, and towards this the worshipers were now directing their attention. The medicine man also had a large sack full of the buttons. These he would distribute to each Indian as that Indian's name was called. This was repeated until the round of the two semicircles had been made several times. As each Indian received a button he would place it in his mouth, grind it between his teeth, then spit it out into his hand, roll it into a ball, hold it out in prayer towards the furnace, and then, throwing it back into the mouth, swallow it. All the time this was going on the "tom-tom" was giving forth its muffled sound, the gourds were rattling, and the worshipers were accompanying the sound with a swaying of the body and a discordant kind of singing in which the refrain, "Hiya! hiya! hiya!" could be distinguished at regular intervals. Over all shone the dim light from the furnace giving a ghastly aspect to the wild, weird scene. Very soon the narcotic influence of the mescal began to have its effect.

6

The men were constantly shutting their eyes and letting their heads fall forward upon their breasts. Then it was that they saw the visions and dreamed the dreams to which Psaitchutel had alluded. Then it was that they saw pictures of the Indian's "happy hunting grounds" covered with lush grasses and beautiful green groves through which wandered the herds of buffaloes just as they had done ere the white man came.

Mr. Melville knew that they would keep up this worship all night long, so after watching it for an hour or so, he and Andres withdrew and returned to the tepee. There John was already sound asleep despite the proximity of the dogs with the fleas he so much dreaded. But these dogs of Psaitchutel seemed to have been quite respectable fellows after all, since the fleas didn't show up in any great force even to Mr. Melville and Andres who were kept awake for quite a while, by the sounds from the mescal revel.

In the night, it began to rain, but as the tepee was very nearly water-tight, they were not disturbed. Near day-dawn, however, Mr. Melville was awakened by a racking headache and opened his eyes to find the tepee filled with smoke. It was so dense that some of them would surely have suffocated but for his prompt action. He knew at once what was the matter. The rain had caused the wind to change suddenly during the night, and the flap at the top of the tepee, called the windward flap, was now turned in the wrong direction. It was beating the smoke back into the tepee instead of giving it free outlet. Mr. Melville rushed at once to the opening of the tepee, threw back the curtain covering it, and, as his lungs drank in the pure, fresh air, thanked God fervently for it. Then groping for the string of the windward flap, he drew it in the right direction. This done, he went back and lay down again, but he did not sleep much between that and day-dawn as the noise of the mescal revel had now broken out afresh.

At daylight, the "tom-tom," operated by the medicine man, began to beat furiously. Next the rattle-gourds joined in. Then the voices of the worshipers broke forth in shoutings and in songs loud enough to awaken every sleeper, except one totally deaf. The noise could be heard a mile or more. But as suddenly as it began it ceased, at the expiration of about five minutes. It was the mescal worshipers' hail to the rising sun. As the noise ceased, the squaws, who had been appointed for the occasion, and who were in readiness, approached the tepee with food for the devotees. As soon as breakfast was served, the worship ended.

Breakfast was also served to the visitors in the chief's tepee very soon afterwards. At its conclusion, the chief sent for Mr. Melville to come and express himself before the mescal worshipers. It was a trying position for the missionary. If he spoke his mind as freely as his inclination directed, there was the danger of angering them and of thus losing his influence among them. This was one side of the question ; on the other, was the cowardice of not speaking out boldly for his Master when he had the opportunity. But on his way to the tepee where the mescal worshipers awaited him, Mr. Melville decided to take a middle course. He would speak kindly to the Indians, yet he would be firm too. He would tell them how sinful was this revel in which only the senses held sway and in which their better nature had no part.

On reaching the tepee, he found a sad state of affairs. Most of the Indians were in too much of a drunken stupor to listen to him intelligently. But he found the chief and a few of the others still in possession of their faculties to a certain extent and ready to hear him.

Mr. Melville began by saying kindly, that as he had been invited to speak to them, he intended expressing his mind freely, but he did it solely for their good and because he felt a deep interest in them, prompted by that spirit which made all men possessing it feel as brothers. The mescal bean, he told them, was a downright poison calculated to injure the mind as well as the body. Its evil influence was fully demonstrated in the drunken condition of those around them. Though they had been as men on the day before, strong, active, and in full possession of their faculties, they were now little more than beasts or worse still, idiots. You might kick them all around the tepee and they would not know enough to resent it. If persisted in, this degrading habit would not only sap the very foundations of life and strength, but also of reason. It was a sad mistake to think that God, the true God, had part or parcel in any such drunken revel. On the other hand, it was certain that he looked upon it with anger and displeasure, since it was so widely different from any devotion enjoined upon those seeking to serve him. Mr. Melville ended his talk by earnestly urging them to turn from their ways of sin to the worship of the one true God and to accept Christ as their Saviour. He promised to come again and to tell them more of this Saviour when they were not so much under the influence of the mescal as they were now. He then sang a hymn and prayed. His heart was filled with rejoicing as he noted the impression he had made. Two or three of the Indians were sincerely aroused, and even the chief seemed to ponder his words. As he was turning to go away, Psaitchutel called after him to be sure to come again.

"Well, that was surely a scene worth riding many miles to see," said Andres as they reached the outside of the tepee. He had been interpreting and his own eye as well as the missionary's had caught the sudden change that had come over those of the mescal worshipers sober enough to listen to Mr. Melville's talk.

"It was indeed," assented Mr. Melville, his heart overflowing with gratitude to the Master who had so helped him.

Saying good-bye to the chief and such of his people as came to see them off, Mr. Melville, Andres, and John mounted their ponies and were soon riding over the plains in the direction of home. The rain during the night had made everything very fresh and sweet. There was no dust, and there was little mud except where they crossed some bottom-land which formed the valley of a small stream tributary to the Wichita. So, they made fine progress, having gallops and races enough to satisfy even John's ardent love of motion.

By five o'clock that afternoon they were at home and ready for the duties of the Sabbath.

CHAPTER VIII.

SUNDAY AT THE INDIAN CHURCH.

THE Sabbath dawned clear and beautiful. Everything was still fresh and sweet from the rain bath. The sky too seemed newly washed, with its glorious deep blue color brought out all the more brightly. The sun shone as though it intended to shine right down into and through everything and everybody until they had become as golden as its own rays. The green plains stretched for miles on every side until away off against the horizon the two color lines, those of earth and sky, seemed to blend into one, a vivid indescribable purple hue shot with gold. Now and then a patch of wild flowers lent their brilliant coloring to the scene, while the clusters of white tepees looked like flocks of great birds that had come to rest with their wings pointing heavenward.

Long ere the sweet-toned bell in the belfry of the little chapel had ceased its ringing, the Indians began to gather. They came many miles on their ponies. A few had been traveling since sunrise, so great was their anxiety to reach the church in time. One old woman had walked twelve miles and forded the river besides. Her clothing was still damp from the wetting it had received. Her face was scarred and haggard and worn, but there was an eager light in her eyes which told why she had come.

There were men, women and children. Nearly all the men were riding, for an Indian "buck"—the name by which the men are known—never walks even so much as a dozen yards if he can help it. A few of the squaws were also mounted. All rode man-fashion. Sometimes the mother and four or five children would be mounted upon one pony. As the ponies were small, the wonder was how they could carry such great loads. But the Indian mustang is both tough and wiry and has a hardy endurance equaled only by that of the Mexican *burro*. While a few of the Indians were in civilized or partly civilized dress, the greater portion of them were in their camp attire. Both the men and women wore brilliantly beaded moccasins and leggings, and had blankets or sheets draped about their bodies. The buckskin jackets of the men were a mass of beads, buttons, shells and antelope teeth; so also were their leggings, with rows of vividly painted fringe reaching from heel to waist. Around their necks were strings of beads, brass buttons, and bits of metal. While most of the women wore their hair short, that of the men was parted in the center and hung in two long plaits down their backs. These plaits were rolled around with strips of beaver or otter skin, sometimes with the tails of those animals. The faces of fully one half the Indians were painted, some of them horribly so, while eagle, turkey or buzzard feathers were stuck in clusters near the center of the men's heads. Some of the mothers came with their babies on their backs in their quaint board cradles; others again had them in the folds of the blanket slung with a loop between the shoulders, in the center of which baby found his resting-place. When the mothers sat down inside the church, the board cradles with the babies inside were leaned up against the chairs with the points of the boards at the top sticking up above the chair backs like the horns of some animal. Those that were carried in the folds of the blanket still remained upon their mothers' backs, and while the mothers sat upright, gravely and earnestly listening to the sermon, the babies would be screwing their heads from side to side or blinking their eyes over their mothers' shoulders.

There were an unusually large number of Indians present at the services this Sabbath, and it rejoiced Mr. Melville's heart greatly to see among them the old Indian to whom he had given the Sunday tally-stick and the two Indians from the Apache camp. There was also the old woman who had shown such a great delight when she recognized him that first morning he had stopped to preach at the temporary camp. Mr. Melville had a faint hope that Amado too might come, although it seemed highly improbable since it would require a journey of half the night and half the day, steady riding, to reach the Agency in time for these services. But he knew that she had a brave heart, was greatly in earnest, that Tabitosa was away, and that there was a pony at her command. All these things encouraged him to look for her. Aside from wanting to tell her more of "the good way" to which her heart seemed so earnestly drawn, he was anxious to see her and have that talk with her concerning Matouchon. He had told his wife the night before of the circumstances that had first led John, and then himself, to put together link by link the chain of evidence which pointed so strongly to Amado as the mother of Matouchon as well as of Echoschy. The children were so much alike that it was impossible to see them and not surmise the relationship.

Mrs. Melville saw matters as clearly as her husband. She felt assured that the mother of Matouchon had been found. Indeed, she had long had suspicions of her own, though she had not confided them to any one. The strange actions of the woman both times when she had seen Matouchon, and her return the night of the heavy snow for the purpose of looking within the room where the child slept, had set Mrs. Melville's mind busily to work, and the thoughts had brought about convictions. Still she had determined to say nothing until she was sure. She was waiting to see the woman again, but the opportunity had not offered. She agreed with her husband that it was best to see Amado first and have a talk with her. They felt assured she would want to keep the knowledge that Matouchon was her child away from Tabitosa as long as possible.

Like her husband, Mrs. Melville had the earnest desire to shield Matouchon from Tabitosa. Aside from the child herself there was poor Unkama. How great her grief would be when she learned of the matter! Then, too, Mr. and Mrs. Melville were greatly attached to Matouchon, and so were the children. Indeed, the little Indian girl was a prime favorite with the entire household, even with Mrs. Vecht, the stolid German woman who sometimes helped Mrs. Melville with her domestic work. Her cheerfulness, her kindness, her warm, loving nature, and thoroughly sweet temper had won all hearts. It would be such a grief to them to see her returned to the old Indian life and ways. And such a life as it would be with Tabitosa! Both Mr. and Mrs. Melville resolved that it should not be if they could prevent it. So, Mr. Melville looked out anxiously for Amado among the Indians assembled at the church, but up to the time when the text was announced she had not come.

Once launched into his sermon, Mr. Melville's mind became so engrossed with it that he forgot all else. He saw his Indian congregation as a whole and no longer as individuals, though of one thing he was conscious all through the sermon—of the intent faces of the old Indian to whom he had given the notched stick and of the two Indians from the Apache camp. How eagerly they were drinking in every word! The sermon had to be put into both Kiowan and Comanche, and it took a long time, but none of the Indians seemed to grow weary. Throughout the entire congregation, there was not an uninterested face. Even those who had come out of curiosity, merely to look on, sat earnestly regarding the preacher.

But how much of human nature there was in that audience after all! When Mr. Melville remarked that " all had sinned and fallen short of the glory of God," he looked around just in time to see Wolf Face grinning at Antelope and pointing his finger at him, as though to designate him as one of the sinners mentioned, and remind him of some particular sin of which Wolf Face knew him to be guilty. It reminded Mr. Melville of just how prone their white brethren were to judge in the same way, always forgetting the beam in their own eye in their lively concern to extract the mote from their brother's eye.

At the conclusion of the sermon, many of the Indians crowded around the missionary to shake his hand and to tell him how glad they were of the things he had told them. Among them, were the old Indian with the tally-stick and the two from the Apache camp. The former especially was grateful in his acknowledgements. He had evidently not lost a word of the sermon, for his eyes were shining and his whole face was expressive of the emotions it had stirred. His chief thought was with reference to the book called The Testament, from which the sermon had been preached that morning. He wanted to know more about it. He had many questions to ask. He besought Mr. Melville to let him have the book himself and hold it in his hand. Greatly touched, the missionary did so. The old man took it eagerly, wistfully turning it over in his hands and gazing at it as though he could never turn his eyes away again.

" How did that man Jesus, the Saviour, get it to us? " he asked suddenly, turning his eyes upon Mr. Melville's face.

" It was written principally by men who were here on earth with him, and it has come down from them to us," answered Mr. Melville.

" Well," returned the old man earnestly, " it is here, and you have told me how it came here, and I know it came from some one unlike anyone who lives on earth now ; for it is itself altogether different from anything I ever heard. I want to hear more of it. I am coming again, and I am going to keep coming until I learn to walk in the good way of which you have just preached."

" God bless you, my friend," said the missionary earnestly, giving his hand a warm and encouraging grasp.

" And now here is the stick on which you cut," said the old man holding it up to view. " How many notches must be cut next time so that I will know when the day is here on which I am to come again to hear you preach ? "

"Cut six short ones and one long one, my friend, and when the six short ones are counted off, each by a day, then the long one will remind you of the day I preach, which is called the Sabbath, God's Day."

As the old man was turning away, Mr. Melville was pleased, though surprised, to see Amado approaching. He had not noticed her before. She had doubtless come into the church while he had been in the midst of his sermon, and, as she had lingered behind a group of Indians near the door since the dismissal, he had not seen her. She had her oldest child, her son, with her, and both of them gave evidence of having ridden hard and fast, for they were bespattered with mud. As soon as she saw that he was noticing her, she came forward quickly and gave him her hand.

Despite the mud stains, he could see that she was dressed with greater care than usual; her clothing was not only neatly arranged but it was clean. The boy too showed that care had been bestowed upon his apparel. He was a shrewd-looking child and seemed fond of his mother. She now led him up, urging him to shake hands with the missionary, which he seemed quite unwilling to do at first. But some kind words soon brought more of friendliness to his manner.

"I am so glad to see you here to-day, Amado," the missionary said kindly, making the signs that she understood.

She smiled, and in the same way, by signs, made known to him her own pleasure at being there. Then as Andres approached, they continued the conversation without further trouble.

"I am afraid it was a long, hard ride for you," Mr. Melville said again.

She looked at him with brightening eyes, grateful for his interest. "Yes, it was a long ride, but Amado did not mind to make it. There was so much here to come for," glancing around her.

"I hope that you found all that you came for, Amado," the missionary said earnestly.

"Yes! Yes! But oh, there is so much that Amado cannot understand! so much that troubles her here!" laying both hands as she spoke with the old pathetic gesture upon her heart.

"What is it my poor friend that troubles you so?" the missionary asked, closely fixing his eyes upon her.

Amado opened her lips as though to reply, then with a glance towards Andres hesitated.

"If it is Brother Andres you fear," the missionary said quickly, "you need do so no more. He is as much your friend as I. He will help you in any way he can, for he sympathizes with you as well as I."

"Yes, that I do, Amado," added Andres, on his own account. "Tell us what it is that troubles you and let us help you."

"Oh, I am afraid it is something you can not help," she said with a despair that touched them both deeply. "But sometime Amado will tell you," she added, as though after reflection, "but not now! not now! But oh," she broke forth earnestly, "if only you will tell me more of this Jesus, this Saviour, this precious One, who has promised to be a friend to all! Will he be my friend as well as yours?"

"That he will, Amado, that he will!" Mr. Melville said, as he grasped her hand reassuringly. "Only trust him. Let him know that you *want* him for your friend, and oh, how ready he will be to hear!"

"And where does this Jesus, this Saviour live?" asked Amado suddenly. "Oh, if I could but see him!"

"He lives in heaven, Amado, the world above, the place to which he has gone to prepare a home for us. It is impossible for us to see him now, to see him in this life, since that is not his plan for us. But if we are earnest and true, and try to serve him here, we shall go to live with him in the beautiful home he has gone to prepare."

"Oh, I must come again and again to hear you tell of him!" said Amado, with glistening eyes.

"Do so, Amado. Come whenever it is possible for you to come. Don't miss a Sunday if you can help it. But it is such a long, long ride! You surely are not going to try to go back to-day?"

"Yes, Amado must go back. She start pretty soon now, two, three hours or so. Going to Gomb-ba''s tepee to get food and grazing for ponies. But never fear for Amado. Ponies swift. They carry Amado and Kan-ke'-ah home long before daylight."

Just at this point, Kankeah, who had wandered away from his mother's side returned to pull at her skirt, and pointing towards the door, whispered, "Look! Look!"

It was Matouchon to whom he was pointing. As the dwelling and the church joined each other, she had passed through the door into one of the rooms of the house very soon after the services closed. She had now been sent back by Mrs. Melville for several books that had been left on the organ. Kankeah had been standing near the door when she entered. Her noticeable likeness to his little sister Echoschy had first surprised and then astonished him. He was now endeavoring to call his mother's attention to it, but evidently she didn't need this effort on his part. She had already become aware of Matouchon's approach, and was now standing and regarding her with glistening eyes. The missionary could see too that she was trembling. He wondered if she would give forth any sound to betray the thoughts that were surging through her heart.

But she did not. She stood perfectly motionless save for the slight, barely perceptible swaying of her form.

Matouchon entered, obtained her books, and left again without noticing the little group near the center of the church. Neither had she noticed Kankeah, for he had glided to his mother's side very quietly and his hasty "Look! Look!" had not been much above a whisper.

Mr. Melville was glad that Matouchon had not noticed them, for he did not know what scene might have taken place.

He wasn't ready just yet for Matouchon to learn of her mother. He wanted to lay some plans first. The previous night he had determined to speak to Amado with reference to the matter if she came to the church, and in the morning he was still of that determination. But now, for certain reasons, he had resolved to wait; at least, until Amado herself made it necessary for him to speak.

CHAPTER IX.

THE FROGS IN THE MOON.

A YEAR had gone rapidly by, and now the great sorrow that she had so long dreaded had at last overtaken Unkama. Tohausin was dead. At first, it seemed to Unkama that she could not stand the great grief, that it would assuredly kill her. It was a blessed thing for Unkama that she had become a Christian. That helped her to bear it as nothing else could have helped; for now she had the sweet hope of looking forward to a reunion with Tohausin in the beautiful world above.

The little Matouchon had been many times to see them; for true to his word, Dr. Holley carried her, even a little oftener than he had promised. Those were indeed sweet and precious journeys to Matouchon, and with what eagerness she looked forward to them!

As he grew weaker and approached nearer his end, Tohausin seemed to cling to her more tenderly than ever. Sometimes he would imagine her one of his own little ones that had died, and oh, how pathetically he would talk to her then! It made a deep impression upon the child, and always, even to the end of her life, there was a peculiar place in her heart which only Tohausin filled. It seemed indeed to her that he had been as dear as a father could be. Certainly, no father could have been more gentle or tender or considerate. He said, over and over again, that the little Matouchon, his dear little one with the sunshine of the skies in her eyes, was to have half the ponies and cattle on the ranch for her very own, and all the silver dollars which had been given him when he made his trip to Washington, and which were now sewed in his belt.

He died with his head upon his wife's faithful breast, one thin hand clasped between the tender ones of Matouchon, and the other wandering from one face to the other as he tried in vain to dry their tears.

In great state, the body of Tohausin was brought back to Anadarko, but the Indians were not allowed to bury it after their way, a most horrible way in every particular. Even if Tohausin himself had not so earnestly requested it, Unkama would have had no other than a Christian burial. So, in the little cemetery attached to the Agency, he was laid away to rest, and the precious promise of the Christian ritual of the dead, "I am the Resurrection and the Life," was never spoken more feelingly nor with greater assurance of fulfillment than above the grave of the once warlike chief, Tohausin.

And now once more Unkama was at the Agency. It would be too lonely for her at the ranch since Tohausin could not be with her. So, she had put an old Indian and his wife to live there to see after the ponies, the cattle, and everything generally, and once more the yellow tepee pointed its picturesque top skyward from the plain to the right of the mission station.

Her heart had hungered so to have Matouchon with her, but when she saw the influences by which the little girl was surrounded at the parsonage, she was even more anxious than Dr. Holley that the little girl should be benefited by them at least for two years more. But Matouchon was with her dear adopted mother for some time during each day, and very often slept with her at night. Once or twice, at Mrs. Melville's earnest solicitation, Unkama had come to stay with Matouchon, for the parsonage had now another room. Oh, what happy hours those were! and how they warmed and brightened Unkama's widowed heart!

Greatly to the delight of Dr. Holley, Unkama, and the others who loved her, Matouchon was making rapid progress at school. She was not only quick and intelligent but she had a very winning way; sweet gentle manners, which—added to a warm heart—made her a favorite with all. Miss Davis, her teacher, often declared that she had no pupil in school who did her greater credit or of whom she was more fond than Matouchon. But best of all Matouchon was thoroughly straightforward and truthful. No fear of punishment or of gaining the reproach of those she loved could lead her to cover up a fault by means of a falsehood. She was forgetful and she had a high temper when aroused. These two things gave Matouchon many hours of pain and remorse, but she never sought to excuse herself and always bore without protest any punishment to which she was subjected.

Matouchon could now read and write quite creditably. She could also work "sums" as far as division. She had a quick mind for mathematics which soon became her favorite study. She could also speak English quite plainly by this time, and understand the greater part of what was said to her in that language. She spoke the Kiowan, too, quite fluently, for she had learned that from Unkama. From John she had learned many Comanche expressions and also from Mrs. Conover, Willie's mother, who was quite fond of her, and often had Matouchon at her home. Unkama had brought Matouchon one of the ponies from the ranch, a gentle, obedient little fellow, hardy and swift of foot, whom she had named A-chon-ho'-ah. It meant *to go with haste*, and certainly the brave little brown pony deserved his name. Many glorious rides Matouchon had over the plains on Achonhoah's back in company with John and Emma Melville, and sometimes with her dear adopted mother, Unkama. At such times it seemed as if Achonhoah just outdid himself, for none of the other ponies were ever able to quite overtake him.

Troublous times now came to the Agency. A trader by the name of Ormond had killed two of the Indians, being himself severely wounded in the affray. Mr. Ormond claimed that he had been compelled to do it in self-defence, but the Indians did not look at it in that way. They were so greatly aroused at the occurrence and so openly threatened vengeance that Mr.

7

Ormond, though in a dangerous condition from his wound, had been removed to the Agency. But even there he was by no means safe.

Anadarko, as has been stated, was not a military post, but merely a supply station. There were only about a dozen white families in the whole place, with perhaps about twenty men all told. The nearest encampment of troops was at Fort Sill, thirty miles away.

So far, the Indians had done little more than merely threaten, declaring that Mr. Ormond had committed gross murder and must suffer the consequences. The Agent had not thought it necessary as yet to notify the commander at Fort Sill. Besides, he could do nothing of this kind so long as it was an individual and not a government affair. But should the Indians show a disposition to attack the Agency, he had runners in readiness to carry the news to Fort Sill. The men too had all taken the precaution to have their arms in readiness.

Though the Indians seemed to have no plan for attacking the Agency and seizing Mr. Ormond, their actions during the past two days had given rise to some very grave apprehensions. The Indians killed had been Comanches and the men of that tribe were specially aroused. During the last two days they had been coming into the Agency in squads, hitching their ponies to the racks in front of the principal stores, and standing around in sullen silence, or else conversing with one another in whispers. Several times they had been seen to point to the house where Mr. Ormond lay. They had also, many of them, pitched their tepees nearer the Agency. At one point, about a half mile away there were at least three hundred Comanches congregated. The nights were full of the hideous noises of the "tom-tom," the rattle-gourds, and of the revel of dancers. Now and then, these were intermingled with wild discordant whoops as of men in great anger.

It was now the first of the week and Mr. Melville's duties called him away from home. He left with great reluctance.

"I hate so to leave you, my dear," he said to his wife at parting, "until this commotion is settled one way or the other,
but my Master's business must be carried on. However, you
have John, and I am going to send Andres too to stay with
you. I am really not apprehensive of the dreadful things
that others fear and predict. But should the worst come, it
will only be to poor Ormond and maybe to some of those who
seek to protect him. But I doubt even that. But should the
attack be made," he concluded with conviction, "I feel that
no harm will come to my dear ones. The Indians are all my
friends. They know that I mean well. My home would remain untouched by them."

"I share the same feelings," Mrs. Melville bravely declared, "and I am not afraid. Go and do your Master's
work, my husband, and leave us in his keeping. While you
are serving him elsewhere, he will keep watch for you here."

"That is spoken like a missionary's wife, my darling," he
said as he kissed her fondly, took leave of the little ones, and
then went to mount his trusty pony.

The night following Mr. Melville's departure was a cloud-
less one. The moon was full and shining brightly. As far
as the eye could reach the plains were gloriously flooded with
its rays. Even remote objects were distinctly visible. There
were no shadows except those cast by the fringe of trees lin-
ing the river's banks and the clusters of tepees. It seemed to
be one of those still nights, when the few sounds only make
more impressive the following silence. Nearly all the sounds
had ceased at the Indian camps save now and then the crying
of a child, or the barking of a dog. From the fringe of
trees along the banks of the river, the occasional hooting of an
owl was heard; and further out towards the plains, the im-
patient call of a nightbird as it wandered restlessly in search of
its mate. These were all, and save for these, over everything
a profound stillness brooded.

But about eight o'clock, the very demon of noise seemed to
be aroused. There were sharp cries and yells and the fierce

beating of the "tom-tom." There was the noise too of some one every now and then making a loud and exciting harangue. All the sounds seemed to come from the main Comanche camp, a half mile away. That many Indians were there was evidenced by the volume of noise. The noise increased, the yells grew louder and louder, the beating of the "tom-tom" fiercer and fiercer, while, to add to the din, there was the shrill blast of an old army trumpet, which the Indians had obtained from the soldiers at Fort Sill.

Suddenly there came a sound that chilled the blood of every one who heard it and knew what it was : the unmistakable, never-to-be-forgotten Comanche war-whoop! As it fell upon their ears, the men at the Agency closed their stores and went home to place themselves in readiness for whatever might come. The Agent called up his runners and, with their horses bridled, had them standing ready to throw their foot into the stirrup at a second's notice. The fierce blood-curdling sound of the Comanche war-whoop had struck consternation too to the hearts of the inmates of the parsonage, for both Andres and John recognized it and told Mrs. Melville immediately what it was. The smaller children began to cry. Emma's face was very white, but she kept still. Matouchon came and stood by Mrs. Melville, slipping her little hand softly into hers.

"What is it that troubles you, dear white mother?" she asked earnestly. This was the name by which she always addressed Mrs. Melville. "Is it that you are afraid the Indians are coming here to fight?"

"I don't know, Matouchon," replied Mrs. Melville, giving the little girl's hand a pressure in return. "It sounds so, but it may be after all, that they are only seeking to frighten the men at the Agency."

"And will they kill us if they come?" her great dark eyes shining luminously through her fear.

"I think not, Matouchon. The Indians all know the good Docté (the name by which Mr. Melville was known), and many of them love him; they surely will not harm his dear ones.''

" If they should come here to do that,'' declared Matouchon, her eyes shining now like stars and her voice trembling with its weight of earnestness, "I'd make them a little speech—I'd ask them if they could have the heart to harm you and the little ones when the good Docté has done so much for them, and is even now away preaching to their people and telling them of the God who wants to love and save them.''

"That would be a brave thing for a little girl to do,'' said Mrs. Melville admiring the child's courageous spirit, her heart deeply touched too by the affection shining so eloquently from her eyes. " But let us hope that they will not have to be told this; that they will see and feel it for themselves. I don't believe they will trouble us,'' she concluded with conviction, looking around upon the others as she spoke. " Even if they do attack the Agency they will not come here. It is only Mr. Ormond after all whom they want, poor man ! ''

"That too is my opinion,'' said Andres. " They are angered because he has escaped them. I think myself his act was without justification, but as he was nearly killed himself, it seems only humane for the Agent to seek to protect him.''

" I don't believe the Comanches will really fight,'' asserted John positively. " I don't care if there are three or four hundred of them. They are such cowards about guns and pistols, and although some of them have learned to use them themselves, they will run if you just point one at them. They know that the men at the Agency have plenty of firearms and will use them, too, upon the slightest provocation.''

But evidently the Comanches intended something, if not a downright attack; for the noise had increased tenfold if that were possible. They seemed on the move too towards the Agency, for the sounds grew gradually nearer. Unkama came in now to see how they were faring and to be with them should trouble come. From her, they learned that quite a number of

Kiowas and Apaches had joined the Comanches, and that they
were evidently bent on mischief.

And now a strange thing happened; or, at least it was
strange to those who didn't understand it. Within the last
twenty minutes the moonlight had been growing gradually
dimmer until there was a distinct shadow across the face of the
moon. It could not be from a cloud, since there was no cloud
visible. But there it was without doubt creeping gradually
and more determinately across the moon's bright disc. Where
objects had been seen clearly and distinctly some moments before, they now presented a weird and unnatural shape, while
ghostlike shadows began to flit across the plains. For a while,
the Indians had been so absorbed in their warlike preparations
that they had not noticed this change; but now, as it became
apparent to first one and then another, a feeling of alarm took
possession of them and quickly spread.

The Indians had already started on their march to the
Agency, but now noticing the strange condition of the moon,
they had called a halt and were anxiously consulting. What
could it mean? Was the Great Spirit angry with them for
what they were about to do, and was he taking this means to
frown angrily upon them? Evidently it seemed so. They
called their medicine man, ordered him to beat the "tom-tom"
as loudly as he could, while others gathered about a fire, that
was hastily kindled, and began to throw into it various charms
from their necks and clothing. But instead of appeasing the
Great Spirit, this seemed only to increase his wrath, for moment by moment the shadow grew greater and deeper, until
everything far and near seemed clothed with obscurity.

The sudden change in the moon had also been noticed at
the Agency, but as all recognized it as an eclipse, and knew it
to be the total one marked in the almanac for that year, no
further attention was paid to it, except that one of the men remarked, "Now, if the wretches really contemplate an attack,"
the darkness will give them just the opportunity they desire!"
But he knew little of Comanche nature.

At the parsonage too, the eclipse had been noticed and commented upon with very much the same idea concerning the Indians' attack as that expressed by the man at the Agency.

"We'll just dim the lights and keep on the watch, little mother," said John, placing his arm around her reassuringly.

"I don't believe they'll trouble the good Docté's place," reasserted Andres with conviction. "But just listen how furiously the 'tom-tom' is beating, and there are some unmistakable cries. Oh, I do believe they are frightened!" clapping his hands. "They don't understand about the moon. They think it is the Great Spirit and that he is angry with them. Now I see it all! Good, very good!"

Some fifteen or twenty minutes had gone by, when there came a loud thumping at the front door and they could hear the distinct murmur of voices.

"Shall I open it?" asked Andres looking at Mrs. Melville enquiringly.

"Yes. But first ask who it is."

"Who is there?" called Andres in Comanche.

"Friends," came back the answer immediately. "Open the door, we want to speak to you."

He went at once and threw the door open, John closely following him, but as the latter went his fingers were on the handle of a little pistol he had stuck into the pocket of his pants.

"*Ay haitch?* (How are you?)" came the greeting in Comanche as soon as the door was opened, and four Indians crossed the threshold, two of whom Andres knew well. One of them, A-ma-co'-pha, seemed to have instituted himself the spokesman of the group.

"We have come to see the Docté," he said, as soon as he entered.

"He is not here," returned Andres.

The man looked as though a blow had been dealt him. "But we *must* see him," he insisted.

"I am sorry, my friend, but that is impossible. He is now thirty miles or more away from here."

"Then we are all lost!" declared Amacopha despairingly.

John's quick eye took in some unusual situation, and with characteristic alertness he was ready to meet it.

"What is the matter, Amacopha?" he asked, now coming forward. "My father is not here, but some of the rest of us may be able to help you."

Amacopha shook his head. "No one but the Docté can do what we want done," he said positively.

"Well, tell us anyhow, Amacopha," persisted John, "and then we can see."

Amacopha looked at him doubtfully, spoke a few words in an undertone to the others, and then apparently getting a nod of assent from them, said, "The Great Spirit is angry with Amacopha and his brethren. To-night his light shone bright over all the plains. There was not a cloud between. There is not a cloud still in the sky, but lo! a strange thing has happened! There has a great darkness come over the ball of light which the Great Spirit has made to guide his people by night. At first we thought it the frown of the Great Spirit himself, but now we know what it is—he is angry with us, and he has sent frogs to eat up the moon, so that there will be no longer a ball of yellow fire to guide the Indians over the plains at night. It will be eaten up and all will be darkness, darkness for red man and white. We can see that the Great Spirit is very, very angry, and the frogs will perhaps not stop until they have eaten up the stars too!"

"And so you have come, thinking my father might help in some way?" questioned John.

"Yes!" eagerly. "We know that the Docté is good, very good. He can talk to the Great Spirit. He knows how to reach him. We want to beg him to ask the Great Spirit to take the frogs out of the moon. They are eating it up now as fast as they can. Do you not see how dark it is? Just go to the door then and look out. It is dark, dark, and it gets darker all the time. As we came along we could barely see each other's faces. Oh the frogs must not be allowed to eat the moon! for then what will poor Indian do? and white man, too, for that matter?"

John thought a second or two rapidly. He was not sure that his father would approve of what he was about to say and do, but then so much depended upon it. Surely the end, if it could be attained as he hoped, would fully justify the means.

"Well, Amacopha," he said, speaking deliberately and hence all the more forcefully, "it does seem that your people have made the Great Spirit very, very angry. You must have been about to do," looking at him boldly, "something of which he did not approve. Now there are others of us who can talk to the Great Spirit as well as my father. I can do it; so can Andres and my mother. If you will go back to your people and dissuade them from what they were about to do, we will all promise to beseech the Great Spirit in your behalf. We will also mention the good Docté's name and tell the Great Spirit that he too would petition him were he here. This much I can assert, if you will go back to your people and do as I say, in one hour's time every frog will be out of the moon and the Great Spirit will be smiling upon you from his globe of yellow light as brightly as ever."

John spoke with so much conviction that Amacopha withdrew, and in a little while thereafter all was quiet in the direction of the Indian camps. Of course, John knew the eclipse would soon be over. His almanac told him in just fifty-five minutes, as it had now been of forty minutes duration. So, taking advantage of this knowledge he had played this bold game with the superstitious Amacopha and his people. Surely, as he had reasoned, if ever a result justified the method employed to bring it about, this was one; for the lad's quick perception and his presence of mind had accomplished what perhaps a squad of soldiers could not have accomplished: had frightened the Indians and restrained them from the attack. When the story became known, for Andres took care to tell

it, John suddenly found himself the hero of Anadarko.
And ever afterwards the Indians called him, "The Little
Docté."

NOTE.—An incident similar to the one recorded in the foregoing chapter actually occurred at Anadarko. There was an eclipse of the moon,
and the Indians, believing that the Great Spirit was angry with them and
had sent the frogs to eat the moon, visited the missionary in a body and
besought him to hold communication with the Great Spirit and entreat
him to avert the calamity.

CHAPTER X.

ALL was quiet at the Agency. Since the night on which John had made his strategic move with reference to getting the frogs out of the moon, the Indians had shown no further disposition to make an attack. Indeed, they seemed to have disbanded, for many of the tepees had disappeared from the plains. Mr. Ormond had recovered and gone away, and all felt that there was no longer cause for apprehension.

The fall was approaching. The glowing suns of the summer had drunk all the dewy green from the grasses. Many of the wild flowers too had drooped their pretty heads and were dead. But the plains were still beautiful; for though the bright tint of the grass had fled, the grass itself was there, mellow and feathery. At midday, little sparkling rays of light ran over it as though touching it with pure gold. When the sun was setting, its light grew softer and mellower still, until the plains it covered stretched away like some liquid, amber sea. The willows, the cotton-woods, and sweet-gums shooting up here and there along the narrow banks of the Wichita, had already begun to show the vivid touch of Frost's artistic pencil. The squirrels were laying in their winter nuts. The rabbits were scurrying over the plains, leaving the unsheltered spots, and hunting warmer quarters. The wrens, the sparrows, and robins were strengthening the walls of their spring and summer houses. The blackbirds had held convocations and sent out runners to hunt for thicker growths of stubble. Only " Jimmie Browncoat,* " and his mate " Jennie,* " wandered unconcernedly through the stretches of

---

* Familiar names for the partridge or quail.

grasses to fall in large numbers here and there before the unerring aim of the huntsman.

From the tops of the white tepees, the smoke curled straight up in dense volumes, showing that the old squaws had not been lax in bearing their heavy burdens of wood. From daylight until dark, they could be seen passing to and from the river with their backs bent almost double beneath the heavy loads of brush. It was their duty to take the ponies to water, twice each day, and on the return, to hobble them so they could graze without getting very far away. Indeed, they did all the hard work of the camps, even to butchering the meat. This they would do with their arms bloody to the elbows. When too old and sick to work any longer they were cast aside, starved, shamefully treated, and abused in every way.

During the year that had passed, Amado had come several times to the church at the Agency. Gradually the light was dawning, and she had now something more than a mere faint conception of the Saviour who had died for her. Little by little, but surely, he was growing into her heart, and as the image of him grew clearer and clearer, so too her sorrows grew less.

In order to talk with her as he desired, Mr. Melville had had to take Andres into his confidence. But he knew Andres could be trusted. It had been three months now since Mr. Melville had seen Amado with reference to Matouchon. At first, she had been disposed to deny all knowledge of the child or that she had seen anything in her to arouse memories of the past. But on Mr. Melville's gently yet determinately urging her, she broke down and confessed all, her past deed of burying the child—or rather of having it done by an old woman—and of her present feeling that Matouchon was indeed the little one that had been hidden in the sand. Oh, how her mother-heart longed to claim her, but always there was the fear of Tabitosa !

"Tabitosa has one hard, cruel, wicked heart," she said to Mr. Melville. "He beats wife and he beats children. He

" From the tops of the white tepees the smoke curled straight up."

p. 108.

loves none of them, the little Echoschy least of all. Should he find out that she was born thus," holding up her two fore fingers together, " he would even now put her out of the way. And the other little one—the bright-eyed, sunny-faced little one to whom the Docté and all have been so good—oh, he would do her harm too! I don't believe he would let her stay with you. He would go and bring her back to the camp, and how dreadful that would be! He would beat her too as he does the little Echoschy. Perhaps he will beat them both to death ere he is through, and I could not endure that!" Here she broke down completely and began to cry bitterly. Evidently, the mother-heart was warm within her.

"Do not cry so, Amado," Mr. Melville said, seeking to soothe her. "Let us hope for the best. Only a few of us know the secret, and we must be careful in guarding it from Tabitosa. Even Matouchon herself must remain ignorant. It is better for her and better for you. It would only try your heart and hers were it otherwise. But should the worst come," he concluded reassuringly, "why then I will try to find some way out of the difficulty. I shall not hesitate at anything that is honorable to keep her from Tabitosa. In the meantime, Amado, come to see her as often as you choose, only be careful to control yourself. I can see that the little one has a strange feeling towards you now. I have seen her gazing at you wistfully many times. I suppose it is something of the same instinct that God gives to the tiniest fledgling in the nest that makes it *feel* the mother's presence though its eyes cannot recognize her. I know it is hard, but think, Amado, what would have been her fate had not the kind-hearted physician rescued her and provided for her as he has."

One afternoon, Mr. Melville was sent for in great haste to go to Stumbling Bear's village. His son, who had been sick a long time, was dying.

Stumbling Bear, or Tsaittimgear, as his Indian name was, had been chief of the Kiowas for about twenty years. He was now quite old, and having also been sick a great while, he was acting chief no longer. This duty had fallen upon a younger man, "Lone Wolf." But Tsaittimgear was the great man of the Kiowas still, with an influence that reached from the Wichita River to the Wichita Mountains. Hence when it was known that his son was dying, the Indians began to flock to his village from every direction. Mr. Melville overtook scores of them on his way thither.

Between the missionary and the chief, the warmest friendship existed, heightened on Stumbling Bear's part by an admiration that bordered upon the idolatrous. He believed it possible for the good Docté—it was he who had first given him the name—to accomplish almost anything he desired.

Stumbling Bear, for the last two years, had been a regular attendant at the mission chapel, though he had not attached himself to the church. Mr. Melville wondered what it was that kept Stumbling Bear back. He was certain that his heart had been reached and that the old chief was earnestly seeking to change his life for the better. He was always ready to aid Mr. Melville in any plans that he had for the good of his people, and it was through his example and influence that so many of them had now begun to lead moral and industrious lives.

Stumbling Bear's son had been sick for nearly three months. He was dying from slow poison, which had been produced by the bite of a spider. This spider is frequently found in the Territory, and physicians all agree that there is but little hope of recovery when bitten by it. In many respects, it is as deadly as the much dreaded tarantula, though its poison is slower. The spider is a very small black one with a white spot on its back.

Mr. Melville arrived at the village to find it crowded with Indians, either gathered around the chief's tepee waiting for news from within, or else assembled in knots earnestly discussing poor Kop-sait'-ka's condition.

Mr. Melville was not conducted to the chief's tepee immediately upon his arrival, for the young man was in a swoon and the medicine men, summoned by his mother, were seeking to revive him. It was thought by the superstitious Indians that a white man's presence would counteract the beneficial results of the medicine men's conjuring.

But Stumbling Bear was determined that the Docté should see his boy, though he had little hope that he could do him any good physically; for the old chief, sensible as he was, had long ago seen that his boy must die. He knew the bite of that spider too well. But to please the mother, he had sent for the medicine men. He longed, however, for the missionary to come and talk to his boy. So, now when he heard that he was here, he sent for him at once despite the presence of the medicine men.

It was a wild, horrid scene, upon which the eyes of the missionary looked as he entered the tepee.

The two medicine men—perfectly nude with the exception of the skin of some animal, probably that of a coyote, about the waist and their faces horribly smeared with paint—were down over the boy making the noise of wild boars. Then one of them rose up and began waving his eagle wand over his head, chanting some kind of a shrill piercing refrain, while the other remained over the boy. The latter now applied his mouth with suction to the mouth, ears and nose of the boy and began spitting out the blood extracted in this way. He also applied his mouth in the same manner to the chest, drawing blood through the pores of the skin. Next he blew with all his force into the nose and mouth of the boy. Then he spit upon his hands, one, two, three times, and rubbing them together held them over the nose and mouth of the patient.

The other medicine man had stopped his chant and the waving of his wand, and, during the last performances of his companion, had been furiously shaking his rattle-gourds, two in number, around the head of the boy. The young man had now revived and no wonder! Such treatment as that to which he had been subjected was enough to arouse him.

He smiled in faint recognition upon the missionary, and then whispered to his father the request that he be carried out under the brush arbor at the rear of the tepee, where he could look upon the sinking sun. His father lifted him fondly; for, though he was an old man, his arms were still strong, and the poor boy had become so wasted by disease that he was a mere shadow of himself. So his father lifted him as tenderly and as easily as though he had been an infant, and, kindly refusing Mr. Melville's proffered aid, carried him out to the arbor and laid him down upon a bed of skins and blankets.

The Indians now crowded around, but their respect for Stumbling Bear and their desire not to disturb the dying youth kept them from pressing too near. They also took care to leave an opening towards the west through which he could look upon the sinking sun.

Stumbling Bear now motioned to the missionary to approach and speak to his son. Mr. Melville could easily do this as the way was clear, the medicine men having been dismissed. They were now squatting about a fire some little distance away and muttering to themselves as they smoked from the same pipe, passing it, at intervals, from one to the other.

Mr. Melville bent over the dying boy and clasping his hand, said gently, "I am sorry to see you no better, Kopsaitka."

"Yes, Kopsaitka must soon go," he replied feebly, and turning his eyes wistfully upon the missionary's face. "His life will soon run out like the sun that is sinking."

"But the sun will come again, Kopsaitka," said the missionary earnestly. "So when Kopsaitka leaves this world it will be to enter a better and a brighter one if only he will trust Jesus, trust the Saviour."

"How am I to do that?" asked the young man eagerly.

"Listen, Kopsaitka. You have often heard me tell in the church at Anadarko of One who came to die that all who believed in him might be pardoned from their sins?"

"Yes, I have heard but I would not heed," Kopsaitka said mournfully. "The ways of the young men of my people were too dear to me—I could not turn therefrom. Oh, often you have taken my hand and besought me just as you are doing now ; and my father, too ! " he added, turning his eyes with an expression of the deepest affection upon the face of the old chief. " Oh, would that I had listened ! "

" It is not too late yet, Kopsaitka," the missionary went on earnestly. " Only feel that you are sorry for sin—that, if you had your life to go over again you would make it a better one in every way, one lived nearer the Saviour."

" Oh, I would ! I would ! " he cried eagerly.

A deep glow of gratification lit up the missionary's face.

" Thank God for that much ! " he said fervently.

" Now try to realize," he continued, " just what this Saviour has done for you, for all men. He came from his home in heaven to suffer, to die, to shed his blood that in its precious fountain even the deepest stain of sin might be cleansed away. Think of him as *your* Saviour, as dying for *you*. Think of him as waiting to receive you into his beautiful home up there, if only you will believe in him, if only you will say, he is *my* Saviour ; I will leave all in his hands."

" Oh, I will ! I will ! " cried the young man with a joyful outburst, while the tears began to run over his face. " Will you not tell him that I want him for *my* Saviour, that I am willing to trust him, that I *do* believe in him, and oh, that I long so to be where he is ! "

"That I will, Kopsaitka," and in beautiful, feeling words Mr. Melville prayed fervently that the light might grow brighter still as Kopsaitka's feet went down into the dark shadows of the Valley of Death, and that at the end he might *see* and *know* Jesus, and *feel* that he was indeed his Saviour.

There was a peaceful smile upon the young man's face as the prayer ended.

Just then his mother came and, with piercing cries, fell over him entreating him not to leave her.

" Do not grieve for me, mother," he said gently, "I am going to a home so much better than this one."

8

But this instead of soothing her seemed to excite her all the more, and her cries grew louder and more piercing.

Seeing how it distressed the dying boy, Stumbling Bear came and led her away. And now he too stood gazing upon the face of his boy for the last time in his life. It was touching in the extreme to see him. He was a powerfully built Indian, standing fully six feet and a half in his moccasins and with a form of portly proportions. Despite his full seventy years, he carried himself as erect as the arrow-wood tree, the beauty and pride of the Wichita swamps. His hair that was but little sprinkled with grey was, unlike that of most of his Indian brethren, cut close to his head. His face was furrowed and seamed with age and care, but it was a striking face still. He had thrown off his blanket, and the helmet hat he usually wore. His close-fitting shirt, made of black sateen, with a large white figure showing upon it, was opened at the throat thus displaying the powerful muscles and cord-like veins of his neck and chest. He came and stood over his boy, over him who in life had been his hope, his joy, his pride. His face worked, his strong, powerful chest heaved as though with the throes of a sorrow to which it could not give birth. Then the fountain of tears in his eyes seemed broken up and the flood poured forth. Throwing himself down over his boy he placed his hands, one on either side of his head, and in accents of the most touching pathos and tenderness gave vent to the full tide of his love, his despair, his sorrow. The boy was too weak to respond save by a feebly whispered word or a faint smile.

There were now about five hundred Indians gathered. Their mournful faces and bowed heads showed how deep was their grief and sympathy for the chief. They all loved and honored Stumbling Bear. He had been their chief for years and the Kiowas had never had a better. He had led them to victory in time of war, and in times of peace he had been their safe counselor. They had come now to show their respect to him and their deep sympathy in his grief.

Mr. Melville remained until Kopsaitka breathed his last, though it was ten o'clock at night. He remained to help Stumbling Bear successfully combat the pressure that would be brought to bear upon him to have his son buried after the Indian fashion. This would mean to take him as soon as the breath left his body and wrap him in the clothes of the bed on which he was lying—every one of them—and then hurry him away into a deep pit-like hole in the ground, while everything which he had possessed was either buried with him or destroyed at his grave.

The Indians were loud in their protest when they found this was not to be done, but that the body was to be carefully watched that night, after being prepared for burial in the clothes he had worn when well. In the morning it was to be carried in a coffin, which Mr. Melville would send out to the little burial ground belonging to the church at the Agency, and there laid away with a Christian service. They predicted all manner of dreadful things that would come through this shameful disregard of the old ways and customs. A few of the head men even went so far as to hold an audience with Stumbling Bear, first entreating and then seeking to drive him to alter his decision with reference to the manner of the burial.

But the old chief was firm. He said:

" You Indians want me to take my son, my beautiful, brave boy, and bend his knees until they meet his breast; then, ere the breath is hardly gone, you want me to bundle him up like a bale of goods in all those skins and blankets on which he died. What will he look like then? Besides I shall not have one single glimpse of his face as they go to lay him in the grave—I shall not see whether he is peaceful and smiling as he was when he died, or if he is disturbed over what he is seeing in that new world to which he has gone. Oh, the missionary's way is so different. He will leave my boy with me till the morning. By that time, he will be dressed in the suit he was so fond of wearing when he was alive, and he will be laid out so peacefully with his hands folded upon his breast. Then, in the morning, he will be placed in his wooden bed that is so soft it cannot hurt him, and he will lie there as sweetly as a papoose in its cradle. Then when he is put into the ground, he will not be thrown in as though he were some horrid thing of which one is glad to be rid, but he will be let down gently, and the good Docté will say words that will tell the Great God, to whom he has gone, all about him. Oh, it is so much the better way! so much the better way!"

Seeing they could not turn him, they wisely decided to say no more. And so in the morning the body of Kopsaitka, laid peacefully away in its coffin, came to the mission chapel, and from there the funeral services were conducted.

It took all Stumbling Bear's close watching to keep the mother from slashing her face, throat, and breast with a knife, as is the custom of the Kiowan women when they lose a child. Neither would he let her cut off her finger. The only thing to which he would consent was that she might crop her hair. But at the grave she managed to elude his vigilance; and while the coffin was being opened so that the family and personal friends of the dead boy might look for the last time upon his happy, peaceful face, she secured a sharp stone. As the way was opened for her, she rushed to the coffin and bending above it began to slash at her face and throat with the sharp, jagged point of the stone, all the time howling like a mad creature. The blood was pouring in torrents before she could be seized and the stone taken from her.

Another thing too that happened distressed Mr. Melville greatly. The chief had been firm with reference to his son's having a Christian burial. He had refused too to have his personal effects destroyed. But there was one thing he did not combat, doubtless through force of the old superstitions that still clung to him. He allowed Kopsaitka's pony to be killed at the grave. When he feebly protested, the Indians were outspoken in their surprise and indignation. "Would he abandon his son to go on foot through the next world?" they questioned with undisguised astonishment.

This was too much for Stumbling Bear, and so he finally gave his consent to the sacrifice of the pony, at the grave of his son, according to custom.

When Mr. Melville saw the beautiful creature led between two men, and understood what was to be done with it, he entreated the chief to revoke his decision with reference to the slaying of the pony.

"It is a needless sacrifice," he urged earnestly. "The pony has no soul and cannot enter the world where your son is. Why take the life of so beautiful and so useful a creature, and all for naught?"

But Stumbling Bear was immovable, and Mr. Melville felt that the beautiful creature was indeed doomed.

He hurried away as soon as the grave was filled so as not to witness the shocking sight of the pony's being killed. But when at a little distance, he heard his name pronounced, and turned around just in time, unfortunately, to see the glittering knife blade plunged into the pony's throat. With a shriek like that of a human being it careered wildly for a moment or so with the blood spouting in a stream. Then with a final leap, it fell trembling to the earth.

The remembrance of the scene lingered with Mr. Melville for many days thereafter.

CHAPTER XI.

THE LEGEND OF THE TIE-SNAKES.

"O FATHER," said little Lillian Melville, one cold winter night, as they sat up close around the stove in the room that served both as sitting room and study, "do tell us a story; this is just the night for it, as it is too cold for you to sit over there by the table and write."

"What shall I tell my little girl?" he asked, as, reaching over, he took her upon his knee.

"An Indian story, father! an Indian story!" she cried, clapping her hands with delight for she knew by his face that he would tell her just the grandest story he could remember.

"But there are so many Indian stories, my dear; I hardly know which one to tell."

"O father, do tell us about the tie-snakes," said Henry at this juncture, pulling his little chair nearer his father as he spoke and clasping his hands about one of his father's legs.

"O, yes, father, about the tie-snakes, do!" joined in Glover.

"Well, children," began Mr. Melville, "when father was preaching in the Creek Nation before he came out here, he went one Sunday to attend the services of a brother missionary who had some church members to be baptized.* Some of them were whites and some were Indians.

The hour for the baptism came and all the white candidates were there, but, though they waited many minutes, not a single Indian came. All thought this very strange, and were deep in wonder as to the failure of the Indians to put in an appearance.

* The place selected for the baptizing was a point on the Canadian River.

(118)

"They were soon enlightened as to the cause of it by a remark of one of the gentlemen present, a Major Cramer.

"'I am not surprised,' said he, 'that the Indians did not come. Why, have you all forgotten that this is tie-snake hole?'

"'Tie-snake hole,' I asked in wonder, 'why, what can that mean?'

"It was then that he told me the story, which I will put into my own words."

"That will make it all the better," declared Henry emphatically.

Mr. Melville looked down into the face of his little boy, and smiled his appreciation of the compliment; then went on.

"It was in 1800 that the Territory of Indiana was established, and in 1801 Gen. William Henry Harrison—afterwards President of the United States—was appointed Governor. The Territory then included a large tract of country lying north and west of Ohio, but has since been divided into several states and territories.

"Gen. Harrison was very popular with the Indians, but they were cruelly treated by the settlers who encroached upon their lands, and by the speculators who defrauded them of all they could and, what was worse, demoralized them with whiskey.*

" So great were their wrongs and so unfeeling the treatment they received from the whites who were seeking to drive them away from their own lands, that an old chief who hardly ever had anything to say came to Gen. Harrison, complaining bitterly.

"'Why do you not make us happy as our fathers, the French, did? They never took from us our lands; indeed they were common between us. They planted where they pleased, and they cut wood where they pleased, and so did we. But now if a poor Indian attempts to take a little bark from a tree to

* See Drake's Indian History.

cover him from rain, up comes a white man and threatens to shoot him, claiming the tree as his own.'

" By 1811 the spirit of discontent among the Indians, and the desire for revenge that slumbered within their breasts, had grown to such an extent that an outburst against the whites seemed imminent. They were also in many places, upon the edge of starvation, owing to the low price of furs and the inability of the traders to keep the necessary supplies.

" At this time the Creeks lived in Georgia and Alabama. It was while the Western Indians were almost upon the point of an outbreak that there came to the town of the Tuck-a-ba'-ce Creek Indians, a great orator and warrior by the name of Tecumseh, which means Flying Tiger. Tecumseh, though a Shawnee and dwelling with that tribe, was nevertheless, half Creek, his mother having been one ; it was now to her native town that he had come. His present home was in Ohio, where he had been born on the banks of Mad River only a few miles from the town of Springfield.

" Tecumseh had a great scheme in view, that of leaguing together all the Indian tribes from the Lakes to the Gulf for the purpose in common of driving out the white man. He told his Indian brethren that the treaties they and others had made, giving up their lands north of the Ohio River were fraudulent and therefore good for nothing, and these things he could easily prove. The Indians' land, he contended, belonged to all in common, and no part of it could be legally sold without the consent of all.

" Now strange as it may seem, he succeeded in enlisting the sympathy of all the Indians in the South except those of his own town and of two others. On the very day that he made the first harangue among the Tuckabace Creeks and exhibited the bundle of red sticks, which was the emblem of the union of all the tribes for a bloody war, Tecumseh was greatly angered by the manner in which the chief of the tribe received them. Sternly eyeing the chief, he threatened the whole tribe with the vengeance of heaven if they did not join with him in the league. He declared angrily that when he got back to his home he would stamp his foot upon the ground with such force that they could hear it from one end of the line to the other. Then they would know that his anger and his displeasure were still burning against them, and if they did not arm themselves at once, they might prepare for something a great deal worse. The Creeks counted the days that it would take Tecumseh to reach his home, and sure enough, by a strange coincidence, when the time predicted by him had arrived, the whole southern country was shaken by an earthquake. Trees that had stood for centuries, were shaken down ; houses fell and were crushed in like egg-shells; the waters of the great Mississippi boiled and foamed ; while the town of New Madrid was completely swallowed up in its boiling waves."

"I remember hearing my grandfather tell about that time," said Mrs. Melville. "There were certainly some never-to-be-forgotten scenes."

"Of course, the Indians were greatly alarmed," went on Mr. Melville, "and all those of the surrounding country tried to get the three towns that were for peace to go with them to the war.

"But the Tuckabaces gathered in their square grounds, and declared they would not. There they were besieged for three days. Numberless arrows, cast by the other Indians fell in their midst, but no one was hurt. This made the Tuckabaces feel that the Great Spirit was indeed on their side. There was a legend in the tribe handed down from mouth to mouth that the arrows of the besieging Indians lay two inches deep upon the ground, and still no one among the Tuckabaces received so much as a scratch. Even silver-tipped arrows were shot at them but failed to hit.

"On the third morning of the siege, the chief of the Tuckabaces called his son and heir, a lad fourteen years of age, and gave him a message to a chief that lived several miles up the river. This message stated the situation of the Tuckabaces, and asked for aid. As an offering of friendship, the chief sent by his son one of the sacred vessels of the tribe, a small round pot.

"The boy took his companions, two other boys of about his own age, and started off up the river. After going seven or eight miles they became tired, as boys sometimes do, and forgetting the importance of their message and the need of haste, stopped to look about them. Directly, they began skipping rocks across the river, for no other purpose, I suppose, than just to see them skip."

"O father! I've done that many times," interrupted Henry, "and I assure you there's lots of fun in it."

"Well, maybe so," assented his father, "and it is all well enough for idle boys, I suppose; but when one is sent on an errand, especially on so urgent an errand as carried these Indian boys, I think, stopping to skip stones across the water or to engage in any other pastime is not only a foolish but a culpable proceeding."

"What does that mean father?" asked Henry quickly.

"Culpable? It means wrong, blamable, that which calls for reproof—I hope my little boy will take care not to have it applied to anything *he* does."

"I hope so too, father," said Henry earnestly.

"Finally," continued Mr. Melville, "the chief's son, growing tired of skipping stones, concluded he would try the skipping properties of the pot, all of which showed he was not only a silly lad but a reckless one. But the Tuckabaces always contended that it was the Great Spirit that prompted him. Anyhow, the lad threw the vessel and it skipped along until it reached the middle of the river, when suddenly it sank out of sight.

"The boy was in dismay at what he had done. He knew it would be useless to go on without the pot ; and return to his father he dared not. There was but one way open. The pot he must and would have at any cost. So, stationing the other two boys to guide him to where the pot had sunk he swam after it. When just over the vessel, he saw it lying at the bottom of the river. He made a sudden, bold dive, hoping to reach it and bear it up again. But on reaching the bottom he was literally bound hand and foot by the snakes that had gathered about the pot. These snakes were called tie-snakes because they had a way of tying themselves about a person's body."

"O father," said Emma, with a little shiver, "what horrid things! I am sure if I had been the boy I should have screamed out with terror."

"Well, perhaps he did, Emma, though it isn't said whether he did or not. At any rate, the tie-snakes carried him along on the bottom of the river until they struck a sand bar. After lifting him safely over, they went on and on with him, till finally they came to an island made entirely of snakes, though he did not notice this at the time.

"He was carried partly across this island and then brought up before a kind of throne on which sat the king of the tie-snakes. Then he was released. The king invited him to come on the throne, but as he attempted to do so the throne raised up. This occurred three times before he succeeded in getting on the throne. As soon as he had stepped in front of His Majesty, his attention was directed to a tomahawk sticking in a column at one side of the throne. The king told him to take it as it belonged to him, but as he reached out his hand, the column receded. This occurred three times ere he was able to possess himself of the tomahawk. In another column was a large eagle feather, which the king of the tie-snakes told him also to take, but that column receded as the other had done, three times before he gained the prize. On still another column was hanging a wampum belt. This he was also told was his, but again it took the third effort to possess himself of it, for this column receded, as the other had done."

"O father!" cried Henry, clapping his hands with delight, "that is just like a fairy story!"

Mr. Melville smiled.

"So it is, my boy, though fairies don't usually take upon themselves the form of snakes."

"I should think not," commented Emma decisively.

"After all this had taken place," went on Mr. Melville, "the king informed the chief's son that he was aware of his father's troubles; that he knew of the surrounding hostile band that was trying to drive him into a war; that the chief was a friend of the king; that he was acting in the right; and that the king of the tie-snakes would help him. His majesty commanded that when the chief could hold out no longer against the enemy, he must come to the river, to the very spot where the vessel was lost and face the East just at sunrise. When he had done so, his eyes would fall upon the king of the tie-snakes who would be there to deliver him from all his troubles.

"As the king finished these words, he gave the boy to understand that he was dismissed; whereupon the same snakes who had brought him approached, and again tied themselves about his body, preparatory to taking him away. As this was being done he noticed for the first time that the platform, throne, columns, pillars, island and everything were entirely composed of tie-snakes. He was taken up and safely carried out of the lagoon, over the sandbar and to the very spot in the river where the pot had sunk. There he was given the vessel again, and the snakes having untied themselves from about his body, he arose and swam ashore."

"How long had he been gone, father?" questioned Glover at this point.

"Well, that I can't say, since the Indians neglected to tell that part in the legend. But it was a long while; for the boys on the bank grew tired of waiting and convinced that he had been drowned, returned and told the old chief of his son's death.

"The news nearly broke the heart of the old chief, for all his hopes were centered in his son. He grieved much and would not be comforted. He ordered the tom-tom to be

beaten constantly, and the medicine men were required to keep
up their chants, while all the tribe joined in the death song.
His mother even went so far as to slash her arms and breast
with a sharp knife. But one morning—I suppose not more than
two or three days afterwards—just as the performances in
memory of the dead were at their height, the lad suddenly returned. At first, his appearance brought consternation to the
camp for they thought he had come back from the dead. But
when the old chief became really convinced that it was his son
who had returned to him alive, he fell upon his neck and wept
for joy. Then the lad related to his father all that had occurred and all that the tie-snake king had told him.

"During all the time that the boy had been gone the besieging Indians had failed to make any successful attack upon
the Tuckabaces. But on the very night of the day that he had
returned, a great effort was made to break into the camps, and
so fierce was the rush upon the fortifications that at first it seemed
it would prove successful. This was continued for three succes-
sive nights, but still the Tuckabaces kept back the besiegers.
But the peaceful Creeks could hardly hold out long; they
would in time be forced to surrender, for the hostile Indians
were increasing in number, every day.

"So, on the third morning after his son's return, the chief
of the Tuckabaces went to the river to meet the tie-snakes.
He reached there just at sunrise, and, as the tie-snake king
had bidden him, he prostrated himself three times with his
face to the East. As he arose the third time from the ground,
the tie-snake king came up out of the water and stood before
him. He told the chief to go back to camp, continue in the
same course he had been pursuing, and to rest easy for de-
liverance would surely and quickly come.

"That night, no assault was made by the hostile Indians.
The next morning the chief received the startling information,
from some scouts who had been out, that all the men in the
besieging army were lying dead upon the plain. But such was
not the case, for when the chief went forth with a band of his

warriors to reconnoiter, he found that instead of being dead, they were all bound hand and foot by the tie-snakes."

" Oh, goody ! goody ! " cried Lilian, clapping her hands. "Those were pretty good old tie-snakes after all ! "

" I don't think you would have called them good if they had had hold of you," said Glover.

" No, I think not," said Emma, with a shudder. " But those mean old Indians deserved it. Why couldn't they have let those peaceful Indians alone ? "

" They were just like other people, I suppose," said Mr. Melville, " they wanted to go into mischief but didn't want to go alone; they wanted to draw others into it, too."

" But is that all the story of the tie-snakes, father ? " asked Henry.

" No, not quite, my son. One story says that the chief of the Tuckabaces had all the Indians who were thus bound by the snakes put to death ; but another declares that he had only the principal men, or the leaders, slain."

" Well, I should think they deserved it," said Henry sturdily. " And is the story of the tie-snakes a true story, father ? "

" No, my son, certainly not. It is merely a legend, a fanciful story, but nearly all the Indians believe it, especially the Creek Indians."

" But what was the reason the Indians didn't come to be baptized ? " asked Henry.

" Because, my son, the place in the river where the baptizing was to be done, was known as a tie-snake hole and not one of the Indians would go near it."

" But, father, were there really any snakes there ? "

" I don't know, Henry ; maybe so. But I think the preacher knew just where to go, for there were no snakes seen that day."

" Father," said Glover, softly, " I think sometimes the tie-snakes get hold of us ! "

" Why, Glover ! " cried Henry, in astonishment.

"Yes, Henry, they do. I mean the tie-snakes of sin. I've seen people held hard and fast by them. When we do things we ought not, get angry, tell falsehoods, disobey those to whom we should be obedient; then the tie-snakes of sin have hold of us."

"Oh yes, Master Henry," said Emma, "I can see your face falling now! Who was it, I wonder, who had hold of the calf's tail this afternoon, swinging on and hurting and frightening the poor thing very much, and wouldn't let go till mamma had spoken the third time?"

"I guess it was a tie-snake, Emma," admitted Henry, with his eyes on the floor.

"You mean a tie-snake had hold of the calf's tail!" asked Emma laughingly.

"No, had hold of *me*. *I* had hold of the calf's tail."

"Yes, my children," said Mr. Melville, "Glover is right. We all doubtless feel a touch of the tie-snake sometimes."

"But I don't think Matouchon ever does," said Emma quickly. "She is always so good and obedient."

The face of the little Indian girl grew bright with pleasure at this praise. Then she dropped her eyes to the floor as Henry had done.

"You are mistaken, Emma," she said, her voice quivering. "I am not so good as I seem. There are many times I have to go off by myself and just talk to myself and scold myself to keep from doing ugly things."

"Why, Matouchon!" said Emma, incredulously.

"Every heart knows its own trials," said Mr. Melville earnestly. "Matouchon speaks truly. I have seen some of her struggles myself, though she did not know it. It is all the more to her credit that she has these struggles and then comes off conqueror." With these words he placed his hand upon the wealth of glossy black hair, and turned her face so that he could look right down into her eyes. The look he gave her said more than a hundred words could have said and it left a happy thrill in her heart that lingered for many days.

CHAPTER XII.

WHERE IS MATOUCHON?

IT was spring again. Twelve of them had come and gone since the good Dr. Holley, walking across the plains, had rescued the tiny baby from its grave in the sand. The baby was now a well-grown girl, intelligent, womanly, and happy in the love of friends. She knew her history at last, but not that her mother was alive and known. It had been told her from the moment she could understand it, that Unkama was not her mother, but the fact of her burial in the sand and of her rescue by Dr. Holley had been kept from her until the present. Now that she knew it and was old enough to think over it, it made her sad at times, despite the love and care lavished upon her.

Whose little one was she? and whence had she come? Who was really her mother? How Matouchon longed to know! Many nights she lay awake thinking of it. Even with her head pillowed upon Unkama's loving breast there would come thoughts of the real mother. Where was she and what was she like? Would Matouchon ever know? Would she ever see her? And if she did, would something tell her it was her mother? Oh, how these thoughts made her heart throb! Somehow she never thought of her father. The good Tohausin had been so much like her father; and then there was the missionary, whom she called "white father," and kind Dr. Holley too. With all these kind and thoughtful friends, she had never felt the need of any one particular guardian or protector, such as her true father might have been. But always there was that cry in her heart for her mother.

Late one afternoon, as Mr. Melville was riding home from

(128)

the Indian camps, he was overtaken by Amado. She had evidently ridden long and hard, for both pony and rider gave evidence of it. She was laboring, too, under great excitement. Mr. Melville and Amado had learned to understand each other very well now; especially, as they made considerable use of the sign language.

Amado had "bad, bad" news to tell. In some way Tabitosa's suspicions had been aroused with reference to Matouchon. One of the Indians had told him Matouchon's history,—one of those who still recalled the circumstance of Dr. Holley's finding her in the sand. This Indian had been educated at the Carlisle School in Pennsylvania, and was therefore quick and observant. He had visited Tabitosa's camp and remained there for several days. He had noticed Echoschy and been at once struck by her resemblance to Matouchon. He asked Amado right before Tabitosa if the children were not related. Taken off her guard, she could only stammer out an evasive reply which at once drew Tabitosa's attention to her. It was then that the Indian related the story of Matouchon, a part as he remembered it, the rest as it had been told him. To add to the trouble, the old woman who had buried the child, and who was still alive, had become angry with Amado, through some fancied slight, and threatened to tell Tabitosa.

"Oh if she does!" cried Amado, in despair, "what will become of me? Tabitosa will certainly kill me! and he will kill the little ones too!"

"Surely it will not be so bad as that, Amado," said the missionary, reassuringly.

He spoke as calmly as he could, but his own heart sank.

"It may be," he added, "that the squaw will not tell Tabitosa. Let us hope for the best."

"But I feel that she will," Amado said hopelessly. "She is dreadfully angry with me, and I cannot get her to see that I did not intend to offend her."

"Well, it may be you can still coax her into keeping quiet. Do so if you possibly can. But should she tell Tabitosa, then

9

come as soon as you possibly can to let me know. I'll go at once to talk to him. It may be that I can reason him into letting the children alone; and perhaps he will not be so hard on you as you think. Since the Agent succeeded in getting the chief to deal with old Tamraka, the Indians seem to be a little afraid of proceeding in so bold a way with their wives. Another such example as this will assuredly put an end to much of the cruelty now practised."

"But Echoschy! Echoschy!" cried poor Amado, pathetically, "he will assuredly kill my poor little Echoschy. He hates her now, and all because she is not a boy like Kankeah."

"Rest easy, Amado. He will not kill Echoschy. I feel assured of that. She is too large now. His Indian brethren would not sanction such a proceeding as that, and he knows it."

"And Matouchon!" she broke forth again, pressing her hand against her breast, "what will become of the little Matouchon?"

"Trust that to me, Amado," he said, riding nearer and placing his hand for a moment upon hers. "I will protect Matouchon and so will her noble friend Dr. Holley. Indeed, I think he has the best claim to her of any one, since without him she would not be. I believe should it come to a test, the Indians would decide almost unanimously against Tabitosa and in favor of Dr. Holley as the guardian of Matouchon. So, return to the camp, Amado, and act as cautiously as possible. Should it come to the worst, keep out of Tabitosa's way and keep the little Echoschy from him too."

On his return to the Agency that afternoon, Mr. Melville sought Dr. Holley and told him all. The good doctor was very much worried. He showed his perplexity in the number of wrinkles that gathered in a line of puckers between his eyes. The eyes, too, were cloudy with trouble and not bright and sparkling as was usual.

"I can't bear the thought of losing my little one after all these years in which I have grown to look upon her as mine," he said determinately. "I have so many bright plans for the

future when my little girl is through school and can come and
keep house for me," he added, and now his eyes were misty
with an unusual tenderness. "She will grow into a sweet,
true woman I know. She has all the qualities that make one.
Oh, I could not bear the thought of her returning to the degraded ways of her people. The life in the camps, especially
with such a man as Tabitosa for her father, would be almost
like death to her. Oh, it must not be! it must not be!"

"That is just the way I feel," Mr. Melville said with deep
earnestness. "I, too, have grown to love the little one dearly.
In truth, we all love her, from the good wife down to the little
Lilian, and I do not know how we are ever to give her up even
to you, though of course, we must. But the thought of her
falling into the hands of Tabitosa fairly wrings my heart. I
can't endure it. Should this ever be threatened we must find
some way to prevent it."

"You are right, we must! and what is more," added the
Doctor, bringing his hand down determinately upon the table,
"*we will!*"

Three days later, on Saturday, Mrs. Melville said to Matouchon, "It is such a bright, pretty morning I think I know
a little girl who would like to take her pony and ride over to
Go-komb's to bring me some eggs!"

"Oh, that is myself!" cried Matouchon, jumping up quickly
and clapping her hands. "Indeed I should like to go, white
mother, and right away if you want me! Achonhoah was
looking at me only a little while ago, as much as to say, 'Aren't
we to have a race this morning?' I can have him saddled in
a few minutes, white mother."

"Do so, Matouchon, but bear this in mind: my little girl
and her pony must take all the racing they want *going*, for
there will be the *eggs* coming back."

"Oh yes, white mother, I'll be very careful with them," said
Matouchon, earnestly. "I'll not let Achonhoah get out of a
pace coming back never mind how fast his nimble legs may
want to go."

"Well, bring me three dozen and tell A-to-geer to pack them in straw, then you'll be sure not to break any if you are careful. And, my child," she added going out of the door, "hurry all you can. I want to make something for dinner with the eggs. It is only a few minutes after nine o'clock now. You can surely be back by eleven even if you do have to make the journey one way on a walk."

"Oh, I'll be back before then, white mother," Matouchon said positively. "Oh, you don't know how fast Achonhoah can go."

"Well, don't let him go too fast for my little girl's safety," was the caution given her as she went out the door.

It was with a light heart that Matouchon caught and saddled Achonhoah. How pleased and proud she always was to do these little errands for the white mother, especially when Emma was not at home, as was the case this morning. But Matouchon was sent more often than Emma, for Matouchon's pony was much faster and Matouchon always liked to go. It gave her the opportunity to put into action the great desire that filled her heart to be in service, particularly in the service of those she loved.

Gokomb lived on a little farm about six miles away. He was one of the few Indians who had shown a taste for agriculture. His wife, too, was industrious and saving. She seemed to take a great fancy to chicken raising, and as she usually had fine luck with them, she was enabled to supply many in the neighborhood with eggs. Gokomb, too, raised many little crops of first one thing and then another, which he always carried to the Agency for sale. He and the Agent were great friends, and the latter was always encouraging him in his agricultural pursuits. He wished heartily that there were more of the Indians with the industrious tendencies of Gokomb and his wife, Atogeer.

With the basket for the eggs slung on her arm, Matouchon sprang into the saddle and galloped away. As she had to pass right by the yellow tepee, she paused long enough to jump down, run in and give Unkama a kiss on the cheek and a tight little hug around the neck. Then mounting Achonhoah again, she gave him free rein and told him to go. There was nothing he liked better than this permission, so sticking his nose straight out before him as though he were sniffing away at something exceedingly good, he brought his sturdy little legs down upon the sandy road so fast that you couldn't have counted one tenth part of the strokes he made if your life depended on it.

For three miles they galloped on in this way; for, of course, as she was on his back, Matouchon was doing as much of it as he; then Matouchon gave the bridle a gentle pull which was the signal to Achonhoah that he must stop for a while and walk. Besides, there was a turning to be made and Matouchon wasn't quite sure as to just which road to take—so many tracks had been made of late by the woodcarts.

Up to this point, the route she had followed had lain straight across the prairies. Now she knew that she had to turn into the belt of timber. But it was not a very wide belt and the trees were not close together. On the other side, however, there was a second growth and beyond it lay the farm of Gokomb. Matouchon had passed safely through the first belt of timber and was in the midst of the second, when suddenly something happened which caused her to utter a little scream of fright. An Indian in full camp dress, and with his face horribly painted, rode to her side and seized her bridle. At the same time he pointed significantly to the knife in his belt, giving her to understand that he would use it did she dare repeat the scream of the previous moment. Then he turned her pony half around and started straight through the timber instead of across it.

He was an old Indian and there were many wrinkles and scars on his face, which seen through the paint, gave him a more horrible appearance still. But though old, he was evidently not feeble for he sat on his pony as erect as a young war-

rior, and there was grip as well as determination in the hand
which he had placed upon the pony's rein.   Evidently Achonhoah thought so and he resented it, whereupon the man dealt
him a cuff that set Matouchon's heart on fire with indignation.
She would have spoken then if her life had paid the forfeit
the next minute.

"Why do you strike my pony so?" she demanded, looking at him with eyes that were ready to blaze.

The man evidently understood some English, for he answered her, "I strike him because he does not mind me.   I
serve all so," he added warningly, "who dare me."

Matouchon's heart sank like lead not so much at the words
as at the look that accompanied them.   Who was this dreadful man, and where was he taking her?   She was quite sure she
had never seen him before, or if she had she had forgotten it.

He still kept his hand upon the pony's bridle, riding so near
that he touched her at times.

Once or twice, he seemed about to speak ; then, apparently
changing his mind, maintained a sullen silence.

As the ponies went on in the thickening gloom of the timber, Matouchon's heart sank lower and lower till it almost
stood still with dread and apprehension.

Again the questions presented themselves, "Who could this
terrible creature be, and where was he carrying her?"   So
startling were they this time that she unconsciously gave a little scream.

He turned upon her fiercely, bringing his great strong hand
down with a grip upon her shoulder that made her wince with
pain.   At the same time his eyes nearly transfixed her, while
he said,

"If young squaw know what good, she keep mouth still.
She make 'nother cry like that, Tabitosa squeeze life out so !"
and he dropped Achonhoah's bridle-rein long enough to span
her throat with both hands in a most threatening gesture.

So Matouchon knew his name at last ! Her fear increased
two-fold if possible.   She had long heard of Tabitosa as one

of the most tyrannical and cruel of all the Indians on the
Reservation. Then, too, she recalled the terrible picture of the
Indian woman with the bleeding stumps of fingers, and remembered that John Melville had told her that it was Tabitosa,
her husband, who had done it. Oh, what a terrible creature
he must be ! and to think she was in his power ! The thought
was almost unendurable. Of course he was going to kill
her ! What other purpose could he have ? She wondered,
over and over again why he was going to kill her. " What
had she done to him ? " To her positive knowledge, she had
never even seen him before.

The ponies now came to a narrow footpath through the
timber. Here the undergrowth was so thick that they had to
separate and take it single file. Tabitosa motioned to Matouchon to go ahead, at the same time making her a threatening gesture intimating what he would do if she did not obey
him. They went about a half or three-quarters of a mile in
this way, and then suddenly came out into a small clearing of
an acre or so. Here there was an old hut built of cotton-wood
logs and chinked with clay. It had once been the dwelling of
a wood-chopper, perhaps of several of them, but now gave
every sign of having been for some time deserted.

Tabitosa dismounted, unsaddled his pony and tied him to a
stake by means of a long rope that he carried. A second rope,
in time, did the same service for Matouchon's pony. Then
Tabitosa shouldered the saddles and motioned toward the hut.

Inside, there seemed to be some preparations for living. A
fire was smouldering on a rudely improvised hearth set below
an aperture in the roof. Near by, hung a slab of bacon ; while,
in one corner, were a sack of meal and a jug of molasses.
Some strips of smoked beef were on a cross-piece near the fire.

" Sit down," said Tabitosa, sharply. " Sit down. Tabitosa
talk to you. You see here meat, meal, all to live five, six days,
maybe a week. By that time squaw child's friends glad
enough to get her. They pay Tabitosa, twenty-five, fifty,
maybe, a hundred dollars to tell where she is."

So this was the game the wicked creature meant to play!
He had captured and brought her here to keep her until her
friends, the good missionary, Unkama, Dr. Holley, and others
paid a reward for her release.

But she would not stay here, she would not stay a moment
longer than she could help. This she resolved. She would
break away; she would yet make her escape, and mounting
Achonhoah, would flee as the wind. She knew the way very
well. She had not been too frightened to take note of it as
they came along.

As though he read her thoughts and fully divined her
plans, from the hasty look she gave about her, Tabitosa said
roughly,

"You no get away. You no go from here till Tabitosa say
so; till money paid. Tabitosa himself watch. He no sleep
as you think he do. Then when Tabitosa gone, gone to see
squaw child's friends, then another come here and watch in
Tabitosa's place."

Matouchon's heart sank at this news. What was she to do?
A thought struck her. Tabitosa showed so plainly that it was
money he wanted, maybe, she could herself pay the price.
There were the big silver dollars, fifty or more, sewn into the
belt which Tohausin had given her, and which she kept locked
away in her own little trunk. If Tabitosa would only let her
go, she would get them and bring them to him. But when the
plan was proposed, Tabitosa glowered upon her fiercely and
shook his head with such emphatic decision that the eagle
feathers fairly danced about.

"No, no, no!" he said. "Tabitosa no such fool as that.
Tabitosa let you go, then that the last of it. You not come
back. I know that well 'nough. Tabitosa not taken in by
squaw child. When Tabitosa ready, him go himself. That
to-morrow morning," he announced determinately.

In the meantime, all was consternation and alarm at the
mission-house. Eleven o'clock came, and with it no Matouchon. Then twelve, then one, and still there was no sign

of the bonny little pony and his rider anywhere across the plains.

Mrs. Melville went again and again to the door to scan the grassy stretches, glowing fervidly in the midday sun, until her eyes fairly ached.

"What can have become of the child?" she questioned anxiously. "I feel sure some accident has happened to her or she would have been here long ago. It can't be that Achonhoah has thrown her? No, he is quite too gentle and faithful; besides Matouchon is far too careful a rider. I do wish Mr. Melville would come. As soon as he has had dinner, I am going to send him to Gokomb's in search of her. How I wish John was here!"

But John had chosen that particular day to go fishing with Willie Conover.

One o'clock was the dinner hour at the mission-house. It was a half hour later than that, when Mr. Melville came in. He had been detained at the Agency helping to extricate some Indians from their troubles. He was much disturbed when his wife told him about Matouchon and her long absence.

"I will go at once to Gokomb's, as soon as I have had dinner," he said determinately. But in two hours he returned, filled now with the deepest alarm and consternation. Matouchon had not been to Gokomb's nor had the old Indian or his wife seen or heard anything of her. It was all certainly very strange and mysterious. Mr. Melville had gone out of his way in several directions to make close enquiries but without success. He had now returned determined to lay the matter before Dr. Holley, and with him to agree upon some plan of action whereby to recover the missing child.

When Dr. Holley heard of Matouchon's disappearance, he had but one opinion. Especially was he confirmed in this, through recalling what Mr. Melville had previously told him of his recent conversation with Amado.

"This is Tabitosa's work, I feel sure," he said decisively. "There is no other conclusion, considering the late aspect of

affairs. The child knows the country too well to be lost; the
pony is gentle and reliable, and there is no one else but this
miserable, wretched father of hers who would seek to do her
harm. The scoundrel! if I could just get my fingers on
him!" and Dr. Holley's usually mild blue eyes glowed with a
fire that boded no good to the villainous Tabitosa.

"We must hurry," he said again, decisively. "Even now
he may have done the child some hurt. But I can't believe
he'd be quite so reckless as to put her out of the way. Even
his own people would be against him for that, now that the
child is so well-grown. He is too big a coward to risk the
consequences. But my poor, precious little one," he added,
while his eyes glistened and there was a sob in his throat
which showed plainly how dear she was to him, "there is no
telling what she has already suffered at his hands. We must
find her as quickly as possible."

"But suppose, when we have found her, he will not release
her?" said Mr. Melville, hesitantly.

"We must find a way," returned Dr. Holley, decisively. "I
know the old rascal so well that I feel sure this will bring him
over," and as he spoke Dr. Holley took a small handful of
coin from his pocket and shook it together suggestively.

"Can you go with me to Tataquitnamse's camp?" he asked
the missionary suddenly.

"That I can and will," Mr. Melville returned heartily.
"There were some matters pressing, but everything of that
kind is of secondary consideration now until we have found
and rescued this poor frightened child. We ought to start
as quickly as possible."

"We will. My own pony is bridled and at the door. I
will send a runner for yours with a message to your wife. I
must keep you here for some preliminary arrangements.
Every minute is an hour now until that precious little one is
found."

CHAPTER XIII.

JOHN TO THE RESCUE.

FIVE o'clock that afternoon brought John home from his fishing trip. He was so much earlier than usual that it surprised his mother a little. It surprised her so much in fact, that before she had told him the bad news about Matouchon, she said,

"Why John, what brought you back so early? I didn't look for you for two hours yet, though I was wishing for you with all my heart."

"Well, mother, for one thing we got tired of fishing, because you see we soon had all we wanted. The fellows bit unusually well to-day. See what a fine string! Another reason, little mother, was that we got awfully hungry. While crossing a foot-log, I actually let our lunch fall into the creek. What have you for dinner, mother? I feel that I could eat almost anything."

"I have a fairly good substantial dinner for my boy. Eat it, John; take plenty of time, and then I have something to tell you."

She turned away from him at these words for fear he would see the anxiety in her face. She knew how impetuous he was, how ready to act. Besides he loved Matouchon almost as well as if she were his own sister. He was tired, too, from his trip as well as hungry. She would wait until he had rested and eaten before she told him.

John sprang from his chair with a little sharp cry when at length his mother told him.

"O mother," he cried reproachfully, "why didn't you let me know sooner? Here I have wasted all this time! I see

Mrs. Vecht coming. I am so thankful; now I can go and search for Matouchon without leaving the little mother unprotected; for mother, I feel that I, too, must go and look for Matouchon."

"I feel so too, John. Indeed, I was longing for you to come. Somehow, I have the impression that your father and Dr. Holley have gone in the wrong direction. If Tabitosa has seized Matouchon, as we think, I feel sure that he is concealing her somewhere until he can decide what to do. It may be, that the wicked creature has shut her up alone in some dreadful place to frighten and torture her. It would be just like his mean, cruel nature to do that. O John, you must find that place and release her. But don't go alone. Get either Willie Conover or Andres. But stay! the quicker and better way would doubtless be to go to Gokomb's and get him to accompany you."

"I guess it would, little mother. I am going as fast as Spot will carry me. I am glad he is fresh. It will take me just five minutes to put on saddle and bridle, and then I am off."

A few minutes later, he led Spot round to the door, kissed his mother, hugged her tight around the neck for a moment or so, and then swinging into the saddle leaped the low fence and went galloping away.

It was now nearly six o'clock. The sun was fast sinking. In a little while, it would be gone and there would be nothing but the light of the stars to guide him on his journey. But John was brave. He felt at that moment, that he would gladly go alone. What courageous young knight starting out on a quest such as this, could bear the imputation that he feared to go alone? For just a little while, John had the inclination to give the sturdy Gokomb no part in this knightly undertaking. But there was his mother's request, and, with loyal John, this far outweighed everything else. He rode along over much of the way Matouchon had gone only nine hours before. Indeed, there were the tracks of her little pony in the loose sand, so very close to where Spot every now and then put his own flying feet, that once or twice he actually stepped in them.

John went on until he came to the belt of timber. Here he slackened his pony's pace for a few moments while he searched for the path. He seemed to have missed it in some way. Doubtless he had ridden too high up. John knew that there was not only a path but also a wagon road through this belt. If he couldn't find one, he could assuredly find the other. But he preferred the path as it was the nearer way. Strange to say, however, he could find neither, and while he rode up and down in the search, the sun sank out of sight. Twilight had now come and the belt of timber was in deep gloom. Failing to find the path or the road, John sturdily set his pony's head towards the timber, determined to ride through it at all hazards. There were open plains on the other side he knew, and somewhere in the midst of these Gokomb lived.

It was not only a hazardous but a difficult undertaking, to ride without a path at night through the timber, as John soon found out. Several times he was almost torn from his pony by the overhanging limbs and vines and more than once he would have gone headlong against a tree but for Spot's wonderful instinct.

Suddenly, when in the very midst of the timber, he heard a sound that made even his brave young heart stand still a moment. Some one was coming through the underbrush, coming directly towards him. He could hear the noise plainly. It was a horse, and doubtless a rider.

John checked his own horse and remained listening. What should he do? Should he hail the rider or not? If an enemy, would not his situation be perilous in the extreme? But on the other hand, suppose it were a friend? What joy that would be! especially, as he was undoubtedly lost in the timber and had no other hope of getting out. So without stopping to consider matters further, John called out in cautious tones, "Hello!"

There was no answer, but the noise made by the feet of the

horse seemed to have stopped. John felt a cold chill strike him. Was it an enemy, after all, and was he now planning an attack? Determinately, John grasped the handle of his little pistol and drew it from his pocket. He would at least die as bravely as he could.

But while he sat there, almost stone still and with the muzzle of the little pistol pointing straight before him, there came a sound that set John's heart to ringing as though a dozen silver joy-bells had begun to pour forth therein all their music. It was the whinny of a horse, and well John knew that whinny.

The horse was Achonhoah!

" Matouchon! Matouchon! Matouchon! "

He called the name over and over again; almost shouting it in his gladness.

There was still no answer. Just as his heart began to stand still again with dread, he discovered the reason of his failure to get an answer to his call. The pony had now come close up to him and was joyfully rubbing his nose against Spot's neck, while Spot, too, was joining in the delighted whinny of recognition.

Achonhoah was riderless, and not only riderless but the saddle too was gone from his back. From his neck there dangled a short piece of rope. As John examined it, it gave every evidence of having been bitten through.

" I do believe the smart, knowing fellow gnawed himself loose! " declared John. " I always said that pony knew things like folks. He has actually bitten through the rope that he might get away and come and tell us where Matouchon is, eh, old fellow? "

As though he understood every word, the pony began to whinny excitedly.

" Bless your bones! " said John, and tears, tears of joy were actually in his eyes.

" I do believe you are going to do what I want. Achonhoah, where is Matouchon? At what place have you left her, old boy? and is she safe? "

By way of answer Achonhoah whinnied again, and left off his caressing of Spot to rub his nose vigorously up and down John's legs.

"Achonhoah!" and now John reached down and got one arm about the pony's neck. "Achonhoah, old fellow, where is Matouchon? I know you want to tell me. You are almost ready to speak now. There! you *are* speaking; I feel sure of it. It is only stupid I who can't understand you. You will have to lead me. Turn round, old fellow, and go back the way you came, so! Ah, I knew you would understand me. See how much quicker you are than I. Yes, indeed, we are off. Go cautiously, old fellow, for there are enemies about us and not friends, I know."

As though he understood every word of this conversation—and who shall say that he didn't?—the pony turned himself round and began to make his way back through the under-brush, John closely following.

They went along perhaps fifteen or twenty minutes in this way. It was very dark. Only outlines were discernible; for the pale light of the moon penetrated only here and there through the thick growth. Sometimes, the thick shadows enveloped them so that John could just make out the form of the sturdy little pony moving along in front of him.

As though he understood fully all that was expected of him, and, what was better, knew himself what to do, Achonhoah kept steadily on his way. Now and then, he would turn his head to one side to see if John was following. Whenever John detected this movement he would give a low, cheery whistle of encouragement, to which Achonhoah never failed to respond with a cautious whinny.

In about twenty or twenty-five minutes from the time of starting, John could see that they were approaching the edge of the timber; for the moon's rays began to penetrate more distinctly now through the growth. In a little while he could see plainly that there was a clearing ahead. A cry escaped him as he almost at the same time caught sight of the glimmer of firelight just across the space. Soon the hut was clearly visible, the light shining through its many chinks.

John felt that he must now indeed be cautious for he did not know what person or persons were within the hut. In the excitement of meeting with Achonhoah and the subsequent following of the pony hither, John had forgotten all about Gokomb and his mother's injunction not to go alone. For the first time, the rashness of what he had done came fully to John. But it was too late now to reconsider, to turn back for help, unless on examining the inside of the hut, he found the inmates quite too many for him to deal with alone. Then John felt that for his own sake as well as for the successful issue of the search—to say nought of the safety of Matouchon herself—he must go for aid, before seeking to release her.

John never once doubted that Matouchon was within the hut. Everything induced him so to believe. The meeting with the pony and the subsequent action of that intelligent little creature in leading him thither, were all too conclusive. He felt sure that he had come upon the place where Matouchon was concealed. Dismounting and throwing the bridle over his arm, he cautiously approached the hut. When within ten or twelve paces of it, he stopped and issuing a low command to Spot, threw the rein back over the pony's neck. At the words, Spot stopped and stood immovable. Achonhoah also remained close beside him.

Reaching the door, John peered in. He almost gave a shout when he noticed only one person with Matouchon; but the next minute his spirits sank, as he saw that it was Tabitosa. John knew well the character of Tabitosa. He had heard of him and his cruel, heartless deeds again and again, and he recalled so vividly now the sufferings of poor Amado.

Matouchon was sitting near the fire and gazing into it. She had been crying and the tear-drops were still glistening on her long lashes. Over against the wall of the hut, with his shoulders propped against the logs was Tabitosa. He was wide awake and on the watch, but John saw with delight that the belt that held his knife and pistol had been removed and lay some little distance away.

Tabitosa was only about six or eight feet from the door and sitting with his side towards it and his face turned in the direction of Matouchon.

In a moment, John had resolved upon his plan of action. Success hung almost solely upon his getting the door open without noise. John's heart was nearly in his mouth as he reached out his hand to push against the door. Would it creak? or worse still, *hang*, and give him much difficulty in opening it? To his joy he noticed that it was not fastened— only propped by means of a piece of scantling and that instead of metal hinges, it swung on rough ones contrived of leather. It was but the work of a few minutes to sever these hinges noiselessly with his knife. This was rendered quite easy because of a wide crack between the door and its facing. Quick as a flash, John had thrown the door down and stood facing the startled Tabitosa, pistol in hand.

"Move an inch and I'll shoot you as I would a panther!" declared John, his eyes blazing. "You mean, wicked old wretch, I'd like to put an end to you anyhow!

"Now, Matouchon, I can't turn round so as to show you how rejoiced I am that I've come in time to save you from this horrid old villain here; for I have all I can do to keep my eye on him. I'll certainly blow the top of your head off, Tabitosa, if you move an inch. But you can tell how glad I am, Matouchon, just from my voice; I know you can. The first thing you must do is to get that belt over there with the pistol and knife in it. Now come here and buckle it around my waist. So! that is it. I'd like to see your face, Matouchon, but now I must keep my eyes in another direction. Whatever you do don't get between me and Tabitosa. Now take your saddle, and run and saddle Achonhoah. When that is done, mount. When you are mounted, whistle, and be sure to keep Spot right beside you."

In a few minutes Matouchon's clear musical whistle rang out.

10

John called to her, "Jump down, Matouchon, and run here; I need you again."

She was quick to obey.

"Take that lasso cord from Tabitosa's saddle. So, that will do. Now, Tabitosa, hold out your hands."

Tabitosa glowered and refused to obey.

"You had better do as I tell you," said John, determinately. "It will be the best way, Tabitosa, if you want to get off with a whole hide. I don't want to use this on you," with a nod towards the pistol, "but I certainly will if you don't do as I tell you. Hold out your hands and cross them."

Evidently, Tabitosa soon saw that there was no safe course save to obey, so he sullenly held out his hands, crossing the wrists one over the other.

"Now, Matouchon, wrap that cord round and round them, tying it as tight as you can, but not so tight as to cut. Tabitosa will soon find his way to some one who will untie it, I dare say, but he'll not make much headway in his pursuit of us. Now, Matouchon run again and mount. Be sure to drive out Tabitosa's pony before you. Give Achonhoah the rein; he knows the way. I'll be with you in a few minutes. If Spot shows any inclination to follow you, before I have mounted you know how to make him stand.

"I'm going back towards the door now, Tabitosa, but remember I'll have you covered with the pistol every step of the way. You had better not attempt to follow if you know what is good for you. But when I am mounted you can do as you please."

John had barely gained Spot's back when Tabitosa reached the doorway and sprang out after them.

"Ride, Matouchon, ride as fast as you can!" John called out after her, "and be sure to drive Tabitosa's pony before you."

Giving rein to Spot, John dashed on after Matouchon.

Now that the dreaded pistol was away from his line of vision, Tabitosa seemed to lose all fear. He was evidently greatly aroused, too, because Matouchon was about to escape him so easily.

He started after them as fast as his strong long legs could carry him. He was a swift runner, and doubtless would have caught them before they got out of the timber, for there he could travel faster than the horses. But he had the disadvantage of running with his hands tied, and fate seemed determined to be harder even than this against him; for he had not gone many paces when he stumbled and fell.

John thought this a good opportunity to give him some additional fright; so, turning in his saddle, he pointed the pistol high over Tabitosa's prostrate form and fired three times in rapid succession.

At the very first shot there was a loud howl from Tabitosa, but John knew he could not be hurt.

"I wish I could sting him a little without doing him any serious harm," John said, as he turned again to ride after Matouchon. "But I'm not marksman enough to try that, especially at this distance. However, I don't think he'll try to follow us now," and John was right. There were no further signs of Tabitosa, though he kept looking back every now and then.

"You can turn his pony round now and let him go back," John said to Matouchon as soon as they were safely out of the timber. "And now Matouchon we must ride at a sharp pace, or the rascal may yet devise some plan to overtake us."

It was not until they were in sight of the mission-house, a mile away across the plains, that John found time to talk to Matouchon. Prior to that, they had been riding too rapidly. Matouchon now gave him a full account of her capture by Tabitosa. She also told him how Tabitosa had intended to keep her until her release.

"The despicable villain!" said John, clinching his hand. "But ain't I glad, though, he was foiled?"

"But he may do something yet," ventured Matouchon, timidly.

"Oh, no, he won't," declared John, promptly. "Don't be frightened, Matouchon; he won't dare harm you again."

"But it was not of myself I was thinking."

"Well, of whom, then, Matouchon?"

"Of you. Tabitosa will be *so* angry, he will try his best to hurt you. Oh; he is dreadful!"

"Oh, he'll not hurt me," asserted John, with all a fearless boy's confidence. "He won't *dare*. I think I gave him enough of myself to-night. He won't want to come about me again."

But when they heard of the matter, his father and Dr. Holley were of quite a different opinion.

"You have certainly angered him greatly, my son," said his father, "and Tabitosa's is a nature that never forgets nor forgives. I fear he will yet do you injury. But I would not have had you act otherwise," he concluded, his eyes glowing. "It certainly was a brave deed, and I am proud of my son."

His mother, too, showed how greatly she rejoiced in his courageous behavior. It did not take her long either to forgive him for not going for Gokomb as he had promised. "I know you forgot it," she said, "in the excitement of meeting with the pony. It is all right, John. I am indeed thankful to God that he let no harm befall you; thankful to him, too, that I have my little girl home safe," and with these words there were both a kiss and a close hug for Matouchon.

The days passed on, and as they saw or heard nothing of Tabitosa—except that he had gone with a party of Indians several miles below Fort Sill to treat with the Government Agent with reference to some lands—they all began to feel easy again, save Mr. Melville. He couldn't get rid of his first impression that Tabitosa in his anger would not soon forget or forgive. He would yet seek his revenge, if not upon John directly, then in some other way.

CHAPTER XIV.

A CROOKED RAIL AND A SERMON.

IN his life as missionary to the wild tribes on the western plains, Mr. Melville had every opportunity of studying their character. He saw phases of it which perhaps no other, not similarly placed, could have seen. There was much that was bad, but, at the same time, also much which was good. Like his white brother, the Indian had his shortcomings and his commendable points.

Had Mr. Melville been asked to give his opinion with reference to the " Indian Question," he would doubtless have handled it a little differently from the way in which others had done. Close observation of the Indian and of his surroundings had served to fix several strong convictions within his mind. What pained him more than anything else, was the great difficulty he had in reaching some of the more prominent of the Indians. This was doubtless owing to race prejudice. Hatred of the white man was still a deeply fixed principle within the breast of the Indian. The years during which he had been a ward of the government had not served to lessen it. It still slumbered like the fire, smothered under the ashes, ready to blaze up at any moment. Though he had, in many instances, been treated by his white brother kindly, the Indian still looked upon him suspiciously. The missionary himself, though greatly beloved, had now and then, something of this kind to endure. This distrust in the mind of the Indian had been brought about chiefly through the action of bad whites, herders, and traders; men whose sole aim in life seemed to be to deceive the Indian and to speculate upon his credulity. Mr. Melville felt that as long as this class of whites had the opportunity to prey upon the simplicity of the Indian, there would be no remedy for this state of feeling. These whites not only defrauded the Indian, but they set him a terrible example of immoral conduct. When the missionary would remonstrate with some Indian for his loose way of living, he would again and again be met with the answer, " Your white man do this way." The Indian's own mode of life tended to this immorality. Herded together, as they were, men, women, and children, in the close quarters of a tepee, it was little wonder that they led lives of filthiness and degradation.

" There is but one remedy," Mr. Melville would say again and again to Dr. Holley. " The Reservation should long ago have been abolished and the Indians settled in homes with respectable white families in their midst. The Indian will learn civilization by object lessons and by contact as he will learn it in no other way. Give him a sober industrious white neighbor, and he will soon be catching the same spirit himself. Up to this time, save in a small degree here and there, the important factor of civilization—example—has been kept out. From such whites as he has chiefly seen, the Indian has imbibed evil instead of good. The white man's vice coupled with the Indian's superstition, form a compound that is like fighting fire to handle. Only the grace of God can reach and dissolve it."

" It is a pity," said Dr. Holley, " that the government could not issue restrictions to keep this demoralizing class of whites off the Reservation. But alas ! the regulations they now have in force with reference to the settlement of the whites in the Indian country, are such as to invite the very class that is dangerous ; while, on the other hand, the very best element of civilization is kept away. I agree with you that the Indian must be permanently settled before he can become other than he is. No people of such continuously wandering habits can ever be developed into anything like respectable citizens so long as they retain those habits. There is nothing whatever in the present mode of managing them to develop self-reliance.

The help given them by the government only encourages laziness. It has been forcefully said that the best help in the world is self-help. That is what these Indians need—encouragement to self-help. Nay, with some, it must be more than encouragement, it must be an absolute, out-and-out forcing them to it."

" Yes," replied Mr. Melville ; " there is a policy which if pursued would open this whole country first to civilization and then to Christianity. These Indians can be civilized and Christianized too. We already have several illustrious examples in those who have come forward for membership in the church, and who have allowed themselves to be directed and moulded into a sober and moral course of living through the help and example of the better class of their white brethren. This added to their genuine religious convictions, have made of them entirely new creatures. There never was any wisdom in the efforts to keep the Indians and whites separate. Let the government encourage the settlement throughout this Reservation of the right class of whites; let the Indian live on terms of brotherly intercourse, in helpful relations the one to the other, with the better element of their white brethren, and only a few years will show the difference."

" I see more and more clearly every year," added Dr. Holley, " the great mistake made by the government in dealing with these Indians as wards, and at the same time, treating them as a separate nation. If they are wards of our government, they can't be a separate nation ; and if they are a separate nation they can't be wards of the government. Now which are they? The government says they are both, and at one time deals with them as wards and at another as a nation —a dangerous policy to pursue with any question, a course weak and vacillating. They should be made *subjects* and citizens of the United States at once. As the case now stands, the United States is absolutely powerless to deal with many of the crimes that occur here among the Indians. The result is a state of lawlessness that, in some instances, borders upon anarchy."

"You are right," commented Mr. Melville, warmly, "and it is this very policy pursued by the government that hinders the work of the church and prevents the real civilization of the Indian, to say nothing of his Christianization. There is no reason in the world why the government should not place these people upon their own resources, at the same time throwing about them the strong restraining arm of the law, which is about every other citizen of the United States. With such restrictions, and with the proper management, the majority of these people would in time become not only self-reliant and self-supporting, but also useful citizens of the government. They have every inducement here to industry, for this is as fine a section as the American continent can show ;— a soil and a climate adapted to the production of almost everything that could be named."

The present laziness of the Indian men was one source of the deepest pain to the good missionary. The squaws were really hard-worked ; for, when it came to labor of any kind, they had it all to do. They led the ponies to water, brought wood and made the fires, cut and stripped the beef, brought water, and did everything else that required work about the Indian camps. When the camp was on the move, they had to carry the tepee poles, the heavy rolls of canvas, the cooking utensils and all else, while the men rode along on their ponies with no greater weight in their hands perhaps than a quirt.*

When he needed anything done about the mission-house or yard, it was hard for Mr. Melville to get any of the Indians to assist him except those in his church who were sincerely striving to walk in the right way. But these were not always available.

One portion of the fence around the mission station, had long needed attention. On a certain morning, Mr. Melville determined to delay work on it no longer ; so he sent for an

* A Mexican whip made of horse-hair and leather.

Indian Braves.

Indian by the name of " Short Horse " to come and help him.
" Short Horse " was stout and healthy and fully able to do
what was required of him, Mr. Melville knew. But " Short
Horse " returned word that he didn't feel like doing anything
that morning, and advised sending for " Prairie Dog."
" Prairie Dog " was pitching quoits and said he couldn't quit.
At last, Mr. Melville succeeded in getting " Spotted Wolf " to
come. "Spotted Wolf" was a big, tall Indian who looked
fully capable of shouldering not only the post-hole digger, but
the good missionary along with it. Yet when the instrument
was pointed out to him and he was shown the way to use it,
he declared he didn't believe he could get up the dirt at all.
Besides he didn't like the way it made his hands feel. The
missionary finally blistered his own hands by taking hold to
show him, but in reality doing nearly all the work himself.
Finally, as the holes were dug and they were getting ready to
put the posts in, a companion of " Spotted Wolf " came along
and began to call him "a squaw-man " for doing work. This
so nettled " Spotted Wolf " that he dropped the post at once,
and no inducement could prevail upon him to remain.

Mr. Melville's next experience in fence building was, when
he undertook to put a rail enclosure around his corn-patch.
He had one of his own Indians, " Big Paul," to assist him
this time. Paul was not so large as his name would imply. It
was simply that there were two Pauls in the family and he
happened to be the bigger Paul of the two. But Paul was of
good size, considerably larger than the missionary. Paul
hadn't been long in the church. He was not only a new convert, and a rather weak one as Mr. Melville knew only too
well. Paul had one weakness that it was hard for him to overcome ; this was the passion for gambling. He had every opportunity to indulge this passion, as gambling was extensively
carried on by the Indians and low whites throughout the
Reservation, though to a certain extent, secretly, because of
the government restrictions. Paul had lost money again and
again and also his blankets and his ponies, but his losses seemed

never to teach him a lesson. He went on to the next game of chance as madly intoxicated with it as ever. This evil passion seemed to shut out and to obscure whatever else was noble in Paul. It kept him back from the true religious life he would otherwise have been enabled to lead. It was the one bad tendency that kept him astray, the false stone in the foundation that threw the whole structure out of shape. As long as Paul allowed himself to be swayed by this passion, he would never be a Christian, no matter how hard he might struggle in other ways.

In helping Mr. Melville with the fence, Paul, without noticing, got in a crooked rail. It was very crooked, but Paul put it in its place on the fence. Next he put a straight rail above it. The straight rail was so very straight and the crooked rail so very crooked that when they came together there was a considerable hole between them. Indeed the hole was so large that a pig might easily have crawled through it. Even "Big Paul" could have stuck his head and perhaps his shoulders partly through it. Paul gazed at the hole dubiously. It would never do to let it stay that way he knew. So he took down the straight rail and turned the crooked one over. Then he laid the straight rail back again. It was all the same, only the hole was at the bottom now instead of at the top, for there was another straight rail between the crooked rail and the ground.

As Paul was standing again dubiously regarding his work, the voice of the missionary spoke to him:

"There is but one way, Paul, my friend. You must take out the crooked rail or the hole will still be there and the entire panel wrong, even though you placed a dozen straight rails above the crooked one. It is the one crooked rail that makes all the trouble, and that alone; the one crooked rail that prevents the straight rails from performing their part as they should.

"And it is not only so with rails, Paul, but it is so with people. Once let anything wrong get in the heart and the whole structure is wrong. One bad habit may lead a person astray no matter how many good ones he may have. It is always the one evil tendency that gets the upper hand of the nobler ones. The only safe plan then, Paul, my friend, is never to allow the bad habit to enter nor the evil tendency to gain a footing.

"Take away the crooked rail now and you will see how quickly the straight ones will drop to their places, and the whole panel be in shape."

Paul did as the missionary advised. There was a very serious expression in his face as he stood regarding the fence.

"That rail, bad rail, sure enough!" he said indignantly, as he tossed the crooked rail away. "Him no good but to burn. Leave him here and pigs and dogs and all crawl through, and fence same as not here for all the good it do."

"Yes, my friend, you are right; it will do no good; for, as long as the crooked rail is there in the fence, the hole will be there and the corn at the mercy of hogs and other small destructive animals. But remove the rail, as you have seen, and all goes right. So, Paul, we must remove the cause of evil from our hearts; for not until then, can they be right; not until then, can they help us truly in the good way that we would go in the good life that we would lead."

"Paul got bad rail in him heart," said Paul suddenly, and looking at the missionary in a way both helpless and appealing.

"Yes, Paul, my friend, I know you have," returned the missionary, laying his hand earnestly upon his shoulder; "and you must get it out at once, Paul. When 'Coyote Joe,' and 'Wild Dick,' and 'Spotted Tail,' and all those bad whites and Indians ask you to play, to risk your money and your blankets and your ponies, you must say 'No,' Paul, that you must, and you must mean it, too. But the best way, Paul, is to keep away from them. Don't go where the temptation is, then the inclination in your heart will be the easier to overcome. As long as the crooked rail was kept out of the fence, then the fence was all right; but just the moment it was put in, then the fence was all wrong. So the moment you yield to the temptation, Paul, you have the crooked rail in your heart. Keep it out. You will soon be able to conquer the inclination if you keep out of the way of temptation. Ask God to help you. Come here to me and I will help you."

The missionary could see that Paul was deeply impressed and an earnest prayer went up that the convictions might prove lasting.

CHAPTER XV.

IN THE COUNTRY OF GRASS-HUTS.

ONE Saturday morning, Mr. Melville said to his wife, "I have to go over the river to-day, about ten miles away, to preach to some Wichitas. As they are not in school I believe I will take Matouchon and Emma with me. Just give us lunch enough, good wife, to do three hungry people for one meal, for we'll be back late this evening. Call them to get ready and tell Emma to hunt up the little kodak that was sent to John. I think I'll try my hand at taking some pictures. They'll doubtless be glad to use them in our missionary magazine."

Emma and Matouchon were wild with delight when they heard they were to accompany Mr. Melville on his trip. Matouchon soon had Achonhoah ready. He seemed to understand that this was a splendid occasion, for he pawed the ground impatiently while he waited for his little mistress to get ready. Emma was to ride John's pony, Spot, as he was faster and in every way better fitted for the journey than her own little one who wasn't much out of his colthood, as yet. They were soon off, taking a trail that turned in to the right of the Agency and led to a ford of the river a half mile away.

As they rode along, they chatted gaily, for all were in the best of spirits. Even the grave missionary seemed determined to lose his gravity for this day, at least, and to be a child with the others. So he laughed and talked with them and humored all their fancies with the abandon of a boy.

"I declare father's better than any boy in the world," said Emma over and over again, confidentially; "anyhow, I'd rather go with him than twenty boys!" and Emma meant every word she said.

They went down the sharp incline and forded the river in great glee, laughing merrily as the water was splashed all about them.

The banks of the river were very steep at this point on both sides. Indeed, it is thus with nearly all the streams in the Indian Territory. The banks are steep, even precipitous, and the streams narrow and shallow.

The pony of the Territory has a steep climb up the banks of these streams and has all he can do to keep his feet steady under him going down. But, though small, he has a full stock of hardiness and endurance, and sure-footedness, too.

On crossing the river, the road led through a tangled mass of bamboo vines and of canes. It was now summer and everything was in full, rich flower. Especially were the colors vivid and brilliant here in the swamp. The china-berries, the elms, the box-elders, the sugar-berries, and cotton-woods were vying with each other in the beauty of blossom and richness of foliage. The ground too was covered with myriads of wild flowers, some hugging it closely and creeping along through the mosses and low-growing grasses; others again shooting upward with symmetry and grace as well as bloom. Every opportunity was given the travelers to study the wild flora of the country shown here in its full magnificence.

On coming out of the woodland and on to the prairies again, the little girls were very much amused at the quaint appearance of a house that was situated upon a knoll and looked straight down upon them. It had all sorts of queer shaped rooms, and was built here and there about the ground after no particular shape or fashion.

"It belongs to an Irishman by the name of Sherrill," Mr. Melville said, in answer to Emma's question. "He has been twenty years building it, and it isn't finished yet. Every room is built after a particular pattern of his own and, as you can see from the outside, there are no two alike. It is even more noticeable from the inside."

"Why, what made him build such a house, father?"

"Oh, just to be odd, I suppose. Besides, he has lots of money and does not know what to do with it. He married an Indian woman. She is dead now. She was the last of the Anadarko Indians, the full-blooded Anadarkoes I mean. You know the Agency takes its name from them. At one time they had a great deal of land hereabouts. Sherrill's wife's share brought him a fortune, which he has added to in one way and another."

"Well, he may think that jumbled-up house mighty pretty, but I don't!" declared Emma, emphatically. "I'd a heap rather have our own little one over at the Agency; it looks like it has some sense about the way it is built, at least. Father," suddenly, "if Mr. Sherrill has so much money, why doesn't he give some of it to the mission? We do need it so bad for work among these Indians."

"He does give money to the mission, Emma, but not to our mission. He is a Catholic."

"O father! Then he gives it all to that fat, horrid, old Catholic priest. No wonder he was smiling so last week! Father, the Catholics give a great deal of money to keep up their missionaries out here, don't they?"

"Yes, Emma, much more than the Protestants do, very much more. This priest and the one higher up the river seem always to have what money they want for every thing. Both churches are finished, and there are Sunday-school rooms besides, with all the necessary out buildings."

"O father! and you can't even get a study, a little room to call your own, and the church is not half big enough for the Indians who come now! What do the Protestants mean, father? Why do they not give as the Catholics do?"

"I don't know, Emma; they lack zeal principally, I suppose. The Catholics, it is said, are the most zealous church people in the world. They give as they pray, regularly and systematically.

"I have been trying for two years," he continued, as though he were speaking more to himself than to Emma, "to

get our Board to establish a school out here in connection with
the church.   In properly training the young lies one of our
greatest hopes as to the future of the Indian."

   " But what about the Government Schools, father ? "

   " The Government Schools are well enough, but they do not
give that religious training which is such a vital need.   To
found a school where the children are trained religiously, is
the opportunity of the church in these mission fields.   The
Catholics recognize it, consequently both priests have a school
ready to begin operations."

   " But why will not our Board establish one, father ? "

   " Because they haven't the funds, they say.   The people of
the church have not been liberal in their gifts this year, not so
liberal as they were last year.   The receipts have fallen off
considerably.   They lack the zeal of the Catholics, you see."

   " Yes, father, and it is a downright shame !   I do wish the
whole church could know how things are out here ; how the
Catholics are going to get the biggest part of this Territory, if
they don't mind.   Father, why do you not write to the papers
about it ? "

   " I have, Emma, again and again.   I have gone over the
situation until it seems to me that the heart of the church *must*
be moved unless it is cold, *dead !*   My hope now of the school
is through the Woman's Mission Board.   I have been corres-
ponding with their Secretary for some time.   Many things now
point auspiciously towards an early realization of my desires.
These noble women are both zealous and wide-awake, and I
believe have the funds to begin work, at least on a small scale."

   " Oh, I do hope they will start the school ! " said Emma,
earnestly.

   They rode on for some moments in silence until a little sharp
exclamation from Matouchon caused them to turn and glance
in the direction in which she was now gazing.

   An Indian woman, almost nude and bent with age, was
standing near their path and ravenously devouring the partly
decayed offals of a beef, which had been thrown aside when

---

that animal was butchered. Her hair was perfectly white, her face a mass of seams and wrinkles, while the sight of one eye was entirely gone and that of the other partly so. She was fully eighty or eighty-five years of age. As familiar as he was with such sights, the missionary could not repress a cry of horror. Emma too cried out sharply. It was such a sickening, revolting sight.

"The poor creature is almost starved to death," said Mr. Melville. "I doubt if she has tasted food for several days. We must give her some of our lunch right away," and he made preparations to dismount.

"Yes, father," returned Emma, quickly, "let's give her every bit of it. I am sure we can make out till we get supper."

"No, Emma, that would not be prudent. She might eat so ravenously of it that she would kill herself. I will give her enough to satisfy her present sharp hunger, and then we will think of some other way to help her."

The old woman had now grown aware of their presence. She had moved a step or two nearer to them, but had not thrown down the beef offals or ceased to gnaw upon them.

"Here is something far better than that," Mr. Melville said kindly, as he held towards her a large sandwich made of two generous slices of bread with a thick layer of broiled beef between.

She did not understand the words, but her sight, dim as it was, saw the food.

She snatched it eagerly, threw away the offals, and began devouring it as though she could not get the sweet, wholesome morsels down fast enough. Mr. Melville gave her a second sandwich but remained firm in his refusal of the third; though the old woman begged so piteously that both Emma and Matouchon burst into tears.

Finally, Mr. Melville made her understand, by signs, that if she would leave the beef offals alone and go back to her camp, he would come to see her again in a day or two, bring her more food, and would then do all he could for her.

11

In the same way, by signs, she told him of her troubles.
Like most of the old squaws, when she became useless, she
had been left to shift for herself. Now and then, a morsel of
food, a bone, or a scrap of bread, was thrown to her ; but,
oftener, she was left to get sustenance as best she could. Half
the time she lived on the refuse left on the prairies when the
beeves were butchered.

Mr. Melville knew that this was not an exceptional case.
Only the day before, he had had a startling experience. Three
Kiowas, stout, strong young men, and men who bore a very
good reputation among their fellows, had called at the parsonage to get Mr. Melville to go with them to the Agent's office.
They wanted him to intercede with that official so as to have
him give them three or four of the old worn-out government
mules that were considered of no further good, and had been
turned out to pick up a living as they could. Mr. Melville
felt favorably inclined to the mission ; so he went readily with
the Indians. They did not tell him for what purpose they desired the mules, but he supposed they were going to try some
little experiments in planting and wanted the mules for the
plow.

At Mr. Melville's solicitation, the Agent granted the request
of the Indians. But it occurred to him to ask what the mules
were to be used for, before letting them go. His own and the
missionary's horror and indignation can better be imagined
than described, when the answer came that *they wanted the
mules to kill so as to feed them to the old squaws !* *

Mr. Melville and the girls now entered a stretch of prairie
covered with tall grasses, in many places above the backs of
the ponies, but as a road had been opened through our travelers had no difficulty in getting along.

On coming out of the thicket of grass, they suddenly saw a
queer village before them. It was built entirely of grass.
There were about a dozen huts and half as many provision

---

* This incident actually occurred at Anadarko.

sheds. The huts were from sixteen to twenty feet high, conical in shape, and about forty feet around the base. They were dark and gloomy-looking, not having at all the picturesque and attractive appearance of the cloth tepees of the Comanches and Kiowas. The people, too, seemed to partake of the nature of their huts. They were very filthy-looking, with begrimed faces, tangled hair and tattered clothing. Instead of hastening to meet the travelers with faces brightened by curiosity and expectancy, as so many of the Indians do, they stood around with sullen countenances, scarcely making a sound.

But the dogs were not so silent; they rushed out to greet the new arrivals in a noisy, yelping pack. It took a considerable time to quiet them and drive them back. Then they did not retreat far, but only around the corners of the huts, whence every now and then, a nose could be seen sniffing the air suspiciously. Mr. Melville soon made himself so agreeable that he was invited by three of the men to enter their huts.

The first hut into which our trrvelers went, was one of the largest in the village. From base to top, it was woven entirely of straw, twisted in and out through ribs of willow splints. The one opening, through which our travelers crawled to enter, looked more like the entrance to the burrow of some animal than anything else. There was no outlet at the top through which the smoke could escape, as in the tepees of the Kiowa and other Indians. The smoke had to find its way out between the straw as best it could; consequently, nearly the whole inside of the hut was begrimed with soot. This gave a gloomier appearance than ever to the interior, where, at midday, it was almost like twilight.

In this hut there were two men, their wives, and ten or twelve children. There were also fifteen or twenty dogs that had entered upon the heels of the travelers, and were making themselves familiar with every appointment of their persons. At first, Matouchon and Emma had been considerably frightened at this familiarity, but, when the men gave them to understand that the dogs would not hurt them, they felt more at

ease. But they took care to keep close to Mr. Melville, so as
to have him near at hand in case of need.

Mr. Melville was greatly pleased to find that one of the
men understood some English. He had picked it up around
the Agency and also from his oldest son who had been to one
of the Government Schools, and who was now out on the Reservation with a party of cattle-men.

In this way, and with the help of some sign language, Mr.
Melville managed to carry on a conversation that was for the
greater part understood. He hoped that in a little while, his
interpreter would come. Then he could proceed with his
preaching. Until then he had to do the best he could.

Some two or three Indian men now came in. All were
highly pleased when Mr. Melville finally made them understand that he wanted to take their pictures. Both men and
women began to make great preparations for it. But two
young girls who belonged in the hut seemed determined to
outdo all the others in the effort to array themselves. Evidently they intended to put on every scrap of their possessions.
Doubtless they wanted their friends to see, by means of the
picture, the full extent of their wardrobes.

Mr. Melville succeeded in getting all the others out of the
hut but the two girls. They still lingered. He had finally to
go back to the entrance, put his head inside, and insist on their
coming.

As he now returned to rearrange his group against the side
of the hut, he found that in the moment he had been away all
had gotten out of order. While he was waiting for the girls
to come, he began stepping backward so as to get his picture
properly focused within the little glass indicator. As he was
doing this he looked up at the sun so to see if he had the light
in the right direction. Just at this moment, the two girls came
to the entrance and stepped out. When they saw Mr. Melville
glance upward at the sun, they gave a cry and darted back
again into the hut. There was also a commotion in the group
that had been arranged for the picture. It broke up in com-

plete confusion. Several of its members did not stop until
they were entirely behind the hut. Only two men remained,
the old man who understood English and one other.

When Mr. Melville questioned the former as to the meaning
of all, he answered that the girls and other Indians, on seeing
him look up to the sun, had concluded that he intended to put
a spell upon them, and so had fled in fright.

No coaxing could induce them to return. They now looked
upon the little black case in which the instrument was enclosed
as a box of bad medicine into which a spell had been drawn
from the Spirit in the sun, and which would be thrown upon
them the moment the instrument was directed towards them.
Mr. Melville had to content himself with photographing the
two Indians and the grass huts, with a few of the dogs thrown
in for variety.

In looking about him, Mr. Melville was pleased to see that
several of the Indians had set out little orchards, principally
of peach and plum trees. There were also a number of grape
vines. Evidently, these Wichita Indians had determined to
do what few of their Kiowa and Comanche brethren had not
yet shown inclination to do, make permanent settlement.

On Mr. Melville's making enquiry as to how they were led
to set out the orchards, he learned that it had all come about
through the persuasion of the old man's son who was now out
on the Reservation with the cattle-men. He had seen the
stock men setting out little orchards here and there, and at
once taken to the idea and felt that it would be a good plan
for his own people.

The interpreter had now come, and so, seeking a shady spot,
Mr. Melville gathered the people around him for the preaching. There were about thirty men, women, and children in
all. He felt sure this was not more than half the population
of the village; for he could see many heads peering here and
there around the corners of the huts. It was not until he had
safely slung the dread kodak across the saddle of his pony,
that Mr. Melville could induce those that showed a desire to

come to draw nearer to him. Their eyes kept turning every now and then towards the pony as though fully expecting to see some terrible thing overtake it through contact with that dreadful box. But, as nothing happened, they after a while began paying less attention to the pony and more to the sermon.

Mr. Melville was fortunate in having a good interpreter. Many of the Indians seemed impressed, but every now and then, he could hear the click of the tongue and the word, " kitty, kitty, kitty ! " " Kitty," he knew was the Wichita negative. They used it for every form of dissent or disapproval—no, not, none, don't, won't—every kind of negative assertion in the Wichita language was represented by the word " kitty."

But as the missionary went on and endeavored to grow clearer and clearer in the words he was saying, he was encouraged by noting that the utterance of the word grew less and less ; finally it had ceased altogether and every face fixed upon him had rapt attention in its gaze. They were a gloomy looking people usually, but they were a people easy to arouse ; or, at least, so it appeared from the missionary's experience with his present audience. He was certainly never given more attention nor appreciation.

When he had finished, they all crowded around him, entreating him to come back again and tell them more of Jesus, the wonderful Saviour of men. A few had heard of him before, among them the old man whose son had learned to read at the Government School. This man was exceedingly anxious to have a picture of Jesus.' Doubtless Mr. Melville's explanation with reference to the kodak had suggested the thought. If the picture of one person could be taken, why not also that of another? He asked Mr. Melville if he had one. Mr. Melville told him that he had two or three, but that they were at the mission station. The man said he was coming to get one, that he was coming soon ; for he was anxious to see how this Jesus looked who pitied all men. Mr. Melville assured him that he would certainly give him one if he came.

The interpreter accompanied Mr. Melville back to the mission station, and doubtless it was a good thing, since, on the way, quite a startling little occurrence took place. It was just as they had passed through the swamp and were preparing to ford the river. Mr. Melville had drawn his pony aside to let Emma and Matouchon go ahead, when a sharp cry from Matouchon caused him to look up suddenly. There on the bank astride of his pony was Tabitosa, in full war paint, and looking as ugly as it was possible for him to look, which was very ugly indeed. He seemed to be waiting for some one, doubtless for them; for, on catching sight of Mr. Melville, he opened his mouth as though to speak. Then seeing, for the first time the interpreter, he apparently changed his mind.

Mr. Melville spoke to him, but Tabitosa gave him only a sullen grunt. Then glowering fiercely upon them all and giving Matouchon a threatening look, he pulled up his bridle and moved off in the direction they had just come. Matouchon was trembling so that she could hardly sit on her pony. So, Mr. Melville told them to wait a little while before they went down into the ford. In the meantime, he endeavored to soothe and quiet Matouchon. He had another part to perform too, that of replying to a battery of questions from Emma. She was highly indignant when she learned that the Indian who had just left them, was "the horrid, wretched creature," as she termed him, who had captured Matouchon and from whom John had rescued her.

"Why do you not have him arrested, father? He just ought to be made to suffer for such meanness!"

Mr. Melville could not tell her, especially as Matouchon and the Indian were present, of the claim that Tabitosa had upon Matouchon, or how, in the sight of both Indians and Agent, Tabitosa would have a right to do as he pleased with his own child. So, he only said :

"That is easier to talk about than to do, Emma. There are many things in the way. These Indians stick right up for each other, you know, which would be truly commendable if it were always for the right thing. Thus the arrest of Tabitosa might bring about no end of trouble to others. So it is best to pass it over unless he tries the same thing again. Then I think patience will cease to be a virtue."

CHAPTER XVI.

ISSUE DAY.

THEY saw Tabitosa again, the very next day, which was
the regular semi-monthly period for the issuance of supplies to the Indians.

Issue days at the Agency always fall upon the first and
middle of the month and are the occasions of the assembling
of several thousand Indians; all those, in fact, upon the Reservation. The stores are kept in two long, shed-like buildings
known as supply-houses. In these buildings are piles of flour,
bins of sugar and coffee, barrels of vinegar, and boxes of
dried fruit, soap, soda and other things. From the two
houses, fully 12,000 pounds of flour are distributed each issue
day, in addition to a proportionate supply of sugar, coffee,
dried fruit, etc.

The Indian men do not condescend to receive these supplies; they think it beneath their dignity. So the women are
sent. It is highly amusing to note the various contrivances to
which they resort in order to provide means and ways of con-
veyance for the supplies. Old skirts tied together at the ends,
pant-legs similarly treated, old hats and bits of blankets form
receptacles for the flour. As to the other supplies, they bundle
them up *pellmell* in some portion of their clothing. An un-
failing place of deposit is in that space not filled by the baby
in the cavity of the blanket at the mother's back.

The beeves are issued from the pens, which are about a mile
from the supply-houses. Here the men are seen in all their
glory, mounted upon their ponies, and decked out in eagle
feathers and paint, with their buckskin leggings and moccasins
resplendent with brilliant fringe, glittering buttons, shells, and

bits of metal. From 160 to 175 beeves are given out each issue day. The Indian tribes are divided into bands. Each
band has its band-man or leader. The bands gather, in turn,
about the gates of the stock pen. The beeves are then turned
out in the proportionate number. As the beeves rush through
the gates and out on the plains, they are at once set upon by
the band of Indians who begin yelling and whooping like mad
creatures, spurring their ponies on to the chase, and wounding
and maddening the cattle by firing small shot into them.
When they have had sufficient sport of this kind, or when the
poor tortured creatures fall to the ground from weakness produced by the wounds, then they are dispatched by larger balls
from pistol or rifle.

When the beeves are shot down, the women are required to
come and do the butchering. The men never condescend to
this. It is a common sight to see these squaws, at such a time,
with their arms bloody to the shoulders. Truly the scenes
connected with issue day at these Agencies are sickening and
revolting in the extreme. It takes a stout heart and a steady
and strong nerve to enable one to look upon them unflinchingly.

Again and again has the government been remonstrated with
with reference to this cruel and cold-blooded system of issuing
rations of beef to the Indians; but always they have the same
reply ready: that any other plan would entail an additional
expenditure, an amount so great as not to be thought of under
the present appropriations. There are in the Indian Territory,
five government supply stations, or Agencies. It costs in the
neighborhood of $500,000 to keep up each annually, or two
and a half million in all. Many thousands would be added to
the expenses did the government attempt to butcher the beef
and deliver it in portions.

The Indians are alone to blame for the cruel and sickening
method now pursued. Each band could receive its number
of beeves and, then retiring with them to some secluded spot,
proceed to do the butchering decently and in order. But as
long as the present cruel sport has the least suggestion in it of

the old time chase of the buffalo, then will the Indian's desire
to engage in it remain. As Indian law, with reference to these
matters, and not government law, prevails on the Reservation,
there is really no way, save the one previously mentioned, of
putting a stop to these savage and disgusting scenes. But one
mark of promise is, that the Christian Indians, with but rare
exceptions, heartily condemn, and, what is better, refuse to
engage in it. Thus in the proportion that God's grace enters
their hearts and shows them sweeter and gentler things, in the
same degree will these barbarous and revolting customs cease.

While many of the scenes witnessed on these occasions,
especially those at the pen, were always exceedingly trying to
the good missionary, still these gatherings of the Indians afforded him opportunities he dared not slight.

On the particular issue day of which we have previously
made mention, Mr. Melville went early to the supply-houses,
taking with him John, Emma, Matouchon, Glover, and Henry.
The children had begged so hard to accompany him, that he
could not refuse. He gave his consent readily to their going
as far as the supply-houses. Here they were to turn back,
while only John and himself went to the pen.

It was while they were standing near the supply-houses
watching the stream of Indians going in and out, that they saw
Tabitosa again. He came galloping by on his way to the
pen. A few paces beyond them he reined in his pony so
that he might take in the scene about him. Just then, he saw
for the first time the group near the steps. He scowled fiercely
as his eyes rested upon John, and, it seemed to Mr. Melville
who was watching him closely, that the hand holding his riding whip was raised for a second or so menacingly. But he
said nothing of this to John.

John was one of the last of the group to see Tabitosa ; as his
time and attention were taken up in watching the manœuvers
of some Caddoes, who were endeavoring to carry between them
an old pair of army pants closely packed with flour. When
John did see Tabitosa, it was merely to give him a mocking

smile; but that smile enraged Tabitosa as words perhaps could not. His face was a picture ugly to look upon as he turned and rode off towards the pen muttering to himself.

"I hope he's gone for good!" said John. "I don't want to get close to him again, for I don't believe I could keep my fingers off of him so well next time, the mean, cowardly old villain!"

"Yes, John," said his father, earnestly, "I think you had better stay away from Tabitosa. He would not hesitate to do you harm if he had the opportunity."

"I know that, father; but I am not afraid of him. I don't think he could ever get the best of me; I'm too sharp for that."

"Don't be too sure, my son. He may yet take you unawares. I am so sorry you had to use violence with him."

"It was the only way, father."

"Yes; I feel sure of that; but he will never forgive it. Just keep away from him, John, that is my advice to you."

As they walked around the supply-house, they came upon a group of squaws engaged in playing an exciting game of chance, known among the Indians as *gudelpha*. The women were so much interested that they had set down their supplies, regardless of the fact that two or three dogs were now nosing them to their hearts' content. The game was played by means of flat sticks marked red on one side and black on the other. They were grasped in the hand and thrown suddenly upon a stone placed in the center of an outspread shawl. If the sticks fell with the red side uppermost, it counted five; if the black, nothing. Whoever scored a hundred first took possession of all the spoils. These consisted of brass buttons, beads, trinkets, and even copper cents, nickels, and dimes which had been put up by the various players. One Indian had even put down the handkerchief from around her neck. It was of coarse silk, but must have cost, at least, fifty or seventy-five cents.

"The poor foolish thing is certainly going to lose it," said Emma, looking at her sympathizingly.

" Well, Emma, if she does," said Mr. Melville, "it will be a small matter indeed in comparison with what some lose. Why I have known women to put down the last blanket or shawl they had, and even their children's clothes. It is terrible enough to see men gamble, but when it comes to women, it makes the heart sick indeed."

Just at this moment there was a sensation among the women, especially the young women. Even those engaged in the fascinations of *gudelpha* stopped for a moment to take in the overwhelming picture. A young "buck" had ridden up, ostensibly to ask where the Agent was, in reality to exhibit himself before the admiring feminine gaze. Both himself and his pony were painted, his pony in spots, himself both in spots and stripes. The bridle of the pony was ornamented on both sides with heavy plates of German silver. The reins were made of hair, elaborately twisted, and dyed in a variety of colors. In the tail of the pony, almost from the roots to the tip, were woven little tassels of the same colored hair ; at least, a dozen different shades. The saddle like the bridle fairly glittered with its platings of silver.

"It cost more than the pony, perhaps twice as much," Mr. Melville said to John. "What a foolish boy!"

The boy caught the look cast towards him and his saddle, but not the words, and thinking both were meant for admiration began to pose more conspicuously than ever by turning his pony back and forth and making him prance under the touch of the spur.

The boy's hair was long, reaching almost to his waist, and was thrown back in two plaits over his shoulders. Around these plaits were elaborately wound stripes of the skins of panther, beaver, and wild cat. His moccasins were heavily beaded, and from the heel of each hung tassels made of buck-skin strings dyed a brilliant red, yellow, and green. His face was a mass of paint. Even the hair, the eyebrows, and eyelashes were thickly coated with it. From his head rose two eagle feathers, also smeared with paint. But to cap all, he carried over his head a lady's parasol of bright color.*

Just as the boy had struck his most imposing attitude, an old squaw rode up. She was in every way a contrast, and a most striking one, too. She had an old saddle on her pony, but little more than a saddle-tree—"squaw saddles" they call them in the Indian Territory. But for the number of blankets both under and over it, it could not have been ridden at all. She rode it astride, as all the squaws do in the Territory. Her moccasins had but few beads and no fringe. They were like herself, worn and old. Her hair was short and had no covering. She carried a blanket under her arm, doubtless for the purpose of conveying her rations, but had neither blanket nor sheet around her. Her clothing was soiled and torn. Through several of its rents, her skin was showing. As he caught sight of her, the boy turned and said something harshly. The old squaw at once dismounted and started towards the supply-house, leaving her pony standing, watched by a child who had been riding behind her.

"Why, the squaw is the boy's mother!" said John, indignantly. "I heard him so address her. He ordered her to go and get the supplies without any waiting. I declare, I'd like to get my hands on him! What a miserable young brute! I wonder if he intends her to lug that blanket of supplies from the house back to the pony, and get up without any help. I declare if he does, I am going right over there and help her myself and tell him what I think," and John's eyes flashed ominously.

"No; John," said his father, earnestly; "you must not meddle. That is the worst course in the world whereby to reach such cases. You must not be too hard upon the boy. It is the way he has been raised. His own father has doubtless taught him this air of contempt and arrogance towards his mother and the other women of the camp. Let us, on the other hand, pity him, and pray that he may soon learn the

* This picture is real.

better way. I have seen this boy once or twice at the mission church. The next time, I shall make him a special object of notice, and see if I can not drop a good seed or two in his heart by talking earnestly to him. But come now, let us go. We will walk back as far as Mr. Cash's store with the children; then we will turn towards the pen."

Mr. Cash, or "Hard Cash" as he was called, kept a small store a few hundred yards from the supply-house and to the right of the Agency. He was a shrewd, hard man, as his name implied, and drove some sharp trades with the Indians. Many of those of the better class had quit dealing with him long ago, and transferred their patronage to the other merchants who were without exception straightforward in their dealings. Mr. Cash had long been known to adulterate his flour and sugar, to weaken his vinegar, to put sticks and gravel in his coffee, and not only this, but to deal out short weight as well. Mr. Melville had felt for some time like giving the dishonest merchant an earnest talk, but felt his courage fail him every time he planned to do it. It certainly would take a bold advocate to handle so delicate a matter.

As they neared the store, they saw Mr. Cash out on the piazza, surrounded by a little group, and gesticulating wildly. In front of him, was a Caddo Indian by the name of "Lame Horse." It was upon him that Mr. Cash seemed to be expending all his wrath. As soon as "Lame Horse" could get a chance to speak, he said:

"Me but walk white man's road. Me but do one way what you do 'nother. Me come here, me heap swap (buy of) you. Me give you heap money, you give me little *chuckaway* (food). *Chuckaway* too no good. Heap water, little *chuckaway*. Heap sticks, and still little *chuckaway*. If me rascal, then white man rascal too; all same, me and white man; all the same, me and you, for all the same road we go."

"That's so, Cash!" called out a big, brawny-looking cowboy. "Let the Indian go, he's certainly got the best of you. We all know you do doctor the chuckaway that you sell 'em."

The merchant looked as though he could knock the speaker down, but as there were one or two more of his fellows standing around, he thought better of it. He merely glowered at him fiercely, and then giving "Lame Horse" a push that sent him spinning off the piazza, walked back into the store.

From Charlie Ahatone, who was standing near, Mr. Melville learned the cause of the trouble. "Lame Horse" had sold Mr. Cash a sack of corn which had been purchased by weight. Afterwards, when the sack was emptied, it was found to have a stone of considerable size in it. For a wonder, Mr. Cash had failed to detect this at first, a great oversight on the part of a man of his usual shrewdness. When he did find it out he was very angry, as we have seen.

"It is just such examples as this, on the part of the whites," said Mr. Melville to John, as they walked on, "that completely dishearten me. The Indian learns from example when he will perhaps learn from nothing else. It is all powerful with him. Now I feel sure in saying that this Caddo would never have thought of placing the stone in the sack of corn if he had not himself been served in a similar way by this dishonest man, Cash."

"Can nothing be done, father, to make Mr. Cash mend his ways?" John asked.

"I don't know, John. I am seriously thinking of calling the attention of the Agent to the matter. But I don't want to make the man my enemy. Still, both justice and the welfare of these Indians demand it. I do wish his trade could be so broken up that he would be forced to quit. A dishonest man has no right to thrive."

A brilliant and picturesque sight was presented at the pen. Fully three thousand Indians had gathered. Nearly all were on horseback, though there were several buggies, wagons, and other vehicles. The most of these contained women and children, for, on this day at least, the husband and father scorned to ride in any other way than befitted a warrior, astride of his pony. There were Comanches, Kiowas, Apaches, Caddoes,

Wichitas, and many others. Horses and horsemen were re-splendent with fringes, feathers, silver mountings, beads and paint. Every warrior had his gun. In addition, there were slung to the pommel of the saddle, pistol and dirk-knife. Sev-eral bands had already received their share of beeves and were now racing away over the plains after them, brandishing their guns and yelling like mad creatures, while before them ran the frantic brutes, many of them wounded and streaming with blood.

As Mr. Melville and John neared the pen, a poor tortured cow, escaping from its tormentors, ran almost in front of them. It had been shot in the head and throat, and the blood was pouring from its nostrils. John uttered a little cry, while Mr. Melville covered his eyes. The fearful sight had made them both shudder and turn away. At that moment, a government employe approached and with his pistol mercifully ended the poor brute's sufferings.

"Such a sight as that makes me heart-sick for this people," a voice said at this moment near to Mr. Melville.

Looking around, Mr. Melville saw Carpio, a Mexican In-dian,* who very often interpreted for him when he went to preach among the Comanches.

Carpio was an old man, sixty years of age or more. As he had been captured when but eight years old, he had been long among the Indians. Indeed, he felt almost as one of them; for, unlike Andres, Carpio had never found his people, and his eyes had never again looked upon the sunny skies of the land whence he had been stolen. So he really knew little of any life outside that of the Indian camps. Since he had become a Christian, which was three years before, Carpio had been of great help to Mr. Melville. He was quite intelligent and could both read and write; for the old Indian who had brought him up had sent him to one of the schools even after he had grown to be a man. Though he started late, Carpio made all the more of his advantages. He left the school after having spent three creditable years there.

---

* A Mexican captured in childhood.

12

" You are right, Carpio," Mr. Melville said, deeply moved by the scenes around him.   " I often ask myself if it can long continue.   Surely not.   Surely God will, before a great while, turn the hearts of the most of these people towards him.   I am both hoping and praying for it," the missionary concluded earnestly.

" And there are those who are helping you," Carpio added feelingly.

" God bless you, Carpio.   I know you are one of them."

At this moment Tabitosa rushed by on his pony, in hot pursuit of a cow that seemed about to escape him.   He did not see either the missionary or his companions; he was too intent on his chase.

The thought came to Mr. Melville to ask Carpio a few questions.   " You are down about Tataquitnamse's a good deal now, Carpio ; how is Tabitosa doing ? "

" Tabitosa is a wretch and a coward," said Carpio hotly. " Instead of taking men like himself to fight with, he bestows all his blows and harsh words upon women and children.   It is said in the camps that he treats one of his wives and one of his children worse than if they were dogs.   He always was mean to all of them, but he is meaner to these two than to any."

" He ought to be handled for it," Mr. Melville said warmly, as he walked on up towards the pen.   He feared to linger longer talking to Carpio, lest in his indignation he should betray something of what he, Dr. Holley, and the others desired to keep to themselves as long as they could.

CHAPTER XVII.

THROUGH BILLOWS OF FIRE.

" JOHN," said Mr. Melville one morning, "two of the calves escaped during the night. They must be hunted up to-day lest they wander too far off and get lost entirely. As soon as you have eaten breakfast, get your pony and go and look for them. I had intended accompanying you, but am called off to see a sick Indian. Willie Conover will doubtless be glad of the opportunity to go with you."

As soon as he had eaten his breakfast, John saddled Spot, and, mounting, started off after Willie Conover. But Willie had gone to the wood-camp, twelve miles away, so Mrs. Conover informed him, and would not be back before night. There was nothing for John to do but to go alone.

It had been an exceedingly hot, dry summer. Now, at the end of August, the plains were parched as though from the heat of an oven. In many places it seemed to John as though the stubble almost fell apart at the touch of his pony's foot. Owing to the copious rains of the spring, the grass had grown luxuriously all over the prairies. In some places, it was of unusual height and rankness, well matured now through the heat of the sun.

"This is pretty good material for a first-class fire," John said reflectively. "I hope no shallow-pated Indian with more matches than brains will take it into his head to fire the grass for the fun of the thing, as I've seen him do again and again. But with this grass it would be no fun. Why it is as dry as powder!"

John rode on a mile or so carefully looking about him for his calves; but not a sign of them could he see. He even went as far as Gokomb's, but still could hear nothing. On coming out of the timber, he took a line directly across the prairies, very much the same route he and his father had taken the morning they started to the Comanche camp. He had ridden about three miles, when he noticed a heavy smoke rising off against the horizon.

"Some superstitious Indian is setting fire to a hut in which another has died," * John said to himself.

But soon the smoke began to spread in such a way that John knew it could not be from a house.

"It is a prairie fire, I do believe," he said again, scanning it now uneasily. "Well, I hope the poor calves haven't been caught near it. I must hurry and get them out of it."

So saying, he urged Spot to faster speed, keeping him headed in a direction somewhat to the left of the fire. But the fire seemed to be spreading rapidly, not only in a forward direction but also to left and right.

Soon John became unpleasantly aware of its nearness, for whiffs of the smoke driven before it, had now entered his lungs and begun to make him cough. It seemed to him also that the heat itself was perceptible, although the fire must be at least a half mile away.

"It is time to be getting out of this," John said with decision, and with these words slipped his fingers along the bridle-reins nearer to Spot's neck so as to turn him speedily around.

But before John could do this something came down with stinging force upon Spot's glossy flank once, twice ; while a most blood-curdling screech rang forth. The pony gave a mad plunge that almost unseated John, then went rushing headlong towards the approaching fire with the mad unearthly screech still ringing out behind it and continuing for the space of several seconds. With a swift turn of the head that almost

---

* It is still the custom among the Indians on the Reservation to burn the house as soon as a death has occurred in it. They think it brings no end of ill luck to let it stand.

wrenched it from the neck in the mad plunges the pony was giving, John had a lightning-like glance at the cause of the pony's flight and the source of all these mad unearthly cries.

An Indian had stealthily approached him from behind. As John had been about to turn his pony, the man had suddenly brought the keen ends of his quirt with stinging force down upon the pony's flank. At the same time he had given vent to those unearthly yells, which, added to the smart of the blows, had so frenzied the pony that it was now dashing headlong like a mad creature towards the fire.

As swift as had been the glance, it had been of sufficient duration to show John that the Indian was Tabitosa !

With a sick feeling at his heart, John realized Tabitosa's terrible purpose: so to madden the pony that he would plunge headlong towards the fire and probably be surrounded by it before his rider could stop him or dismount. To make the pony's fright all the greater, Tabitosa had followed some little distance behind shouting and screeching. The work had been well done, for Spot was a mettlesome and high-spirted pony, gentle and sweet-tempered under kind management, but just of the nature to get completely beside himself at such treatment as this; especially as, in all his life, he had never experienced anything like it. It was no wonder, then, that he was now rushing madly towards what seemed certain doom, not only for himself but for his young master utterly deaf to that master's persuasive cries or firm tugs upon the reins.

John knew it would be certain death to attempt to leap from the pony's back at the wild speed he was going ; besides he loved his pony with all his heart, and there was a courageous, loyal prompting in that heart that made him determined to stick to Spot at all hazards. If Spot died, then John felt that he wanted to die too. There has been many a noble, tender-hearted boy who felt just that way about his pet.

Oh, why did not Spot obey that coaxing voice ? those tugging hands upon his reins ? It seemed that he was indeed mad to be so utterly oblivious of the loved presence that had

never yet failed to have influence over him. As both pony
and fire were rushing on to meet each other, it seemed only too
evident that the dread catastrophe must soon take place.

The heat of the fire was now perceptible. John could feel
its scorching breath getting nearer and nearer. He could hear
also the distant crackling and roaring of the flames. The
smoke too was choking him and filling his eyes giving them a
smarting, painful feeling. Numerous small animals now came
scurrying by him, rabbits, prairie dogs, and such creatures.
Each was rushing away and making a brave effort for its life,
which seemed all the sweeter now since danger threatened it.
Oh, how earnestly John prayed that he too might have a
chance! How dear his life seemed now that he was about to
lose it! and oh, in such a horrible way! He had a stout,
young heart, but even stout young hearts quail before such
terror as this.

On rushed Spot, and nearer and nearer came the fire. Clouds
of smoke were about them now, tongues of flame shot up only
a few hundred yards away, while the rushing and roaring sound
beat all about them like the leaping waves of the sea. John
shut his eyes and closed his teeth together. Another prayer
went to God, then a cry that almost rent his chest in its deep
paroxysm of grief as it came up.

"O father, mother, sisters, brothers, good-bye!" Then
the next moment, John's cry of despair was changed to a little
shout of hope as his eyes, now unclosed, caught sight of a little
opening in the smoke just to the left of him. In an instant
John knew what it was. The fire had struck a barren, that is,
a place where no grass had grown or else where it had been
mowed.

John, of course, did not know which it was then. He only
realized that from the position of the smoke and from what he
knew of prairie fires, the flames had struck a barren and that
fire and smoke were both circling round it. With the realization, came the knowledge that within the barren lay his only
chance for salvation. With all the strength at his command,

he tugged at Spot's bridle-rein, heading him gradually but surely towards the opening in the smoke.

At last, Spot seemed to realize his young master's presence upon his back as well as to have the inclination to obey the directing voice and rein. Quicker than it takes to write it, he had changed his direction and plunged towards the opening in the clouds of smoke. A very sea of fire seemed about horse and rider for a moment. Billows of flame leaped here and there, appearing almost to meet above their heads. The smoke rushed past them engulfing them. The crackling and the roaring sounded horribly near, almost within their ears. Then, the pony, blinded by the smoke, overcome by the heat, reared, plunged headlong, and went down with John on top of him, both scorched and singed but safe.*

There had once been a water hole near the center of the barren and it was not yet altogether dried up. There was still some mud at the bottom, and into it horse and rider went, Spot first and John on top. There they lay for a moment, stunned and partially blinded by smoke.

When they both got up and John had looked around him, he saw that a merciful Providence had directed them here. They had entered almost at the edge of the barren but plunged diagonally into it. The barren was only about sixty feet across and from seventy-five to a hundred in length. All about them from this space and beyond as far as the eye could reach the fire had made a clean sweep of everything. The roots of the grass were still burning and smoking. John knew he must wait an hour or more yet, before he could venture out, or Spot's feet would suffer.

It was now after ten o'clock. John had been out since half past six. The heat of the sun was growing unbearably warm. John made Spot lie down, and, unstrapping the gum coat that he always carried at the back of his saddle, he placed himself

---

* A missionary in the Indian Territory once had an escape similar to this, but he was not driven into the danger by a revengeful Indian.

by the pony and threw its protecting folds over the head of each of them.

Any one passing at that moment, would have been greatly amused at the picture presented by John and his pony, yet they looked exactly like what they were, two of the best of comrades who thoroughly understood each other. Spot's face had a quaint appearance as it, every now and then, poked itself out beside John's. It had a knowing look too, as though he were trying to say that he very well knew what a good thing he was at present enjoying.

"Well, old fellow," said John, "that was an abominable trick that wretch, Tabitosa, played us, and in your pain and fright, my poor fellow, you came very near putting an end to both of us despite my protestations."

At these words Spot looked very grave as though he understood their full seriousness.

"You see, old fellow," continued John, "I just couldn't make you understand that it was I on your back. That came from thoroughly losing your head, Spot, my boy, an exceedingly dangerous piece of business for either beast or man."

Again that grave look on Spot's part accompanied by a rather sober dropping of the lids of the eyes, which seemed to say in the clearest horse language imaginable, "That is all so, my master."

"But, poor fellow," and here John's arm went round Spot's neck in a hurry, "I know you were in such pain from those outrageous blows—something new to you, Spot, my beauty—and in such a terrible fright from that unearthly yelling, that you didn't have your senses for a single second."

"That I didn't, master," said Spot's eyes as plainly as could be.

"And I just know those blows are smarting yet," John continued as he threw the covering off his head for a moment and let his hand slip around to Spot's glossy hide, following it on his knees. "Yes, there are the marks of them, two great whelks! O, Spot, my poor darling," and here John's voice broke in a sob that didn't take one whit from his manliness, "if ever I lay hands on that wretch I am going to make him feel what you felt!" and John gripped his fingers in a way that showed just how determined would be the blows if ever he could lay them across Tabitosa. He little dreamed how soon he was to have opportunity to put his threat into execution.

In an hour or so John felt that they could move on by picking their way cautiously over the burnt prairie. At the distance of about three-fourths of a mile, they came to some ploughed fields where the fire had spent its force.

Here John found some cattle men gathered, some with their stock in little droves about them; others, sure that many of theirs had been lost in the fire, and all preparing to go in search of those that had escaped and stampeded to some distance.

John gave a little shout when he saw Andres among the cattle men. The young Mexican was greatly excited when he learned of John's thrilling experience and narrow escape. With Andres were Mr. Conover, Willie's father, and a Mexican Indian called Watchecado. Watchecado was powerfully built. He stood six feet some inches in his moccasins. He was in partly civilized dress; that is, he had on a pair of pants, but over them his leggings were strapped. He wore a shirt and vest; around the latter, a beautifully embroidered belt in which were stuck knife and pistols. About his neck, was a collar elaborately worked with beads. In shape it was like those Good Templars wear, only smaller. On his head was the Mexican sugar loaf.

Like Andres, Watchecado had been stolen when quite small. When the Indians had come upon him and his little brothers and sisters playing in the bushes, he had remained hidden for awhile. Hence the Indians gave him the name of Watchecado, which means crouching down and trying to hide. As Watchecado never remembered his Mexican name, he kept the name that the Indians had given him.

John did not tell Andres and his friends of the part Tabitosa had taken in his thrilling experience until the cattle men were left behind, and they were riding over the prairies together.

The indignation of all was outspoken.

"He must be punished," said Mr. Conover decisively. "Such a wretch should not be allowed to go at large. Something must be done with him even if the government does get into trouble by it. I feel sure all the Indians of the better class will be down on him about this."

"That they will," said Watchecado heartily. "There isn't one of them that will uphold anything so low and mean as this, to say nothing of the murder he evidently intended."

"I feel sure the Agent will deal with him this time," said Andres emphatically. "He has long needed handling of some kind. His terrible cruelty to his wives and children ought to have been investigated and punished long ago, but the government felt it could not meddle there."

"Why, there is the rascal now!" said John suddenly.

All glanced up as he spoke, and sure enough, there, not more than fifty paces away, was Tabitosa.

He did not see them at first as he had his back partly turned. When he did catch sight of them, he seemed desirous of getting away, but they were too close upon him. As his eyes rested upon John, Tabitosa gave a start, while a little gasping cry came from him. He evidently thought him a visitant from the other world. However, he soon recognized that it was John himself alive and well, and doubtless wondered by what miracle he had escaped.

"There is just one thing I want to do," said John, his eyes blazing and his fingers tightly gripped about the handle of his quirt; "I want to give him, right across his naked hide, two such blows as he laid on the flanks of my pony here. I want him to feel the smart of them as Spot had to feel it."

"That is too little," said Mr. Conover emphatically, his own eyes blazing. "If I were you I'd double it, nay treble it.

His back will be a good place. We'll cut his shirt off for the purpose."

All the while he had been speaking, Mr. Conover had been riding nearer to Tabitosa, having previously given Watchecado a look which he well understood. Before Tabitosa was at all aware of their intention, they had reached him, one on either side, and while Watchecado quickly pinioned his arms, Mr. Conover cut the entire width of his shirt from the back.

"He is ready now," Mr. Conover said to John. "Chastise him all you want and be sure you lay it on well."

John urged Spot to the side of Tabitosa's pony and raised his quirt to strike. But what was it stayed his hand? It was surely naught that he saw in Tabitosa's eyes, for they were now raised to his face expressing all the deadly hatred that their owner felt. Neither was it for the lack of any courage. John knew not what fear was. He absolutely had no dread of Tabitosa's after-revenge, although he had seen through experience how villainous it could be. Besides here was Tabitosa, bound and helpless before him, and on either side, a stout, brave defender who would protect John, at all costs.

There was naught for John to do but to bring his arm down and strike, yet he didn't do it. Somehow, at his heart a voice had begun to whisper, faintly at first, but now so distinctly that John was aware of every word. Was this a brave thing to do? Was it the act that his gentle, manly father would perform under the same circumstances? Was it the deed for him who desired so earnestly, who strove so faithfully every day to be like that same manly father and not only like that father but like the One that he and that father had taken for their pattern, their guide—One who had said, "Love your enemies; do good to them that despitefully use you." In an instant, all the accumulated weight of the boy's feeling of hatred, and of his desire for revenge, had been moved out of sight by that powerful lever, the religion of Jesus Christ. The warm, sweet forceful rays of the Sun of Righteousness melted **everything** else before them.

John turned and looked about him into the faces of those around him. There was Mr. Conover's, stern and unrelenting. He was not a Christian, John knew. There was Watchecado's, harsh and unpitying. Neither had Watchecado's heart yet felt the divine touch of the spirit of him who is the Master of Forgiveness. But, oh! there it was in Andres, showing in his eyes—forcefully, eloquently, speaking out in every line of his face. From the very moment John had raised his whip to strike, there had been a pained, surprised expression in Andres' face. He had turned his eyes away. His heart sank. Would the son of the good Docté, the brave and manly lad he loved so well, do this thing? Tabitosa deserved punishment, the severest kind. Andres thought this, felt it, and desired fervently to see it brought about; but not this thing from John, not this thing!

"Why do you not strike?" Mr. Conover said a little impatiently. "Lay it on, lad! lay it on well! You surely are not afraid?" as he noticed John's hand fall.

"No," said John, his eyes glowing, "no, Mr. Conover, I am not afraid, not in the least. But I do so hate to strike him while he is so helpless, and while there are so many of us here who are against him."

"He showed no consideration for you when he had you at his mercy," said Mr. Conover indignantly. "Have you forgotten, lad, that he drove you to the death? that he would gladly have seen you perish in that raging fire?"

"No, Mr. Conover, I haven't forgotten it," and John's face blanched even at the remembrance of the fearful peril into which he had been driven; "but I don't want to strike him while I have all the advantage and he has none. I'll wait until I can have it out with him alone."

"Yes; and perhaps have him sneak upon you, like the villian he is, and put an end to you when there is no one near. Your heart is too soft, lad. Tabitosa deserves no such consideration at your hands. Whatever compunction you may have," he continued, "I, at least have none. If you won't give the chastisement there is nothing to keep me from it," and with these words he brought his keen riding whip once, twice, thrice —four, five times down upon Tabitosa's naked back.

Tabitosa winced but not a sound escaped him, though the blood came from two places.

"Undo his hands and let him go," Mr. Conover said to Watchecado. Then to Tabitosa, "Let this teach you a lesson. You may tyrannize as much as you please over the helpless ones of your own race, since there seems no redress for it even through your own people, but you had better beware how your hatred and revenge extend to your white neighbor, for there is some law there, thank heaven." Tabitosa's only reply was a scowl as he rode away.

When Mr. Melville heard of the fearful revenge Tabitosa had sought upon John, he was deeply stirred. His first impulse was to have Tabitosa arrested at once. But the more he considered it, the greater grew his reluctance to adopt this course. The Agent, he knew, would agree with him in the matter; so would every white man at the Agency and all the Indians of the better class; for John was a great favorite all round. There wasn't one but that would be outspoken against Tabitosa's villainous deed, as well as desirous of seeing him brought to speedy punishment. But Mr. Melville knew well the outburst such a proceeding against Tabitosa was likely to bring about among the more warlike of the Indians. He had seen evidences of it before when the Agent had arrested and confined certain of their numbers. It had never yet been done without bringing menace to the whites. He hesitated to place others in danger, even though right and justice, to say nothing of the safety of his own family, which demanded that something be done with Tabitosa. But it was better that a few should be threatened, than that all should be brought into danger. It was thus that the missionary reasoned; he showed the spirit of his Divine Master by never faltering in his determination, though the few that stood in danger were those who were nearest and dearest to him on earth.

"We will have nothing done to Tabitosa; at least, not yet," he said to John. "As outraged and indignant as I feel, and as earnestly desirous as I am of seeing him brought to punishment, I yet hesitate. Tabitosa has a following of some of the most desperate and dangerous Indians on the Reservation. They would stand up for him without question, and beyond a doubt incite others to an attack against the Agency. There is already a disturbed feeling among the Comanches with reference to the shortness of the supplies given out on last issue day, and some of them are even bitter against the Agent. I have learned since, that it was purely an oversight and the Agent has been doing everything he can to rectify it; but it is hard to convince these Indians. They seem to have taken up the idea that the government wants to evade its part of the contract, and to finally get out of giving them any supplies at all."

"You are right, father," John said heartily. "It would be dangerous to arrest Tabitosa; I have felt that all along. He has just the following to make it warm for us if we undertake it."

"But when I look at you, my boy," Mr. Melville continued, his eyes blazing, "and think what he came so near driving you to, only the mercy of God saving you, it is all I can do to keep my own hands off him. But this isn't right, I know," controlling himself, "and I must try to get in a better spirit by the time I meet him. Still, I expect to talk quite plainly to him. It may be that the grace of God will yet enter and touch his heart and make of Tabitosa an entirely new creature. I must, at least, try to reach him. It is my duty, although he sought to do this terrible thing. It is my duty as it is the duty of each one of us to reach out a hand to save a soul we see groping in the darkness, notwithstanding how desperately wicked that soul may be—the more desperate it is, the more urgency there is upon us to the duty."

CHAPTER XVIII.

ALAS, POOR MATOUCHON!

THE worst had come for Matouchon. Tabitosa had laid claim to her as his child and the Indians had sustained his claim. It is true that the chief was not present at the council, neither were several of the best of the Comanches. Some of them were with the chief in Washington; others had gone on a mission to the capital of the Cherokees. The council had been hastily called together. Tabitosa had taken care as to this, and also to have all his friends present.

Neither Mr. Melville nor Dr. Holley knew of the council until it was all over and the decision had been rendered. They did everything they could to induce Tabitosa to change his determination to take possession of Matouchon. They even offered him money, two or three times the amount he had mentioned to Matouchon in the hut; but Tabitosa now had evidently some other plan in view. At least, money seemed to have no power to turn him. He wanted Matouchon, and Matouchon he was determined to have.

It was a terrible blow to Matouchon, the most terrible that could have come to her. It fell with double force. She was not only amazed, horrified at the knowledge that Tabitosa was her father, but her heart was pierced, broken at the thought that she had to leave her sweet home, the friends who were all in all to her and go and live in the horrid Indian camps. It was enough to break any heart, even a stout, reliant one, and Matouchon's was so clinging, so tender!

"Oh, must I go, white mother?" she moaned, clinging to Mrs. Melville's skirts, "*must* I go and live in that horrid place and leave all those I love so here? Oh, it surely cannot, cannot be! You will not let me go!"

(191)

Mrs. Melville's own tears were falling and her throat was so choked with sobs that she could scarcely speak, but she managed to say,

"I would not if I could help it, Matouchon, but it is beyond our power to keep you. We dare not oppose Tabitosa. The Indians have said that he must have you, and their word, you know, is law. Oh, my poor child! My whole heart aches for you. God help and keep you, Matouchon! How you, raised as you have been, are to endure the life there, I cannot see. But you must be brave, as brave as you can. And think! there will be your poor mother and sister and brother. You must help them all you can, especially your mother. It may be that God is taking you there for just this purpose. Pray to him, Matouchon, for he can give you strength and courage as no one else can."

As hard as was the parting from Mr. Melville and his family, it was even harder when the time came to say good-bye to Unkama. Matouchon clung to her as though she could never take her arms away from her again. On the other side, Unkama's grief, too, was pitiful to witness. Matouchon was as dear to her as her own child could have been. Indeed, had she not been the only mother the little one had ever known? Had not her bosom been the first soft sweet pillow and the only one upon which the baby head had ever lain? Had not her lips taught those of the little one the first word they had ever uttered? And was it not Unkama's hand that had upheld and guided the wavering feet when first they were learning to step? Though Nature itself had not planted the mother love within Unkama's heart, still it came through years of the sweetest association of the tenderest devotion, and no child could have been more fondly loved by its own parent than Matouchon by Unkama. It was like wrenching the very heart from her breast to see her go.

The last one to whom Matouchon said good-bye was Dr. Holley. It was a sad parting from him, too. He had been her earliest benefactor. He had tenderly cared for her and watched over her through all these years. He had supplied all her wants; given her many things that are a delight to young hearts. In one sense, she was more peculiarly his than anyone's. She had always loved and reverenced him, and now that she was about to leave him and realized all that he had been to her, all that he had done for her, she broke down completely and, clasped in his arms, wept as though her heart were broken, which indeed it was.

His own heart was bleeding for her, but he kept calm that he might comfort her. Unlike the others he held out a hope to her—oh, it was such a sweet hope! Doubtless the others, in their distress, had not stopped to think of it. He had great faith, he told her, in Quan'-nah, the Comanche chief. Quannah was not only his friend, but was an Indian of many fine impulses; one, too, who liked to see right prevail and justice done. If there was any hope of setting the matter right, of getting Matouchon back to them again, it was in Quannah. As soon as Quannah came back from Washington, Dr. Holley, would see him. It would be three weeks or more yet. Until then she must try to be as brave as she could.

Somehow this sweet hope that Dr. Holley held out to Matouchon, took much of the darkness and despair from her heart. She, too, had firm faith in Quannah. She had heard the missionary say that Quannah was one of the most agreeable of men and had many fine traits.

Dr. Holley rode with her to the camp of Tataquitnamse. He would not let Tabitosa carry her alone, for he did not know what villainous thing might be attempted on the way. Tabitosa was such a mean wretch, Dr. Holley had no opinion of him whatever. It pierced his heart that Matouchon had to be given into his keeping at all; but if she were once safe at the camp, she might find some protection there which she could not have on the prairie. Besides, Dr. Holley wanted to see and talk with Tataquitnamse, to lay the positive injunction upon him that he keep Tabitosa from abusing Matouchon so far as it lay in his power.

13

Tabitosa had a small wagon in which were Matouchon's things, for both Mrs. Melville and Unkama had insisted that Matouchon should take all her neat, nice clothing as well as her clean bedclothes. Tabitosa objected at first, but finally agreed, and so had brought the wagon for the things. Dr. Holley and Matouchon rode their ponies. More than ever now did Matouchon cling to Achonhoah. He was the one friend, the one link out of the past that she could keep near her.

On their way to the camp, they passed by the place of Quannah, or Quannah Parkers as was the chief's name in full. He had quite a settlement around him. His own dwelling and outhouses took up several acres. He had not only a dwelling house neatly arranged, but he had also a large tepee and a brush arbor. The tepee he occupied in the summer, still cling-ing to his old Indian instincts; the brush arbor was for the missionary whenever he came to hold preaching. Quannah had quite a fine herd of cattle grazing upon the plains. Within the dwelling enclosure, were several stables and barns. There was plenty of life visible about the place though Quannah him-self was absent.

"When is the chief expected home?" Dr. Holley stopped to ask of a young intelligent looking Indian, who was letting the bars down for some calves to go through.

"Not before another moon yet," was the answer. "The affairs on which he has gone are long and trying. They will keep him."

Tabitosa, who overheard the question and the reply, glanced suspiciously at Dr. Holley. Then as an inkling of the Doc-tor's desire to see the chief dawned upon him, he set his teeth together and began to shake his head ominously, as much as to say that some one else as well as the Doctor would have an in-terview with Quannah.

It was ten o'clock at night when the camp of Tataquitnamse was reached. Tabitosa took the Doctor and Matouchon straight to his tepee. There were several squaws lying around with their feet towards the smouldering fire. One squaw sat on the ground with her head bent forward, almost entirely enveloped in the folds of her blanket. As they entered the tepee she turned her face towards them. It was Amado! She gave a little gasping cry when she saw Matouchon and partly extended her arms. Then, with a moan, she sank back again and drew the blanket over her head. Matouchon sprang forward, knelt at her side, and for the first time in her life, clasped her arms around her own mother's neck. Then the two sobbed together. Tabitosa scowled fiercely; then walking to the other side of the tepee threw himself down, motioning to Dr. Holley to do the same.

That night Matouchon slept in the arms of her own mother on the sweet, clean bedclothing that she had brought. On the other side was Echoschy, who by Matouchon's request, had been awakened so as to change to the new bed. There she fell asleep with the hand of her sister clasped in hers.

The parting from Dr. Holley, the next morning, was a bitter trial to Matouchon, perhaps the very bitterest in one sense that she had yet known; for, with his going, she saw the last link severed that bound her to her old home and to the dear friends there.

" My little Matouchon must bear up and be very, very brave," he said, as he kissed her for the last time. " I will come to see you when I can, so will the good Docté. He told me so. And I have spoken to Tataquitnamse about you. He surely will not let Tabitosa abuse you if he can prevent it. Cheer up, my child. Let all the sunlight you can, come into your eyes. This poor mother of yours will need it, and so will the little sister. And remember, my dear, what I told you about Quannah."

She stood and watched him till the clump of cotton-wood trees shut him and his pony from view; then, she broke down and cried with her whole desolate heart.

" Why do you cry? " a voice asked her, and, looking up, she saw Echoschy. Matouchon had learned Comanche from

both John and Willie Conover, so she could speak it very
well.

"I am crying because my heart is broken," she replied,
thinking even in her grief to lay a gentle hand upon Echoschy
and to draw her down beside her.

"What has broken it?"

"I have had to leave my home and friends that I loved and
come here where I know no one but Tabitosa, and oh, he is
dreadful!" Here Matouchon's sobs overcame her and she
broke down again in tears.

"But they are only your friends and we have your blood,"
Echoschy said reproachfully; "at least so both you and my
mother have told me. Can it really be true?" she broke off
in a startled way and giving her sister a wide, dazed kind of a
look that smote Matouchon to the heart. There was so much
of the feeling of the wide difference between them in it.

"It is really true," Matouchon answered, and now the hand
that had been in Echoschy's slipped up about her neck; "and
you must not think that I do not love you, and did not want to
come here after I found you were my sister and Amado my
mother. Oh, I did! I did! I did want to see you and to
know you, and to tell you how my heart was wrung to see you
this way! But it is Tabitosa who is so terrible, and all about
the camp is so bad, so dirty. Oh, so different from everything
over yonder," and, at the remembrance of the sweet, clean
home she had left, a home filled only with love and gentleness, Matouchon's tears broke forth afresh.

"It *is* beautiful there," Echoschy said wistfully. "I saw
it all once through the door."

The words went to Matouchon's tender heart like the stab of
a knife. Echoschy had seen it only through the door; she had
not been inside. And yet they were sisters? The same mother
had borne them. If things had been reversed and Echoschy
had been rescued from the sand, would not Matouchon to-day
be in Echoschy's place? The thought made Matouchon very
pitiful, and oh, so humble? She drew Echoschy to her and

began to cry over her, caressing her and calling her all the sweet names her tongue had at its command. Bewildered, amazed, Echoschy could only lie in her sister's arms, her starved heart feeding upon these caresses as it had never fed upon anything before.

The sisters were now nearly thirteen years old, and well-grown for their years, though Matouchon was a little the taller. Both had fine figures, however, and could Echoschy have been dressed as Matouchon was, she would have been almost as attractive in appearance. But Matouchon's face had that softer, more refined look which only gentle raising and education can bring. The one was still the savage, untutored, wild ; the other the savage, too, by birth, but oh, how changed and bettered and ennobled by the sweet and refining influences of life and the all-powerful religion of Jesus Christ !

" Tell me some of the things you saw and did over there," Echoschy said wistfully.

" Oh, there were so many sweet and beautiful things," a sob rising in her throat in spite of her, at the remembrance, " that I scarcely know where to begin. O Echoschy, if you could but know the white mother and the good Docté, and Unkama, and all. Oh, they are so good ! so good ! And every morning and every evening there were sweet prayers to the Father in Heaven, and songs about Jesus, the Saviour who died for us. And sometimes, they would tell me to read in my own little Testament, and then the white mother or the good Docté would pray. And they were all so kind to me and let me do just what they did, and they gave me so many beautiful things. Ah! I know just what I'll do ! " she broke off, as though a sudden thought had struck her. " Some of them shall be yours, yes, that they shall ! I'll put them on you to-morrow."

Echoschy's eyes glowed at the promise and she clasped her sister's hand fondly. Then she said,

" What was the little Testament of which you spoke and in which they had you read ? "

Oh, how that question stabbed Matouchon's heart! Was it possible that Echoschy knew nothing of the Word of God, of the Testament of Jesus, the Saviour? If she did not, then how glad she was she could read it to her!

"I will show you the little Testament when we go back to the tepee, Echoschy, and what is more, I will read to you in it."

"What are you two lazy cubs doing here?" a gruff voice said to them at this moment, in Comanche, and looking up they saw Tabitosa standing over them, his brows knit, his eyes shining fiercely like those of some savage animal. "Get up!" and with this he bestowed a rough kick upon each one; "get up, and if you can't find anything else to do, go and catch the ponies that were hobbled and have now gotten away. Hurry up! stir your lazy bones or the ponies will be out of your reach before you know it," and a second kick, even more savage than the first, accompanied the words. The tears filled and overflowed Matouchon's eyes; her lips quivered. Never before in her life had a kick or even a rough word been bestowed upon her. As keen as was the pain on her bruised limb, it was even keener in her heart. But poor Echoschy seemed to take it as nothing unusual. Indeed, they were bestowed upon her, so many of them and so often, that she had grown as used to them as she had to every other degradation of her hard camp life. But somehow as she looked at her sister and saw her wince with the pain and the tears fill her eyes, she felt a hardness, a bitterness, a resentment in her heart against her savage father, such as she had never felt in her heart before even for herself. The new sister's love was warmly stirring her bosom.

p. 198.

CHAPTER XIX.

CHRISTIAN AND SAVAGE.

THE two sisters walked on, side by side until the outer edge of the camp was reached. There they paused for a moment. Matouchon's eyes were on fire. She was thinking indignantly of the cruel kicks bestowed by Tabitosa. The smart of the blows still lingered. She knew that the flesh was bruised; that the marks would be there for many days. It was even worse for Echoschy; for Tabitosa was even more brutal with her. She reached out her hand and drew Echoschy to her. As she did so the latter winced. Matouchon's hand had fallen about her sister's hip. "Oh, I have hurt you!" she said, her voice full of the keenest regret.

"No; Echoschy is not hurt, that is not much," correcting herself. "It was only when your hand fell on the spot where the pain is."

"Oh, how mean and cruel of him!" Matouchon exclaimed, her eyes blazing. "And to think he is our father!"

"Do not the white men kick their children so?" Echoschy asked, a wistful expression in her eyes.

"No; they do not," Matouchon returned emphatically; "not that I have ever seen. When the children are naughty, they are punished, but never by cruel kicks and blows. The white men, especially the Christian men, are kind to their children—to their little girls as well as to their boys. Indeed, they love their girls just the same as they do their boys."

"Oh, how I wish I had a father like that!" said Echoschy, while the wistful look in her eyes deepened.

"The white father says it is this way in all Christian lands," Matouchon continued. "Where men know of the

true God and have learned to love him, they keep the law of
love toward all things, especially toward the weak and helpless. Their women and children are tenderly cared for, and
are not beaten and abused as they are among the Indians."

"But some of the Indians are kind to their wives and
girls," said Echoschy earnestly.

"Yes; I know, because some have naturally kind hearts.
But nearly always you will find that those Indians, who are
considerate of their women are the Christian Indians, those
who have God and his sweet law of love in their hearts. Oh,
how I wish they *all* had it!" her eyes expressive of deep feeling. "I love my people, and I do long for the day to come
when they shall all know of the one true God and learn to
serve him. What a different people they will be then, and
how happy their women and children!"

"And will it make a different man of Tabitosa, our
father?" Echoschy asked, her eyes full of a wistful desire that
no words could express.

"Yes; it can, if only he will let it. We must pray, Echoschy, pray fervently that it may come to him and make him a
different man."

"Pray?" echoed Echoschy; "Pray?" her whole face
having the expression of one groping in the dark. "I do
not know what you mean!"

The words went to Matouchon's heart like the cut of a
knife. For a moment she had forgotten her sister was what
she was. The vast gulf of difference that lay between them
had not loomed in view while she had been talking. She
only knew that they were together, that a strong tie had
grown between them even in this short space, and that they
had interests and desires in common, the chief of which was
that their father might become a different man. But now
as never before the full force of the difference between
them came to Matouchon. It struck her almost as a blow.
It made her heart sick. Her sister had not yet seen the first
faint dawnings of light. She was still an untutored, wild

savage, with all the superstitions and degradations of her race clinging about her. She knew not even how to pray. The very word itself was an unknown one to her. All the better and truer impulses of Matouchon's heart—and they were many—came to the surface as these realizations dawned upon her. All the sisterly love within her was aroused. She was willing to endure the hardships, the trials of this wretched camp life, even the blows and abuses of Tabitosa for weeks to come, if only she might bring the light to this groping soul, put sweet music into the heart through which coursed the same blood as through her own. And there was her mother! Matouchon thought of her, too, at this moment. How doubly strong were the ties that bound her to the camp, though it was in woe and bitterness to herself!

But the pause during these thoughts had already been too long. There were Echoschy's eyes still wistfully, enquiringly regarding her. She bent towards her sister, and, placing an arm around her neck, drew her nearer as she said: "The God whom the Christians love and serve, lives up there, away beyond the sky," pointing upward as she spoke. "He is kind and true and good. Though we cannot see him, we *know* that he is there, because he has told us so in his Testament, the book I have promised to read to you and to my mother. But this is not all. Once, many, many years ago, he sent his Son, to die for those who were in sin and darkness. The name of this Son was Jesus. We call him our Saviour because he suffered a cruel death on the cross to save us from our sins.

"Though God lives away up yonder," continued Matouchon, "still he is ever about us. He knows what is taking place on this earth just the same as up yonder. When we are sick and in sorrow he knows it. But he has taught us to come to him in prayer, to tell him about it ourselves. Then we ask him, for the sake of the Saviour who has died for us, to heal our sickness and to take our sorrow away."

"Oh, what a great kind God he must be!" exclaimed

Echoschy fervently. "And does he always answer when he is thus asked?"

"If it is for our good he does."

"Then I am sure he will answer us if we ask him to make a different man of our father, Tabitosa. To-night when it is all dark about the camp and there is no one to see us, I will get you to show me how to pray to this God. If the Indians saw us they might think we were working some spell. They would be sure to tell Tabitosa, and how angry he would be! He would doubtless beat us both. Oh, how dreadful that would be for you!"

"And why not just as dreadful for *you?*" asked Matouchon earnestly.

"Because Echoschy is used to it," she returned, with a pathos of endurance that cut to Matouchon's heart with the keenness of a knife blade.

"But that does not take away the pain when the blows fall," Matouchon answered, her heart on fire now as she recalled the extreme cruelty of the blows that had been so recently given. "I will do as you request, Echoschy," she continued. "To-night when all have wrapped themselves in their blankets and lain down as usual with their feet to the fire, we will steal out and go to the cotton-wood trees yonder. But I do not believe all the Indians would inform against us," she continued after a pause, "nor would all look upon it as a spell. There are some who would know what we were doing. The white father has preached here, I know. I heard him say so. Do you not remember some of the times, Echoschy?"

Thus reminded, Echoschy easily recalled that she had seen the White Father there and that he had preached to the people in the camps several times, but she had been allowed to go only twice.

"And do you not recall," continued Matouchon, "how on these occasions the white father would lift his face to the sky and fold his hands, and say words while all the others were silent?"

Echoschy remembered that he had.

" Well, he was praying then, talking to God as we will talk to him to-night when we go to the cotton-woods."

" What do you suppose the white father was saying ? " asked Echoschy, with sudden, deep interest.

" He was asking God, I am sure, to forgive the people their sins for the sake of the dear Saviour who had died for them, and to send the light so that they might never more walk in darkness. But we have stood here long enough, Echoschy ; we must go and search for the ponies, else there will be more blows for us. Where do you suppose they are ? "

Echoschy drew herself to an erect position and let her eyes sweep with strong glances the plains to the right and left of them.

" There are three of them away off yonder near the water hole," she said after a moment.

" How many are there astray ? " Matouchon asked again.

Echoschy brought her hands together and began to count on her fingers; " *Semus* (one), *wa-hot* (two), *pi-hit* (three), *hi-ye-ro-quit* (four), *mor-wet* (five), *har-wi* (six), *tars-choque, seven* ! " she announced in conclusion. " There are three yonder. You go get them because they are in sight. Echoschy will hunt the other four."

" But that is not just," Matouchon protested. " You are giving me the lighter task."

" No, no," Echoschy persisted. " You will not find it a light task when you come up with the ponies. They will want the fresh grass near the water hole, and you will find it hard to drive them away. Echoschy goes to search for the others because she knows the country better. It might be you would be lost if you went out of sight of the camp."

" Oh, I have a clearer head than that ! " declared Matouchon emphatically. " I have often gone miles over the prairies alone."

" But not around here. There are many marshes and quicksands. Echoschy knows these as you do not. Besides she has an idea where the ponies are, which you have not. Altogether it is better for Echoschy to go in search of those that cannot be seen."

Matouchon saw it was useless to protest further. Besides she recognized in this arrangement the true sisterly devotion and generosity that had prompted it. She felt more than ever the new thrill of affection at her own heart.

Outside the camp the two sisters separated, one turning to the right and the other to the left.

It was a day in late October and 'the chill winds that heralded the approach of November were racing over the prairies. Their keen stings made Matouchon shiver even through the warm clothing she wore. She thought with a pang, of Echoschy, whose clothes were old and worn and, with the exception of the shawl about her head and shoulders, there was but a thin calico waist between her and the cold. Matouchon would gladly have taken something from her own body, but there was nothing of which she could well divest herself, as, on leaving the tepee, she had not brought shawl or wrap of any kind. She resolved, the very moment they returned with the ponies, to put some of her own clothing upon Echoschy.

The ponies were much further away than Matouchon had thought. It was doubtless that they were on the move all the time and had increased the distance to some extent ere she reached them.

Echoschy's parting injunction had been to get between them and the water hole without letting them see her, if possible, and then to suddenly drive them back. Matouchon endeavored to follow this advice closely, but the wind was blowing from her towards the horses, and they soon sniffed her approach. When she ran up to them to turn them towards the camp, they scattered in every direction. They had slipped their hobbles and their feet were perfectly free. Thus they had her at great disadvantage. As fast as she would get one turned in the right way, another would be scampering off in an entirely

p. 205.

different direction. When she would start after him, the others would turn and follow. Soon they had led her entirely away from the water hole and out of sight of the camp.

After scampering about for half an hour or so, like wild animals, the ponies gradually came together and began picking the grass along the edge of what seemed to Matouchon at that distance a small ravine. As she came nearer she saw it was a ravine and that it marked the bed of a dry water course.

As she was cautiously and patiently making a circuit of the place so as to get around the ponies, all the time keeping her eye upon them, she came near stumbling upon a figure lying at full length in the grass. It was Kankeah. He was as surprised to see Matouchon as she was to see him and started up with an exclamation. He had evidently been on the wait for some small game, for he still held his bow in hand with the arrow half drawn.

"*Haca po mea ?*" (Where are you going?) he asked, gazing at her curiously.

She replied that she was making a circuit of the ravine so as to get to the other side.

"*Hin a waughkt ?*" (What are you looking for?) he asked again.

"I am trying to get around the ponies over there so as to drive them back to the camp."

The boy raised his head and for the first time seemed to be aware of the presence of the ponies. Then he gave a grunt and lay down again upon the ground.

Matouchon had seen Kankeah at the tepee the night before, and knew that he was her brother. How cold and indifferent was this treatment in comparison with that of Echoschy! and yet there was the same tie of blood between them: she was his sister. She wondered if he were like all the rest of the Indian boys and men, taught to show little emotion in the presence of women and girls; or if it were really his own indifferent heart, after all, prompting him to this course. He was obliged to know that she was his sister. His mother had told him, and though he had not spoken a word to her on that previous night or given her a look, she somehow felt that it was because of the presence of Tabitosa. Now that he had met her away off here on this prairie where there was no one to see, he surely would say some kind word to her, he surely would tell her that he was glad she had come to live with them and that he had another sister. How affectionate John was with Emma! and if he went away to stay but one night, he always kissed her good-bye. And sometimes he kissed Matouchon, too, though she was not his sister. Nor was John the only one who thus showed affection to his sister. She had again and again seen other of the white lads around the Agency kiss their sisters, when meeting them after an absence or when parting with them. Oh, why should there be such a difference in the way women and girls were treated in the white families and the way they were treated here in the camp?

Matouchon knew very well that she did not expect Kankeah to kiss her. To tell the truth, she would have been startled had he done so. But she did want him to be kind to her, to notice her, to tell her he was glad she was his sister. But instead, here he had turned his back upon her with an air which said plainly that she was of such little moment to him that it mattered not where she went nor what she did.

Another thing that cut Matouchon to the quick was that he showed no disposition to help her in getting the ponies back to camp, though he must know it was a new undertaking to her and would assuredly prove difficult. How different this was, too, from the way the white boys treated their sisters! Think of John sitting down on the grass and letting Emma drive the ponies in! The thought was too much for Matouchon as well as the rush of remembrance of the Christian home she had left. The tears sprang to her eyes and began to roll down her cheeks.

CHAPTER XX.

MATOUCHON MAKES A FIND.

SO completely did the tears shed by Matouchon obscure her vision that for some moments they blinded her as to the direction she was taking. As soon as she regained sight, she noticed that instead of skirting the ravine she had followed along its edge. It was a wonder she had not fallen into it; but some instinct seemed to guide her. But if she had fallen, she would doubtless have received only a shaking instead of a hurt, as the ravine at no part was more than five or six feet deep.

As she paused upon its edge and dried her tears she caught a sudden sound. At first she thought it was made either by the horses or Kankeah, but both were too far away. Again the sound was made, and now she knew that it proceeded from the ravine some little distance ahead of her. About ten paces in front of the point where she was standing the ravine made an abrupt bend. She felt sure the noise came from the other side of this bend. As she stood there she heard it once more, and felt assured now that the cry or groan, whichever it might be called, came from a human being. It was that of a person in distress; evidently some one weak or sick, for the cry was not strong.

She walked rapidly towards the spot on which she had her eyes fixed. There in the ditch lay an Indian, old, feeble, and apparently half dead, though, strange to say, his eyes were very wide open and he had partly propped himself against the bank.

"What can I do for you?" Matouchon asked, as she sprang down the bank and stooped above him.

In the excitement of finding him, Matouchon had forgotten herself and addressed him in the language that came more readily to her tongue in English. Greatly to her surprise, he answered her in the same language, though somewhat broken.

"Get Indian out of this. White Plume grateful. Love young squaw all his life. Eyes not good. While walking fell into ditch. Leg bad hurt. White Plume wants to go to Tataquitnamse's."

"Why, that is the very camp where—where I—where I am!" Matouchon couldn't say "live" to save her life. The word would have died in her throat even if she had given it birth in her mind.

"Then get White Plume there," the Indian cried eagerly.

"But how in the world am I to manage it?" Matouchon asked, gazing about her in dismay. "Can you walk?"

As though the better to answer her, the Indian attempted to rise, then fell back again with a groan.

Matouchon tried to help him. She was young and lithe and her arms were strong. She succeeded in getting him to a standing posture, but as soon as he attempted to bear his weight upon his feet, he fell down all in a heap again with a sharper groan than ever.

Matouchon was just wondering what she should do and if she could not, through some means, prevail upon Kankeah to help her get the old man out of the ditch, when a sudden gutteral exclamation caused her to look up. There stood Kankeah at the edge of the ravine gazing down upon her. He had evidently followed her, either out of curiosity or with the mean desire to enjoy her struggles with the ponies. Evidently the old man was an unexpected sight. Matouchon forgot herself, Kankeah's attitude, and everything else in her desire to help the old Indian. He seemed to be painfully hurt, and he was shivering so with cold!

"Will you not come down, Kankeah, and help me get the old man out of the ditch?" she asked appealingly. "He has hurt his leg so he cannot walk. But it may be that once he is out of the ditch, he can crawl.* He is so anxious to get to Tataquitnamse's."

For answer Kankeah only stared at her and twirled his bow a little derisively about his head. He had been educated to believe that the old were to be left to take care of themselves. They were better out of the world anyhow, than in it.

Matouchon felt her heart glow with indignation. For a moment she did wish she were a boy so that she could give Kankeah the thrashing he deserved. But for the sake of the poor old man, she curbed her temper and made one more appeal.

"Do you not see that he is old and helpless, that he must die if we leave him here? What kind of a heart have you, anyhow, to stand there in that cruel way and laugh at the misery and helplessness you see?" For Kankeah was by this time laughing derisively and describing upon the ground with the point of his bow the serpentine movement known as crawling.

"Help him yourself," he replied, "or let him get out of the ditch as the snakes do."

With these words he turned partly around and began shooting his arrows straight up into the air. As they would come down, almost where he was standing, he would turn on his heel, pick them up, carry them to a point just above his nose and make a mocking gesture with them toward Matouchon.

She realized fully now that it was useless to expect any help from Kankeah. Whatever was done she would have to do it herself or else return to the camp for help. The latter was not to be thought of until she carried the ponies in, for would not Tabitosa punish her severely if she went without them? So turning from Kankeah, she bent again over the old man. Once he had doubtless been a fine tall Indian, as straight as the arrow wood, and as active as the mountain deer. But now he was very old, and the once tall form was

---

* It is not an unusual sight to see very old Indians who are unable to walk, crawling about the plains.

14

bent and his limbs trembling with weakness as well as cold.
He had lost so much flesh, he was little more than skin and
bones. Matouchon noticed with satisfaction that it would not
be a great task to lift him. But though she might lift him on
a level, still it would be a task well-nigh impossible to get him
up the bank unassisted. Still she felt that she must try. As-
suring him that she would do everything she could for him,
she went up the water course a little distance to reconnoitre.
There, to her joy, she saw that the bank grew less and less
steep. At one point, about fifteen or twenty paces away, it
was not more than four feet deep. If White Plume could crawl
to this spot, she felt sure that she could pull him up the bank.

Going back she explained the situation to him. Then assisting him to his knees, she supported him as best she could
while he slowly and painfully crawled toward the shallow. It
fired Matouchon's blood more than ever to note that Kankeah
kept pace with them along the bank, all the time making that
crawling movement with his bow, and calling upon the old
man to hurry or the snakes would overtake him. Matouchon's
palms were fairly tingling to " do royal battle " upon Kankeah's mocking face. But she dared not strike him. She
knew only too well what the penalty would be from Tabitosa,
even if Kankeah himself did not almost kill her. So she made
a brave effort and controlled herself, giving all her time and
attention to the old man, and trying not to see Kankeah or to
hear him either.

When the low place in the bank was reached, Matouchon
guided White Plume as near to its foot as she could. Then she
bade him with her help, to bring himself to a standing posture
and to lean against the bank. This he did, standing upon one
foot, for he could not bear the pain of the other when he attempted to use it.

Leaving him in this position Matouchon sprang quickly up
the bank. Then giving herself time to draw several long hard
breaths, she bent downward and caught the old man by the
shoulders. Though he seemed a full-blooded Indian, he was,

nevertheless dressed in half civilized costume. That is, while he wore the usual moccasins and leggings, he also had on a white man's shirt and coat. The coat was of military cut, stout and strong and with many buttons. By running her hands under the collar and down towards the shoulders Matouchon had a firm grip. Calling to the old man to aid her all he could by using his hands and knees, and to look out for his injured foot, she tugged away bravely and with all her might. It was a heavy strain, but not too heavy for her to endure, and in a few moments, she was rejoiced to see the old man lying safe at the top of the bank. Although her hands smarted and burned from the friction of the pull, and her face felt very hot, she had done herself no other damage.

"Now," she said, bending over the old man encouragingly, "now that you are out of the ditch, do you think you can crawl to the camp, a little bit at a time?"

"How far?" he asked in a quavering voice.

"I do not know just how far it is, but I think about two miles."

He sank back with a groan of dismay.

"Old as White Plume is," he said, "he has never yet had to go like the snake upon the ground. Always White Plume has had his legs till now, though often they shook under him like the reed when the wind blows it. Now that one leg is like the staff when broken and of no more use; what is there left but to crawl? Two miles! How can such distance be made in so feeble a way and with such pain?"

She glanced down upon him, her eyes full of pity. "I know it will be hard and painful," she said, "but I will help you all I can. You need go only a little distance at a time. Then by way of a change you can try getting along by leaning on me and hopping with one foot. Maybe by changing so you can make the distance at last."

So they started. He tried it first crawling, she encouraging and helping him all she could. But it was a slow and laborious mode of proceeding at best, and she could see how he was suffering by the drops of perspiration that stood out like beads all over his face. She next encouraged him to stand and to try hopping upon one foot by leaning upon her. Though this seemed better than the other way at first, still the jar that the hopping process gave the injured foot made the pain even greater than when he tried holding it up and crawling along. So he fell to crawling altogether after a while, stopping to rest at little distances and to wipe his pain-distorted face.

All this time Kankeah was following them and making all kind of mocking suggestions; and tantalizing them by proposing various impossible things, such as waiting for a carriage and horses to come along and even suggesting the railroad train. Finally, when he saw he could provoke no retort from Matouchon, and that neither she nor the old man was paying any heed to his mockery, the sport lost all its flavor. He turned away in disgust and went back to the pursuit in which he had been engaged when discovered by Matouchon, that of killing birds and whatever other small game came in his way.

When Matouchon and the old man had gone about a half mile in the painful way described, White Plume sank down with a deep groan declaring he could not go a step further. Matouchon was deeply moved. She did not know what to do. But, finally, a plan made itself clear in her brain. A few steps away there was a small clump of cotton-wood trees. Dragging the old man hither as gently as she could, she brought him some dry grass, made him a pillow, and then said, "I will go to the camp and bring help. But first I must drive the ponies in or my father," with a quivering lip as she pronounced the word, "will punish me. I see that the ponies have followed us a part of the way and are once again at the water hole. If you lie here I think I can soon drive them in and bring help back with me."

But driving in the ponies was more easily said than done. Matouchon was new to them and they were evidently suspicious of her. She had just the experiences of an hour before. Despite her best efforts they got away from her and scattered in various directions. As she was chasing them about, running now here and now there, and almost ready to drop with fatigue, what was her joy on seeing Echoschy approaching!

"Oh, *you* have had the hard time after all, it seems!" she said, as she came up beside Matouchon. "Echoschy has never seen the ponies do so before. It must be because you are new to them. Hie there, Yetse, Baabo, and Yinhin! Ugly creatures to act as you do. Are you not ashamed of yourselves? Go home now like pretty things and show that you are sorry for what you have done."

The horses, as though they understood every word, and following the direction indicated by her swaying arms, began to move slowly off toward the camp. They were doubtless also led to do this, because Echoschy had, while talking to them, placed herself in their rear and was using many coaxing words after her scolding ones.

As the horses moved away, Matouchon had her first chance of speaking to Echoschy. She had been denied'this opportunity when the latter came up, since Echoschy had passed on toward the horses before she concluded her speech to Matouchon. Now Matouchon, gaining her ear, told her all about the old Indian she had found in the gulley, and pointed to where he was lying under the clump of cotton-woods. "How *can* we get him to the camp?" was the question with which Matouchon concluded.

"We might get him on one of the ponies," suggested Echoschy.

Matouchon's face showed her surprise and incredulity.

"Why, they are so wild we could never induce them to go near him!"

"You think the ponies wild because they acted so when you tried to drive them. But they are not so wild as you think. Two of them are just a little frisky, but the other one is Echoschy's own little pony. She will come to Echoschy when Echoschy calls her. Oh, she is as gentle and sweet as the breeze that blows from the south! Are you not, my own

Yinhin? Come now, and show how you can mind when you are called. Come then, Yinhin! So-yo! So-yo! Yinhin! Come, my own girl. Now then, my beauty!" The pony thus addressed had stopped at the very first sound of her name. As the caressing tones grew louder and stronger and more coaxing, she pricked up her ears, threw her legs into motion, and began to trot towards Echoschy. By the time the last endearing sentence was out, she stood with her nose on the shoulder of her mistress.

She was a beautiful creature, though her somewhat thin sides and the scars here and there upon her body showed that she was either not kept in the best condition or that she was subjected to hard usage while in service. She was larger than the common Indian ponies, taller and longer, and much more shapely in every way. The head was gracefully carried, the neck arched proudly, while the deep, lustrous brown eyes possessed both intelligence and spirit.

As Echoschy stood caressing the horse which seemed so gentle and docile, Matouchon spoke her surprise. "The horses ran about so, I would never have thought there was one so gentle among them."

"It was because she was in rather bad company. Is it not so, Yinhin, my girl? If Echoschy had only thought to tell you their names! But she did not think of that! It is too bad she did not. Then you would not have had so hard a time."

"Oh, that is such a beautiful pony!" Matouchon said again, stooping over as she spoke to caress the glossy flank. "I believe it is even prettier than my own Achonhoah. You have not seen Achonhoah yet. I must show him to you when we go back if I can find where they put him. I love my Achonhoah as you love Yinhin. But is the pony really yours?" she concluded a little abruptly.

"Yinhin is really Echoschy's, though she cannot claim her. Carpio gave her to Echoschy. Tabitosa will not let Echoschy claim her. He wants her himself. He rides her all the time, and he beats her too. See the scars upon her coat. O my pretty thing!'' and overcome with the sorrow of it Echoschy bowed her head upon Yinhin's neck and sobbed aloud. Then recovering herself she went on, "But many times out here on the prairies Echoschy has her to herself, and she rides her too, and teaches her many beautiful tricks. Sometimes when no one sees, Echoschy will show you. But there is the old man! We must go and try to get him on the pony."

"I do not see how we are going to do it," said Matouchon a little gloomily. "He is so old and so badly hurt, he is nearly helpless."

"Maybe together we can lift him."

"Up to the pony? I don't believe it. Why it is about impossible! We are not giants, Echoschy. Oh, it is too bad he has fallen and hurt himself so! And once we get him to the camp what *are* we going to do about it? Will not Tabitosa, our father, beat us for carrying him there? You know how they look on old people, especially when they are helpless."

"Tabitosa is not there," said Echoschy quickly. "When Echoschy got back to the camp with the ponies, they told her that he had been sent for in a great hurry to go to Fort Sill, and that he could not return under three days."

"Oh, I'm so glad!" cried Matouchon, feeling like she wanted to clap her hands in her joy.

"The old man says he is a friend of Tataquitnamse," she continued. "We will take him to Tataquitnamse, and he will know best what to do with him. But let us hurry. I fear the old man has begun to think by this time that I have quite run away and left him. But what are you going to do about the ponies?" she turned to ask Echoschy.

"Leave that to Echoschy. While you hold Yinhin, Echoschy will start them back towards the camp."

CHAPTER XXI.

WHAT IS THE CHARM?

AS they came up to where the old man lay, they saw that he was quite restless and evidently much chilled by the cold winds, though he had tried to screen himself as best he could behind the trees. He was muttering words to himself and gazing intently at something he held in his hand. As they came up to him they saw that it was a small leather pouch securely fastened. To the pouch was attached a stout buckskin string which was tied about the old man's neck.

"It is something the witch-doctor has given him," said Echoschy, her eyes distending. "He is asking it to help him get up and walk."

Matouchon gazed at her sister in sorrow. Oh, how her heart ached as she read all the superstition to which the eyes gave expression! What a fervent prayer was that in which Matouchon asked to be led to say just the right thing! Matouchon knew that nearly all the Indians wore charms, either those given them by the witch-doctors or others that they had procured themselves through certain suggestive circumstances. She had heard the white father say so again and again. These charms were generally bits of stone or wood, the teeth and claws of different animals, seeds, shells, queer-looking beads, and sometimes tiny bottles of liquids that the witch-doctors made them believe had been procured by the help of the Great Spirit himself.

But the charm carried by the old Indian seemed to be none of these. It had more the appearance of a thin flat substance, for the sides of the pouch were but little distended. Moreover, it seemed to be of an even thickness throughout.

"*Ner marbone pars uwite,*" (I want to look at it) Matouchon said to the old man, as she came up and extended her hand as though to take the pouch. These words she said not through curiosity, but because she wished to make the charm the subject of a conversation that she hoped would do good both to the old man and Echoschy.

" No ! No ! " he cried much startled that she had observed him ; and with the words he placed the charm hastily into the bosom of his shirt.

" What is it ? " she asked, bending her eyes earnestly upon his face.

" White Plume cannot tell ! White Plume must not tell," he cried excitedly. " If other hand touches it, it will lose its charm. The white man who gave it to White Plume said it was for White Plume alone."

" The white man ? " echoed Matouchon, in much astonishment.

" Yes, the white man ! Oh, it has on it the mark of a great hand. But White Plume cannot tell ! White Plume must not tell ! " he reiterated. " The time is not yet. Only when White Plume is dead can any one else look at it. Then it must go into the ground with White Plume ! "

" But what good can it do to wear it there ? " Matouchon asked, pointing to his neck. " What good can it do to wear it at all ? What did the white man say it would do ? "

White Plume closed his eyes a moment as though to think. From the expression of his face it was evident that he would have preferred not to talk about the charm at all, lest by so doing it might lose the very virtue ascribed to it. Had not the white man said it was for White Plume alone ? By allowing another to have part in it, even though but to talk about it, might not some of the spell be lost ? But he felt that he must answer the question in some way or she might ask it again. Besides White Plume felt very grateful to the young girl. Had she not helped him out of the ditch ? and not only that, but had she not also guided him to the trees ? and was she not here now for the purpose of helping him to the camp ? So he said, " White Plume wears the charm because the white man said it would bring him great good."

" But how can it do that? It is but a senseless thing. It has no life. It cannot help you in any way. Just now when you were in the ditch did it get you out ? "

This seemed to be a puzzler at first to White Plume. But suddenly his eyes gleamed. He answered,

" It sent young squaw to help me."

" No ; it did not. If anyone sent me it was the good God up there, who felt sorry for your helplessness and pain. But I would have found you anyhow," concluded Matouchon, in the most matter-of-fact way. " I was going in that direction to drive the ponies."

" Do you not believe in the charm the old man has ? " asked Echoschy suddenly, and with deep wonder in her eyes.

" No ; I do not. It is doubtless a piece of cloth or paper. It seems so from its shape. How can such things help us when we are in sorrow or pain ? or how can they bring certain things to pass ? Only God can do that. Oh, if you would only quit trusting to the charm, and trust in God ! " Matouchon said earnestly. " He can do you more good than all the charms in the world."

" But he is so far away, I cannot get to him," White Plume replied helplessly. " I have heard the white man say he dwelt up there, away up there, far beyond the clouds."

" But he knows all we do, and he hears all we say. He has an eye that can reach to this earth and a power mightier than I can describe."

" But White Plume wants to *see !* How can he know unless he *sees ?* "

Here was the same old crying out after something tangible, solid, something that eye could see and ear could hear—the same old cry that hundreds of times had issued from the Indian heart when brought face to face with the spiritual. No wonder the worship of charms and of images—the tangible, in short—had such a hold upon them !

Matouchon paused a moment thinking intensely. At the same time her lips were moving in prayer to God. Not only was this groping soul to be enlightened, but there was also that of the sister beside her. Again and again she had heard the good Docté, the white father, use striking illustrations when speaking to the Indians at the church. One of them came to her now.

"White Plume," she said, "take your hand and place it upon your side, upon the side where you can feel something beat. White Plume knows that that is his heart. He has learned to call it by name. He needs no one to tell him it is there. He *knows* it is there though he cannot *see* it. And why? Because he can *feel* it. So it is with God. We cannot see him yet we can feel him, feel him in every breeze that blows, in every flower that he has made ; feel him in the sun that shines upon us, in the rain that falls ; feel him here in our hearts."

Both White Plume and Echoschy seemed impressed. They were thinking earnestly. A great throb of joy went to Matouchon's heart. She continued : "When we see something that is done we know that some one has done it. The tepee is there because hands have placed it there. The fence stands around the camp because the men have brought the poles and built it. So with the flower that grows on the prairie and the stream that flows through its banks. They are there because God's hand has made them. So too with the breeze we feel; it is here because God's hand has sent it. The fire in the tepee does not come by chance. Some one must kindle it? So with that great blazing ball of fire up there," pointing to the sun. "Some hand must kindle it. Whose? Could the hand of man do it? You know that it could not. Not the swiftest arrow that was ever shot could reach that blazing ball, let alone the hand that sent it? So that we know some other hand than man's must kindle it day by day. That hand is God's."

Matouchon stopped here and for a few seconds gazed earn-

estly at her audience. She could see that the impression had
grown even deeper. The old man's eyes were very bright; so
were Echoschy's. Indeed the latter was looking at her sister
with all her heart shining through their depths. "Then you
must see how great is the God who has done all this," Matouchon continued, "greater than any creature or any thing
on the earth, greater than all the charms ever made."

At the word "charms" the old man's thoughts seemed to
center once more upon the talisman in his bosom. He clutched
at it nervously, muttering words that Matouchon did not understand. She wondered again what the charm could be. Doubtless a written paper he had picked up somewhere around the
Agency, she decided. She knew well what a reverence the
Indians had for "marks that talked." *

It was now high time to return to the camp. Indeed, they
had lingered much longer than they intended, Matouchon's
conversation with the old man taking up the time. Yinhin
had grown restless, and it had required all Echoschy's coaxing
to detain her, especially as the other ponies had now gone on
towards the camp.

"How are we to lift him?" Matouchon asked, with a nod
of the head toward White Plume. "I fear we never can get
him on the pony."

"Oh, yes," said Echoschy confidently. "Echoschy will
show you."

With these words she led Yinhin close up beside the old
man. Keeping one hand in the long flowing mane, she placed
the other upon Yinhin's right flank, giving with it an up and
down movement and at the same time uttering a low peculiar
cry. In a few moments, greatly to Matouchon's astonishment,
the gentle, obedient creature had extended herself along the
ground with all four of her feet doubled under her.†

It was an easy task now to get the old man upon her back.

---

* Writing.

† Many similar tricks are taught their ponies by the Indian boys and
girls.

At another low cry from Echoschy and an encouraging pat, Yinhin arose to her feet and then stood perfectly still awaiting orders. Gently grasping her by the forelock, Echoschy led her slowly towards the camp, while Matouchon walked at the side, her strong young arms holding the old man's foot as tenderly as possible.

In this way they reached the camp in about three quarters of an hour from the time of setting out. The ponies had already been driven ahead and were safe within the inclosure when they arrived. There was much stir and great curiosity excited as the strange procession came in, but neither Matouchon nor Echoschy would answer any questions until they had seen Tataquitnamse.

He recognized the old man at once. He said they had been great friends at one time, though they had not seen each other for years. He told the sisters to which tepee to take him, sent word to the squaws that they must see to all his needs, and dispatched a messenger at once in search of the medicine man.

The messenger returned in the course of a half hour or so saying that he could not find the medicine man anywhere, and that he was surely not in the camp as every tepee had been visited.

Then Tataquitnamse determined to call several of the head men together and let them decide what to do. They surely would know. The old man was suffering too much with his foot to wait for the medicine man. The men went and looked at him; turned him over and over, asked him questions, ran their fingers along his body and even into his hair, then returned to make their report. In their opinion he had as much cold as anything else. Therefore he needed "steaming." After that, the foot could be dressed in clay mixed with water in which the roots of a certain plant had been boiled, and he would be all right. To the carrying out of this prescription, Tataquitnamse gave his consent, and at once sent four of the men to execute it.

These men went to the tepee where the old Indian was lying. Their first proceeding was to divest him of every particle of his clothing. But there was one thing he would not let them remove. This was the leather pouch fastened about his neck. When they had at first attempted it, not knowing exactly what it was, he had shown such a decided tendency to be belligerent, that they had been considerably exercised. When they found out what it was, they made no further effort at molestation. Doubtless each one had a charm of some kind upon his own person.

After divesting him of his clothes, they rolled him in a blanket and hurried him to the steaming-house. This house stood on the outer edge of the camp. It consisted of a frame work of poles stuck in the ground and bent over until the structure assumed an oval form. The frame was covered with blankets, four or five deep, thus making the inside of the house perfectly air-tight as soon as the opening in front was closed. In one corner was a bed of straw. On this the old man was placed perfectly nude. Then numerous hot rocks that the squaws had been engaged in heating, were brought and piled near the straw bed. Then while the other three self-instituted doctors filed out through the opening of the steam-house, one remained to pour a bucket of water upon the almost red-hot rocks. This he did in great haste and as hastily made his exit, closing the opening tightly behind him.

The steam generated by thus pouring the water upon the hot rocks did rapid work, for when, twenty or twenty-five minutes later they pulled aside the blankets and entered, there lay the old man with the steam and perspiration issuing from every pore and almost dead with suffocation.* Now, instead of taking him at once and drying him off and putting him to bed, they carried him to where a barrel of water was standing and proceeded to dip him in once, twice, thrice, head downwards, as we have seen hogs dipped at slaughtering time. Then they took him back to the tepee and without replacing his clothes

* This steaming process is quite common among the Indians.

left him to dry off as best he could. But they took care to
wrap the sprained ankle in the prepared clay.

When Matouchon heard of the treatment to which the old
man had been subjected, she was truly indignant, for she felt
that it was the very worst thing that could have been done.
By to-morrow, he would certainly show it. If it were really
cold he had, this treatment was enough to kill him. She determined to go to see Tataquitnamse about it and to beg him
to do something else for the old man, if he were really sick.
She thought the best thing was to keep him in the tepee as
warm and as comfortable as they could and to doctor his leg.
She had heard Doctor Holley talk so much about the cases he
had attended that she felt sure this was the way. She would
get up courage enough and go and tell Tataquitnamse so. But
first she thought she would wait and hear all the young man
had to say who had brought the news, and who was now talking to her mother. He was one of those who had helped to
strip the old man in the tepee, and at this point was telling
about the leather pouch the old man had around his neck and
of how quickly he had shown a disposition to fight when they
had made the attempt to remove it.

"He kept it on all the time he was in the steam-house," the
man concluded, "and it even went into the barrel with him."

"Poor old man!" Matouchon said to herself; "it's a pity
he hadn't shown even half as much determination to defend
himself, as that worthless thing; then he would never have
gone into either the steam-house or the barrel."

It required a heap of courage to go to see Tataquitnamse,
but Matouchon finally accomplished it. But all she got for
her pains was a frown and the words "he guessed the men
knew what they were about. The kind of sickness the old
man had, needed just such treatment and no other."

When well away from Tataquitnamse's presence, Matouchon wondered again and again at her courage in seeking him
on the errand she had. But her life among the white people,
and the kindness, care, and consideration she had received, had

made her not only free and easy in her manner but perfectly fearless.

Matouchon had not forgotten her determination to dress Echoschy in some of her clothing. She had put the determination into execution very soon after their return, even while, the so-styled doctors were steaming and ducking the poor old man. The dress she selected to put on Echoschy was one of dark red woolen stuff with bright buttons and a row or two of glittering braid around the skirt and the edges of the jacket. It was the dress of all others that Matouchon liked best to wear herself, for, despite her bringing up, Matouchon still retained enough of her Indian nature to have a fondness for bright colors. The selection of this dress, her favorite, to put upon Echoschy was as good an evidence as could be wanted of the noble impulses that were stirring at Matouchon's heart with reference to Echoschy.

At Matouchon's earnest solicitation, Echoschy gave herself a thorough preparation from head to foot. The greatest task was to reduce her locks of matted hair to anything like order. They needed other attention, too. This Matouchon patiently and carefully gave them. When all was done she looked quite a different Echoschy. Matouchon could not repress her exclamations of delight. But Amado looked sad. When questioned by Matouchon, she replied that she was thinking of what would happen when Tabitosa returned. He would never let Echoschy go dressed up that way, never, never! Indeed Amado had her doubts as to whether he would even let Matouchon wear the clothes she had brought. Once or twice the night before, and even that morning before the sisters had left the tepee, Amado had seen Tabitosa surveying Matouchon's attire with a scowl. But she prudently refrained from saying anything of this to Matouchon, thinking the trouble would come soon enough anyhow. There were three or four days of peace and happiness granted. She would let the poor young creatures have all the pleasure in them she could.

So she tried to rally from her sadness and to join in the de-

light with which Matouchon was now regarding Echoschy.
The latter did indeed look a different person. The resemblance
to Matouchon was now more marked than ever, though the
face still lacked the softened, refined expression Matouchon's
had. All the pretty clothes in the world, however could not
have changed that. Echoschy, too, seemed ill at ease. She
didn't wear the clothes as though she liked to wear them.
To tell the truth, she didn't feel anything like so comfortable in them as she thought she'd feel. The skirts were too
long and they bothered her. She couldn't half walk in them.
There was a tightness too about the jacket that she didn't like.
It seemed as though it had her arms partly tied to her body.
And such a way as it had of sticking close to her waist. Why
it would never give her the least bit of chance to belt it in!
In short Echoschy was the savage Echoschy still despite the
clothing.

Echoschy walked about a while to please Matouchon and assumed all kinds of postures, even to letting herself fully into the
various airs and graces proposed by Matouchon. To please her
sister still further, she even went visiting among her acquaint-
ances in two or three of the tepees, but soon returned, with a
disturbed face and an uneasy air. Some of the squaws had
guyed her unmercifully, but this she loyally refrained from
telling Matouchon.

Somehow the dressing of her sister in the clothes in which she
had longed to see her, hadn't proved either the gratification or
the success of which Matouchon had dreamed. Echoschy herself had not taken to the new dressing as Matouchon had hoped.
Instead of seeming pleased, delighted, she had, on the other
hand, appeared ill at ease. The glad, joyous expression that
Matouchon had expected to see in her eyes was altogether wanting. Matouchon could not but notice the alacrity with which
Echoschy doffed the new clothes to put on the old ones, the
time having come for her to do some work about the camp.

"I believe you like your own clothes best, Echoschy,"
Matouchon said a little reproachfully.

15

Echoschy's eyes fell. She was so sorry her sister had noticed it.

"But I guess that is natural," Matouchon continued, trying to find the excuse. "I guess it is because you are not
used to them yet. When you wear them a time or two they
will feel all right." Echoschy replied that she supposed this
was the reason; that she would try again to-morrow, and that
she was so glad her sister had given her the beautiful dress.

Somehow the scene that had just taken place showed Matouchon almost more than anything else could have done the
difference between herself and her sister. Oh, what a work
there was before her to bring that groping soul up to the
light; to arouse heart and mind to the full reception of the
sweet graces of gentleness and refinement!

But as far apart as the sisters had seemed during the scenes
of that afternoon, they were assuredly close together in
spirit, if in naught else, when as the evening drew on apace and
the whole camp was wrapped in slumber, they stole softly
out of the tepee and wended their way to the small clump of
cotton-wood trees, there to pray in common for Tabitosa, their
savage father.

CHAPTER XXII.

"THE WHITE MAN'S WAY THE BEST."

IT was as Matouchon had feared. The treatment to which the self-improvised doctors had subjected the old Indian, White Plume, had done him more harm than good, save the benefit rendered by the clay to his injured foot, which now seemed to be healing.

But otherwise the old man was much worse. Indeed, he was in a high fever and, for most of the time, he was out of his head and rambling away in a manner that seriously alarmed those who had the watching of him. He seemed to know two or three languages, and would talk first in one and then in another. Many of the expressions used in his delirium were in English. Noting this the squaws who had him in charge went for Matouchon, thinking she might make something out of them. But Matouchon had to go two or three times before she could catch anything clearly. Then she had to put it together piece by piece. Much of the talk was about soldiers. Indeed, White Plume himself seemed to have been a soldier, and not only a soldier but he seemed to have been in battle. He would start up wildly when he thought he heard the sound of the cannons. There was much talk, too, about a great man who often rode in front of them all on a grand white horse that pawed the earth and almost sent forth fire from his nostrils. Whoever this man was, White Plume evidently looked upon him as the greatest soldier he had ever seen. There was not one of the officers at Fort Sill, from the sergeant up to the commandant, who could in the least compare with him.

These ravings showed that White Plume was a very sick

man. It distressed Matouchon to see how very ill he was·and
to realize that what the medicine man was doing did no good
at all. Somehow she had taken quite an interest in the old
Indian, for he seemed so sick and helpless. Doubtless the
circumstance of her finding him in the ditch had something to
do with her pity and her interest. But aside from this there
was something about him that showed that he was above the
general run of the Indians, much gentler in manner and neater
in appearance. Besides, Tataquitnamse had shown plainly
that he regarded the old man as his friend and that he was or
had been an Indian of much consequence. So he ordered that
the best attention be shown him and sent the medicine men to
take care of him.

How it provoked and disgusted Matouchon to see the senseless mummeries and the revolting performances carried on by
these medicine men ! Again and again she longed for Dr.
Holley. How quickly he could make the old Indian well
again ! Sometimes she felt like sending for him or even for
the physician at the Fort, but she was afraid of what Tataquitnamse might do or say. She wondered why the physician at
the Fort didn't hear of the sickness and come to the camp. It
was in his territory. But then she supposed he ought to be
notified. She could see very well why this wasn't done. The
medicine men were jealous of any one who encroached upon
their rights ; they were particularly so of a genuine physician.
So they kept the fact of the sickness away from the authorities
at the Fort, and went on practising their disgusting rites and
doing a vast amount of injury with no good at all.

There was much sickness in the camp just at that time. The
old man's case was not the only one. There were several
women and children sick and two or three men. There had
also been three or four deaths attended by the usual horrible
savage rites. In the tepee next to that occupied by the old
man there was, among others, a child sick that Matouchon felt
sure would die. Indeed, the death-damp was already on its
brow. Matouchon felt so sorry for the poor young mother.

It was her first little one, and the only one, and she was beside herself at the prospect of its death. Matouchon did all she could to comfort her, but in that wild, untutored heart it was a grief such as no balm could reach.

Matouchon was so indignant with the medicine men. She did think that when they saw the child's last hour had come they ought to have left the poor young mother alone with her babe. But instead of that, they went on with their revolting performances. Indeed, it seemed that the nearer the child got to death the more revolting and disgusting these performances became. There were two medicine men; tall, powerful looking Indians. They were nude from the neck to the waist save that they wore, slung over their shoulders and confined about their throats with cords, a kind of mantle that reached almost to their heels. They had feathers in their hair, and rattle gourds and various charms and medicines in their hands. With the exception that their foreheads were stained a deep red, the rest of their faces were unpainted.

While one of the medicine men sat by the fire pouring something on the coals that caused a dull blue smoke to ascend, the other approached the child, threw the blankets back, stripped it of every vestige of its clothing and then prostrated himself over it on his knees and hands. Then he applied his mouth just above the child's heart. He kept it there for some little time, making a considerable display of performing the act of suction. In a moment or so, having drawn all eyes to himself he spat out a mouthful of plaited hair which he pretended to have extracted from the child's heart. This was the evil spirit that had been troubling it, he declared. This done his final performance was to ring a bell in the face of the child to keep the evil spirit from going back.

With this last barbarous performance, the child's own spirit went out of it, and the mother, seeing its eyelids quiver and its little body twist and distort itself in its last death agony, threw herself with wild cries upon it. In an instant they had dragged her away, and before the child's breath had more than

left its body they had bundled it up in the blanket in which it
died and hurried it away to the rudely dug hole in the ground.
Then while the friends of the parents came around to weep
and to howl and to show their measure of grief by the depth
and compass of the noise they made, the squaws prepared the
knives, sharpened to an edge like a razor, with which the poor
young mother was to perform those barbarous rites without
which no mother's grief in this savage land is considered genuine. With one, shining and heavy and sharpened like a
cleaver, she chopped off the first joint of the forefinger of
her left hand, and with the other, smaller, finer, and gleaming
as a razor newly whetted, she slashed arms and face and
throat and breast, all the while screaming and screeching and
throwing her body about like some maddened creature.
With the blood flowing from head to waist, and running in
rivulets down her clothes, she presented a truly horrible and
ghastly sight.

Matouchon almost fainted before she could make her way
out of the tepee and shut from sight the fearful picture. Oh,
how terrible it was ! When would these poor creatures ever
learn that these fearful practices were as unavailing as they
were barbarous ? When would the light dawn in their darkened minds and lead them to gentler and better things ? How
different was the Christian's way of showing sorrow, of expressing grief ! There were tears and moans and even cries
for the dead : but no savage drawing of blood or mutilation
of the body. And oh, what a sweet hope they had of meeting
their loved ones hereafter ! Matouchon did wish she could
tell the poor young mother of this, tell her in such a way that
she could feel it in her heart. If only she could bring her to
look upon her baby as not really dead. Matouchon resolved
to try, but she knew she would have to wait at least a day or
two until all the barbarous rites attendant upon the child's
death were concluded, for until that time the mother would be
in close custody of the squaws.

Meanwhile the sickness among the Indians grew more and

more alarming. Almost every day there was a death in the camps. Even the Indians themselves were fast beginning to show their distrust of the powers of the medicine men. The old Indian, White Plume, had made a brave battle for life, but he was now assuredly very near death.

Matouchon longed more than ever for Dr. Holley. Dared she write to him? What would Tataquitnamse and the other Indians say if they found out she had summoned him? Just as she was in the midst of these doubts and fears, to her great joy he came. Poor Matouchon had undergone such a strain, and this new life had been in many respects such a severe trial, that when she saw him she could only throw herself on his breast and weep. She felt the less restraint in doing so inasmuch as only Amado and Echoschy were in the tepee at the time.

He comforted her in a loving, fatherly way, called her his dear Matouchon, his own little girl, and promised to do all he could for the sick Indians. He had only come to see her, however, he told her, and to pass a day and night. But if the matter was as urgent as she told him, he would see Tataquitnamse and arrange to stay three or four days. He would also dispatch a messenger for his brother physician at the Fort.

Dr. Holley saw Tataquitnamse. The chief was only too glad for him to remain, and to send for the other physician. To tell the truth, like so many of the other Indians, he had begun seriously to doubt the ability of the medicine men to cope with the diseases. He was also greatly alarmed at the number of deaths. Why, if it kept on thus the camp would soon be depopulated! So he not only gave Dr. Holley permission to remain and to send for his brother physician, but he also set himself heartily to work to further their efforts.

In only a day or so, the change for the better in the sick was very noticeable. In two days there had been but one death, and this was of a patient almost gone when the physicians took hold of him.

As one by one the sick Indians began to recover, and some

of them even to get up and walk about, praise for the white
medicine men was heard on every side. "The Indian's way
may be well enough," commented a grave old man, "because
it is the only way he knows; but there is a way, it seems, even
better than the Indian's, and that is the white man's. Yes;
the white man's way is the best," he repeated. And soon
this phrase was on many lips, "The white man's way is certainly the best!"

It is needless to describe Matouchon's great happiness at
having her dear adopted father with her. The sweetest hour
of all the day was that near its close, when he came to the
tepee for a season of needed rest, and instead of giving himself up wholly to that rest, spent the time in conversation with
Matouchon. There was so much to tell her, for it was now
several days since she had left the Agency and the loved ones
there.

They were all well, he told her, only the good Docté seemed
determined to kill himself with work. He had just been on a
preaching tour to the Indians that had covered more than a
hundred miles. He had completed it in four days and returned in time for his Sunday duties at the church. The white
mother and John and Emma and all had sent her many loving
messages; but best of all was that from the good Docté. He
was coming to see her! He hoped to be there in a few days.
Matouchon's heart would be in a thrill all through those days
of expectancy.

The Doctor brought news, too, of Quannah. How rapid
were Matouchon's pulse beats when he disclosed it! It was
said that Quannah would soon be at home; that the business
on which he had gone to Washington would be completed
earlier than he had anticipated. "Then, my child, I shall
make it a point to see him; the very moment I know he is at
home. I shall take pains to place before him the great injus-
tice of that council that gave you to Tabitosa. I shall tell him
freely of the comment it has created; of how only a certain
faction of the Indians was present, chiefly Tabitosa's friends;

of how the chief being absent, an old man was selected to preside over the council who was quite in his dotage and totally unfit in every way. Be brave, my child; it cannot last much longer now."

She looked up into his face with shining eyes, and he could see that in their depths which told him plainly how severe had been the trials of this life to her. The time had been only a few days, but those days had left their mark indelibly.

Then he told her of Unkama. The name had been on her tongue many times, and her joy was great when it was reached. Unkama was still in the yellow tepee at the Agency. She had sent a whole wealth of love to her precious Matouchon. There was a sick baby in the tepee whose mother had to be constantly at the Agent's house, or Unkama would have left long ago to seek Matouchon. She would certainly come in a few days now, doubtless with the good Docté. At those words Matouchon's heart bounded more than ever. Both at one time! What a joy it would be!

Besides the love, Unkama sent her many messages of cheer, for Dr. Holley had told Unkama of his hope with reference to Quannah, and she shared it. She knew Quannah well, and felt sure he would do all he could to have the decision revoked. He would see some way out of it; something to justify him in changing the guardianship of Matouchon. She was Tabitosa's, it was true, by a tie of blood, but then Dr. Holley had rescued and raised her. He was really more entitled to her than Tabitosa, who would have dashed her brains out when a baby had it been left to him. Quannah would assuredly see it this way. So reasoned Unkama, and she was not alone in her belief. Many of the Indians themselves agreed with her. All this was enough to make Matouchon's heart very happy, outside the fact that she had her dear doctor-father there with her.

But the time soon came for his departure. He had been nearly a week at the camp, and had done all he could for the Indians. Besides his duties at the Agency demanded his re-

turn.   All of the Indians who had been sick were well on the
road to recovery except White Plume, and his chances were
now good.

The old man had a severe case of pneumonia, Dr. Holley
told Matouchon.   It had undoubtedly been brought on by the
reckless treatment he had received at the hands of the self-instituted doctors.   It had really been enough to kill him, and
it was a wonder it had not.   It had taxed the combined skill
of the physicians to arrest the progress of the disease, but now
with care and good nursing he would in all probability recover.   Matouchon at once instituted herself his nurse, and was
very attentive as to the instructions given her with reference to
the medicines and other things.   The old man was now perfectly clear in his mind, and showed great pleasure when Dr.
Holley told him to whose care he had committed him.

Once or twice while attending him the doctor had noticed
the pouch about his neck.   He noticed too how every time his
hand, in examining the patient came in contact with the pouch,
the old man even in his delirium, seemed to be aware of it.
Once he had chanced to mention the circumstance to Matouchon.   She had then told him all she knew.   The doctor
shared her opinion that it was a paper of some kind ; one the
old man had undoubtedly picked up around the Agency.   "I
would have examined it," Dr. Holley concluded, "had he
not shown such a decided tendency to defend it from examination.   I respected his solicitude concerning it all the more because of his helplessness."

All this time Tabitosa had been away.   On leaving he had
declared his intention of returning in three or four days.   But
the time had now extended into two weeks, and there was
still no sign of him.   Those who had gone to Fort Sill had returned with the intelligence that he was not there.   He had
only remained two days, then he had pushed on into the
country beyond.   As he had taken considerable ammunition
with him, it was surmised that he had gone into hunting-
camp somewhere.   He was doubtless after skins, which sold

for a very fair price at the various agencies. But whatever were
the reasons for his absence, one thing was certain : his non-
return gave joy to more than one heart. Especially were Matouchon, Echoschy and Amado made happy by the delay. The
tepee had not been like the same place since he had taken himself away from it. It seemed almost like a civilized home, for
it had been thoroughly cleaned from top to bottom and all the
bedding and other furnishings put in the best of order. Matouchon could sleep anywhere now without that feeling of
loathing that had at first been with her, for every blanket was
as clean now as soap and water could make them.

There was also a difference in the appearance of both
Amado and Echoschy. They were as clean looking as the interior of the tepee, and their clothing too was much better
cared for and more attractive in every way. Matouchon had
brought with her several pieces of calico and woollen cloth,
gifts from both Unkama and Dr. Holley. Indeed, they had
been lavish in the matter of clothing. The most of these
pieces Matouchon made up into dresses and underwear for her
mother. She was quick with both needle and scissors, for Mrs.
Melville had taken great pains to instruct her in these womanly
accomplishments. She sewed, too, for Echoschy. The latter
had now grown less uncomfortable in the clothes Matouchon
prevailed upon her to wear. Even the dreaded crimson dress
was now worn with some approach to gracefulness. But despite the charm it was supposed to lend, Echoschy still appeared the savage in many things. However, there was one
thing that was producing a change. Matouchon noticed this
with deep joy. She had begun to teach Echoschy to read, and
her pupil was making rapid progress. She could even spell
her way through many of the verses in the little Testament that
was such a treasure to Matouchon, and such a source of deep
joy to them all when read aloud every morning and night by
its owner.

There was but one source of unhappiness in Matouchon's
heart at this time, and this was concerning her mother.

Amado had not been well for some time.   Now she was droop-
ing perceptibly.   Matouchon who had noticed this before Dr.
Holley left the camp, had spoken to him about it.   At first,
he had entertained the matter lightly, saying it was only a bad
cold Amado had caught.   But after a while he had seemed
more grave about it and he had begun to treat Amado regularly.
On going away he had carefully instructed Matouchon about
her mother's medicines.   Amado was now quite weak and for
a considerable part of each day kept her bed.

It was a great satisfaction to Matouchon that, during
nearly the whole of her father's absence, Kankeah kept away
from the tepee.   He only came now and then for his meals,
which he took in sullen silence.   It was learned that he slept
with some boy-friends at another tepee.   His mother seemed
pained by his behavior and tried to talk to him once or twice.
But he never seemed to pay any attention to her, soon ridding
her of his presence, much to Matouchon's relief.   Somehow,
it never seemed to her that she ought to try to work on Kankeah, too.   He had such a forbidding way.   She felt sure he
would repulse her.   Then, too, her heart was still sore over
the shameful way he had treated her.   Probably after a while,
when that feeling had worn away, she might put forth earnest
effort in his behalf also.   But not now.   She just couldn't approach him.   He had been so ugly to her and so cruel to the
old man.   Poor Matouchon ! as sincere as were the endeavors
she was making toward the living of that higher and better life,
into which she had been brought through the Christian rearing
of those in whose hands she had been placed, still she had
enough of the old Indian nature left to bear keen resentment
of wrongs inflicted.   Perhaps it was not altogether the Indian
nature.   Others of us have been that way even with our claim
to ancestry more civilized.

At last Tabitosa returned, and at the most inopportune time
he could have selected !   Those making a thorough study of
the subject might have been led to declare that there was
some wicked instinct of Tabitosa's thoroughly diabolical na-

ture that prompted him to put in an appearance just as he did. Amado was much better that afternoon. She had been sitting up nearly all day. But still she looked sad and thoughtful; too sad Matouchon thought. So in order to cheer her mother and to draw from her a smile or two, she and Echoschy dressed up in the best they had and began to parade around with all the airs and graces of the white ladies at the Agency.

Just as they were in the midst of their most overwhelming company manners, showing how Mrs. A. received Mrs. B. when she came to see her, and how Mrs. B. in turn posed before Mrs. A., the flap covering the opening to the tepee was suddenly raised and in stalked Tabitosa! His eyes fairly glared as he took in the picture. Then as he noticed also the changed appearance of the tepee, something very much like an oath escaped him, for Tabitosa had been around the agencies and the fort a great deal, and instead of learning the white man's good ways had learned his bad ones.

Striding toward the two girls he gave each a cuff on the face that sent her spinning over backwards on the blankets. Then turning toward Amado, he was on the point of treating her to a similar blow, when Matouchon, quickly recovering herself, interposed a determined hand.

"Strike me again if you will, but don't, *don't* lay hand on her! Do you not see that she is sick?"

Tabitosa wheeled quickly and fixed his eyes in a savage glare on Matouchon's face. Then he caught her roughly by the shoulder and dragged her in front of him, raising his powerful arms for the blows she had invited through her interference. But somehow they didn't fall. There was that in her eyes that stayed him. Doubtless it was a spark from the same fire that glowed in his own, though more courageously enkindled. Instead he satisfied himself by shaking her roughly once, twice, thrice, and flinging her from him. Then he picked up the camp clothes Echoschy had dropped when she arrayed herself in better. Throwing them toward Matouchon, he cried,

"Put those on! They are what you ought to have had long

ago ! And you," to Echoschy, " will keep what you have on. Don't dare put on any others ! I will beat you within an inch of your life if you do. We'll see now who is the lady and who the Indian drudge. Living with these stuck up dogs of white people has given you big airs indeed. But I, Tabitosa, your father and ruler, I will show you the Indian blood is still there if I have to draw every drop from your body to prove it ? "

With these words he flung himself down in front of a pan of meat placed before the fire and began to devour it raven-ously—even as a hungry dog—without waiting for the bread Amado rose to bring him.

Echoschy crawled nearer Matouchon, and putting her arms around her, whispered through her tears, " O Echoschy *so* sorry ! She wishes it had never been ! She just can't bear to do what Tabitosa says ! "

" But you must," Matouchon replied, as she returned the caress, " or he will beat you worse than ever. I do not mind it. It will not be so dreadful as you think. I am only too glad we got off so easily ! "

CHAPTER XXIII.

THE COUNCIL RENDERS A DECISION.

TABITOSA remained for five days at the camp, five of the most terrible days Matouchon had ever spent. Indeed, there had never been anything like them in all her life before. Tabitosa seemed determined to make her drink the cup of wretchedness to the last drop. He stormed at her, he kicked her, he made a perfect camp drudge of her, and did everything else within the compass of his mean soul to humble and terrify her. When Amado and Echoschy went down on their knees to him, with the tears streaming, and begged him piteously to abuse them in any way he pleased so he spared Matouchon, it only had the effect of arousing him to greater brutality. Tataquitnamse was gone, or Amado would assuredly have appealed to him. But amid it all Matouchon bore herself heroically. Despite the wretched apparel which Tabitosa compelled her to wear, she looked the same Matouchon still. No attire, however coarse or uncouth, could take from or obscure the natural sweetness and refinement of expression. Underneath it all there remained that which Matouchon had been made through the power of Christian education, and the all-redeeming grace of God. The pearl might be dragged through the dust heap, but there was no power in the dust to quench its lustre. It was the pearl still, despite its rough usage.

Opponents of mission work among the Indians have this plea with which to lay self-excusing unction to their narrow souls: "Those Indians that have been educated and brought up in the ways of the white people slip back again into the barbarous habits and customs when they return to their homes."

(239)

As evidence of this they cite the example of the daughter of one of the Nez Perces chiefs, educated at Carlisle; or again that of two of the most promising pupils sent out from the Hampton Virginia School.

Nowhere do the records show this to be the rule. It is only the exception. Where one has slipped back into the old savage ways, scores have gone on to nobler and better living. And not only have they reached this life themselves, but they have led others into it, fathers, mothers, brothers and sisters. In short, where the education and Christianization of the Indian have proven a failure in one instance, they have in a hundred others proven a success. Let those who doubt this give the matter honest investigation. Let them write to the missionaries of the various churches now operating in the Territory. Better still, let them go and see for themselves. Let them enter the tepees of the Christian Indians and note what changes have been wrought there, very often through the influence of but *one* member who has found the better way and gradually led the others into it. Further, let them go into the neat cabins scattered at intervals over the prairies, and, sitting down in these civilized homes, hear the story of their founding and of their growth through the sweet persuasiveness and earnest, forceful living of some loved child sent to one of the mission schools.

The Indian is an Indian, beyond doubt, and in some respects he will never be anything else but an Indian, even with all the education that can be given him; but give him the education, and, at the same time, touch and sweeten his heart with the pure religion of Jesus Christ, and you will have a new Indian so totally unlike the old that you will hardly know him.

Matouchon had received the education, and along with it the sweeter and nobler influences. It had been no surface work. The rootlets had sunk deep within her heart bringing forth many flowers of grace, which the rude shock of this wretched camp life had not the power to crush. They bloomed as flowers still, with all their sweet fragrance, despite their surroundings.

On the morning of the sixth day Tabitosa departed rather suddenly. Matouchon who chanced to hear a part of a conversation between him and an Indian that had just come to the camp, thought she knew very well what carried him.

Quannah had returned. He had been back from Washington only two days, yet the news of his arrival had spread rapidly. Matouchon's heart beat so that it almost suffocated her. How much Quannah's return meant to her! She wondered how long it would be before he could summon the council and hear all the evidence. Oh, if she could only see some of the dear ones from the Agency! Her prayer was not more than uttered before it seemed answered. Unkama had arrived, but not at the camp. She had too great a dread of Tabitosa for that. She was with a band of Kiowas who had come from the Agency, and who were going back again in a few days. They had pitched their tepees but a short distance from Tataquitnamse's camp, and Unkama had sent Matouchon word that she would be there in a little while, and that she was going to beg that Matouchon might return with her and stay for the two or three days the Kiowas remained. Unkama was emboldened at the last minute to make this request through having seen Tabitosa taking a course toward the Agency.

"Matouchon must hurry the old clothes off!" Amado said decidedly, as soon as she knew of the coming of Unkama.

"But suppose *he* returns before I can get them on again?" Matouchon asked.

"Amado thinks he will not. He took his gun, his hatchet, some skins. That means he will go to the Agency before he comes back, and that he will be all night on the road. Amado cannot bear for Unkama to see you that way," and her eyes filled with tears.

Matouchon threw her arms around her mother's neck. "Poor mother!" she said, for she had learned to call her by

16

that sweet name, "this seems to grieve you more than it does me. I can bear it better than you think."

"But oh, the cruel blows! and for *you!*" said Amado, and she covered her face with her hands, overcome even by the thought.

"They are brutal and they are like the one who gives them!" Matouchon said, her eyes flashing. "But I can bear even those, for it cannot be long now. Quannah has come, and he will hold another council. All the white people think so, and so do many of the Indians."

At the words Amado covered her head and sank back upon the blankets. As a deep sob escaped her, Matouchon for the first time realized just what her going away would mean to her mother. Quannah's decision would bring happiness to one, but oh, what misery it would bring to that other heart—the one of all others to feel it the keenest—the mother's.

Matouchon threw her arms around her mother and tried to comfort her. She talked to her in the most endearing way. So occupied was she, she did not note the lapse of time. She forgot to change her clothing. She still had on her old camp dress when Unkama lifted the curtain of the tepee and came in. Matouchon flew to meet her, kissing and hugging her between smiles and tears.

Unkama returned the caresses, the tear-drops glistening upon her own cheeks. Then holding Matouchon at arm's length, she gazed at her in astonishment. "Why does Matouchon have on such as this?" she asked quickly, her hand touching the wretched attire as she spoke.

Matouchon's eyes fell. Then as gently as she could, for she well knew how the recital of it would arouse Unkama, she told her of Tabitosa's stern command, omitting much of his brutal treatment. But Unkama guessed it. Her quick eyes took note, too, of the bruises showing upon the arms and neck, which Matouchon did her best to hide by means of her ragged clothing, but ineffectually.

Unkama's indignation knew no bounds. But for the presence of Amado, she would have given vent to it much more energetically. But consideration for Amado restrained her somewhat. But it did not restrain her from taking Matouchon in her arms and crying over her as though she were a baby, at the same time vowing vengeance upon Tabitosa. Amado, too, joined in the weeping, and for the next few moments there was a flood of tears from the three.

Unkama was the first to grow calm as she had been the first to give way. There was a voice of hope stirring in her heart. In the midst of her sorrow she remembered the news she had come to bring. In all probability Tabitosa would soon have a stop put to his brutality, toward this one victim at least. Unkama clinched her hand as she thought of what he had already managed to do in the few days Matouchon had been at the camp. But the end, without doubt, was near. Unkama managed to convey to Matouchon a part of the sweet hope that was stirring in her own breast. But the words had to be low and necessarily hurried on account of the proximity of Amado, for Unkama fully realized what the giving up of Matouchon would mean to her. Unkama could judge this by the pain that had been in her own heart.

What she managed to tell Matouchon was that Quannah was really at home, and that Dr. Holley had lost no time in seeing him. Indeed he had placed the matter before him as Quannah passed through the Agency on his way to his home. Quannah had assured him that the right thing should be done. He would call another council of the Indians just as soon as he had attended to some matters that were pressing. He would see to it this time that the very best men of the tribe were present and that Dr. Holley's claim was given full consideration. More had been said by Quannah, enough to show Dr. Holley that all the chief's sympathies were with him.

As much of this as she could, Unkama conveyed to Matouchon. Her heart was full of keenest sympathy for poor Amado. Therefore she was very careful not to allude to the subject so that she could hear.

When Unkama found that Tabitosa was gone and would probably remain away a day or so, she was very readily persuaded by Amado to change her plans with reference to Matouchon and to remain at the tepee with them, at least until Tabitosa returned. The next three days were days of deep joy to Matouchon. She had resumed her own clothing, and despite the bruises that still made her wince whenever her mother or Unkama pressed her in a closer embrace than usual, she was again her old bright, cheerful self.

Matouchon took Unkama to see the old sick Indian, White Plume, whom amid all her troubles she had never neglected. He was now a great deal better and was sitting up for most of the day. He seemed to take to Unkama at once and to be quite talkative with her. Among other things he told her that he had once worn a great hat such as the soldiers at the Fort sometimes wore when they went for long distances through the sun. In it was a big white feather a soldier had given him, and that was how he came to get his name. He told her also that he had been a long distance from home, away over in the country where there were great wildernesses of thorn bushes, and tall stiff plants with sharp points that stuck like swords.* It was the country where the Indians used to get their captives. From this description, Unkama felt sure that he was talking about Mexico. It seemed too, from his conversation, that while he was there he had done some fighting, but just who or what it was he had fought Unkama couldn't well make out. The only point that was clear was that it had been a long, long time ago—so long, in fact, that White Plume had grown to be an old man since.

Great was Matouchòn's joy, the third day after Unkama's coming, to see the white father at the camp. He had come to preach to the Indians and would be there that night. In the sight of them all he took Matouchon in his arms and kissed her and called her his own little daughter. She could scarcely see his face through her happy tears. Later, when they were

* Cacti.

together for a little while, he confirmed the good news Unkama
had told, only he made the intelligence he brought much more
emphatic.   He had seen Quannah himself just the day before.
He was making preparations to call the council and assured
the good Docté that it should be now in a few days.

He had so much to tell her of the dear ones at the Agency,
and with what eager ears she drank in every word !   One piece
of news he brought her interested her particularly, though it
was not with reference to any of the dear ones at the old
home.   Matouchon had heard him talk again and again of the
school he was so anxious to see established by the Mission
Board of his Church.   It seemed the school was to be a reality
after all, for the Board had just sent him word to lay claim to
the tract of land that had been offered, as steps would be taken
toward the erection of a suitable building.   The missionary
was so happy over this that his eyes fairly glistened as he told
Matouchon of it.   How long he had desired it, and how fervently he had prayed for it to be brought about !   Now he
was to see the fruition of his hopes and prayers.

"It will be a great thing for the Indian children," he said
earnestly, "especially for the girls.   So many of them will be
reclaimed from the vicious ways of the camp!"   But this
wasn't all he told Matouchon.   There was another piece of
good news still.   The women of the Church had also been
stirred by the letters he had written to the various publica-
tions, and they too were going to take a part in the proposed
missionary operations.   A camp-worker was to be sent out
under their auspices.   Her special line of work was to be
among the women and girls at the camps.   She would make
daily visits to them, reading to and praying with them, and
otherwise helping them to a better life.   She was already on
her way and would doubtless arrive the first of the coming
week.

It was hard for Matouchon to part with both the good
Docté and Unkama on the same day; but her heart was
buoyed with the sweet hope with which they filled it.

" It will not be long now before I have my own little girl
again," the good Docté had said as he bent over her at parting, while Unkama had whispered,

" Ere the great sun rises and sets many times now, all this
will have ended for Matouchon. Then what joy to the hearts
and homes of those who love her ! Unkama's heart is swelling even at the thought ! "

But somehow there was a dark cloud amid all this sunshine.
Matouchon's thoughts dwelt much with her mother. With all
her effort, she could not get them away. Her anxious eyes, too,
read Amado's face. How much of sorrow and suffering she
saw there ! Amado was now really sick. She had managed
to keep up wonderfully while Unkama was there. It was
doubtless the excitement of the visit ; the proximity of one
who stood in the relation to Matouchon that Unkama stood.
Then, too, Unkama had so much to tell of Matouchon's baby-
hood and subsequent years. Amado drank in each word
greedily, hungrily. What she suffered, only her mother heart
knew.

Now that Unkama was gone she seemed to sink back into
her old state of despondency. It would be idle to suppose that
Amado knew nothing with reference to what was in progress
concerning Matouchon since Quannah's arrival. We have
seen how Matouchon herself had let certain words drop that
were sufficient to give an inkling of the truth to her mother.
Besides Amado had now and then caught certain signs and expressions and faintly murmured words that had told her much
despite their caution. It was the same as though she had
heard the whole story.

A slow fever now set in, and Amado was very ill indeed.
One of the worst symptoms was a distressing cough that nothing seemed to relieve.

Tabitosa had not returned and Matouchon was heartily glad
of it, as it allowed her to have things about the tepee in her
own hands. Kankeah, too, was gone. He had been sent for
to go to one of the wood-camps. Thus there were only Ma-

touchon, her mother and Echoschy in the tepee, though near by there was another tepee owned by Tabitosa and the squaws were now and then dropping in. Matouchon at once devoted herself to her mother with Echoschy's help. Her first step was to beg Tataquitnamse to send to the Fort for the physician.

Dr. Wall was very candid with Matouchon. He told her at once that her mother was seriously ill. In a day or two she knew the whole truth. The disease was consumption. The lungs had been weak for some time. Hard work and exposure had done the rest. Oh, what sorrow these words brought to Matouchon's heart! There was a great lump in her throat, but somehow she could not cry at first. When at last she did give way to tears, it was where no one could see.

In her mother's presence she felt that she must be as cheerful as she could. Neither did she tell Echoschy the whole truth.

Matouchon had not been with her mother long enough to give her, like she gave Unkama, that full, overflowing devotion that would have been hers had the circumstances surrounding their lives been changed. But the ties of nature were strong, and the bonds uniting mother and child were growing closer day by day. Now and then, despite herself, Matouchon felt just the least bit of hardness in her heart against her mother. Had she not abandoned her and sent her to her death in the sand? How *could* she have done it? But then came the remembrance that the poor mother had been driven to it. It was death in either case. She could not help herself. With all a mother's love she had sought to save one rather than see two die. How could Matouchon blame her? She did not blame her. Bitterness or ill-will could not long dwell within a heart like Matouchon's. It is a question as to whether they had ever really existed there. But whatever may have been the feelings, not a single trace of them remained when she saw her mother lying so weak and ill, her whole frame racked by that terrible cough. With all a loving daughter's care and gentleness she set to nursing her.

Quannah had at last called the council. The day had been
definitely fixed. News of it had been sent to every camp.
The Comanches were requested to give full attendance. The
place of holding the council had been so selected that it would
be as nearly central as possible. When the day came there
was a great stir in the camp. Nearly every man prepared himself to attend. They set forth at daylight with Tataquitnamse
at their head. Owing to the distance some of them would
have to go, the council had been called to meet at night.

Matouchon knew well what the stir and departure meant,
for word had been sent her. But her heart was too sad with
reference to her mother to feel the deep joy she would otherwise have felt.

It was the largest council that had assembled for some time
among the Comanches. Quannah had taken care that it
should be. He had made special effort to have the old men
of the tribe present, those that represented the best element
and were looked up to as oracles of wisdom.

Tabitosa, too, was busy, so busy, in fact, that he had not returned to his camp since leaving it. He soon became aware
of the feeling against him with reference to the manner in
which the other council had been held. He saw, too, and that
plainly, that the Indians of the better class did not approve of
the way in which he had gone to work on that occasion.
Neither did they approve the verdict that had been rendered.
The truth is that outside his own particular following of kin-
dred spirits in wickedness and cruelty, Tabitosa was not at all
popular on the Reservation. Too many knew him for just
what he was, cowardly and brutal. The more tender-hearted
among them shuddered at the thought of one so gentle and
sweet as Matouchon being in his power.

Tabitosa saw well enough that unless he rallied his clan and
rallied them in full force, the day would go against him. So
he spent every hour he could of the intervening time in the
effort to do this, and what was more, he used all the cunning
he could. So well did he succeed that when the council met,

he had every man there that had been present on the former occasion and a few who were not. He made a strong showing and waged a hot battle.

The girl was his, he argued. What if she *had* been thrown out in the sand? The mother had done it and not himself. *He* had not cast her away from him, neither had *he* sought to put her to death. Therefore she was still *his*.

Some of the Indians tried to break down this argument by declaring that he would have put the child to death; yes, both of them, had he been present at their birth. But in face of this Tabitosa stubbornly persisted that he had *not* put them to death, nor even attempted to do so, which certainly settled the matter. A murmur of approbation went around at this, and Quannah looked grave.

Then up rose an old man of considerable standing in the tribe. Indeed, his word was valued next to that of the chief. Even the chief himself sometimes deferred to it.

Wankenah was an old, old man, seventy-five or more, though his form was but slightly stooped; neither was his hair so white as that of some younger than himself. But somehow there was an air about him of great age, and of wisdom combined with age. When he arose to speak every eye was turned upon him. His voice was strong and clear, and it rang through the assembly.

"There is that," he began, "that seeketh to destroy as well as that that seeketh to preserve. The one has its origin in evil, the other in good. The one is as the shadow of night; the other as the brightness that heralds the morning. Where the evil maketh its way is terror and darkness and *death;* wherever the good, joy and all the sweetness of *life!* A man's heart may seek to do a wicked deed, yet if there is that that stays him against his will, it is the same as if he had done it. A serpent may have its fang ready for the approaching fawn, which perchance it unwillingly sees escape, yet the poison is in the fang. Thus Tabitosa, our brother, had he found the two born at a time, would, through the old cruel custom of his tribe, have put them to death. It makes no difference that he did not. It was only because some one else had played the destroyer before he came.

"Though absent he would nevertheless have caused the child's death, by other hands, perhaps, but by hands acting through fear of the consequences at his return. My brothers," and here Wankenah threw his head still further back and let his piercing eyes sweep the sea of faces, while each syllable he uttered was distinctly audible to every ear, "my brothers, it is well known that by a law of this tribe he who *sanctions* death forfeits all claim."

An excited murmur arose at this, and the chief had to call the council to order before Wankenah could proceed.

"On the other hand," continued Wankenah, "if *life* be aught, and we know that it is all in all, then should not the saviour of life claim that life as his? The child, Matouchon, was given over to Death and Death would have found her but for *him*," pointing to Dr. Holley, "but for *him*," he repeated more impressively than ever, "*her saviour!* My brothers, I sum up in these words the claims of Tabitosa and of our white brother: the one would have *destroyed*, the other *saved!* The one as slayer would have spoiled and wasted; the other has cherished and sustained. The life is his because he made it life when it would have been death; therefore give him the life."

"Yes! Yes!" "Give it to him." "It is his!" sounded on all sides.

The chief saw the most auspicious moment for decision had come. Therefore he lost no time in putting the vote. It was overwhelmingly in Dr. Holley's favor. *Matouchon was his!*

CHAPTER XXIV.

MATOUCHON RENDERS A DECISION.

IT was after midnight when the council adjourned. Dr. Holley's heart was in a happy glow as he thought of Matouchon. She was his, all his now, and no earthly power could take her from him again! The Indians had spoken and Quannah had ratified it under his own seal. How the Doctor longed to see Matouchon and tell her the news! He would go as soon as day dawned, he said to himself. He never dreamed that any one else would be before him, yet such was to be the case.

Mr. Melville was not at the council. He had fully intended to go, but at the last minute he had been summoned many miles in an opposite direction. However, John and Willie Conover and Andres were there, and throughout the assembly there were no more interested spectators than they. Indeed, John's heart was in a tension of suspense. It would be simply awful if Matouchon were given back to Tabitosa! But John had more faith in Quannah than to believe that.

When the decision was rendered he couldn't sit still a minute longer. He jumped from his seat, swung his hat into the air, and then went to hugging both Willie and Andres as hard as he could. They were almost as much excited as he.

"And to think *she* has to wait until the middle of to-morrow before she hears the news!" said John regretfully. Then a sudden gleam shone in his eyes.

"Willie," he said quickly, "is your pony fresh?"

"As fresh as yours," returned Willie. "You know we came together, and got here at noon to-day. They have been resting and picking ever since. Why, John? What makes you ask?"

"Oh, I have a plan in my head; that's all. Just wait a minute and I'll tell you. I want Andres to get a little farther away," he continued in an undertone, "for I know he'll oppose it. He'd doubtless be right, too, as he always is," John continued frankly. "But I just can't help doing it. Why I believe I'd go wild if I didn't!" and John showed the excitement he felt in every quickened nerve of his body.

"It isn't anything dreadful, I know," said Willie confidently, "for you aren't given to that kind of thing. I don't believe Andres would be as particular as you say," he added. "I imagine, John, it is something in which we ought to have his help."

"Oh, no," said John, "we can manage it by ourselves. There, Andres is out of range now! Well, Willie to put it into as few words as possible, I am just wild to be off with this news to Matouchon. I can't wait till morning. By starting now—it is not yet one o'clock—we could be at the camp easily by eight, and not push our ponies too hard either. Yes, that is it, Willie; I want you to go with me. That was the reason I asked about your pony. Come! let us saddle and be off. The moon will give us light for the most of the way."

"I think we had better tell Andres," said Willie, with conviction. "Not that I'm afraid!" his eyes flashing. "You know better than that, John. But it would be so much better to have Andres with us. He would know the best way to go so as to make the quickest time. Then, too," continued Willie, "I don't believe the good Docté would like it if we went without Andres."

"No," said John suddenly, "he wouldn't. You are right Willie. In my fever to be off I had forgotten about that! We'll ask Andres, but," despondently, "I fear he'll oppose it."

And so Andres did at first. He thought it something of a wild undertaking, and said so frankly. But after a while, catching the spirit of the boys, and feeling himself how great must be the anxiety of Matouchon, he consented to go. But first, he made a stipulation that they must not be hard on the ponies. He would set a gait at which to ride, and they must follow it.

So they sprang to saddle and were off, riding merrily under the stars, with the broad light of the moon making the way almost as clear as though it were day. Did ever cavalcade before carry more glorious news than this?

The morning began to draw on. The light of the stars grew fainter and fainter. The moon had said good-bye and left them only its shadowy face; still the cavalcade rode merrily on; still the hoofs of the good ponies made music upon the loose soil; still the cheery bits of song or joyous whistling rang forth from the riders. What were the miles of the seemingly boundless prairie? what mattered the night and its dreary suggestions? What cared they for the chill that swept the air and lodged with keen stings in the very bones? Did not they carry that within their hearts that warmed the body and kept their spirits bright?

The day began to redden the east. All the prairie seemed awakened to its coming. The very blades of grass caught the new hope of the dawn, every pendant dewdrop seeming to twinkle afresh. The clouds enveloped themselves in their robes of vapor, and stole silently away. In the northeast the low line of mountains began distinctly to show itself against the horizon. Life and light and rich promise were in the coming day. So, too, there was gladness, and a gratitude inexpressible, in the hearts of those who bore the news to Tataquitnamse's.

The full glow of the morning! The sun shining upon a million millions of dewdrops, the sky one solid arch of smiling blue; and there in full view the camp of Tataquitnamse!

John felt his heart leap. It almost came out of his bosom.

"Andres, Willie," he said, "do let me ride on ahead and tell her the good news alone. There may be something she will want to say. So many eyes may embarrass her. Matouchon was always so timid."

"All right, John," said Willie quickly. "Go ahead, old fellow. We know how you feel about it. Matouchon has been brought up with you like your sister. Give Spot the word and go! Neither Andres nor I will think anything of it."

"No, that we won't," said Andres heartily. "Go, lad. We'll follow you slowly."

John needed no further urging. Neither did Spot. Indeed, that wise pony seemed to know by intuition what was expected of him. He gave his body a sudden decisive shake, threw his legs out at graceful angles, and then went speeding away like an arrow shot from the bow.

The camp was fully astir by the time John reached it. He sprang from the saddle, threw his bridle reins over his arm, and leading Spot, entered the enclosure. He had no trouble in finding the tepee of Tabitosa. A young Indian pointed it out to him as soon as he made inquiry. Approaching it, his heart almost stood still, for there, just a little distance away was Matouchon. She was approaching the tepee and carrying a load of wood. She had on her old camp dress, but despite its unsightly appearance, John knew her at the first glance. There was no mistaking that little air with which Matouchon carried herself, an air peculiarly Matouchon's own, as graceful as it was natural.

John sprang to her side, and reached out his hands to take the wood before she was aware of his presence. Then she almost dropped it before he could get possession of it, so surprised was she.

"How did you get here?" she asked breathlessly.

"Why, on Spot, of course," returned John laughing. "Don't you see your old friend, Matouchon!"

"That I do," returned Matouchon heartily, giving the pony a hug and a kiss, the latter of which he returned with compound interest by running his silky nose up the full length of her face.

"And you came from—" Matouchon could not finish the sentence.

"I came from the council," answered John quickly, finishing it for her; "right straight from there, Matouchon. I could not wait after the decision was rendered; no, not an hour, I felt I *must* come and tell you. So, I got Andres and Willie to come with me. They will be here directly. Oh, it is glorious news indeed we bring you, Matouchon! The council has spoken. It has given you to Dr. Holley."

"Oh!" she said, and that was all. She couldn't speak. Her heart was too full for utterance. But a glad light shone in her eyes that spoke more than a volume of words. Then John was surprised to see a look of unutterable sadness come into her face.

"We are all so glad," he went on to say. "I fairly shouted when the decision came; so did many others. You ought to see the Indians, Matouchon, how glad they are; I mean the better ones. Wankenah did the most of it. Such a grand speech as he made! But Dr. Holley will be here directly to tell you all about it and to take you home, too, Matouchon, you are to come back to us!"

John expected to see her eyes glow again at this, and to hear words expressive of her gladness. Greatly to his surprise she stopped him with a gesture of pain, while there was an expression of unspeakable wretchedness upon her face.

"I cannot go," she said decidedly.

John started and drew back almost as though she had struck him a blow.

"Why, Matouchon, what *can* you mean?" he asked in astonishment.

"Throw down the wood here," she said, pointing to a place near the entrance to the tepee, "and walk a little distance with me, and I will tell you." Evidently she was afraid that some one within the tepee would overhear them.

John obeyed, and wonderingly followed, still leading Spot by the bridle. In a secluded portion of the camp, twenty-five or thirty paces from the tepee, she stopped, and turned her eyes upon him. They were swimming in tears.

"Oh, it is *so* hard for me to do this," she said, "but I *must.*"

"What is it, Matouchon? What is it you *must* do?" and John's tremulous voice showed his deep concern.

"I must stay here. I cannot go back there," pointing toward the Agency; "at least, not now."

"Why, Matouchon, what *can* you mean?" It was the second time John had asked the question; but his deep anxiety kept him from noting the repetition.

"There was a time when this news would have made my heart glad, all glad; but not now."

"And why not now?" John asked hurriedly.

"Because there is a change. Because it is not as it was. There is one sick who needs me, whom I cannot leave. She will suffer if I go; and my heart would never be glad again for thinking of it."

John looked at her enquiringly.

"It is Amado, my mother. She is sick, very sick indeed. She will probably die, and before a great while," a little sob in her throat. "The doctor said so. Then how *can* Matouchon leave her?"

John broke out hotly. He was but a boy after all, and his impulses generally got the better of him. "But, Matouchon, what claim can she have upon you? Didn't she abandon you when you were a helpless baby? Didn't she give you to one with instructions to put you to death? Think! if it hadn't been for Dr. Holley you would have perished in the sand. Indeed," continued John warmly, "this was the ground upon which the Indians gave you to him; *he saved your life.* What claim, then can this savage mother have upon you?" he repeated.

"She is *my mother*—" a whole volume could not have spoken more—"and she loves me. It will break her heart if I leave her. She was cruel then, I know? She had to be. But oh, she is so different now, so changed! You will see for yourself."

" Perhaps so," assented John. '' But oh, what a horrid place
this is for you, Matouchon ! " he broke forth afresh. "You
hardly look like yourself at all, and such wretched things as
these are you have on ! Why do you wear them ? Where are
your own clothes ? But you needn't tell me," he continued as
he saw her eyes drop, " I know. It is Tabitosa ! Matouchon,
how *do* you stand it ? And now to think when you could leave
it all you will not. O Matouchon, have you no thought of
others who love you, too ? There is Unkama, and Dr. Holley,
and my father, and mother, and all of us. Have you forgotten the old times with us and how it nearly broke your heart
to leave us and come here ? Matouchon what *can* have
changed you so ? "

" I am not changed," she said, her voice unsteady, her lips
quivering, a look of unutterable woe in her eyes. "I love
you all yet, just the same as I ever did—oh," her words giving
way to a cry of anguish, "do you not see how *hard* this is ?
Do you not see my heart is breaking ? " With this cry she
buried her face in Spot's silken mane, and throwing her arms
around his neck, burst into a passion of sobs.

John was seriously alarmed. " Matouchon, *don't*," he entreated. "Only stop crying, and I will not say another word.
I just couldn't understand how you could do it ; how you
could give up those who love you and had cared for you to
stay here with those who didn't. And who not only didn't
love you and don't, but who do everything they can to abuse
you," he concluded, his eyes flashing.

She raised her head to gaze at him. Her own eyes were
almost invisible through their tears. " There is only *one* who
abuses me," she said. " The others are kind, *so kind*."

" But this does not give them a claim upon you."

"I know it does not ; but it makes my stay here much less
hard. Think ! it is my own blood they have in their veins.
Matouchon must never forget this ; never ! never ! no matter
what comes. Neither must she forget that it is her *own mother*
she is asked to leave, and that she is sick—sick almost to

17

death.   Let Matouchon ask you a question," she continued,
her eyes fixed earnestly upon his face; "could *you* leave *your*
mother if she were thus?   *Would* you do it?"

"Certainly not!" returned John vehemently.   "How can
you ask me that, Matouchon.   Don't you know it without the
asking?   But it is not a similar case," he continued emphatically.   "The two won't do to go together at all.   My mother
never cast me off when I was a helpless babe, but instead has
been to me all my life just the best and dearest mother a boy
ever had."

Matouchon looked at him sadly.   She knew only too well
the difference he pictured.   Had it not made itself apparent
in her own starved heart many, many times?   But she was
loyal.   More, she was generous, and the love for her mother,
though late in coming, had made its way to her hungry heart
at last.   However short the time it had there abided, she knew
its worth and sweetness all too well to cast it from her..   What
had the earth, after all, to offer her that could compare with
that? because in all the world there was not anything just like
it.

"I know what you say is true," she answered.   "I have
felt it many, many times.   But you will find *her* so changed.
As I have said, you will hardly know her.   She is all a mother
could be now—that is a mother," correcting herself, " who
has had so little chance to learn.   But it is all there *in her
heart.*   That speaks to me, oh, so gently and sweetly.   How
then *can* I leave her, especially now when she is sick and needs
me?"

John's eyes began to show tears, and there was a catch in
his voice as he said, "Forgive me, Matouchon.   I feel now that
you are right.   Don't think my heart a hard one because I
couldn't see it at first.   It was an awful disappointment to
hear you come to such a decision.   Have you thought,"
he asked quickly, "what Dr. Holley will say? how he will
take it?"

"Yes; many, many times, and my heart has almost broken

thinking of it. Oh, he has been so good to me! I owe him
so much. I owe *him* more than any one else in all the
world. I owe him my life. How *can* I tell him what I have
decided to do? And oh, it will be so hard, so hard not to go
back with him when he comes!"

It was even harder than she anticipated.

He came a few hours later, his face radiant, his heart
running over with gladness that she had been given back to
him again, that she was all his now! He could hardly believe her when she told him of the decision she had made.
"Why, my child," he said, "you are certainly out of your
mind. Stay here in this miserable camp, and with that
abominable man who heaps so much abuse upon you, and will
continue to heap it," he exclaimed, his eyes directed to her
wretched attire, "when you have it in your power to go back
to your friends, to go back to me again!"

The last words were too much for her. They brought
only too clearly to view the full value of all she was giving up.
She could only throw her arms round his neck and burst into
tears. For the moment she was speechless.

"But I *must* do it," she said, as soon as she could find
voice, "it is my duty to do it. She is *my mother*, and she
needs me so. There is no one else who can do for her
what I can do; and it will not be long," her voice sinking
to a whisper over the last word.

No; it would not be long. The trained eyes of the physician could see that plainly when they looked at her some
moments later. Amado would probably last a month or two,
but that would be all.

When he came to weigh Matouchon's reasons well, and to
know fully the motives that prompted her, Dr. Holley no
longer opposed her in the decision to remain at the camp.
Indeed, he began to take a different view of it altogether
and to honor and admire her for the love and loyalty shown
her mother. Now he had come to think of it, he wondered
how he ever could have supposed Matouchon would take any

other course. She would not have been Matouchon if she had.
Deep in his heart he acknowledged now how keen would have
been his disappointment in her had she acted otherwise.

He could see the great change in Amado; how gentle she
was and how she clung to Matouchon. Better still, her
groping mind was fast coming to the light under the young
girl's leading. Amado would yet find him who was "the
way, the truth, and the life," ere she died.

There were many little ways in which Dr. Holley felt he
could brighten the path for Matouchon; one way in particular
—indeed the chief one of all—was to see Tataquitnamse and
have him put Tabitosa on warning. Tabitosa must now remember that Matouchon was no longer his, and that if he
dared abuse her he would be prosecuted to the full extent of
the law. The chief promised to give the matter close attention and to keep Matouchon, as well as the other inmates of
the tepee, under his protection; so far as he could.

Dr. Holley also arranged to have many comforts sent to the
camp for Matouchon, and delicacies for her mother. Then
after seeing Dr. Wall, and begging him to give Amado's case
the best attention he could, and promising to come himself
whenever he had it in his power, Dr. Holley tenderly took
leave of Matouchon and went back to the Agency. All
they could do now was to wait.

When they heard of Matouchon's decision, the Indians
were loud in her praise, even many of those who had been
on the side of Tabitosa. She was certainly a fine, brave,
young squaw, and it was well that she had been given into the
hands of one who would have so thoughtful a care as to her
future.

But of all the words spoken to her none were sweeter than
those of the good Docté when next he saw her, which was
only a day or two after Dr. Holley had left the camp.

"You did right, my child," he said, holding her hand in
his and looking straight down into her eyes; "you did right,
and God will bless you. And it will be a double joy that will

come to your heart in after days, Matouchon ; not only the
joy of the remembrance of having crowned your poor mother's
last days with love and attention, but also the joy of the
knowledge of having guided the poor weary soul home to the
mansions of its Father."

"O white father, do you really think *that ?* " she asked
brokenly.

"That I do, my child. And I not only think it ; I know
it. Can I not see the change ? Any one can who tries. Most
of all *I* can, because I know only too well how pitiful used to
be the gropings of this poor soul in its darkness. Now all
seems so clear. She is no longer restless and uneasy, and
seems to catch my meaning so well when I talk to her. Happy
Amado ! she has at last found anchor, and it is your hand,
my little Matouchon, that has brought her there ! This were
worth staying for if no more."

"White father," and here Matouchon raised her face down
which the happy tears were streaming, " white father, I would
rather have you say these words to me than any others in all
the world."

"I say them with all my heart, my child," he returned
earnestly, and with his hand in blessing upon her head, " for
they are true."

CHAPTER XXV.

BLACHITO AND HIS MISTRESS.

THE winter was now well advanced and the winds were sweeping over the prairies. There was ice, too, along the streams, and the snow had fallen in many places.

Amado was slowly passing away. She was now so weak that she scarcely left her bed for any length of time. Matouchon was her close and devoted attendant. Echoschy, too, was all love and gentleness, caring for her mother tenderly in Matouchon's absence. Only once since the meeting of the council had Matouchon left her mother for any length of time. This was to go and see the dear ones at the Agency. She was now back again and installed at her mother's bedside.

Tabitosa had the grace now to leave them for the most part alone. When he was at the camp, he generally passed the time in the other tepee. This was doubtless owing, in a considerable degree, to the influence of Tataquitnamse.

They saw Kankeah, too, but little. He seemed to prefer to stay with his father. But sometimes he came into the tepee, generally at such times when he knew there was something extra nice cooking. Matouchon always treated him kindly and spoke to him as pleasantly as she could. He had stopped showing her the sullenness he had formerly, and now and then gave her civil answers to her questions. Once or twice, greatly to her surprise, he had brought some birds to be prepared for his mother.

Kankeah sometimes came in while Matouchon was engaged in reading the Testament to Amado and Echoschy. On such occasions she had endeavored to make the meaning of the passages as simple as possible. More than once, to her joy, she had noticed him listening intently. How she longed to win his interest and then his affection! For was he not her brother? Did not the same blood run in their veins?

On Matouchon's visit to the Agency she had learned of the coming of Miss Helen Brewson, the camp-worker sent out by the Woman's Board of the Church, which the white father represented. Matouchon had not seen her, as she was away engaged in her work at the time, but she had heard from several sources how delighted they were with her, Indians and all. She was so kind, so cheery, and so sympathetic. She knew just how to go right to the heart, and though she had, as yet, learned little of the languages, still the progress she had made in reaching the women at the camps, was wonderful. At Mr. Melville's request Unkama had gone with her to a number of the camps, and also John and Willie Conover. The latter were with her during Matouchon's visit at the Agency.

"Oh, you ought to see her!" Unkama said enthusiastically. "She is *so good*, and she seems to see just what is needed. She can look right down into a sick heart and know what medicine to give it. And she don't seem to think herself above the Indian. She will sit right down on a pile of dirty blankets, as though it were the nicest seat in the world, and hold a poor sick baby and try to quiet and comfort it, all the time talking to the mother and pointing her to the good way. Oh, she is as sweet as the flowers in summer and her voice like the tinkle of the waters flowing over the pebbles. When she goes to the camp of Matouchon, then it will be to make her happy."

During her visit to the Agency, Matouchon saw also the ground selected for the new school. Already the foundations for the building had been placed in position. But the work had to proceed rather slowly, owing to the difficulty with which the lumber was procured. There was in this section of the Territory no timber fit for building purposes. The principal tree, the cotton-wood, was so soft and porous as to have little durability. Therefore all the lumber for the school building had to be hauled from the railroad station thirty-five miles away. But the Board had provided the money, and Mr. Melville was pushing matters as fast as he could. If things went on as he hoped and had planned, he would be ready to open the school in about three months. The Indians themselves, especially those that belonged to his church, were greatly pleased over the prospect of the school and the good it would bring about, and were helping him all they could. Some of them had teams and were now assisting in the hauling of the lumber. Others again had gone to work clearing up the ground and helping to get the timbers for the foundation in position.

From those who were passing back and forth between the Agency and the camp, Matouchon heard again and again of Miss Brewson and her work among the women and girls of the camps. Miss Brewson had proved, too, that she had something else besides sweetness and gentleness. Her recent encounter with a drunken Indian, who had endeavored to stop her pony in the road, showed plainly that she had plenty of nerve. Indeed, nerve and pluck seemed to be two things eloquently characteristic of this little woman, who from love to her Master had come to face all the hardships and dangers attending mission-work in these savage wilds. In order the better to reach her various posts of labor, she had now gone to live all alone in a little house away out on the Reservation. It was thirty miles or more from any permanent human habitation. She had only the wild cats and wolves for close neighbors. While passing the night in her cabin, which she often did, she had the music of their howls all through the hours, as these wild animals prowled about her doors.*

Matouchon heard all this with bated breath and rapidly beating heart. What a grand woman she must be! She wanted to see her more than ever now. Of course, she was a great big woman, with eyes that just blazed when her courage was aroused, and a voice of which even the wolves would stand in fear.

* This experience is of actual occurrence.

One afternoon Matouchon had gone for a ride on Achonhoah. She did this quite often now, at Dr. Holley's request, so as to give her the exercise of which she stood so much in need after the hours of close confinement beside her mother.

The day was an unusually mild one for the winter. The sun was shining brightly from a clear sky; the winds were calm, while only here and there was a patch of snow visible. The air was just cold enough to make it bracing. The ride was truly enjoyable. Matouchon gave herself up to it fully. Achonhoah seemed to catch the spirit of it, too, and his pretty feet barely touched the ground as he went skimming along.

Matouchon guided her pony toward the ravine where she had found the old Indian. Many times she had seen it in her rides since then. How things had changed now! If any one had told her on that day, when tearful and well-nigh breath-less she had endeavored to run the headstrong ponies into camp, and when she had stood with reddening cheeks and swelling heart under fire of Kankeah's mocking, taunting bat-tery—if any one had told her then that she would remain at her present post of her own will, she would not have believed it. It would have been too impossible even for thought. But the test had really been made. The power of choosing, either to go or stay, had been given her, *and she had stayed!* What was more, there was at this hour no regret in her heart that she had so chosen.

As she rode on all the incidents attendant upon her finding of White Plume in the ravine came vividly to her mind. The old Indian had perplexed her much, and he was still a subject of speculation. Whence had he come? and what was in the little pouch about his neck? It was rather strange that, as good friends as they had become, he never spoke to her about it now. Doubtless he remembered what little faith she seemed to put in it as a charm. Perhaps if he showed it to her she would again make light of it. It was a source of wonder to Matouchon herself as to why she thought so much about the contents of the pouch. Why, it really was foolish! Didn't

numbers of the Indians wear charms of various kinds? then
why should she suppose this old man had one in any particular different from those commonly used?

White Plume had fully recovered, but he had not left the
camp. Indeed, he seemed determined to attach himself to
Tataquitnamse, and the chief appearing not at all unwilling,
the old man had now become a permanent member of the
chief's household. But he passed many hours in the tepee with
Matouchon, Amado, and Echoschy. At such times, if Matouchon happened to be reading in the Testament, she had no
more attentive listener than White Plume.

Matouchon rode past the ravine, then guiding the pony to
the left and decreasing his speed, she turned into a well-de-
fined roadway. This she knew was the track leading to Fort
Sill. She had not gone far, when suddenly Achonhoah gave
a sharp neigh. Matouchon had her head down, but she raised
it quickly. There just a few paces ahead of her a shaggy pony
had come to a stop in the road and was looking at Achonhoah
with eyes that said plainly,

"How do you do, old fellow?"

Achonhoah returned the look with interest, then by way of
being more social still, added another neigh in very decided
horse language. The look meant, "I'm pretty well thank
you," and the neigh, "The same to you old fellow!"

Attached to the pony there was a light road-cart, and sitting
erect on its seat was a small figure, the merry eyes of which
seemed enjoying to the fullest the meeting between the ponies.
Then they were turned upon Matouchon.

"Ay haitch!" (How d'ye do?) she said gaily in Comanche. Then under her breath, "I wonder if she understands
English? She looks as though she might."

The words were spoken in a low tone but Matouchon heard
them. Close attendance upon her mother had trained her ear
to catch the softest sounds. "Yes, ma'am, I do," she returned quickly. "I know English well."

Such a look as came over the gay little woman's face then!

It was like the sunlight rippling down over the water that had already been in a smile. "Well, that's lucky? Who would have thought it away out here? Ride nearer, my dear, and let me have a good look at you."

Matouchon readily complied, and while she was herself under inspection she also inspected.

It was such a sweet face, that on which she looked. It hadn't a wrinkle, at least none were visible at that distance. The skin was as smooth as a child's and almost as fair. The brow was broad and fine, and above it were soft masses of wavy hair. Matouchon was surprised to see that they were well sprinkled with gray. How strange this was when the face seemed so young ! And there were the eyes, keen bright eyes, and how they were glowing as they gazed at her !

" I do not know to whom I am talking," she said quickly; "but I will tell you at once who I am. Helen Brewson, camp-worker among the Indians."

Matouchon's eyes were vying now with Miss Brewson's in brightness. Could it really be? Why, where was the big strong woman Matouchon had pictured to herself? *This* the woman who had lived all alone on the prairie with the wolves and wildcats? Impossible ! Matouchon was quite overcome with the surprise of it all, but she managed to stammer, " I am Matouchon. I——"

But she got no further than this. Miss Brewson interrupted her with a quick little cry of delight. " Matouchon? Why I might have known it ! I have heard all about you at the Agency, you see, dear. How fortunate that I should meet you here ! Now I shall have no further trouble. It is to your camp I am going. Won't you get in and ride with me and lead your pony? We can be more sociable then."

As Miss Brewson got up to change to the other side of the cart, Matouchon saw that she was taller than she had at first supposed. Still, she was far from being the " great big woman" Matouchon had pictured.

Matouchon glanced askance at the shaggy little black pony.

"Do you think—do you think he can carry us *both?*" she asked hesitantly.

For answer Miss Brewson broke into a merry peal of laughter, and, bending over, gave the pony a little flick on the ear with her riding whip. "Do you hear that Blachito," (Little Blacky) she said. "Do you hear how she is slandering you by expressing doubt as to your ability? Now, old fellow, the best way to get even with her is to convince her of her mistake."

By way of answer the pony turned his head and gave his mistress a look which said as plainly as pony language could, "All right, mistress, just get her in and we'll show her a thing or two." "You see he is doing his best to answer you," Miss Brewson said to Matouchon. "He assures you he is quite able. Just get in and try him. Now then, Blachito, old fellow," shaking the reins over his back as Matouchon climbed into the road-cart, "Off with you, and remember what is at stake—your reputation, good fellow."

The pony shook his ears vigorously, and throwing his trim little legs out gracefully, started off at a brisk trot.

"He seemed such a little fellow," said Matouchon apologetically; "I was afraid he couldn't do it."

"Oh, he's bigger than he looks, in capability, I mean. There's plenty of *go* in Blachito. Isn't that so, old fellow?"

He threw back his head and arched his ears at this, and said as plainly as pony could, "That is so, my mistress."

"I was doubtful of his ability myself at first," his mistress continued; "that is of his ability to do the work required of him, for it is often very hard work indeed. But since I've tested him through these weeks, I know what's in him. He is hardy and he is willing. Sometimes I wish he wasn't quite so willing, for he is likely to be abused should he fall into hands that are not considerate. And oh, he is so trusty!" she continued, her eyes shining. "I think I can depend upon him in almost any emergency. He has been put to the test again and again. Many a rough, dangerous crossing he has carried me over safely. You ought to see him at such times! I have only to say, 'Charl a Blachito, kish, kish!' (Good, Blackie, steady, steady!) and he will throw his weight against the light cart and take me steadily to the bottom, though sometimes the slope is so steep it looks almost as though I were going over his head.

"I remember one day in particular, I had been riding for hours in the pouring rain, and came to the Little Wichita to cross it. I knew there was danger of my horse's falling, but I knew also I must cross, since there was no place I could stop, and I was alone. So, speaking a few encouraging words to Blachito, and lifting my own heart above to the Fountain of Strength, we started down the steep bank, the wet sand slipping and sliding beneath Blachito's feet, till it really looked as if we must go tumbling down at any moment. I watched Blachito closely. He seemed fully to realize the danger and to be watching accordingly. When we were safely down the steep bank and across the stream it seemed to me a burden had rolled away from Blachito's shoulders. So knowing and so faithful as he is, bless him!"

"You love him very much, do you not?" Matouchon asked, gazing a little timidly into the soft bright eyes so near her own. "I know you must," she continued, "for I love Achonhoah," turning back to give her pony a caressing touch as she spoke, "almost as well as if he were another person."

"That I do!" Miss Brewson returned heartily, in answer to the question. "Why we are the dearest of friends! Many have been the nights we've passed all alone on the prairie together. Why, I talk to Blachito then as though he were a person sure enough; and you ought to see how he understands me!"

"I've heard about that," said Matouchon quickly, referring to "the nights all alone on the prairies." "Oh how did you do it? How *did* you ever stay out there alone? and you so small and weak, too! I thought you were a great big person!" she broke forth impetuously.

Miss Brewson laughed merrily.

"'*A great big person?*' Well, that is too good! As if only a great big person could be brave! Why, child, the most cowardly person I ever saw was a great, big Indian nearly seven feet tall; the bravest, a tiny scrap of a boy that I could easily lift with one hand. So, you see, size doesn't have anything to do with courage. But you don't think I'm *so very* small do you?" she broke off suddenly, while her eyes seemed fairly dancing with amusement.

"No, ma'am; not now. Not so small as I did at first. When you stood up a little while ago to let me get into the cart, I saw you were taller than I thought."

"That is always the way, Matouchon; folks think I am rather small until they see me standing up. I guess it's the way I have of straightening my shoulders when I stand. Somehow when I sit down I will give them a droop. But tell me something about the camp to which we are going, Matouchon. Are there many women there?"

"Yes, ma'am, a good many."

"And have they shown much disposition to learn of the better way, Matouchon? I know Mr. Melville has preached there a number of times."

"Yes, ma'am? I think several of them have. I am so glad you are going there to talk to them!" and Matouchon's face glowed as the words were spoken. "But there are others," she continued, "whose hearts are so hard. They make sport of the preaching and even make faces at the white father when his back is turned. And oh, they are so low and disgusting in their lives! It seems nothing can change them."

"Nothing but the grace of God," said Miss Helen softly. "We must try to give it to them, you and I, Matouchon, for I want *you* to help me."

"Oh, it is so little I can do," Matouchon said tenderly.

"It is more than you think. I have heard of *one* thing, of *one* work that has been a glorious work indeed. O my dear, what a good, true, brave girl you have been!" and here the gloved hand of Miss Helen that was not driving, was laid gently and caressingly upon Matouchon's knee. "Such a heart of gold as you have, Matouchon!"

"O Miss Helen!" Matouchon could say no more. She was crying.

"And how is the mother now?" Miss Helen asked softly, after a moment's silence.

"No better. She gets weaker day by day. The end will soon come."

"And when it does, Matouchon, what a sweet feeling of peace will be in your heart that you made the choice you did."

"I only did what I thought was right, Miss Helen."

"The highest and noblest motive that could actuate to duty, Matouchon. If more of us felt it and acted upon it, what a glorious world it would be! But tell me, Matouchon, is there a place at the camp where I can stay for a week or so? I have my hammock and some bedding under the seat and a box of biscuits and some canned beef. So you see the most that I'll need will be shelter."

"Why, Miss Helen," said Matouchon quickly, "you can stay with us, that you can! We have a whole tepee almost to ourselves, mother, Echoschy and I. Everything is nice and clean, Miss Helen, and we'll be so glad for you to stay."

"Thank you, Matouchon. How nice that will be!"

"And Miss Helen," continued Matouchon, "you won't need the box of biscuits and the canned beef, at least not much. We have a box full of nice things which the dear ones at the Agency have sent, and they keep sending all the time."

"And do you think, Matouchon, you can go with me sometimes when I go to talk to the women in the tepees? You know I do not understand their language well. Do you think you can leave the mother for a little while now and then to go with me?"

"Oh, yes, Miss Helen. I leave her now some every day, to take exercise and for other things. Echoschy loves to be left with her, and she knows almost as well now as I do how to wait on her."

"Then we'll do some glorious mission work together, Matouchon. How glad I am you can help me!"

"And how glad I am, Miss Helen, that you are going to be with us, right there in the tepee with us. Oh, it will mean so much to mother, and to Echoschy too. There are so many things you can tell them that I cannot."

And as the days went on it proved a blessing indeed to have this sweet pure soul in daily contact with their lives. How good she was and how cheery and sympathetic. How much sunshine she brought them and how ready she ever was to take earnest part in all that pleased or interested them. And if there were, too, any little sorrows, how quickly she joined in them!

To Amado she was both a joy and a blessing. How the sick woman loved to lie and listen to her as the sweet, clear voice read so feelingly the many beautiful and comforting passages of Scripture! There was none that thrilled Amado's soul more than this one: "I am the resurrection and the life: he that believeth in me, though he were dead, yet shall he live."

But Miss Helen did other things for Amado besides reading the Bible to her. She talked to her; long and earnestly, and how beautifully Miss Helen could talk! And she sang to her, too, in a deep rich voice, every note of which was music. There was one hymn Amado loved best of all. It was this:

> "The King of love my Shepherd is,
>   Whose goodness faileth never;
> I nothing lack if I am his,
>   And he is mine for ever.
>
> "Where streams of living water flow
>   My ransomed soul he leadeth,
> And, where the verdant pastures grow
>   With food celestial feedeth.

" Perverse and foolish oft I strayed,
 But yet in love he sought me,
And on his shoulder gently laid,
 And home, rejoicing, brought me.

" In death's dark vale I fear no ill
 With thee, dear Lord, beside me;
Thy rod and staff my comfort still,
 Thy cross before to guide me.

" Thou spread'st a table in my sight;
 Thy unction grace bestoweth;
And oh, what transport of delight
 With which my cup o'erfloweth!

" And so through all the length of days,
 Thy goodness faileth never:
Good Shepherd, may I sing thy praise
 Within thy house for ever."

—*H. W. Baker.*

18

CHAPTER XXVI.

HOW MANATOAH WAS WON.

MISS HELEN remained at the camp and its vicinity for nearly a month. She found much work to do, and she did it bravely, trusting God for the result.

Matouchon found some time every day to go with her to the various tepees. She was of great assistance to Miss Helen. Indeed, Miss Helen could not have gotten on well without her, for she knew very little of the language as yet.

One of the hardest battles Miss Helen had was to teach the women cleanliness. She had to get at it gently for fear of offending them, and thus losing her hold upon them; for she *had* a hold upon them already. The love and sympathy she so plainly showed them had won that. They were indeed, keenly susceptible to kindness. She could do almost anything with them through kindness. There were, of course, exceptions to this rule, as is generally the case. Some of the women mocked her. They even did so openly. Others again gave her a sullen silence when she entered the tepees. But Miss Helen was too brave a soldier of the King to let such as this discourage her. She had come to this work expecting drawbacks and dangers and hardships, and expecting them she met them courageously. She was ready, too, for sacrifice and suffering. There was a blessedness in enduring these for her Master. Had he not endured them for her?

There was one custom among the Indians that pained her heart more than any other. This was the custom of child-marriage. Tender children were given in marriage to men old enough to be their fathers or grandfathers. She had seen several mothers of only thirteen or fourteen years. How dreadful it all was to Miss Helen! How fervently she prayed

that it might be changed. Only the day before her heart had
been painfully wrung by a case she witnessed.

A little girl of eleven, Tah-paro by name, had been given
in marriage by her parents to an old man of whom she stood
greatly in awe. He was not only a forbidding looking creature, but he was said to be cruel, too. The morning of the
second day after he had taken her to his tepee, Miss Helen
met her wandering about and crying bitterly. "What is the
matter, my poor child?" she asked gently.

"Ner peah par suwite" (I want my mother), sobbed Tah-
paro. And this was ever the cry of these frightened little ones
torn away from home and from a mother's care.

The Indian mothers love their children deeply, passionately.
Miss Helen had seen many instances of this. Likewise she
had seen many instances of paternal love. She wondered
again and again how they could let this cruel thing go on,
loving their children as they did. She supposed it was all because it was a fixed custom of the tribes. Even if the father
did not yield in the beginning, there was always something to
reach and break down his opposition in the end. Miss Helen
had had experience of a case of this kind.

Man-a-to'-ah was a happy little Indian girl at one of the
camps where Miss Helen had lingered for a week or so teaching. She was only ten years old, and her greatest joy was to
play at housekeeping with a very dead looking wooden doll
and a decidedly live puppy. The puppy she sometimes tied
up in her shawl and carried at her back as though it were a
baby. But nicest of all, Manatoah and her sister both had the
very cutest of ponies, and nothing delighted them more than
to go out with their father to round up, and bring in his ponies.
How fearlessly they rode on such occasions!

One evening as Manatoah and Norwa came racing up on
their ponies they noticed an old man, whom they knew, talking to their father.

"Get down, Manatoah, stake the pony, and come here,"
said Ton-a-we'-na her father.

Manatoah did as she was bidden, but with slow and reluctant step, coming in with a heavy scowl on her face, and utterly refusing to shake hands with the old man as her father commanded. Only too well she knew what he wanted, for he had been there before on the same errand.

" My daughter," said Tonawena, " this, my friend, has come again to see if you will not go with him to his tent."

For answer Manatoah burst into a passion of tears, threw her arms around her mother's waist and clung to her. Her father's hand placed gently on her head was pushed roughly away, and no words from him or presents from the old man, We'-ter, could induce her to look at him.

Tonawena couldn't bear the sight of his child's tears, and his heart melted. Neither could he bear the thought of parting with her to this old man whom he did not regard with much favor. " You see my daughter's heart is very weak toward you," said Tonawena. " It may be her heart will grow stronger after awhile," he added kindly.

Weter rose slowly to his feet, wrapped his blanket closely around him, and bestowing a scowl upon the weeping Manatoah, said : " Kish ! kish ! (wait ! wait !) In two moons I come again. Then she go with me to my tent," he added emphatically. The next moment the sound of the pony's feet was heard as he galloped rapidly away.

Manatoah thought often of the old man's words as she watched the moonlight steal in through the opening of her tent, and she would cover up her head and cry. But in a few days all these thoughts were lost in fears for little Norwa, who was very sick. Their mother had done all she knew of for the little one. She had fixed the steam-tent with the hot rocks and laid the little one within, and then, when the perspiration poured off, had run with her to the little stream and dipped her in. Still the hot fever kept coming day by day. She put all the medicine charms in the tent around her bed. Still it did no good ; and now, to-night, Tonawena said : " I will go to Wich-a-tos'-ka's tent and talk."

Wichatoska was the medicine chief that lived at the foot of Mount Scott.

Tonawena's fleet-footed ponies soon carried him over the fifteen miles of moonlit prairie to Wichatoska's tent. Going in he seated himself on the ground, took out the pipe, lighted it without a word, and drawing a few whiffs, passed it to Wichatoska. He took it and smoked it out in silence.

"My friend," then said the medicine chief, "your heart is heavy ; what you want ? "

"Yes, my little one is very sick. Go with me to my tent and make her laugh and play again, and I will give you three ponies."

Wichatoska went at once. As they neared the tent they heard the death wail given by Tonawena's squaw. Going in, the medicine man knelt by the dying child. He straightened little Norwa on the bed, and, opening her slip, passed his hands all over her chest and body. Every now and then he would wave his hands toward heaven, then toward the north, south, east, and west ; then downward toward the earth, uttering strange discordant words, utterly meaningless to his anxious-hearted listeners. Then he would tremble all over, shake Norwa, and make a strange noise like the growling of some wild beast of prey. All this was to frighten away the evil spirits that he thought had taken possession of the child and were killing her.

But as he worked with her little Norwa grew limp in his arms, and he laid her down dead, just as the bright sunlight of the morning streamed in at the tent.

The friends and relatives who were camped near, now came in, and the loud death wails and screams made a scene hard to describe, but much harder to forget, once it was witnessed. They gathered around Norwa, each trying to touch her somewhere ; stroking her little hands, patting her face, and talking to her poor dead body. All this time they were screaming, tearing their own hair, and beating their chests. The mother and near relatives, stripped to their waists, began to cut their arms and faces until the blood flowed all over them. Then a near relative took a knife and cut off the hair of Norwa's mother and sister, placing it in the little girl's hands to be buried with her. In the meantime they had dressed her in a beaded buckskin slip, with beaded moccasins coming up over her knees and trimmed up the sides with little tinkling bells. Then they wrapped her up in the bedclothes on which she died, and corded up the bundle ready to start right off to the burying ground.

Just as they were ready to start, the old man Weter, who had been camping near for days, came up with a handsome blanket. He tenderly wrapped it round the little corded bundle, pressing it to his heart as if it was the dearest treasure he had in all the world, and clinging to it till those who were starting out to bury it had to force his hands loose from the cords. Then he flung himself down on the ground and rolled and screamed and beat his chest, his tears flowing like rain, and his sobs seeming to come from a breaking heart. Thus he went on long after all the other mourners had utterly exhausted themselves and stopped.

When all in the tent, save this old man, had grown silent, Tonawena according to Indian custom, went round distributing presents to all who had mourned with him. To one he gave a blanket, to another something else, and so on as they wished.

Norwa's little pony was now sent out to the grave to be shot there. Her saddle, clothes, and toys were heaped up outside to be burned. All had taken what they wished, and Tonawena came last to Weter, who was still lying on the ground. "My friend," said Tonawena, "you have cried a great deal; your heart is very sore, and my heart is very strong toward you. What can I give you?"

Weter slowly rose to his feet, and crossing the tent took the hand of Manatoah in his own. "Give me your daughter," he said; and though she could not bear even the thought, neither she nor her father dared refuse under the circum-

stances. So Weter took her at once to his tent, and thus he
won in spite of her own and her father's wishes the little Indian maiden, Manatoah.

Miss Helen knew this was not an unusual case. More than
one little Indian maiden had been won in this way—given as
a present to him who had mourned the longest and the loudest
at the funeral of some member of the family. It was a custom
of the tribe, and as such none dared break it. Another law
of the tribe was that if a man married the oldest daughter, he
was entitled to all the others. Oh, how savage and cruel were
these customs! and how the heart of the good little missionary ached as she thought of them! It seemed to be the penalty woman had ever to pay in lands devoid of the precious
light of the gospel. The only hope, then, for these wretched,
degraded Indian women and girls was to kindle this light within
their hearts and homes and as speedily as possible. How fervently Miss Helen prayed and how earnestly she worked to
that end. She seemed never to tire. Early and late she was
seen on her rounds. There was no ear that would hear it, no
heart that would receive it, to which she failed to carry the
precious gospel message. There was no tepee too wretched for
her to enter; no blanket-bed too filthy to receive the pressure
of her knees if some poor creature lay there famishing, dying
—famishing without the Bread of Life, dying without the
knowledge of it. The very joy of knowledge in her own heart
made her all the more desirous that others should share that
knowledge. If she could, she would have taken every hun-
gering soul into the banquet. She would have shared to the
last crumb even if her own soul had known the pang of hunger.
But there was no danger of that so long as she had that inex-
haustible Fountain of supplies ever within. If her zeal and
her love could have compassed them and compelled them
through the very force of *their insistence* to come into the
feast, there would not have been a single soul left a-hunger-
ing.

CHAPTER XXVII.

THE CHARM DISCLOSES ITSELF.

IN her missionary work among the women and girls at the camp, Miss Helen found a strong and helpful ally in Carpio. Our readers will remember Carpio whom they met for the first time on issue day. Carpio had been away on a long journey, in which he was employed by the government as guide to a surveying party. But he had returned just a few days before Miss Helen came to the camp. As he spoke English well, and was willing to do everything he could for the good of his people, Carpio was of considerable help to Miss Helen. He generally went with her to the tepees when Matouchon could not, and acted as interpreter.

During these journeys they often saw the old Indian, White Plume. Miss Helen had grown much interested in him. She had heard from Matouchon a full account of the manner in which she had found him. White Plume, too, had added to the narrative by telling something of his life before coming to the camp. He had been employed for a year or more at the Fort; but getting too feeble for the work required of him, and hearing that his old friend Tataquitnamse lived only about two days' journey from the Fort, he determined to make his way to him.

White Plume took a great fancy to Miss Helen from the very first, and seemed disposed to give her more of his confidence than he had yet given to any one, except perhaps to Matouchon. But to Miss Helen he had told some things he had not told even Matouchon.

From what he had himself said from time to time, and from information that Carpio had been able to give her, Miss Helen judged that White Plume was fully seventy-five years of age.

(280)

p. 281.

Yet he didn't look so old, especially now that he had recovered from his sickness and was given the best of care.

White Plume had told Miss Helen that he was neither Kiowa, Comanche nor Apache, but was a Choctaw. However, he had left his home and friends when quite small, and he did not believe any of his family was now living. Indeed, his father and mother were dead when he left his home. He had been brought away by an old Indian whom he called Swift Arrow. He had wandered around with Swift Arrow for a number of years, till he was grown, in fact. They had gone all over the country, it seemed, to many strange places White Plume could not call by name. Finally, they had gone to a place where there were a great many soldiers. From White Plume's description, it seemed an army in camp. Swift Arrow had been employed by them as a guide. All went well until one day Swift Arrow's pony grew suddenly frightened, made a dash against a tree, and left Swift Arrow lifeless upon the ground.

After that White Plume had taken Swift Arrow's place, only he did more than even Swift Arrow had done, he went regularly into the army. It was then he wore the bright clothes, and the great hat, and the long white plume of which he never tired of talking. And if his narrative was to be fully believed, it wasn't all playday-soldiering he did, for there were rough marches, desperate straits, battle, and blood! White Plume had even a bullet mark to show. There was the furrow where it had torn its way from the elbow almost to the shoulder.

Matouchon had told Miss Helen about the little leather pouch, White Plume seemed to guard so carefully. But it didn't take the hold upon Miss Helen it had upon Matouchon. It was, without doubt, some worthless article that he had clothed with a virtue it did not possess, and thus found in it a charm against evil. Miss Helen had been long enough at the camps to discover how well-nigh universal was the Indian's attraction for talismans of this kind. When Matouchon added that she felt sure that it was a bit of paper, Miss Helen was all the more confirmed in her opinion. She well knew the

feeling with which the ignorant Indians especially regarded
written characters. She had seen more than one of them pick
up a portion of some old letter thrown carelessly from the
Agent's office. The bit of writing had been as carefully treas-
ured as though it held a fortune within its compass.

Once or twice Miss Helen had seen White Plume's fingers
nervously playing with the strings that fastened the pouch
about his neck. At one time he seemed on the point of speaking to her about it, then suddenly checked himself.

One morning, not long after this, she was talking to Carpio
in White Plume's presence with reference to superstition—how
it was one of the strongest things that held the Indian man or
woman back from the true way. "Why, I saw a sick woman
not long ago," said Miss Helen, "who had the claw of an
eagle wrapped in a small bit of skin, and she was mumbling
over it and entreating it as though it had the power to relieve
her of her pain and sorrow."

"And does not the white sister (the name by which Miss
Helen was known in the camp) think it did?" asked White
Plume suddenly.

Miss Helen fixed her eyes earnestly upon him.

"No;" she said, speaking slowly and emphatically, "I
feel sure it could not. There was nothing in that senseless
thing to render either help or sympathy."

"But I knew of an eagle's claw that could do many things,"
persisted White Plume. "An Indian over at the Fort had it,
and he said he would not take a great heap of money for it."

"What could it do?" asked Carpio quickly.

"It could tell him the way when he was lost, and it kept all
the evil spirits from troubling him. Once when he had a great
pain, it even cured that."

"White Plume, my friend," said Miss Helen gravely, "I
do wish I could bring you to see how foolish all this is. Even
the claw of a live eagle could not do any of the things you
say, how much less then could that of a dead one!"

These words seemed to impress White Plume. Seeing her

advantage Miss Helen followed it up. "I have seen the Indians carry about such senseless things as stones and bits of wood that they believed had some charm connected with them. When they were sick they pressed them against their poor feverish bodies. When the clouds came and the lightnings flashed, they prayed to these stones and sticks as though they had ears to hear, and eyes to see, and hands to help. Now, White Plume, you know they had none of these things, neither ears with which to hear, nor eyes to see, nor hands to grant assistance. How then could they do anything? Oh, it is so foolish to suppose they could! Only God can hear and answer prayer; only God can still the troubled heart and lead wandering feet aright."

"I know this may be true about sticks and stones, but not about other things," said White Plume positively. "There is the paper with that on it which talks (writing). I have seen myself much that such can do. I have that here," his fingers fumbling with the string at his neck, "which has helped more than once. It was given to White Plume by a white man who said some day it would bring him great fortune."

"In what way has it helped you, White Plume?" asked Miss Helen, turning her eyes full upon him.

"It has helped in more ways than White Plume can remember," he declared positively. "He will tell you one, one that happened only a little while ago. It was when White Plume tried to get here from the Fort. He fell into the ditch, and did not know what to do. Then he took out the charm and begged it to help him, and it sent the girl with the stars in her eyes. She got him out of the ditch and brought him here. But for that, White Plume would have died there maybe."

"But Matouchon was after the ponies. She would have seen you anyhow, she told me."

White Plume looked unconvinced.

"No, no!" he kept repeating. "It was this! It was this! I know it was this!" All the time he was murmuring the words his fingers were playing with the string about his neck. Once he lifted the pouch plainly into view.

" White Plume," Miss Helen said, feeling a sudden little impulse of curiosity despite herself, " let me see what is in the pouch. I can then tell you whether it is anything of value or not."

White Plume looked at her doubtfully, and shook his head. A moment later he seemed to be making up his mind to some course. " Do you think you could really tell about it ? " he asked hesitantly.

" Tell whether it is of any value or not ? " questioned Miss Helen quickly. " That I could ! At least, it is worth a trial, White Plume."

White Plume evidently was beginning to think so. Truth to tell, his mind hadn't been quite at rest for some time with reference to the charm. Ever since Matouchon had spoken so lightly of it, and shown so clearly how there was something else far better than this, he had had serious doubts with reference to it. Was it really nothing of a charm after all? Had he been deceived in supposing it had led Matouchon to him? He could have it all set at rest now if only he would let the white sister examine it. He had great confidence in Miss Helen. Indeed, it was more than a confidence. It was a feeling of decided reverence. Along with the other Indians he looked upon her as a kind of superior being, for had she not come to tell them of One mightier and more glorious than any other of whom they had ever heard ? And had she not said that *he* had sent her ? Yes, White Plume would let her see the charm. She could then set all doubt at rest with reference to it. So, he slowly unfastened the string from about his neck, drew the pouch up from his bosom, and, leaning over, put it in her hand.

The pouch was of well-worn leather, about four inches in width and six in depth. On three sides it was securely stitched with stout linen thread. On the fourth or upper side it had a buckskin strip run through it like a draw string.

Miss Helen had to untie this and to pick it out stitch by stitch before she could get to the contents of the pouch.

As the string was removed, she beheld the edges of a folded bit of paper. On drawing it out, she saw at once that it was much soiled and worn, and crumpled, too, as though with many foldings. But even at the first glance Miss Helen could see that it was no common piece of paper. It was of heavy linen, having a decided resemblance to parchment. Its fine quality was also shown in that it had not worn apart at the creases where so often folded. An official looking seal came to view as Miss Helen opened it. Great was her surprise, but it was to be greater still.

Now, Miss Helen was a woman of fine mind and of a decided business turn. More than this, she had a valuable fund of general knowledge, and a tact for taking such things in as would escape the average woman's understanding, speaking from a practical point. Therefore it took her only a few moments after the paper was unfolded to glean therefrom a clear comprehension as to its nature. The document was, in short, an honorable discharge from the Army of the United States, dated September, 1847, and bearing White Plume's Indian name in full. Further, it was signed officially by Winfield Scott, General Commanding.

White Plume's eager eyes read every expression of her face as she closely scanned the paper. "What does the white sister see?" he asked quickly, as a little exclamation escaped her.

"I see that, White Plume, which tells me that this may be a very valuable document indeed," she answered readily.

"Did not White Plume say so?" he asserted triumphantly.

"No, no, White Plume, you misunderstand!" she said earnestly. "There is no charm about the paper, none whatever. Believe that," her dark, expressive eyes fixed beseechingly upon his face. "It is only that the paper is of value to you because it shows that you have been a brave soldier, White Plume, and that you fought long and well."

"That I did," said White Plume earnestly. "And is that what it really says?" his eyes riveted upon her face.

"Yes; this, and more White Plume. It says that you were honorably discharged—that is that you came out without any-thing against you. What a fine record that is to have, White Plume! I wonder how many of us who are fighting in an-other kind of army, the army of our King, can have such a thing as that said of us when the battle is over—'honorably discharged?'

"But I will put the paper back now," she concluded, "and you must keep it safely, for there is no telling what value it may be to you yet. Only, White Plume, you *must* get that idea out of your head with reference to its being a charm. It is nothing of the kind. It is only a piece of paper that gives you a good character, and tells what a brave White Plume you really were. I will find out definitely about it for you. Ma-touchon told me only this morning that Dr. Holley would be here to-morrow. You must let him see it, White Plume. He will tell you just what good it will be to you."

That afternoon when Dr. Holley came and greetings were over, Miss Helen said to him, "You remember, Doctor, the sick old Indian, White Plume, by name, whom you attended when there was so much sickness here two or three months ago?"

"Yes," answered Dr. Holley; "very well. Why? Is he sick again?"

"Oh, no; he is in fine health for one so old. It was with reference to a little matter concerning him that I wished to speak. As soon as you feel disposed, I wish you would go and see him."

"All right," said the Doctor cheerily. "I'd like to renew my acquaintance with White Plume."

"He has a paper I want you to examine," continued Miss Helen.

"A paper? What kind of a paper?"

"It is a discharge from the army, and a fine one too."

"From the army? Why! which army?"

"The United States army campaigning in Mexico."

"In Mexico! White Plume in the Mexican War? Why, this is news?" exclaimed Dr. Holley in astonishment.

"Yes, he certainly was in the War of 1847. He has the paper so to prove. It says, ' honorably discharged,' and what is more, it is signed by Winfield Scott, General Commanding."

Dr. Holley's face now expressed more astonishment than ever. It was no use for him to accompany it with words. It was a full battery of exclamation points in itself.

"How did you come to see the paper?" he asked suddenly.

"We were talking about charms. I, of course, expressed emphatic disbelief as to their efficacy. White Plume defended the point warmly, declaring he had one about his neck that had helped him again and again. As proof he cited the incident of his falling into the ditch. He had entreated the charm, and Matouchon had appeared to rescue him. As no argument seemed to convince him, I asked him to let me see the charm. I know not what other impulse I followed save one of curiosity. At first he hesitated. Then when I said that I could tell him whether or not it was really anything of value, he seemed partly persuaded and finally untied the string and laid the pouch in my hand."

"So this was really what was in the pouch about his neck, the pouch concerning which Matouchon used to have so much curiosity?" said Dr. Holley quickly.

"Yes, the very same. I opened it and found the paper. It is as I tell you."

"I will go there directly," declared Dr. Holley. And he did.

In about a half hour he returned. He found an expectant group awaiting him, for Miss Helen had told Matouchon and the others the nature of the paper White Plume had for so long carried in the pouch about his neck.

"Did you find it?" began Miss Helen.

"Just what you said," he answered; "an honorable discharge from the army."

"And is it of much value?" asked Miss Helen again.

"That it is!" answered Dr. Holley earnestly. "Why, by this paper our old friend is plainly entitled to a pension."

"I surmised as much," declared Miss Helen, showing her pleasure.

"And," continued Dr. Holley, "as it has been a good many years that our friend has been carrying this precious document around—forty-five in fact—it is quite a snug little amount of pension money to which he is entitled." Here Dr. Holley stopped to do a little figuring—"Something over four thousand dollars, in reality," he announced.

A chorus of exclamations greeted this announcement.

"Oh, I am *so* glad! *so* glad!" declared Matouchon, clapping her hands. "Why now he can have all he wants!"

"And something else I imagine he won't want," said Dr. Holley: "a number of sharks flocking around him and trying to get a bite at his prize. But they shall not make prey of him if I can help it. I will protect him all I can. I will see that he gets this money, too," he continued, "with as little expense to him as possible. There shall be no pension-agent gobbling in the matter either," he concluded positively.

"Did you tell him the truth?" asked Miss Helen. "White Plume I mean."

"Partially. I thought best to break it by degrees. He knows that he will get some money through the paper, but he has no idea how much. I thought best, too, to caution him to keep the matter to himself, for awhile at least."

"Poor old White Plume!" said Miss Helen thoughtfully; "How truly he represents human nature after all! Here he was, ragged, poor, uncared for, driven to seek his daily bread from the hands of others, when all the time he carried about his neck that which would have given him everything in abundance if only he had known its value and claimed what it promised. How forcefully this speaks of the unclaimed promises of God! So many he gives us and so few do we claim! So rich, too, are they in value! We know not just *how* rich until we come to test them!"

CHAPTER XXVIII.

WHITE PLUME MAKES AN OFFERING.

DESPITE Dr. Holley's caution, the news of the prospective fortune of White Plume soon spread throughout the camp. The old man himself had doubtless told it, for he was quite too full of it to keep it. He just couldn't do it. It bubbled out in spite of him.

As Dr. Holley surmised, he was soon surrounded by the sharks. Suddenly friends sprang up of whom he had never heard. Many were the protestations made to him of the sincerest attachments. He was invited to tepees where he had never been before, and made much of by people who, prior to this time, had not really seemed aware of his presence in the camp.

But Dr. Holley was on the lookout for just such a state of affairs, and was prepared to meet it. He had White Plume's interests sincerely at heart. He was determined to see that he did not suffer through these sharks. So he made arrangements to remove him to the Agency, where he could take personal supervision of both the old Indian and his affairs. It would be some little time, he told Miss Helen and the others, before he could satisfactorily adjust the matter of the pension. Until then he would see that White Plume had the best of care, and that he didn't become entangled by any rash promises to professing friends.

Great was the speculation throughout the camp as to what White Plume would do with the money when he obtained it. Some said he would build him a fine house and live in it like a white man. Others asserted that he would buy a grand herd of ponies and a whole prairie for them to run on. But there were some who declared he would do neither of these things,

19

but that he would give the money away, perhaps to some white person who knew how to get around him. He was such a foolish old man. What did *he* know about money or its value! Why he'd just as soon as not lay down half of it for a blanket and a rifle if they chanced to attract his eye!

As to White Plume himself, he was non-committal on this subject. He was never heard even once to say what he would do with his little fortune when received, nor even with a part of it. Perhaps this reticence was for the best of reasons. He did not know himself. He seemed to trust it all to Dr. Holley. Beyond a doubt, judging from present indications, when the time came and the money lay in White Plume's hands, he would closely follow the Doctor's advice with reference to its investment. At any rate, it was evident that White Plume was gradually beginning to entertain in his heart a certain sense of distrust as to the genuineness of the many ovations of friendship that were being made to him. Some of White Plume's so-called friends had again and again styled him " a foolish old man." In this they had made a great mistake. White Plume was not foolish. On the other hand, he had more than once demonstrated that he could be not only shrewd and calculating, but also determined.

The evening before the morning he was to leave for the Agency, he went to see Matouchon. He seemed to have a tender spot in his heart for the young girl and a debt of gratitude, too. Well he might! for had she not both rescued him from the ditch and patiently nursed him through his sickness?

" White Plume never forget what the girl with the stars in her eyes has done for him," he said at parting.

" O White Plume, my friend, you need not make the debt so great," she said quickly. "It was but little, after all, I did."

" It was not little; it was *much*," persisted White Plume. " But for *you*, White Plume would have stayed in the ditch, maybe *died* there."

"Oh, surely not so bad as that, White Plume; some one else would have chanced along."

"No!" he declared, "or if they had, it might have been some one like that boy who only stood by and mocked. Such as he would have left White Plume to die. But young squaw's heart was tender. It could not bear to see the old man die, or even to lie there enduring the pain. And it was not only tender," he continued, "but it made the thoughts come to the head as to how it could get White Plume out of the ditch, and to the camp. Then when he came and was sick, how good the young squaw was to nurse him! No, White Plume never forget it! never forget it!" and he went away still murmuring the declaration, "White Plume never forget it!"

They heard from him in about a week after he left the camp. He had reached the Agency safe, and was happily established there in a Christian Indian family with whom Doctor Holley had placed him. Again they heard from White Plume a week or so later. There was no doubt as to his getting the pension. Proceedings had already been instituted, and, the arrival of the money was but a question of time.

And now in the sorrow that overshadowed her, Matouchon had no further thought of White Plume. The end had come for Amado. Already her feet were touching the farther shore.

Miss Helen was not there when the discovery was made that Amado was dying. But Matouchon sent in great haste for her, and, to her great joy, she came in time. It had been nearly a month since she left the camp, but she was not a great distance away. There was such a glad light on the poor pinched face as the eyes caught sight of Miss Helen. "Is the way clear, Amado?" Miss Helen asked earnestly, as she knelt beside her and took the cold hand in hers.

"Yes; clear, all clear! Oh, it used to be *so* dark! and Amado thought she *never* could find it. But first the good Docté pointed it out, and then this precious one here," her hand upon Matouchon's, "led her into it. Oh, Amado's tongue cannot say the words that would tell how precious *she* has been ! ''

The words thrilled Matouchon's heart as no music could have done. Well she knew who was meant; and oh, what joy it was to have her mother say this ! She tried to answer, but the sobs choked back her words. . She could only stroke tenderly the hand that lay in hers. A few moments passed. Then Amado spoke, addressing Matouchon. ''Oh, the joy and light you have brought ! Amado blesses you, and the God of whom you have taught her, will bless you, too.''

Then as she caught sight of Echoschy who was sobbing beside her, she continued, her eyes fixed entreatingly upon Matouchon's face, ''Take care of *her ;* all that you can. *He* will be so cruel ! ''

''I will ! '' declared Matouchon vehemently. ''I will do *all* that is in my power.''

Amado lay still for a moment, her eyes closed. Then she opened them and said to Miss Helen :

''Sing !. Sing to Amado ! Sing that about the Good Shepherd and the pastures green.''

In a clear rich voice Miss Helen began, the tones growing deeper and more tender as her own soul caught the emotion of the beautiful hymn. Now and then a quiver passed over Amado's eyelids. This was all, but Miss Helen could see that she was listening intently.

Miss Helen reached the fourth verse :

> '' In death's dark vale I fear no ill
>   With thee, dear Lord, beside me ;
> Thy rod and staff my comfort still,
>   Thy cross before to guide me.''

Slowly Amado's eyes unclosed. A light not of this world shone in their depths. A smile parted her lips. She raised her hand as though to place it in that of some one she saw before her. Her whole face now was enkindled with the radiance.

"I fear no ill! I fear no ill!" The words came almost as a burst of triumph. With their utterance the last of Amado's strength seemed to leave her. She lay motionless. There was scarcely a tremor throughout her whole frame, not even upon the lips where the smile still lingered. A moment she lay thus, and then the soul that had groped in the darkness, the soul that had hungered, groped and hungered no more. It had found the Shepherd of shepherds and with him "the pastures green."

Tabitosa was not at the camp when Amado died. He had gone on another trapping and hunting expedition the week before, and there was no telling when he would return—perhaps not until spring was fairly open. Thus Matouchon could follow her desire with reference to Echoschy. This was to take her to the Agency. But first she thought it best to gain Tataquitnamse's consent. The chief could stand as a kind of shield between her and her father. It might be that, through the chief, some arrangement could be made with Tabitosa which would leave Echoschy permanently with Matouchon's friends. They wanted her so much for Matouchon's sake, and Matouchon's heart was overflowing with the desire to see Echoschy at school.

The building for the mission school was now almost completed. Mr. Melville had told Matouchon that it would be opened in the spring. But if it should not be, Matouchon resolved that Echoschy should go to the school at the Agency. The good Docté would surely arrange it. Matouchon still had the belt of silver dollars Tohausin had given her. This should all be spent in helping her sister, she determined; though sometimes the thought came to her that the larger portion of her treasure might be needed to buy Tabitosa's consent. That he might not consent at all under any circumstances nor through any bribe, never seemed once to enter Matouchon's head. She was so secure in Tataquitnamse's promise that she was convinced he would manage Tabitosa.

Matouchon felt that Echoschy *must* go to school; that she

must have both head and heart changed through a knowledge
of better things. These better things in Matouchon's estima-
tion included not only what Echoschy would gain at school,
but also what she would learn every Sunday in the little chapel
where the good Docté preached. Matouchon clung all the
more ardently to these desires through having witnessed a most
painful scene just subsequent to her mother's death. She had
missed Echoschy, and on going to search for her, had found
her with a sharpened knife preparing to cut herself on arms
and throat and breast. Indeed, she had already gashed herself several times on the arms, and the blood was flowing in
streams. It was a terrible shock to Matouchon. In the
months she had been with them she had earnestly endeavored
to lead her sister, as well as her mother, in the better way.
There had been several talks especially to Echoschy, and daily
readings from the little Testament. Echoschy had appeared
so truly interested and so earnestly desirous of doing right.
But alas! it seemed now as though none of the teaching had
gone deep enough to pluck out the old roots of superstition
and degradation. Matouchon had yet to learn that it took
more time than a few months, or even years to accomplish this.
Nor was the teaching all, as long and as patient as it might be.
It needed something further still. It needed the grace of God
in the heart, the spirit of fire to burn in the impressions as the
patterns are burned into china. Before that how easily they
blur, though they may be ever so patiently and skillfully
wrought!

As Matouchon now recalled this painful scene, her heart was
in an agony of desire for Echoschy. How fervently she longed
to see her become a Christian!

Unkama had taken Echoschy to live with her at the yellow
tepee, and the sisters were daily together. The spring had
come, and with it the finishing of the mission school. And
now Matouchon learned that the Woman's Board of the Church
had effected an exchange with the General Board, whereby the
school at Anadarko had passed into the hands of the former.

So, then, the school was to be run all by ladies, with Mr. Melville as superintendent. How glad Matouchon was! It was arranged that both she and Echoschy should attend the school.

Everything was now in readiness and awaiting the coming of Miss Gregby who was to have charge of the school. In a few days she came. Some family matters had been the cause of her detention. Matouchon's heart warmed to Miss Gregby at once. She felt sure she was going to like her. She had such quick, cheery manners, such a pleasant face and bright eyes.

"She is a fine manager," said Mr. Melville. "She has tact as well as skill, and I feel sure she will make a great success of the school, for I have seen her tried."

Miss Gregby, it seems, had taught a year or more in one of the Government schools in another portion of the Territory, and there Mr. Melville had seen her several times while on his travels.

Mr. Melville had already published far and wide among the Indians the fact of the opening of the school. Consequently, when the day came, there were almost as many applicants as the building could accommodate. In another week there were more. Miss Gregby had had to turn three or four away. "It was so hard to do it," she said to Mr. Melville, with her eyes very nearly in tears. "Is there no way to enlarge? Even *one* more room would be a blessing."

"I don't know," he replied, "I will write and see, but I'm afraid the ladies have undertaken all they can at this time."

And so it proved. An answer came back from the secretary, regretful but decisive. The Board had made every possible outlay on the building at present. It had indeed been a strain to do even that much.

Daily Miss Gregby had to listen to the pitiful pleading story of some mother who longed to save her little girl from the wretchedness of life at the camps. How harrowing it was to her kind heart to have to listen and to refuse! How she pitied the mothers, and yearned to take their little ones to the shelter of this Christian home ! "Sometimes I feel actually like giving up my own bed !" she said one day to her assistant, Miss David, and now there were surely tears in her eyes.

Miss Gregby and Matouchon had grown to be warm friends. Neither Matouchon nor Echoschy as yet remained at the school at night, but they hoped to do so after awhile when more space could be provided. Now they walked the mile and a half each day from the Agency to the school, and from the school back to the Agency again. Miss Gregby often called upon Matouchon for little acts of assistance in the schoolroom, and almost every afternoon Matouchon lingered for a talk with her teacher. She knew how distressed Miss Gregby was over the children that had been turned away. Matouchon's tender heart ached, too, in sympathy. One day she asked Mr. Melville how much money it would take to build the rooms Miss Gregby so longed to have.

"For two thousand dollars all the necessary improvements could be made," he replied. "A big item is the hauling of the lumber."

That same afternoon Matouchon was at the yellow tepee. Her heart was so full of sorrow with reference to the smallness of the schoolbuilding and the number of children who had to be turned away, that she longed to pour out the recital in Unkama's sympathizing ears. She was surprised to see White Plume there. From the conscious looks both he and Unkama gave her when she entered, and the little start they made prior to this as she raised the flap of the tepee, Matouchon felt sure they had been talking about her. But as Matouchon knew she was a favorite with both, her heart told her it was nothing they would have feared her own ears to hear.

"Oh, I must tell you how sad it is about the school," said Matouchon, going to Unkama's side and beginning the subject at once, so full was she of it.

"Sad ?" echoed Unkama. "Why I did not think anything could ever be sad *there !*" and she smiled at Matouchon.

" Oh, it isn't the school exactly or anything that happens in that," returned Matouchon ; " but it is about the poor children who can't get into the school. It is so dreadful to see the mothers bringing them and begging Miss Gregby to take them, and she *can't*. She cries about it sometimes, and even talks about giving up her bed, and even half of her room. But that wouldn't do much good if she did. There are *so many !* "

" Is it because she hasn't the space that she can't take them ? " asked White Plume suddenly.

" Yes," said Matouchon. " She needs at least three more rooms. Then she could take twenty or twenty-five more children."

" Why do not those who have the school in charge put the rooms there ? " asked the old man again.

" Because they cannot. They have not the money. They have already done all they could. The good Docté wrote them, and that was their reply. He says that it is true, for they are noble ladies, and would gladly do more if it were in their power."

" How much money would it take to build the rooms the School Chief* needs ? " asked White Plume slowly.

" I asked the white father, and he says it will be at least two thousand dollars. It costs so much to haul the lumber here from the railroad. Oh, it just cuts Miss Gregby to the heart to have to refuse the mothers who come ! " Matouchon cried again, turning toward Unkama. " They do beg her so ! They tell her how dreadful it is at the camps, and how they long for their little girls to be taken in and cared for, and kept clean and taught the good way ! And it *is so* pitiful, too, to see them bringing their sick babies to Miss Gregby to be doctored. They love her so much, and have so much confidence in her, they think she can help them if she only touches them. Oh, I'd just give *anything*," broke off impetuous Matouchon, " if *I* could build those rooms for Miss Gregby ! Why don't some of

---

* The name by which the Indians had begun to call Miss Gregby.

those rich people back yonder in the States give the money, some of those who have plenty of it? They *must* know of this, for the white father has written of it to the papers!"

"Would it please the girl with the stars in her eyes as much as she says, to have the money to give to the School Chief for the rooms?" asked White Plume, fixing his eyes upon her intently.

"Yes, White Plume, it would, that it would!—even more. Oh, if you could see the poor mothers who come and beg, I'm sure you'd feel so too."

"Then White Plume will give young squaw the money."

Matouchon fairly started from her seat. What were the words she had heard? Surely she was dreaming.

"Why, White Plume, what *can* you mean?" she cried, looking at him with eyes that glowed now as though all the stars of the heavens were really in them.

"White Plume means the words that he has said. He will give the money; he will give it for the sake of the young girl with the stars in her eyes and the pity in her heart. The pity helped White Plume out of the ditch, and now it is reaching out after her people."

"O White Plume!" Matouchon's heart was too full for further words.

"Yes," the old man continued: "White Plume has felt ever since this money came that a part of it—half at least— ought to belong to the young squaw with the tender heart. But for her the bones of White Plume might be even now lying in the ditch. She found him and carried him to the camp. There he was nursed and helped till he seemed another White Plume. From the very first when they told him he was to have money, White Plume thought of the young squaw. But he did not know how much the treasure was to be; therefore he kept silent. Now that it has come, and it is far more than White Plume needs, he is more than ever resolved that the young squaw shall have part. He had just come here to talk about it," he concluded, nodding toward Unkama.

"Yes," said Unkama, with eyes and lips vying with each other in their smiles, "he was just talking to me about it when you came in. He wanted my advice as to how to manage giving you the money. I was so surprised, I hadn't recovered sufficiently to answer when Matouchon herself appeared. Now the answer is to be with her."

"Oh," said Matouchon, her eyes again flashing stars, "do you think—do you *really* think I ought to take it?"

"Yes, my Matouchon." replied Unkama earnestly, "I do. Considering the good you are to do with it, Unkama says yes, yes, again and again. White Plume has more than he needs. He will still get one hundred dollars every year, the Docté says. This with what is left will keep him up as no other Indian out here is kept up, except the chief. Then he knows he has always the yellow tepee when he wants the beef cooked as he loves it, and a soft clean bed with his feet to the fire," she continued cordially. "When he first talked to me about the money, I was not so certain. I knew my Matouchon would not consent to use it for herself. But now this about the school makes me see just how she cannot refuse it."

"No," said White Plume earnestly, "young squaw must not refuse it. At first White Plume wanted *her* to have it and no one else; but now he sees how this other way is best. The young squaw still shows the tender heart as she showed it to White Plume. It will bless her, and it will bless her people. She shall have the two thousand dollars from White Plume to build the rest of the school and to take in those who are crying to come. The money is here," removing the very same leather pouch from his neck that Matouchon knew so well. "White Plume asked the good Docté for it. It is now the young squaw's to do with in the way that it will make her the most happy."

With these words he placed a roll of bills in Matouchon's hands.

For a few seconds there was a silence. She could not have uttered a word had her life depended upon it. Then she

looked at him with eyes, the very radiance of which penetrated
to the core of his soul.

"O White Plume," she said, as soon as she could speak,
" I never, never could tell you what joy you have given me by
this offering! And the best part is, it not only makes *me*
happy but it will make many more. I can just see Miss Gregby
as she will look when I tell her. I want to run right away now
to let her know."

" But my Matouchon will of course wait till morning, seeing that it is nearly dark now," Unkama said with a smile.

"Oh, yes, I *must* wait, I know ; but how long the morning
will be in coming! O White Plume," turning to the old man
again, " you must go up there with me! You must go up
there in the morning. I want Miss Gregby to see and know
the one who has brought such joy to us all."

The old man shook his head slowly but determinately.
" No," he said, " no: White Plume will not go now. He
will wait till the rooms are there and the mothers do not have
to come begging in vain, and the smiles are on the faces of all.
That will be the time for White Plume. Besides," he added
suddenly, " it is not White Plume that makes the offering, but
the young squaw. White Plume gives the money to the young
squaw, but the young squaw gives it to the school. Then it is
to the young squaw the thanks ought to come, not to White
Plume."

" No! no !" declared Matouchon emphatically, " it is White
Plume who gives all this joy. O White Plume how good of
you to do it! God surely will bless this offering."

CHAPTER XXIX

THE curtain of the tepee was suddenly lifted and a clear voice cried cheerily, "*Ay haitch!*"

Matouchon sprang forward to greet the newcomer. It was Miss Helen.

"Well, it seems I have come upon a circle that has heard good news of some kind," declared Miss Helen. "Such beaming faces!"

"O Miss Helen, it is enough to make the face beam!" returned Matouchon, the tears of joy ready to start afresh. "Yours will beam, too, when you hear it."

"Then let me hear it at once," demanded Miss Helen. "I am just longing to share in the beaming."

"Miss Helen, the two thousand dollars have been given and the rooms will be added to the school."

Matouchon was so excited that she had hard work to make her voice steady.

"Oh, then," returned Miss Helen, with a look of relief, "the Board has reconsidered its decision?"

"No, it was not the Board. It was some one out here."

"Some one out here?" repeated Miss Helen incredulously.

"Yes, Miss Helen."

If Matouchon did not soon get more voice, she would be unable to speak at all.

"Why, who *could* it have been?" Miss Helen's face showed plainly how mystified she was.

"It was White Plume."

Matouchon had her voice at last, and oh, how she did make it ring as she said these words!

"*You?*" cried Miss Helen, turning quickly toward the old man.

"Yes," he replied, his face beaming. He already felt doubly repaid for what he had done. Even if Matouchon had not shown the joy she had, Miss Helen's radiant countenance would have been sufficient.

"Why, bless you, my friend!" she cried as she took his hand to press it earnestly. Then she added, "What impelled you to do it?"

"It was the young squaw with the stars in her eyes and the pity in her heart," declared White Plume, looking at Matouchon. "From the minute White Plume heard he was to have some money, he felt that a part of it ought to be the young squaw's. For had she not come to help White Plume out of the ditch? and did she not nurse him afterwards? White Plume came this very evening to talk to Unkama about the money he wanted the young squaw to have. At first, White Plume wanted *her* to have it, to have it all for herself. But when she came and told about this school, and the mothers who were turned away, and the children who were sick, and the School Chief who cried over it all, and declared with her own tears coming that she'd rather have this money to give to the school than anything else, then White Plume saw just what was to be done to make the young squaw happiest."

"And he *has* made me happy, Miss Helen," cried Matouchon. "Oh, so happy I have no words to tell it!"

"I can see that without the telling," declared Miss Helen. "O White Plume, my friend, that was a treasure indeed you carried around your neck. See the joy it has already given; but there is more to come, I can assure you."

"Yes, *much* more," added Matouchon, "O Miss Helen, I can hardly wait for morning, I am longing so to tell Miss Elizabeth."

"Why wait till morning?" asked Miss Helen, suddenly, and with a meaning look that made Matouchon's heart leap.

"Because I did not think I could possibly see her to-night," returned Matouchon.

"But you can," declared Miss Helen. "Come, Matouchon, I will carry you over myself. Blachito is without. His legs are just longing to trot the distance between here and the mission school !"

" How will I get back ? " asked Matouchon suddenly.

" Get back? Why you will not want to come back till to-morrow after school."

" But there is no place for us to stay there to-night," persisted Matouchon, showing her dismay.

" We'll *find* a place," asserted Miss Helen. " Why, don't you know we'll all be too happy to sleep, and if we do try it, there's my hammock for you, and I'll crowd in with Miss Gregby and Miss David. I guess ' three will be company' for once," and Miss Helen showed her white teeth in a radiant smile. " Come, Matouchon, it would be a shame to let Miss Elizabeth go to bed this night without hearing the good news. I feel like running every step of the way myself to carry it to her."

" But I must first go and give these to the white father," said Matouchon, showing the roll of bills and suddenly becoming conscious of her responsibility. " Then, too, I want to tell them I am going."

" Of course," said Miss Helen. " I was about to propose that."

Matouchon kissed Unkama, and pressing White Plume's hand earnestly, told him again of her great joy. Then she followed Miss Helen from the tent.

At the gate of the mission house they met John Melville. He had just been out to drive the calves home and was leading Spot into the yard. " Why, Matouchon," he cried, " what *is* the matter with you? Such a smiling face I never saw ! Why you look as though every body you knew and didn't particularly love had suddenly died and left you their fortunes."

" Well, no one has died," said Miss Helen gaily, " but she has the fortune all the same."

" What ! " said John in astonishment. " Why, surely, Miss Helen, you are fooling me ! "

"Oh, no, John : that I am not ! Get her to show you what is in her hand."

"Why, let's see," urged John, in much curiosity, as he went nearer to Matouchon.

She opened her hand and showed him the roll of bills lying there. It was so large she could not more than half close her palm.

John almost fell over against Spot in his astonishment.

"Why, Matouchon," he cried, his eyes distended, "have you been robbing the government safe?"

"Oh, no; nothing so bad as that," she said with a smile; "though I'll admit this came from there."

"Well, what *does* it mean?" looking from one to the other with an expression which said plainly, "don't keep me in suspense any longer, but please tell me."

"White Plume has been making an offering," said Miss Helen. "You know he drew four thousand dollars on his pension? Well, he has given Matouchon two thousand of it."

Such a whistle as John gave then! It brought Tinhim and a half dozen other dogs rushing toward the mission house gates. They had actually heard him from their frolicking ground just this side of the yellow tepee.

"Why, how rich you are, Matouchon!" he cried staring at her, as though he could hardly believe what he heard. "You can just have most anything you want now. I'm glad of it, Matouchon; yes, that I am!" and John threw his hat into the air, and falling upon Spot fairly made him snort, so hard did he hug him.

"But I am not going to spend any of it on myself," said Matouchon quietly; "no, not a dollar of it."

John stopped hugging Spot to stare at her again.

"Why, Matouchon!" he cried.

"Yes," she said decidedly, "it is for the mission school and not for me. Miss Gregby can have the rooms now she so much needs."

" O Matouchon," said John quickly, " I am *so* glad ! That is the best after all. I know you'd rather have it *that* way than any other. I've heard you say again and again how you longed to see the rooms built, and how you did wish *you* could do it ! And to think you *are* to do it after all ! O Matouchon what luck ! That old fellow, White Plume, is just a grand success through and through, that he is !" Then he added, " How glad Miss Elizabeth will be ! I do wish I could see her face when she is told."

" We are going over there to tell her now," said Matouchon, her own face fairly aglow.

" Are you ? Then I believe I'll go, too. You won't mind taking me along, will you, Miss Helen?"

" No ; indeed, John. Really we'd be glad of the company of so brave a knight."

They found Mr. Melville within. His joy was almost as great as Matouchon's had been when he was told of White Plume's offering.

" Bless the old fellow," he said. " He couldn't have made a better use of his money if he had studied and planned for a year. This offering will bring joy to more hearts than he knows. It certainly has brought a large share of it to mine. I will at once write to the Secretary of the Board," he concluded, " and notify her of the gift. Her's will be one of the hearts made glad, I know, for she wrote me how pained she was that the Board could do nothing further at present for the school."

It was dark when they set off for the mission school. Blachito seemed fully aware of the importance of the news he carried, for his trim little legs fairly sped along over the ground. John rode in close attendance, like the gallant knight Miss Helen intimated he would be. Spot, too, seemed to catch the spirit of the occasion for he pranced so John could hardly hold him in check. It seemed as though he wanted to speed away on the wings of the wind, to leave poor sturdy little Blachito far behind, and to be the first to get in with the glad, good news.

20

They met groups of the Indians coming to the Agency. Some gave them pleasant greeting; others again passed them sullenly by. As late as it was a crowd of Indian children were playing in the road. John who was now in advance almost galloped upon them before he saw them.

"*Behainty! behainty!*" (Get out of the way), he shouted as loud as he could.

They ran away with flashing eyes and clinched fists crying, "*Zaiddlebah! Zaiddlebah!* (Oh you bad thing!)"

There were rows of sand houses the children had made in the road. The feet of the ponies dashed into them, and so they were speedily demolished. Such news as these ponies carried could not be delayed, no not for an instant, by such frail things as sand houses, even though they did represent the patient toil and radiant speculations of childhood.

John took the low bars of the mission school gate without dismounting. Then he leaped from Spot's back and stood holding the gate open for Miss Helen and Matouchon.

The children were filing in to supper. They could see that, as soon as the front door was reached. Going into the teachers' room, which at this time was deserted, Miss Helen and Matouchon removed their wraps, bathed their hands and faces, and then rejoined John who had also performed similar ablutions at the wash place on the side piazza. Then they went in to supper.

The children had already taken their places and the room was crowded. Miss Gregby's clear, strong voice was heard leading in the beautiful, grateful words of the blessing she had taught them. The Indian children stood reverently and with bowed heads. There was not a whisper, nor a disturbing noise anywhere throughout the room. Mr. Melville had indeed been right when he pronounced Miss Elizabeth Gregby a fine manager. Though she had had the school but three months the discipline was well-nigh perfect. This was truly remarkable for Indian children used to the disorder and wild ways of the camp.

The blessing over, each seat was taken quietly; neither was there any rattling of knives and forks.

Miss Helen, Matouchon and John had lingered near the door until the children were seated. Then they entered and approached the table where Miss Gregby sat. The dining room was the only apartment in the house that had space to spare. It had been built with a view to the additional tax that would be put upon it when other rooms were erected. There was therefore plenty of room for the newcomers at the table where Miss Gregby sat. She was undoubtedly surprised to see them, but greeted them heartily with a warmth that showed that they were welcome, though unexpected.

Before entering the dining room, Miss Helen had whispered to Matouchon and John, " We will not tell Miss Gregby the grand, good news until she is in her room and all the duties of the evening are over. I want her to have the opportunity to enjoy it to its fullest."

They nodded assent, and tried to appear as unconcerned as possible when they took their seats at the table. But it was a poor effort. The telltale expression would come every now and then in spite of them. Even Miss Helen looked conscious, so much so in fact that Miss Gregby said suddenly, looking at her intently, " I think you folks must have heard some big news over at the Agency. Your faces say so at least."

Miss Helen blushed, Matouchon started, while John almost upset his coffee.

" Oh, yes," said Miss Helen recovering herself; " we did. We are going to tell it to you after supper."

" All right," returned Miss Elizabeth, " but can't you give me a hint. I'll have a time with my curiosity now you have aroused it."

" No danger," answered Miss Helen with a smile. " You can wait; I know you can."

Several times Miss Gregby caught herself wondering what the news could be ; but it is safe to say that, even with her widest speculations, she never came anywhere near the truth.

After supper, all the children stood, while Miss Helen offered a fervent prayer of thanks to God for all his blessings through the day, and of earnest pleading to him to have the care of them through the night to come. Then the children filed out by tables, one behind the other, keeping step thus through the halls and up one flight of stairs till the principal schoolroom was reached. There three quarters of an hour was given to study by all but the little ones, who were excused after fifteen minutes and went away in charge of Miss David.

At the close of the three quarters of an hour, Jennie, one of the Indian girls, went to the organ, and played a simple evening hymn. Jennie had been at one of the Government schools, and was a quick, bright girl who assisted Miss Gregby in various ways. Those of the children who could sing joined in the hymn. The Indian voice is not harmonious; on the other hand it is quite discordant, being shrill on the high notes and guttural on the lower. But Miss Gregby had taken great pains with her charges, going over and over again the words and the air with them. They really sang quite creditably now, especially those who had been in school from the opening.

After the singing the Commandments were repeated in concert, Miss Gregby stopping to lay special stress upon the fifth one. She invariably did this. Her great desire was to impress upon the children their duty to the aged. She had seen so many painful evidences of a far different training in the camps.

Then the Lord's Prayer was slowly and impressively repeated, and at its close the children marched in file to their dormitories.

On her way downstairs Miss Gregby stopped at the door of one of the dormitories. Here the smaller children slept. Miss David had charge of them. They had finished all their lessons for the night and were going to bed. Twenty or more little white-robed figures were kneeling and lisping the Lord's Prayer. The part that would have thrilled even the coldest heart was that almost every other pair of lips used a different language. Kiowa, Comanche, Caddo, Apache, and even Mexican—all were represented and more. But as different as were the languages, the sentiment in each young heart was the same. Each pair of lips murmured, "*Our* Father who art in Heaven."

Miss Gregby stood looking at them with tender, wistful eyes. How crowded they were! and how close the little beds stood together! The last possible one had been crowded in. There was scarcely room for the little occupant of each to turn around while she was disrobing. "And to think there are as many more in the camps, longing, nay *begging* to come in!" she said sadly.

She went downstairs to the little apartment used both as a sitting room and for the general transaction of business. She found Miss Helen, Matouchon, and John there awaiting her. Andres Martinez, too, had come in. He had recently been engaged as interpreter for the school, and proved a valuable assistant.

"You look sad," Miss Helen said solicitously, as Miss Gregby seated herself, her lips giving utterance to a distinct sigh of weariness. Her sorrowful face was quite a contrast to the bright, cheerful one she had shown while at supper.

"I feel so," Miss Gregby admitted. "I have just come by the dormitory of the smaller children. They are so crowded that it is really uncomfortable for them. And it is the same way in the schoolroom. I could not but notice it to-night."

"Bad, too bad!" said Miss Helen sympathizingly.

"But this isn't the worst of it," Miss Gregby returned sadly. "Daily I have to turn applicants away. The scenes are truly distressing. The poor mothers beg so, and do not seem to understand that what they ask is impossible. Their own tepees are so small and crowded that this great house—for so they regard it—seems of vast proportions. Oh, if the Board *could* but give me the room I need!"

"Have you never thought that some one outside the Board might give you the money?" Miss Helen asked suddenly.

"Why no! What could make me think so? There's no likelihood of that I'm certain."

"But there *might* be," persisted Miss Helen, her gray eyes fairly glowing.

"Oh, no; there's no such good fortune in store. If I thought there *could* be, I'd be the happiest creature on the earth!"

"Then *be* the happiest!" cried Miss Helen, and now she was so excited she fairly danced around Miss Gregby's chair.

Miss Gregby looked at her in amazement. "Could the dear little soul be going demented?" she asked herself. And what, too, was the matter with Matouchon, and John, and even Andres? Matouchon also seemed to have a difficulty in keeping still, Andres was moving his head from side to side and wriggling his knees, while as to John, no unbroken Indian pony could far surpass the antics in which he was now indulging.

Miss Elizabeth looked from one to the other in astonishment, then straight at Miss Helen while she asked,

"What *do* you mean?"

"Just what I said!" declared Miss Helen. "If the gift of the money to enlarge the school would make you the happiest creature on earth, as you have said, then *be* the happiest, for it *has* been given!"

Miss Elizabeth almost sprang from her chair.

"You are surely jesting," she said.

"No, no; I wouldn't jest over a matter like this. Tell her about it Matouchon."

"Miss Elizabeth, dear Miss Elizabeth," said Matouchon, her voice unsteady with emotion and her eyes misty with happy tears, "the old Indian, White Plume, whom I helped out of the ditch and carried to the camp when I was at Tataquit-namse's—the same one who drew the four thousand dollars as pension money—well, he has given two thousand dollars to add the new rooms to the school."

"Through you, of course, child? The gift was made by White Plume because he felt grateful to *you* and wished in some way to repay you?"

Miss Gregby's voice was so husky with emotion it was barely audible. Her hands, too, closely clasped in her lap, showed her emotion.

"Yes, Miss Elizabeth," Matouchon returned modestly in answer to the questions.

"God be praised!" said Miss Gregby, while the tears of joy rained over her cheeks. "Child," placing her arm around Matouchon and drawing her to her side, "somehow I felt you would be a good angel to the school. But this news seems *too* glorious to be true," she said after a pause.

"Doesn't it, Miss Elizabeth?" cried John. "I felt that way myself when I first heard it. But the money is on hand, nevertheless. I have seen it with my own eyes, and at this very moment it is lying safe in the vault at the government office, where my good father returned it for safe keeping almost the moment Matouchon gave it to him. To-morrow he is going to write the Board and ask them to let him begin work at once."

"I feel sure they will," said Miss Gregby. "They are very anxious about the school. I saw the letter of the secretary to your father, where she wrote how distressed they were because they could not advance the money now."

"It will soon be the vacation of the school," said Miss Helen; "then all hands can go to work."

"Yes, indeed!" declared John. "I am going to help, too. I can bring water and saw planks, if I can do nothing more."

"I think *I* can do more," said Andres with a smile. "I learned to put up framing very well when they were building before. That new addition shall have every spare moment of *my* time this summer."

"Good for you, Andres," said John heartily. "I'm with you, though we must have a bit of time now and then for a gallop or a fish."

"All right," said Andres, "of course we'll do that. At the same time we'll help push the building on as fast as we can."

"That we will!" said John. "Miss Gregby, I just want to see you when that building is finished. I just know you'll bubble over with the happiness of it."

"You couldn't see me any happier than I am now, John."

"Well, maybe not. But that will be the reality you know!"

"Yes, a most blessed one."

"Blessed indeed. We'll all share your happiness, Miss Elizabeth. We are so glad about it now we can't tell it in words. But I must say good night. I'm sure it is no use to add, 'pleasant dreams.'"

"No, indeed," declared Miss Gregby with a happy laugh. "If we sleep at all, John, it will be to have such dreams as it is safe to say have never occupied this mission house before."

He bade each good night by name. Then mounting Spot galloped away carrying a light and happy heart with him, but leaving much happier ones behind.

CHAPTER XXX.

CONCLUSION.

SIXTEEN years have gone by since the Government physician, Dr. Holley, found the little Indian baby in the sand. The little baby is now a tall and graceful girl. I feel tempted to write this " is " in italics, because you see there is so much of actual occurrence in this story, and so many of my characters are real, even to Spot and Blachito, that really, I feel strongly inclined to go further still and borrow the little girl's emphasis, calling this a " true-true story." But I can't *quite* do that.

Echoschy is still at school, but Matouchon has finished the course and is now taking private lessons from a governess in one of the families at the Agency. How happy she is that she has been made a regular assistant at the school.

The mission school, looking much larger and handsomer through its smart new addition, sits now like a thing of beauty upon its elevation, smiling out upon all the prairie round. The tepees come every now and then to cluster about it, looking up trustingly into its face as though assured of the welcome it gives. Regularly twice a month when the issue day has rolled round, the tepees make their appearance, stealing in with the night-fall, and looking next morning, with the rolls of canvas spread, like hovering birds. But there is one tepee that never leaves its place, on the slight elevation of ground just to the right of the mission school. This tepee is yellow, with gaily decorated top and sides. Here Unkama spends her summers. In the fall she is at the ranche, and in the winter safely housed with her beloved Matouchon at the mission school.

Dr. Holley, too, is there, that is at night, for a snug little office he has now built for himself in the yard. His great

happiness is in giving his services free of charge to the children of the mission school, and his deep joy in having Matouchon near him to render the many sweet and loving services
she knows so well how to render when he comes in wearied
from his work of the day.   He is no longer Government
physician.   He has saved enough to live comfortably for the
rest of his days.   All his work is done gratuitously among the
Indians.   It is whispered that he and Unkama have a plan between them to furnish the next enlargement the school needs.
This will not be long now if the pupils continue to come as
they have been coming through the past months.   Miss
Gregby's radiant blue eyes will glow all the more beautifully
when this does happen, though it seems to her that her heart
is as happy now as any heart could be.

Tabitosa never returned.   He doubtless received some hint as
to how things had turned out ; or it might have been that he saw
larger prospects of earthly gain in the employment he then
had at hand.   At any rate he sent for Kankeah to Fort Sill,
where he had left him, and neither was ever seen again by any
one concerned in our story.

Matouchon's heart ached many times as she thought of
Kankeah.   How she did wish she could have done more toward bringing his darkened mind to the light !   But her trust
was in God, and nightly her prayers went to him in her
brother's behalf.   God's hand could reach over all that intervening space.   Kankeah might yet be saved.   Some seed had
been dropped.   A harvest had often been gathered from even
scantier sowing.

White Plume vibrates between the yellow tepee, the parsonage at the Agency, and the mission school, a welcome and
honored guest at each.   When he saw the completed building
and the rows of bright happy-faced children in the school-
rooms and elsewhere, he rubbed his hands together, while he
exclaimed, " Good ! very good !   White Plume *is* certainly
glad ! "

John Melville is at college.   He is coming home next year,

"a first honor man," rumor says. But John's head has not been in the least turned. His heart still goes yearningly out to his Indian home and the friends and loved ones there. Meanwhile Spot is pining terribly during his absence. His greatest enjoyment is when he meets his friend Blachito, now and then, trotting away over the prairies, sturdily bearing his faithful little mistress on her constant rounds of service in her King's name.

The mission church at the Agency has grown wonderfully. The good Docté is even more beloved. So, too, is the faithful sharer of his joys and sorrow and of his labors, his good wife.

Glover is now a big boy able to ride Spot. This he does with considerable dignity. Emma, like John, is in the States at school. Lillian and Henry still show a fondness for stories in the twilight, and their father humors them now and then. He has even half promised that he will put these delightful Indian stories in a book some time for other little ones. Mabin has grown stronger, and is able to take John's place in many of the light duties around the home.

In the last *Report of the Commissioner of Indian Affairs* I find this statement from the Rev. Mr. Melville:

"The spirit of house-building now among the Indians is most encouraging. This is the longest step forward that I have seen among them. This movement should be encouraged by every one interested. If it continues as it now is the Indians in a few years will all be settled in comfortable homes. This has come about in a great part through having their children at school and seeing the wonderful effects of civilized rearing. The parental pride is touched and aroused. They long to give their children something better than the wretchedness of camp life when they are out of school.

"The school under the auspices of our Woman's Board has made rapid progress. It now numbers nearly one hundred boarding pupils."

Matouchon is constantly at the parsonage home. She still

says "white father" and "white mother" with the deepest
affection. She can never forget nor cease to love these dear
friends who so readily took her to their hearts and home.
Wherever she may be her own heart will ever hold a big
place for them. Through patience and loving care and gentle
yet firm admonition, they have made of her that which had enabled her to stand steadfast and unspotted amid all the degraded surroundings of life in the Indian camp.

And not only have her dear friends done this for her, but they
have implanted also within her heart such principles as through
all her life long, whatever may betide, will enable her to stand
a faithful servant and courageous soldier always for her King's
sake.

Daily she thinks of the hymn Miss Helen taught Amado,
and daily too she sings it :

> " The King of love my Shepherd is,
>   Whose goodness faileth never;
> I nothing lack if I am his,
>   And he is mine for ever."

THE END.

www.ingramcontent.com/pod-product-compliance
Lightning Source LLC
Chambersburg PA
CBHW020936030726
47496CB00005B/1221